EVERYTHING STOOD STILL FOR AN INSTANT

The crack of a gunshot resonated through the wooden buildings around the square like a string snapping inside a piano. Splinters of wood spun into the light, a foot from where Vandenberg stood. He seemed to freeze. An audible intake of breath rose from the crowd. In an instant, the second shot pierced the warm air. Vandenberg was thrown back across the podium. He slumped to his knees, his head almost touching the stage. Then he slowly rolled over on to his side.

Across the square, a little pall of smoke hung around the open third floor window of the west side of a department store.

AFFAIRS OF STATE

Tony Macaulay

HarperPaperbacks
A Division of HarperCollinsPublishers

HarperPaperbacks   *A Division of* HarperCollins*Publishers*
                    10 East 53rd Street, New York, N.Y. 10022

Copyright © 1995 by Tony Macaulay
All rights reserved. No part of this book may be used or reproduced in any manner whatsoever without written permission of the publisher, except in the case of brief quotations embodied in critical articles and reviews. For information address Headline Book Publishing, a division of Hodder Headline PLC, 338 Euston Road, London NW1 3BH.

A hardcover edition of this book was published in 1995 by Headline Book Publishing, under the title *Enemy of the State.*

Cover photograph by FPG International/Mark Reinstein
Cover illustration by Danilo Ducak

First HarperPaperbacks printing: June 1996

Printed in the United States of America

HarperPaperbacks and colophon are trademarks of HarperCollins*Publishers*

❖ 10 9 8 7 6 5 4 3 2 1

*To Daniel, Laura, Matthew, Alice Marika and Aris
with love.*

ACKNOWLEDGMENTS

My sincere thanks to the following people, whose expertise and constant support were invaluable in writing this book: Stuart Mitchell, Brian Thomas, Eddie Shirkie, Steve Cox, Jan Collie, Maggie Phillips, Ed Victor and Marion Donaldson.

T.M.

AFFAIRS
OF
STATE

ONE

Ernst Zeller kicked at the broken earth. The sliver of metal he'd noticed a second earlier was buried again, and he had to stoop down and dig with his fingers. Callused hands scraped rough stone. He cleared the soil around a chunk of concrete. Set into it, half turned on its side, was a soldier's dogtag. A strand of waxed cord was still looped around one end.

Zeller took off his hard hat and glanced across the building site. The riggers were securing the last of the rolled steel joists to a cable that swung from the jib of a tower crane. The engineer checked his watch. In five minutes the shift would be over. He took a Swiss Army knife from the pocket of his donkey jacket, pulled open the large blade and began to work around the dogtag until it came free. When he stood up and turned it to the light, the numbers were still visible.

He looked across to the Brandenburg Gate, floodlit now against the night sky, and checked his bearings again. The flag mast that stood on the site of what had once been Checkpoint Charlie was exactly due north of him. Out of the deep, muddy crater in between, rose the framework of steel that would form the substructure of the new Hassler Hotel. Zeller turned the identity tag in his fingers. There was no way to tell the nationality of the soldier it had once belonged to. Few corners of the planet had seen more violence than this—men of seven races had died here—but Zeller was certain of one thing. It had been buried in the foundations of the Berlin Wall for more than forty years.

The slingers stood clear as the cable began to take the weight of the joist. The wind was blowing in from the Russian steppes now. Zeller buttoned the donkey jacket to the neck. In twenty minutes he'd be in Rudi's, watching Isgarde's white fingers close around the beer pump's bulbous handle, enjoying the tic-toc of her high heels on the flagstone floor as she brought him a frothing half-liter of pils with the schnapps chaser. He'd make his move tonight. The signs had been there for a long time. The heavy-lidded sideways looks she shot him, in those rare moments when eyes were not devouring her every move, they could only add up to one thing.

The jib of the crane swung its load slowly across the site. Tonight he'd go home first. Shower, wash his hair; put on the jacket he'd bought at the weekend.

The ground shuddered beneath him. They all felt it. Steiner and Gotz were thrown off balance by a sudden violent trembling of the earth. There was a low metallic groan and the top of the tower crane, reaching high into the blackness above them, lurched forward. They cowered, braced themselves, waited to be crushed. Three hundred and forty feet above their heads, the cabin hung, seven degrees or more from the perpendicular. The sound of rending steel braces was masked almost instantly, by another. A whistling, a rushing . . . the sound of air forced through the framework of the 260-foot boom as it swept back across the site at terrifying speed. The joist it carried flew back across the site like a missile from an ancient siege engine.

For the seconds that followed, time seemed to elongate, as though measuring duration on some different plane of consciousness. Zeller could see the joist twisting and bucking as it rushed back toward the riggers, hear the sound of cable paying out, gear teeth shearing under violent stresses. Gotz had staggered to his feet. For a split second it seemed the joist, thrown outward by its momentum, would miss them. All but Gotz stood frozen, unable to react. He flung himself forward and the joist sliced clean through him. His head and torso were swept up into the night, then jettisoned into the chill air like trash slung on to a city tip. His lower half, from sternum to toe, stood for a second, fountaining dark life-blood, then folded at the hip and knee into a small heap barely visible amongst the shadows that shrouded the dirt floor.

It took till early Monday morning for two teams of erectors working in shifts to dismantle the crippled crane. A little after 10:15, the last of the concrete railway sleepers used to hold the massive base in place was lifted free and a smaller crane on caterpillar tracks began to remove the base itself. It had been obvious from the start that subsidence under the southeast-facing foot had caused the tower to tip. Now it was clear that a large fissure had opened up in the ground beneath it. A JCB moved into position and began to dig it out.

Insurance investigator Walther Kruger watched as a flat concrete surface began to emerge. At the centre of a wide crack about twenty feet long was a ragged hole the diameter of a dustbin lid. Kruger took a flashlight from the totebag beside him, moved forward and brushed away as much of the dirt around the hole as he could, before kneeling to peer in.

The flashlight reflected off an expanse of muddy water that half-filled the wide pipe. Kruger shone the beam upward around the walls. "It's a section of disused sewer," he pronounced at last, his voice almost lost in the echo.

Zeller pressed his face gingerly with the tips of his fingers. The flesh was still raw from the shave he had had an hour earlier and the cold morning air was making it sting. He unfolded his plan of the area, and turned it to align with the landmarks. The tower crane had been erected at the mid-point of what had once been the Soviet no-man's-land, the thousand meters of barbed wire and anti-tank traps that separated East Germany from West. "A disused sewer?" he asked. "I thought the Soviets blocked 'em all off, in the Sixties to keep the comrades at home."

Kruger leaned back, working on his spine with his fingers. "Not here. You were one dead dissident by the time you got this far, believe me." He began to walk back toward the site office.

Zeller checked the plan as he hurried to keep up.

"There's nothing marked. We made up a composite of all the old services ourselves, from records going back to 1850. I'm certain nothing was missed."

The insurance investigator seemed not to hear. "I want it pumped dry as soon as you can do it. What's planned for this area?"

"Parking for delivery vehicles."

Kruger stopped to let two trucks pass, spraying mud as they turned toward the ramp that led up to the Leipzigerplatz. He looked hard at the site engineer. "Well, shoot in a few yards of lean-mix concrete. Backfill the bastard. In the meantime, I want it covered over with corrugated sheeting or something and the men kept away from it."

The photograph on the packet looked appetizing enough. To describe it as "Traditional Hungarian Goulash" didn't seem unreasonable. Zeller compared the picture with the greasy brown sludge simmering in the saucepan and sighed. He turned up the volume control on the radio. The last story of the newscast concerned a race riot in Munich. No mention of the accident anywhere. Not that he wanted there to be, of course. But you'd have thought . . .

He combed through the clutter around the cooker, searching for his cigarettes, then, with a grunt of irritation, crossed to the living room of the small apartment and began to rummage through his donkey jacket. A stab of pain made him jerk his hand free, scattering a light spray of blood across the carpet. Sucking at the gashed finger he slipped his other hand carefully into the pocket. The dogtag. He laid the corroded strip of metal on the coffee table and sat down.

A sewer. Under ten feet of reinforced concrete . . . He lifted the phone and dialed. "Werner? Ernst."

In Bonn, Werner Wolff covered the mouthpiece of the phone and bellowed at his children to turn down the television. "Good to hear from you. How's the back?"

"Still killing me. So tell me, how's the KLM contract coming?"

"Late. All that snow in January really screwed us up."

"Yeah, us too. Listen, on the Nomura Bank project, tell me about that underground complex or whatever it was you found."

"What do you want to know? We broke into it when we were excavating foundations. There was nothing marked, but the Wall had been over that site by the Brandenburg Gate for so long no one knew for sure what was down there. Held us up for weeks while the city decided what to do. The whole contract came in behind schedule. Cost us a goddam fortune in penalties. Had a hell of a fight with the insurance company. Still isn't settled."

"Schroeders?"

"Who else?"

"Oh, so that's it."

"You got a problem?"

"We had a hell of an accident here this week, Werner. A cave in. I lost a man. Schroeders' investigator is trying to tell me it was caused by an unmarked sewer."

"Where exactly is the Hassler site?"

"About four hundred meters south of the Nomura."

"No sewers there, pal. Russkies blocked 'em all in."

"That's what I told him. Whatever it is down there, he seemed very keen for me to fill it in and keep on working."

The noise that came down the line was somewhere between a laugh and a cough. "I'm not surprised."

"Yeah, well it's due for a concrete backfill at seven A.M. tomorrow and I'm not at all sure I'm doing the right thing. So tell me, what was it the authorities reckoned you found?"

The security guard eased the high steel gate over the broken bricks and concrete that formed the main access road through the Hassler site. "You're early this morning, Herr Zeller."

The engineer nodded and moved the Merc up to the cluster of portacabins in the southeast corner. From the canteen hut, men's voices rose above the drone of rock music. Across the deserted site, the largest of the truck mixers juddered as it turned. Zeller took a flashlight from the trunk of the car and crossed to where the tower crane had stood. A sheet of corrugated steel, held down by two concrete railway sleepers, lay over the opening. Investigator Kruger had insisted on seeing it put in place before he'd left the site. A length of tubing, from a large diesel-powered pump, had been fed underneath it and left to suck all night.

Zeller pulled a crowbar from a wheelbarrow and began to lever one of the sleepers away. A stab of pain in the small of his back made him wince and catch his breath. He gritted his teeth, set the crowbar in position again and put his dead weight against it. It slid sideways like a slab off a tomb. He kicked back the sheet metal, got down on his stomach and shone the flashlight into the hole. The wide pipework had been pumped dry. The smell of damp was almost overpowering. He shone the light around the walls. What appeared to be power cables and telephone lines ran in conduits to his right. Zeller put his foot against one of the steel brackets that held them in place. It seemed solid enough, so he jammed the flashlight into his jacket and climbed carefully down. A broken light bulb was clearly visible through a cracked glass fitting above him. Some sewer, Zeller thought. Water dripped into his hair. No hardhat, damn it. He'd left it in the car. He lowered the flashlight and turned to his right. The passageway beyond stretched into darkness. He moved off slowly, his boots sinking into the inch of slimy sediment that had settled on the floor. To his left was a small room. Zeller edged into it. The ground was littered with rotting wood and rusting metal. He scanned it carefully. The flashlight beam fell on to a small disc the diameter of a Coke can. Zeller stooped down and wiped the mud off it. Some kind of calibrated radio dial. Now he was certain.

An underground Soviet command post. Wolff had said JCBs had ripped into one during the excavation of the Nomura site. Plans of East Berlin border defenses supplied by the withdrawing Soviet army had shown no such installations, but that's what it had turned out to be.

". . . The whole project stopped dead while the authorities poked around it. Three hundred and seventy thousand D-marks. That's what it cost in penalties for late completion of the contract . . . I still say they'd never have got wind of the damn thing if *Der Spiegel* hadn't run that story. Must have been a real slow week for news. They tried to say that what we'd turned up was a bit more of Bunker Two . . . "

The discovery of part of a second bunker, east of the Brandenburg Gate, less than a thousand meters from the complex where Adolf Hitler had blown his brains out in the last days of World War Two, had attracted modest media attention when water supply engineers had stumbled on to it in the Spring of '89. Zeller had seen the report in *Bild Zeitung*. Somehow it had survived intact under the road, for forty-five years. Historians claimed it had once housed the Führer's SS bodyguard.

". . . In the end they shipped in military experts from Bonn," Wolff had gone on. "They confirmed that what we'd found was just an unmarked Soviet installation. Trouble was, by that time I was up to my ass in red tape. What a mess. Jesus, I still wake up in a cold sweat thinking about it . . . "

Zeller moved out into the narrow passageway and walked on. The way ahead was blocked by a massive cave-in. The flashlight showed wide cracks in the roof around it, choked with roots.

The light cut. He thumped the torch with the heel of his hand. Nothing.

Goddamn it! The batteries were almost new.

Sunlight showed through the opening in the roof through which he'd come. He turned and walked back to it. Now at least he could see what he was doing. He unscrewed the end of the torch and prised the metal contact forward to tighten the contact between the batteries, then refitted it.

The light flickered on. He held it steady, staring at the floor that stretched ahead of him into the part of the complex he'd yet to investigate.

How could that be?

Extending through the sludge from where he stood was a line of fresh footprints. Beside it, the prints made by the wearer on his return. Zeller began to follow the tracks. The passageway could only have been pumped dry for a couple of hours at most, he thought. Who could have been down here? He walked on. At the end of the corridor was another room. A length of steel conduit that had encased the overhead cables had broken free of the ceiling. Zeller lifted it to pass, moving the flashlight beam across the walls. The steady drip of water echoed in the stillness. A boiler room. The tracks in the sediment beneath him crossed and recrossed one another, as though the man who made them was looking for something.

Again the light cut. Zeller slapped it with his free hand. The last hit dislodged the end cap and the batteries slid out, dropping into the sludge. He stood there in the blackness cursing, groping around his feet. Then he turned toward the chink of daylight and made for the door. His subconscious mind had logged the length of broken conduit, had already deduced that the jagged end of it would be facing him as he left. It found its voice the same second the rusting metal slammed into his forehead.

How long he'd been unconscious he couldn't judge, only knew that his face was caked with blood and pain throbbed in his head. He was dimly aware of a rumbling above him. He crawled back toward the daylight, choking on the sludge he trawled as he moved, gasping for breath. Twice he was forced to stop and gather his strength before he found himself beneath the opening in the roof of the corridor. With the last of his energy, he pulled himself to his feet and reached for some pipework above him. He swung his right foot on to a conduit and began to lever himself up. His head tipped back. For a moment his skin was warmed by the rays of the sun. Slowly his eyes began to focus. A cry broke from his lips.

The chute from the truck mixer swung in the wind, way above him. Wet concrete rumbled into the wide gash in the earth, almost filling it. Two men in hardhats began to shovel in the little that had missed the hole.

TWO

The stone struck the front offside window of the BMW with a whiplash crack. For a second, Lassiter lost control. The car swerved left and right. Two kids in denims stood jeering and shouting obscenities on the street corner. They couldn't be more than thirteen or fourteen years old. He stamped on the brakes and they raced off. He rolled down the window and yelled after them. Why? he wondered, inspecting the scar the size of a quarter on the window. Just mindless vandalism? Probably for no more reason than that this was Normannenstrasse—until 1989, for millions of East Germans, the Road to Hell.

For the third time that morning the U.S. Customs agent wondered at the wisdom of staying on in Berlin. Lassiter had been on secondment to the *Zollfahndung*—the German Customs Investigation Department—for almost six months, briefing its operatives on the latest techniques his department was using to uncover the hidden assets of convicted drug barons and other criminals. The new special unit he'd set up seemed to be running smoothly enough and Lassiter had planned to be back in Washington by the weekend. He'd been packing his bags when the request for him to meet with a high-ranking official of the *Finanzamt* had come through. It had taken him more than five hours to work through the files delivered by a uniformed messenger an hour later, and almost as long to decide whether he wanted to spend another chunk of lifetime away from home.

He swung left onto a short street flanked by a sports stadium, left again and found himself in the heart of the vast complex that had once housed the *Staatssicherheitsdienst*—the Ministry for State Security—the Stasi.

Few aspects of the tyrannical German Democratic Republic, the GDR, had caught the global imagination more thoroughly than the secrets disgorged by the records of the Stasi. The files Lassiter had been sent could only hint at the reign of terror visited for more than forty years on a third of the population of the GDR by the largest and most efficient intelligence service in Europe after the KGB.

The featureless three-story building at the end of the street had been the "Counter-Dissident Department". From there, Stasi operatives had monitored the activities of more than six million East Germans. Every detail of their marriages, debts, drinking habits, opinions and beliefs was entered into files it took a complex the size of Whitehall to house and process.

A line of people stood in the light drizzle waiting for the doors to open: a handful of the ninety thousand German citizens who had applied for permission to study the files that had been compiled about them. A woman in a shabby cloth coat was breaking chocolate to give to a small child. She ran her hand affectionately around the back of his head as he took it. Her pale face, aged before its time, smiled down at his. It was a simple enough action, but it said a lot. It said, soon I shall know who it was denounced me, spied on my every move, turned my life for years into a living hell. Perhaps my neighbor, my closest friend, perhaps even my husband. Whoever I must cut from life because of that knowledge, I shall still have you. It touched Lassiter.

He parked and crossed the street to what had been the Ministerial Office and Secretariat. From here Erich Mielke, the grand architect of the Stasi, a lifelong communist ultimately as powerful as President Honecker himself, had overseen the whole vast machine with a fanaticism close to the psychotic. Lassiter passed under the canopy that had hidden Mielke's face from prying eyes as he stepped from his black-windowed limousine each morning and crossed to his office.

What would Mielke have made of the young man who sat in reception behind the glass paneling now? His long hair was tied into a pigtail. The T-shirt under the jacket showed Madonna, posed in a moment of simulated sexual ecstasy. He was the quintessence of the capitalism the "Chief Pig" had devoted his life to combating. He took Lassiter down the narrow red-carpeted corridor, past busts and plaques of Lenin, opened the door of an office on the left and ushered him in.

The man behind the desk stood up to greet him. "Mr. Lassiter, do come and sit down. My name's

Kurt Fraenkel. I've been given the task of tidying up matters here." Lassiter shook his hand and drew up a chair. "Sorry about the stink."

The Customs agent sniffed the air. There was a strong smell of wet rot.

"It seems the GDR used cowboy builders on the place," said Fraenkel cheerfully. "The wood in this section's just crumbling away. You get used to it after a while." His eyes flickered back to the file he'd been reading. "You led the team that unearthed the Saddam money."

"I ran the US end of it," Lassiter told him. "The Allies put in teams from three countries."

"Nevertheless, it's not every day you turn up eight billion dollars, I imagine."

Lassiter shrugged. "The brief was 'find and freeze.' There was never a question of the U.S. Treasury seeing any of that money. The administration wanted to wind up the pressure on Saddam and it seemed like a good way. Losing Kuwait and a hundred thousand troops didn't seem to faze him, but we managed to wipe the smile off his face." Lassiter's subconscious mind had already begun to dismantle Fraenkel's face, feature by feature: mesomorphic head shape; eyes were deep set, glassy; a slight vertical strabismus, one eye appearing to point fractionally higher than the other. Fraenkel was a cautious, methodical man who took nothing at face value. He would come unglued under pressure. He was under pressure now. "We've had harder briefs," Lassiter went on. "For a start, there was no laundering involved. Saddam answered to no one back home. He creamed off what he liked, so why bother?" The polished wooden desk glowed a faintly nauseous orange-yellow in the harsh fluorescent light. That and the stench of rot was beginning to make Lassiter wish he'd eaten some breakfast. "Noriega was more of a challenge. He'd had around six billion rinsed through eleven different banks. Had us working double shifts for fifteen months."

Fraenkel stood up and tried to shrug the creases out of the back of his jacket. "Well, we may never know how much the former occupant of this office managed to rinse."

"This was Mielke's office?"

"Uhuh. He ran the whole thing from here. A hundred and eighty thousand informers reporting in daily on the actions and conversations of their workmates, teachers, friends, families. Even their lovers . . . "

Lassiter studied the room. The garish blue of Mielke's chair, the acid green of the walls, the primary red of the carpet: these were the colors of childhood. The colors every twelve-year-old chose for the first bedroom he got to redecorate.

"What they didn't tell him, his agents did. Thirty thousand of them monitored a third of the population with hidden cameras, tapped their phones, extracted the most intimate details of their lives from their letters. It took a ton of money, more than three billion D-marks a year to keep the whole machine turning over."

And he ran it all with the petulance and paranoia of a disturbed child, Lassiter thought.

"This was more than Mielke's office. It was his whole world. He lived here much of the time, slept in the room next door. Always on the job. Obsessed with knowing everything."

"So why didn't he see the end coming?"

"He did, perhaps before anyone. He was a devout communist, but more than anything, he was a survivor."

"Which is why he started lining his own pockets."

"That's my guess. Against the day the roof came in." Fraenkel slid a file across the desk. "The first indication that he might have been skimming off vast amounts of cash from the Stasi budget came in early '90, right after the fall."

"From the mistress."

"That's right. You've had copies of the old bank statements she said were his?" Lassiter shook his head. "Damn it, well you should have had." He passed a file of papers across the desk. "She claims he left them in a closet at her flat. She was frightened of what would happen to her after the fall so she traded them for a ticket out."

Lassiter examined the documents. They showed details of a numbered account in Switzerland, covering a period of nine months in the mid-Eighties. At one point it appeared to have held almost eleven million Deutschmarks.

"Of course by the time we got to it, it was empty." Fraenkel drew on a cigarette as Lassiter worked through the *Finanzamt*'s report. The statements showed mainly transfers to other numbered accounts. These, too, had once held substantial sums, but were also now defunct. Pressed for further details, the Swiss had proved, as so often in the past, to be masters of intransigence, and it seemed from the report that the *Finanzamt*'s investigation had gradually ground to a halt.

"Other than the mistress's affidavit, what is there to link these with Mielke?" Lassiter asked.

"Not a damn thing."

"I take it the man himself is saying nothing?"

"Herr Mielke? Oh, he's said plenty. He told doctors at the prison hospital he had a visitation from St. Anthony of Padua last week. Seems they really hit it off. They watched the giant slalom on TV. Played a little gin rummy. You know, the usual stuff."

"I thought the general view was that he was shamming insanity."

"Well, shamming or not, the hearings on his shoot to kill policy have been a farce. Whether or not they nail him for manslaughter at this point is pretty academic. He's not going anywhere." Fraenkel stubbed out his cigarette. "Come on. I want to show you something."

They moved off briskly through a maze of narrow corridors. "As you can imagine, we've got warehouses full of stuff. Not just here and not just on the Stasi. Relating to every aspect of the East German government over the last forty years. It's going to take our own teams ten, maybe fifteen years to sift through it all. They've turned up a lot of extraordinary material already, but nothing that backs up this Mielke business. There are tens of thousands of Volk in this part of Germany that'd like nothing better than to tear the "Chief Pig" limb from limb for what he's done to them, to their families. The man was a monster. But a thief? Until a month ago my guess would have been probably not."

The far end of the corridor opened on to a vast, windowless filing room. Staffers in grey overalls searched among the dusty shelves.

"Where's the stuff from Leipzig, Greta?" A woman with gray hair wound into a bun and a drawn, scrubbed face tramped off down one of the aisles between ceiling-high shelves bulging with files, carefully lifting her orthopedic sandals over stacks of dog-eared folders. "She's one of the lucky ones," Fraenkel said when she was out of earshot. "Ex-Stasi staff."

"Really?"

"We had no choice when we took this place over. The card-index system alone takes up an area the size of three tennis courts. These old staffers are the only ones who know where anything is. Using these people is not something we shout about, mind you. Like I say, there's a lot of very bitter people in this part of the country."

"Yeah, I saw some on the way in."

"Folk who want the collaborators who informed on them rooted out. Mielke mounted a massive operation in the closing days of the régime to burn all crucial files, but as you see there are still millions they never had time to get to. If there ever was a full list of agents and informers, my guess is it was the first thing to get torched. So, up until a month ago, these files on their agents' targets were the only way we had to identify the agents themselves."

Even in the six months Lassiter had been in Germany he'd seen the witch-hunt intensify. Hardly a week went by when some government official, lawyer, surgeon, industrialist was not "outed" as a collaborator of the hated régime. Once exposed, they instantly became social lepers, ostracized and reviled. Greta was lucky indeed.

"Here, Herr Fraenkel." She led them down an aisle to a dozen plywood crates, stacked against an outer wall. Some were covered in black, sooty fingerprints, others were actually charred.

"That's why this stuff was so important to us," Fraenkel said. "How these ended up in Leipzig, we don't know. Seemed a long way out to stow dead files."

Lassiter knelt down and took out an accounts ledger.

"These are only a small part of what there were, of course. They're the records of salaries and expenses paid to probably a third of the workforce over the last twentysome years—the nearest thing to that list we'll probably ever have. I've had my people going through this stuff, on round-the-clock shifts for three weeks."

"Why do you think these particular files survived?"

"Because no more than a couple of people knew they were there. The key factor may be that at least eight hundred of the employees listed here have one distinct thing in common."

"And that is?"

Fraenkel sat down and lit a cigarette. "They don't exist. They're all figments of someone's imagination."

"You're kidding."

"Figments who over the years received hundreds of thousands of D-marks, paid into their private accounts across the country, which were later transferred to larger accounts at six major banks."

"And eventually drawn out in cash?"

Fraenkel nodded. "Clearly the eight hundred we've identified are just a tiny part of the whole. We'll probably never know the full scale of the operation. The original authorization for these salary payments can't be traced. In fact no one who worked in the accounts department here could ever remember having seen any. Each day, our list of fictitious agents grows longer and so far not a pfennig of the money has been traced."

There was silence for a moment then Lassiter said, "Mielke."

"That's the only conclusion we can come to. I don't see how a scam involving perhaps billions of D-marks could have stayed in place undetected for almost twenty years unless the most powerful man in the Stasi was behind it. I mean the buck stopped with him. Who was there to spy on the chief of spies? Only he had a complete grasp of the workings of the entire ministry."

Lassiter went on leafing through the files. "I guess all that stuff I read about secret units existing within the Stasi itself only added to their lack of an overview."

"Sure. He could be certain that no one department knew enough about the others to have a clue as to what he was up to. I mean, when you stop and think about it, what more perfect organization could there be for running a ghost employees scam than an intelligence agency? The agents in question were listed as I.M.E.s—those in deep cover on special assignments. They would seldom if ever have to visit the Stasi headquarters and would only report in when a new development on their assignments required them to."

"And as they had no assignments, they were never heard from."

"You got it."

"There've been rumblings in the media for weeks about missing Mielke billions. The government have screwed the top down as tight as they can. No one's come out and said anything publicly yet, but it's just a matter of time. You've been here awhile, Jack. I don't need to tell you how things are in this country. The cost of rebuilding the economy of the East is the issue, almost the only issue. People in what used to be the West are bleeding from every pore. Reunification has hit their pay packets. It's changed their lifestyle, and probably the way they'll vote at the next election."

Fraenkel flicked through one of the scorched files. "The government sees the Mielke money as a chance to take some of the heat out of the situation. Politically, a few billion from the East's own coffers, if you like, would be media dynamite. It could be presented as a kind of peace offering that would balance the books a little in the eyes of the electorate. With the polls the way they are, an issue like this could become the key to the government's survival. I don't think I need to tell you we're in a hole with this. Your help right now would be invaluable."

"My problem is, I'd still have to be back in Washington in two weeks to testify at the Pensacola Drug Ring hearing. I have no way of knowing how long that'll take. And once that's out of the way, the department's gonna want me right back on the street."

"You're referring to Agent-In-Charge Capriotti? I may as well level with you, Jack. I've already spoken with him. I can't say he was overjoyed at the prospect of being short-handed any longer than he had to be, but I think I can convince him to let me keep you for a month or two after the trial. But be clear about this: in the end, the decision rests with you."

☆　　☆　　☆

Only now, as employees began to leave the complex for the day, did Lassiter realize how many people were still employed at the Stasi. He pushed the BMW out into the tight line of traffic ahead.

"It's good of you to drop me off, Jack." Fraenkel opened his briefcase, took out a crumpled felt hat, and set to work on straightening it out. "These aren't good places to walk these days."

Lassiter's mind was still on the Mielke case. "There's really only one way to launder money on that scale. Start a bank. Or buy one. These days, somewhere like the Dutch Antilles, Cayman Islands, St. Stephen. Or Cyprus—that's cornering a lot of new business. The important thing is that all the directors and shareholders are locals, answerable only to the local authorities. But obviously in your pocket. You move money in through the back door. No official record's kept of it. It's your bank so it doesn't matter. Then you apply for an unsupported loan, like any customer can. Only this one's real big. The board meets, gives you the once-over and the deal's approved. Of course the loan is never repaid and they don't call it in. If no one complains, and the local authorities usually don't give a damn, the worst thing the board can be accused of is being lousy businessmen. And they can't hang you for that."

The small car farther down the line, a rusting example of the Trabant, East Germany's dismal answer to the Volkswagen, known universally as a "Trabby," threw up a cloud of exhaust and crept uncertainly forward. "Of course, the main man's name never appears anywhere. He'll appoint a financial hotshot of some kind to front the operation for him. The less people involved the better. Often one guy'll handle the whole thing. Act as collector, laundry man, investment guru. How many people would Mielke want to trust with something like this? He'd need a single entity who could deliver all services."

The reason for the traffic jam soon became clear. The only exit from the complex was along Normannenstrasse. As the Trabby turned on to the main ring road, Lassiter got a clear view of the woman's face. The driver was Greta, the old Stasi staffer retained to work in the Records section.

"See, the operator, the 'rinser' as we call him, keeps the only books," Lassiter went on. "In this business, unless you're working from a tip-off— around eighty percent of our information comes that way—or you can actually show money being passed, the only real hope you have of running a trace is to identify the rinser. From all you've told me, this is an old scam, going back thirty years or more. If neither Mielke nor his family have the money, and you say they haven't, it's probably just ticking over right now. In a holding pattern somewhere. Invested in futures, stocks. Sitting in bank vaults. After all that time, the only possible chance you'd have of tracing it would be to find the rinser."

The kids who'd stoned Lassiter's car three hours ago were back on their patch. They'd been joined by four older youths. They stood drinking sullenly from beer cans, watching the traffic snake out of the complex.

Fraenkel said, "The bank statements the mistress gave us show a monthly salary being paid to the account of a man calling himself Krause. He's an obvious choice. Our people tried to run a trace on him but got nowhere."

"I'll look at it again."

One of the youths on Normannenstrasse suddenly noticed the Trabby. All of them immediately began to gather stones. Screaming abuse at the top of their voices they ran between the cars to where Greta's was trapped. Sensing what was to come, she slid down under the dashboard. A salvo of stones pounded the Trabby from three sides, shattering the windows. One of the youths ran forward, cleared a hole through a side window, put in his hand and tried to unlock the door. Fraenkel, Lassiter and other drivers around them got out of their cars and ran forward. The youth's hand was struck with something from inside the Trabby. From his position, way back in the line of traffic, Lassiter could see the youth jerk his hand free and kick at the door in fury. Another kid threw himself onto the bonnet wielding a steel bar and began to rain blows on the screaming woman through the broken windscreen. About a dozen drivers began to close in. One of the youths shouted an order. They slung away their weapons and took off at speed across a stretch of waste ground.

Fraenkel shook his head. "This happens all the time. The old Stasi staff run the gauntlet every day."

Lassiter threw up his hands. "My God, then they should have security guards here."

"They do."

"Well, where the hell are they then?"

"On strike, like everyone else in this goddam city."

☆   ☆   ☆

An archway and part of the perimeter wall were all that remained of the church that had once stood on the corner of Koenigsallee and Taubertstrasse. The ruins of the bombed building had finally been bulldozed in the Sixties and replaced with a ten-story apartment block. Now the blue steel panels that separated the crude concrete balconies were rusted through and smeared with Turkish graffiti.

Rudi Hoffman checked the address again and made his way to the entrance. Germany had been one of the last major European countries to form a sequestration unit, aimed at recovering laundered money salted away by convicted felons. At the outset, Hoffman had viewed his selection for the team with more than a few misgivings. But six months on, after a thorough retraining by the man who'd sniffed out more of the hidden assets of the criminal elite than any in the world, he readily admitted to a fascination with the whole subject. Exhilarated at the prospect of now working alongside his new mentor on the Mielke case, he'd spent most of the previous night ploughing through the files sent over from the Stasi. He checked his watch as he waited for the elevator. He was a little early, but that wouldn't go down badly.

As Hoffman reached forward to press the bell of Apartment 215 for the third time, there was the sound of a bolt being slid back and the door opened a few inches. Lassiter, his eyes red, his hair in disarray, stared blankly at the Customs agent. "Christ, what time is it?"

"Eight twenty. Sorry, I'm a little early." Hoffman shifted his weight on to the other foot.

Lassiter opened the door and struggled into his bathrobe. "I was awake most of the night. I must have slept through the alarm. Give me fifteen minutes." His large feet padded down the tiled floor to the bedroom.

Hoffman peered into the narrow dining room. "So this is where they've had you for the last six months. Cheap bastards."

"Oh, it's not so bad," the American called from the bedroom. "I suppose I've got used to it. At least it's close to everything."

Hoffman crossed into the living room. The half dozen framed botanical prints that, until Lassiter's arrival, had hung on the walls, lay in a corner stacked against a skirting board. In their place was what appeared to be some kind of rogue's gallery. Photographs of faces, hundreds of them: prints, newspaper clippings, squares of paper torn from magazines jostled for wall space from knee height to ceiling. Hoffman began to study them. "Jesus, some case you got here."

"It's not a case."

"What is it then?"

There was the sound of running water. "The Gallery. Faces that interest me."

Third row down, almost hidden behind one of the faded green curtains, Hoffman picked out a close-up of Germany's first postwar chancellor, Konrad Adenauer. Near to it was a crumpled fragment of newsprint showing Jean-Marie Le Pen, the leader of the French National Front. Near the door was a whole montage devoted to the Serbian premier, Slobodan Milosevic. Hoffman crossed the narrow passageway into the kitchen. Here too the faces were beginning to take over. Above the cooker, lines of noses. Around the sink, mouths and pairs of eyes. "What is this, some kind of hobby?" Hoffman called.

"I guess. I hardly know I'm pinning them up most of the time. I don't sleep much, haven't for years. Wake up around four, that's usually it. Sometimes I work, other times I call friends. In the States, Hawaii, other places. Some people doodle, I pin pictures. I first got hooked when I was working as a Customs officer in immigration at Kennedy. Comes in useful now and again. Make some coffee, will you, Hoffman? The stuff's all there by the sink. I've always been into faces. My uncle was a plastic surgeon. He taught me a lot too. He was the face-lift king of Fort Lauderdale. He used to say that "you don't spend a lifetime poring over the few ounces of flesh and gristle that make the face without learning something about the soul.'"

Lassiter came through to the kitchen in his shirttails and rummaged in the washing machine. "Some scalpel artists can read faces like clairvoyants read palms. The big difference, Uncle Frank used to say, is that the lines on a hand are pretty much set from the beginning. Sinner or saint, they hold their pattern." He extracted a pair of socks and turned back for the bedroom. "But a baby's face is as smooth as his ass. Look at it again in forty years and it'll tell you about the way he's lived, and therefore something about his future. Uncle Frank could tell you how every line, crease and puff on a man's face got to be there and what it signified. See that close-up, second down, third from the left, near the breadbin. What does it say to you?"

There was a pause while Hoffman searched for

the clipping. "Tough sonofabitch," he called back at last. "Ruthless, efficient."

"That'll do. Abe Lincoln said, "The dear Lord gave us our face but we make our own mouth." That's the mouth of Tariq Hassan, head of the Libyan secret police. He has a filing cabinet all to himself at Amnesty International." There was the hum of an electric razor. "You couldn't make me some toast could you, Hoffman? Toaster's shot, you'll have to put a dinner plate on the lever thing to hold it down. Now, what about the mouth next to it?"

The photograph had been cropped to show only the eyes nose and mouth. "Similar kind of guy. Killer, psychopath."

Lassiter laughed. "It's the mouth of Kenneth Branagh, the British actor. I saw him take out Laertes at the Barbican in London a few years back, but I hear the company speak pretty well of him. See, the mouths of the two men are similar, but there are key differences in the faces. Branagh's eyes are set farther apart, the upper lids aren't covered as they are in Tariq. Neither do the eyes themselves slope downward. Branagh is ambitious, a perfectionist, sure, but unlike Tariq he's a passionate man. He can be impulsive at times, let his heart rule his head. That's the last thing you could say about Hassan." Again the razor hummed. "The Libyan's ears sit lower on his head too, see? That means he's methodical, idealistic. The clue to the whole thing lies in the area between the mouth and the columella—that's the base of the nose. In Tariq, that space is narrow, the cleft in the flesh is deep. That combination often indicates cruelness, meanness of spirit. Now try the face below it."

"Monroe . . . Madonna. No, it's that model . . .

Chrissie somebody, the one who had the big affair with the U.S. attorney general. She just did that picture with De Niro."

"You got her. That's how she's looked for the last five years, since the collagen injections gave her that big-lip pout. Doesn't tell you a lot. The shot next to it, shows how her mouth looked before."

"Wow, a real hard type. Close to the . . . columella. Cold and ambitious."

"See, different scenario again. The face tells the story, but you need the medical history to crack it."

The montage of mug shots in the bedroom was still a fairly modest affair. Lassiter's attention shifted to the face across from him. It was a strong face. The configuration of lines on the forehead meant the man's life had been dogged by money worries. That barely detectable pattern of creases under the eyes had to be due to stress with a sexual partner. Puffiness around the cheekbones: the man drank. There was dullness in the eyes here too. So what did it all add up to? Lassiter pondered the question for a second. He pulled closer, inspecting the face in the shaving mirror one more time. A man at the end of his rope. Yup, that was it.

Hoffman stood in the doorway with two mugs of coffee.

"Thanks. Just put mine there." Lassiter ran a comb through his wiry salt and pepper hair. "To really get an insight you study the way a man moves and uses his face too. A man who continually strokes the side of his nose is subconsciously hiding half his face from you. He probably couldn't level with you if he tried. A man whose eyes go momentarily out of focus and look to the left when he speaks to you is probably lying.

"Okay, so a guy's cruel or secretive or ambitious . . . It's all good stuff, but where does it take you?"

After a minute, Lassiter said, "There's a face by the light switch in the living room. Guy with a panama hat."

Hoffman sipped his coffee and walked back down the corridor. "Yeah, got it."

"What does it say to you?"

Hoffman studied what was clearly a copy of a polaroid shot. "Well, he looks kind of pleased with himself."

"To me it says arrogant, vain." The phone rang. Lassiter crossed the bedroom and picked it up.

"You sleeping in this morning?" Erika sounded tired.

He reached across and shut the bedroom door. "No, just running late. How's it going?"

"Still on the Scheckler case. I've been trying to extract DNA from a decaying particle of human tissue, weighing something under a hundredth of a milligram, for three days. It's times like this you feel your life's narrowing, you know what I mean?"

"Yup. But it would be nice to nail that bastard for the killings."

"I already know he's a murderer."

"How so?"

"Well . . . " There was a pause. "He looks like one."

"That's a scientific conclusion?"

"No, an opinion. Forensic scientists do have personal opinions, you know." She sighed. "When I was a child, I used to imagine myself surrounded by giant sunflowers and squirrels, making cakes and gingerbread all day. Look at me now, nearly thirty, digging around in people's nail parings and the stuff that comes out of their private parts for a living. This is not a life, Jack." He laughed. "Am I seeing you tonight?" she asked.

"Sure."

"Well don't book anywhere, we'll eat in."

"Sounds good to me. Look, I can't talk for long, I've got Hoffman here. But . . . well, it looks as though I'll be coming back after the Pensicola hearing. I don't know for how long . . . "

"That's great!" There was a catch in Erika's voice. "I've spent the last three weeks trying to adjust to the idea of losing you."

"Well, it depends on how this new case pans out. We'll talk about it tonight."

"Okay." Her voice was a whisper. "I love you, Jack." She hung up.

Lassiter put on his jacket, picked up his attaché case and made for the door.

"The guy in the picture with the big opinion of himself, who is he?" Hoffman asked.

"Rahid Aziz. Saddam Hussein's rinser. He stuffed away nearly eight billion outside Iraq."

"So that's him."

"Switch the lights out, will you?" Lassiter carried a rubbish bag from the kitchen out to the communal hallway. "Like I told you, you don't get a trace on that kind of deal unless you get the rinser. If we'd had that photograph to start with, it would have made things a hell of a sight easier." He locked the door behind him and the two men walked to the elevator. "We had some bank statements of an account we suspected was his. There was only one traceable debit: to a tailor in Bangkok. He gave us a description. Seems our man'd had a couple of smart suits run up for himself while he was there. But the photofit we put together got us nowhere."

The men squeezed into the shabby lift. A small woman with two dachshunds moved shopping bags to make room for them. "A year later we traced a man we thought was him to a hotel in Nicosia. Missed him by minutes. When we took his room apart it seemed like we had nothing, but the key to finding him was a tumbler of water he'd left by a mirror in the bedroom. It turned out to be saline solution, made with table salt. There's only two things you use saline solution for. As an emetic—it works immediately, so you'd expect to find it near the john—or as a disinfectant. The local man on the case reckoned he was using it as mouthwash. But it made a connection. The photofit showed a man wearing a hat. That's when I went back to the tailor's statement. He said our man came in for three fittings. He never once took off the hat."

They walked out into the parking lot and made for Lassiter's car. "A college friend of mine always wore a hat, baseball cap, something. He was embarrassed by his baldness. Then he had a transplant, cheered him up a lot. I remembered he used to have to bathe his scalp with saline solution for a week after each set of implants were put in." Lassiter moved the BMW out into the line of cars that stood bumper to bumper down Koenigsallee. "I ran a check on transplant clinics in Nicosia." He chuckled. "That didn't take too long. It turned out some big London guy had retired there a few years back and was doing the odd job to keep his hand in. One thing most of those surgeons do as a matter of course is photograph their patients' heads at each stage to give them the 'before and after' effect. Seeing the new hair coming through buoys the patient enough to go through the discomfort of the next stage. I figured our rinser was just vain enough to let him take the shots. I had pictures of the surgeon's most recent patients sent to the tailor in Bangkok and he gave us Aziz. We picked him up at Orly Immigration in Paris two months later. It was his vanity that sank him."

"Okay." Hoffman nodded to himself. "I see where all this is leading. The Swiss bank account statements handed in by Mielke's mistress." Lassiter's face registered nothing. "The only traceable debits from it are the monthly ones to the account at the Friesler Bank in Berlin, held in the name of the man calling himself . . . " He checked through his notes. "Otto Krause. You think Krause was Mielke's rinser?"

"You don't pay someone a hundred and twenty thousand Deutschmarks a month to polish the limos."

Hoffman turned over the copy statements of the Krause account. It had been opened in '78 and closed in '89. All the withdrawals had been made in cash, except for one transfer of four thousand dollars, made to a numbered account held at the First City Bank of St. Stephen, in the Caribbean. The *Finanzamt* report made it clear that their investigators had used every means available to follow that lead through to the end but had got nowhere.

"I've run up against this St. Stephen before," Hoffman said. "That's one lead-lined tax haven."

Lassiter allowed himself a smile. "Depends on which direction you're taking a whack at it from. My opposite number at the Drug Enforcement Agency in Washington is real interested in a fella who's a big noise in those parts. The DEA have enough on him right now to extradite him, but he's more use to them in place. So they're talking to him. He sits on about a dozen boards in St. Stephen, including the First City Bank."

"You think he can get us to the microfiche records of the Krause account?"

"The DEA opens for business in six hours. I want the first fax my contact reads to be ours."

The traffic began to move. Lassiter edged the BMW over the corner of the sidewalk and swung left onto the autobahn. Five minutes later they crossed into what had been East Germany. "If one traceable debit can hook Aziz, it can hook our guy. We find him and we find the Mielke money."

THREE

The man with the unkempt hair and beard suddenly lolled over to rummage through the totebag on the bench beside him. Leland Daker refocused the Redfield telescopic sight on his rifle till the crosshairs on the lens lined up with the center of the man's forehead. His right forefinger bore down on the trigger. Satisfied that the man's existence was a sixteenth of an inch from extinction, he allowed himself a slow intake of breath.

Arlen Lydell, a short, wiry man in a blue suit, closed the distance between himself and the governor of Virginia and muttered into his lapel mike, "Vagrant type at ten o'clock."

Daker, hunkered on the roof of an Italian restaurant two storys above him, radioed back, "I already got him." He watched his target grope for his wine bottle a minute longer. "You got him, Ed?"

"Got him."

As the governor moved out of Daker's field of

vision, two city cops closed around the vagrant. "Okay, Ed my boy, it's all yours."

Ed Shale, positioned three roofs farther down the outdoor shopping mall in Springfield, Illinois, saw the Governor and the crowd around him move slowly into view. "Copy." Daker zipped the rifle back in its cover and hurried to the fire escape. By the time he reached ground level, the responsibility for the governor's life had passed to a third marksman stationed at the end of the mall.

"Governor on board." Daker pressed in his earpiece to focus the voice of the chauffeur in the stretch limo parked at the end of the mall. He switched off his radio and moved through the crowd, picking up Shale and the rest of his team as he went. A black Cadillac pulled into the space left by the limo and they climbed in.

"The Orioles got reamed," the chauffeur with a blond crew cut informed them.

"That's fifty bucks you owe me, Shale," Daker said, straining to follow the commentary on the governor's progress on the short wave. They moved up behind Lydell's car, which pulled ahead of the governor's limo.

"Those walkabouts play hell with my ulcer," Daker yawned. "What's next?"

Shale consulted his schedule. "The press call at the Courtney Plaza, St. Louis, in ninety minutes. Lydell's party."

"He's welcome to it. Jesus, what a week!" He ran a hand over his face. "That asshole at the airport this morning's lucky he still has a head! Incidents like that scare the crap out of me." He popped a yellow pill. "This is my last Presidential campaign, so help me God!"

☆   ☆   ☆

"Do I look as tired as I feel?"

Marianne Lassiter held the mirror steady and studied the tanned patrician face in front of her. The green eyes flecked with brown caught hers for a second. "Don't answer that." She watched as Governor Lowell Vandenberg ran a comb through the mane of newly razor-cut hair, shrugged at his reflection and turned his back to her. "Is all the paint out?"

"Yes."

"Are you certain?"

She moved forward to inspect his head as though he might have lice. "Yup."

"Okay. Let's do it." He moved out of the suite into the hotel corridor and was immediately surrounded by a dozen people.

"The man with red hair and the skin problem, sitting in the front row second from the right, is Bren Prendergast," Vandenberg's press secretary announced as they strode down the passageway. "He's with the Illinois *Herald*. Bad news for us. I've put some background together on him." He passed the governor a slip of paper. "The rest of them you know about."

Marianne followed her boss down to the stage entrance of the hotel conference room and proffered the usual glass of Evian water. Vandenberg took a sip.

"What was the gag about the color of the paint, again?" he said, above the sound of taped music. She cupped her hands around her mouth and spoke into his ear. "Okay, got it."

Marianne had been Vandenberg's administrative

assistant for almost seven years. He'd been impressed with her from the time she'd worked for her father, Senator Cattell. The old man's sight had begun to fail when he was in his sixties. In the next years, she had become his eyes. Increasingly, he relied on her to read him the reports, briefs and correspondence that gathered on his desk. She soon learned to select and edit as she knew her father would. Eventually, unable to recognize a face across a room, the senator began to rely on his daughter's memory too. So close was their teamwork that few ever guessed just how disabled he was.

Vandenberg recognized the value she would bring to him. He could readily absorb ideas, key data, strategy, but the day to day minutiae of the job, the names and personal details of many of those he came into contact with, often eluded him. When Senator Cattell finally retired, Marianne moved into Vandenberg's life. Now she was an indispensable part of it.

The governor waited for his cue. A voice echoed over the P.A. "Now I want to introduce you to the man you've come to meet. A man I believe will be the next President of the United States. Friends, Governor Lowell C. Vandenberg."

He had barely reached the mike when the first question came. "I understand a Mr. Walter Kapuzi threw paint at you at the airport this morning, Governor."

"Yup, black undercoat. It's totaled a pretty good suit. But it could have been worse. I mean, he could have thrown yellow or green. Even red! At least he isn't saying I'm a coward, a greenhorn or a commie!" There was a flicker of laughter.

"I understand he was reacting to your inner city development program that favor black communities."

"Is that a fact? Well, I'd say he's got my message a lot clearer than I got his. Sure, some of my inner city program do favor black communities. Others focus on Hispanic-American communities. The aim is to improve urban facilities wherever the need is greatest. The tensions that caused the riots we saw last summer are not special to Chicago. Something has to be done right now to give the people who live in the ghettos of this country some quality of life." Vandenberg switched his attention. "The lady with glasses at the back."

"This state still has some of the lowest educational standards in the country. What would you do to change that?"

"There's not only an urgent need to eradicate basic illiteracy—which I know is high in this state—but to restructure education across the board to meet changing needs . . . "

Political columnist Ethan Oates sat in the back row and studied the man on the stage in front of him. The ventilation in the room was poor. Many of the journalists had taken off their jackets. Now Vandenberg stripped off his, threw it to an aide in the wings and rolled up his sleeves as he talked. He was taller and leaner than Oates had expected and, rather than hiding behind a lectern or desk like most politicians on such occasions, he used the whole stage, "worked" it as an actor might. The face was continually animated. He moved as close to each new questioner as the space would allow and let nothing break his eye contact with them until he was done. A hand would punch the air to reinforce a point here, then would swing out in a sweeping gesture to indicate the breadth of a particular program there, his eyes following it as though a whole cityscape lay before him. The shirt started to discolor with sweat. The steel gray hair fell onto the forehead. But it was as though Vandenberg had concluded that he had vital information the questioner needed and nothing was gonna sidetrack him until she had it all. Now he spun around to make his point to the rest of the room, the eyes searching out faces to gauge a reaction. He was clearly enjoying himself. But the overriding impression was that this meeting mattered to him: hick town or no, they were gonna get the best he had to give.

"He does it well, I'll give him that," Oates said at last to the journalist next to him.

Marvin Kenner, an overweight veteran with a heavily lined face, doodled on his press kit. "He's out of the mold. Another bargain basement Kennedy. A good jawline and a good line in jaw. Okay, he's rich and he's pretty. But what else is he, Ethan?"

"Clean, Marv. He's clean."

"Yeah, like the East River!"

"Says who?"

"My fifty-six-year-old gut."

"We know the Republicans can't deliver that, we've seen it from the figures, heard it from employers. If they can't, then we must. Not just in this state, but nationally."

The man Vandenberg had quickly identified as Prendergast, the minute he walked on stage, didn't wait for a cue.

"Governor, people in the Jewish community

here feel they're picking up a lot of conflicting signals from you. I know having a Jewish mother gives you every right to claim that you're one of them, but you're also very visible in your support of the Episcopalian Church. Some would say you're trying to have your cake and eat it."

Vandenberg's smile faded but there was no anger in his face. "My mother's family were Dutch Jews, my father's were American Episcopalians. My parents died in World War Two and I was brought up in this country by my father's family and with their beliefs."

"I think most Jewish people . . . "

"Most Jewish people, Mr. Prendergast, will tell you that being Jewish is not just about religion. It's also about race. I feel that part of my heritage intensely. Like when I see kids marching up the streets of our cities waving swastika flags. Jewish people here are confused? Jewish people everywhere in this country are confused, Mr. Prendergast. When they see that, they feel that six million of their people died for nothing. Bren Prendergast; Prendergast's an old English name isn't it? And Bren, short for Brendan right? That's clearly Irish. Now let me take a wild guess. Catholic mother, Protestant father?"

Prendergast blinked a couple of times. "Methodist," he muttered.

"I'm sorry?"

"My father was a Methodist."

Vandenberg shot him a wide smile. "So why are you asking me what it feels like to grow up with a conflict of cultures, Bren?" He pointed to a tall man with a mustache.

"You showed fourth in the Maryland and

Georgia primaries, Governor. There's barely four months to go before the Democratic Convention. Your campaign is the least well organized and funded of the five candidates. How do you intend to improve your position in the race in the time that remains?"

"Well, first let me say, as far as the primary here goes, the six hundred volunteers I met this morning seemed pretty organized to me. But, with regard to my general position, you know yourself that this is the closest-run race in the last twenty years. Just a few thousand votes separate some of those placings. In a situation like this, a little campaigning can go a long way. The smallest upset can change things radically . . . "

With his eyes fixed on the questioner's, Vandenberg's peripheral vision took in the face of the woman standing just behind him. She was Hispanic, probably in her early twenties, and there was something familiar about her. As he worked through his prepared answer, a part of his mind searched to fit her into some department of his life, some past event. He focused on her directly. Her expression offered no clue as to her identity. He must have looked into fifty thousand faces in the last months, but something in this one . . .

The questioner, it seemed, was intent on having the last word. Vandenberg brought his mind to bear on what was being said and the woman faded from his thoughts.

Fifteen minutes later, the press conference was over and Vandenberg, his campaign manager, "Ches" Chesterfield, Marianne and two bodyguards were striding through the hotel kitchens, toward the staff exit. Marianne hurried up to the governor's side. "Here's two copies of tonight's speech with the changes you asked for. Oh, and there's this." She produced an envelope. "It came to reception here. I wouldn't have bothered you with it, but it was marked 'private and confidential' so I thought you might want to open it yourself."

The girl lifted her pleated gray skirt and pulled her spotless white blouse down to accentuate her small bust. She smoothed the skirt down and tugged at her white bobby socks before crossing the hotel suite and knocking timidly on the bedroom door. Lowell Vandenberg, dressed in a blue silk robe, opened the door a couple of inches. "No one saw you?" he asked. She shook her head. "Clever girl." He led her quickly in.

The bedroom was lit only by a lead crystal lamp on a secretaire. Champagne stood in an ice bucket on a tray. Vandenberg popped the cork with a practiced hand. "You drink this stuff?" he asked.

"Of course." The girl pouted and took the offered glass. The two kissed gently for a moment; the girl was nervous, awkward, but soon she allowed Vandenberg to unbutton her blouse and push it back to her shoulders, revealing a flimsy teenage bra. The kisses became more intense until he led her, still clothed, to the bed.

What followed was less adult foreplay, more heavy petting. Every advance was met with a small show of resistance. When he slipped his hand into her panties, her hand immediately locked around his wrist. He took a breath and said gently, "I thought you said you were sick of—what did you call it?—'teenage fumblings.' You wanted 'to make love with someone who knows what he's doing.'" The grip on his wrist loosened a little and then released. He pulled her hand into his robe and tried to close her fingers around his erection. She pulled it away. Vandenberg's patience snapped. He slid his hand under the small of her back, lifted her bodily off the bed and threw her over his lap. He pushed her skirt up roughly, then pulled her panties down to her knees. Slowly and deliberately, he spanked her, watching as the white cheeks of her buttocks reddened.

When he'd finished, he threw her on her back and got off the bed. He watched her as he slipped off his robe and finished his champagne, daring her to move. Now she watched him too. His brutish assertion that he was going to punish her still further was met with excited anticipation.

Vandenberg tipped the light so that it lit the counterpane of the bed a little more. For a second it was obvious that the girl curled seductively on it was a mature woman, one who'd clearly played this game before. But by now that no longer mattered. She ran her hands through the thick gray hair as he slid up the bed toward her, lifting her hips toward his face. She spread her legs and pressed his mouth hard into her. Panting hard, she spun over and knelt on the edge of the bed, her buttocks high in the air and waited to feel him penetrate her.

For fifteen minutes, Vandenberg lost himself in the sweating, writhing woman beneath him. Then he turned over and lay on his back, pulling her head gently to his chest. The phone beside the bed rang. The woman yawned and reached for it.

"It's five forty-five, Mr. Vandenberg, we need to leave in forty minutes."

"Okay, Marianne, we'll be ready."

☆   ☆   ☆

It was after midnight when Lowell and Stella Vandenberg left the five-thousand-dollar-a-plate fund-raiser in St. Louis and returned to their hotel. She went straight to bed; he sat in the living room of the suite and went over his briefing notes, to prepare himself for the following day's events. Amongst them was the envelope Marianne had given him. He tore it open to reveal a color photograph—a frontal shot of a naked couple standing in surf. The man was tall with a broad chest. His penis was erect, his hand between the girl's legs. His hair was dark brown, but there was no mistaking the face. Judging by the quality, it had been taken with a telephoto lens.

Vandenberg blinked at the photograph as a door in his mind, that had been closed for fifteen years, swung ajar. He turned it over. On the back, written in ink in a small, neat hand, was a telephone number and beneath it: "Call this mobile phone within seven days. Teresa."

The face in the crowd.

Sweat broke out in beads on Vandenberg's forehead. His bid for the nation's highest office was not fueled by any sudden burst of new ambition. It was the latest move in a game plan that had its seeds in his adolescence. Little he had turned his energies to in more than thirty years had been in the pursuit of any lesser objective. He'd lived through eleven presidencies and, like any apprentice, had striven to learn from the mistakes of his forerunners. One effect of his studies had been to make him obsessive about his own personal image. He'd known moments of great temptation, more than he dared think about. He looked at the photograph again. With this single exception, he'd resisted the urge to get drawn in, sacrificed all, to ensure his private life was above reproach. There could be no Mary-Jo Kopechne, no Donna Rice or Gennifer Flowers in his past . . . Lowell Vandenberg knew most of his own defects and a selective memory was not among them. One night on a beach in Manila, fifteen years ago, had simply not counted in the equation. Until now.

If she's looking to discredit me, break her story to a newspaper, she would never have alerted me this way, he advised himself. He worked to steady his breathing and began to turn over his options. She had to be looking for a payoff. Reason with the woman, maybe bargain with her? Untidy and fraught with risk. In this presidency, there could be no state troopers to dish the dirt on clandestine meetings, no "smoking bimbos" to boast of federal jobs for life in exchange for silence. Pay her off? But was any blackmailer ever paid off? In other areas of his life he had learned that such measures were half-measures. So let her surface, trace her and have her killed. *In extremis,* that had proved a solid option before.

But if she was smart enough to have staged this little exercise—she and a possible accomplice, the photographer—she was smart enough to have covered herself. She must have lodged the negative of the film with someone, probably an attorney. If Vandenberg tried to simplify the equation, the likelihood was the lawyer would have instructions to pass what he had to the media. Until he knew more he could do nothing but comply.

He studied the photograph again. The girl's

head barely reached the man's breastbone. Even in these times, the disclosure of a brief indiscretion so long ago, might not prove fatal. But this . . .

Vandenberg's sense of semirecognition in the press conference had been accurate enough. The woman was a stranger. But he had known—known and enjoyed—the child.

FOUR

The bottle spun high in the air, catching the reflection of the streetlights as it turned. For a second it seemed as though the petrol-soaked rag hanging from it had gone out, but the wind caught it as it fell, and a tongue of flame licked around the neck. The tight cluster of police sheltering beneath their riot shields parted and it smashed harmlessly on the asphalt. A second later, two more petrol bombs clattered onto the shields of the front ranks, exploding at once, showering glass across the narrow street.

The chanting began again with renewed vigor.

"*Ausländischen Dreck, raus! Ausländischen Dreck, raus!*"

Police at the back broke ranks to allow a water cannon to roll forward and deluge the rioters. Ten yards behind the lines, a mob of skinheads were breaking up paving stones with sledgehammers, shielded from view by an upturned car. Hands grabbed at the chunks of concrete and launched

them relentlessly at the wall of shields. A jet of
water sliced into the youths, sending them skidding
and sliding down the gutter.

For forty minutes the rioters, young men aged
between sixteen and twenty-five, had stormed the
barricade, spewing hate, tearing at anything that
they could hurl into the faces of the men who
formed a human wall in front of them. Now as they
fell back and tried to regroup, it seemed the
Brandenburg Gate, floodlit against a starless sky,
five hundred meters to the west, was to be their
bridge too far.

Here the street divided, the left leg bending
sharply southeast. Police strategy had been to close
off the main street at the fork and steer the
protesters down the leg and away from the Gate.
Already the main body of the mob were being
herded into the neck of it by a detachment of police
sitting on their tail. The third retail outlet down the
V-shaped stretch of land that separated the streets
was a department store. It had an entrance at both
ends. By the time the observer in the police
helicopter circling above had figured out the assault
on the store was more than just another act of
mindless vandalism, it was too late. Fifty youths,
some armed with guns, had smashed their way
through the building and out of the other entrance,
back into the main street, twenty yards behind the
police lines. Even the sight of the cornered men
putting on gas masks had no effect. Reserves
moved up. Tear gas canisters were lobbed in from
three directions.

The wind blew off the river carrying the acrid
smell to a crowd gathered behind steel barricades
at the far end of the street. Lassiter clapped his

hand to his mouth, turned around and pushed his way through to the lines of ditched cars that stretched out behind them. Erika sat huddled in her coat in the front passenger seat of the BMW. She sat up with a start as he opened the door. "There's no way through here. We'll have to leave the car and take the subway. We can pick a cab at Jungfernheide."

He checked the security alarm on the car and they set off for Unter Der Linden.

"*Ausländischen Dreck, raus!*" The chanting of the mob spat obscenities down the street. Lassiter pulled back onto the sidewalk as police cars sped past, their sirens wailing. In the six months he'd spent in Berlin he'd learned that *Gastarbeiter,* that once elegant euphemism for foreign worker, had become the dirtiest word of all.

A few hundred meters from here, a crowd of close to a million had danced in the street the night bulldozers had begun to tear down the wall that had divided their nation for close to forty years. Were any of the same people in that mob tonight? Lassiter wondered. Had any of them lost jobs to East Germans? To Poles, Hungarians, Serbs, Bosnians? It was hard to believe that any of the tattooed rabble he had seen charging the police had ever done a day's work in their lives.

Lassiter and Erika began to pick their way through the mountains of trash that spilled out across the sidewalk. Another night without streetlights. The damn city was falling apart. How could a national strike last for a month? Lassiter cursed, felt for the flashlight he'd had to pay almost thirty D-marks for a week before. Ahead of him was a skip, filled with garbage bags. The authorities had covered it with steel mesh to keep trash from blowing around the street. Sparks from a petrol bomb had set alight some of the bags. The mesh glowed red in places. Suddenly there was a muffled thud of something striking it from within. The mesh vibrated with the impact. Then again, the other side of the skip. There was a hissing sound, like steak being thrown onto a grill. It was as though the garbage had taken on a life of its own. There were rats trapped amongst the bags. He could smell them being roasted alive.

"There's a message on my answering machine for you." Erika emerged from the bedroom with her head wrapped in a towel. She bent at the waist and rewound it, tucking the loose end carefully into the top. "Someone called Reubermeyer wants you to call him back at the Washington office straightaway."

Lassiter downed the glass of chilled Gewurztraminer, poured himself another and crossed to the phone.

"What're you doing transferring the charges, you cheap gink." Reubermeyer sounded like he was in the middle of lunch. "This is personal stuff."

"What's the problem?"

"Don't you listen to your messages?"

"I haven't been home for a couple of nights."

Reubermeyer lowered his voice. "I've only had your bank on, that's all. They wanted to know if you changed address in Berlin. They seem kind of anxious to speak to you. I told 'em you hadn't, that you were probably snowed under with work. The things I do for you. You're damn lucky it was me that took the call."

"I'll call them. It's no big deal."

"I hope you're right. Look it's none of my business but . . . "

"I'll handle it, Mo."

"Okay, okay. I'll never understand you, Jack, I swear to God. Ask how much some Third World shitheel at the other end of the planet has got salted away in Kussnacht and you'll tell me to the nearest twenty bucks. Ask how much you spent on restaurants last month, you couldn't tell me to the nearest hundred. I don't know, ever since you split with Marianne . . . "

"Are you done?"

"I guess." Lassiter could hear him chewing on a sandwich. "So they're bringing you back for the Pensacola hearing."

"I'm the only one that saw money passed."

"Watch your back, my boy. Shit, liverwurst again! I hate liverwurst."

"Why don't you ask your wife to put something else in your sandwiches, Mo?"

"What do you mean 'wife?' I make 'em myself, goddam it."

Lassiter crossed the small duplex Erika rented above an optician in Charlottenburg and poured her a drink. "Problem?" she asked.

He studied her for a second. Her face was scrubbed and shiny, her hair scraped back, hidden in the towel. She looked very beautiful to him at that moment. "Nah. You want to eat at Kravitz tonight?"

Lassiter had met Erika on a double date five months before. The forensic scientists he'd been around were not usually known for their levity or eclecticism, and at first he'd found it hard to connect this vital young woman with such a bone-dry profession. The sexual attraction had been immediate—he was soon staying at her place up to three nights a week—but it had taken a little while for them to realize how much else they had in common—a restless curiosity, an indominitable individualism.

Erika was studying the map Lassiter had opened out on the kitchen table. "Are we going on vacation somewhere?"

"I wish. I had to go to three cartographers to get this. There obviously isn't much call in Germany for maps of the Lesser Antilles."

"What do you need it for?"

"The man we think Mielke used to salt away the money he was creaming off the Stasi had a numbered account at a bank here, on the island of St. Stephen." He took another map from his attaché case and unfolded it. "This shows a lot more detail. The DEA got me copy statements this morning. They show that he only ever made three withdrawals from it. All in cash, during '84 and '85. Then he closed the account. The amounts involved were fairly small. That usually suggests a *per diem* account. Mielke's man probably used it to pay for hotels, restaurants, trips to the bordello and so on."

"I suppose credit cards would be too traceable."

"And a local account would save him having to travel with large amounts of cash. The useful stuff was the bank's internal data. It showed that the withdrawals were in local currency. That's when I figured I needed a decent map. When you have so little to go on, it's very easy to see the man you're looking for as a row of digits at the top of a bank statement, instead of as a living, breathing, human being."

Lassiter put a pencil ring around the island's only airport and another around the perimeter of the city of Blanquilla, about seven miles distant. "It always helps to place your man in time and space. Then to try and figure out his movements." He rechecked the address of the bank and plotted it onto the map. "There is only one First City Bank in Blanquilla, and it's right on the airport road." He rubbed his chin. A full minute passed before he said, "You know what this calls for, Erika? Brain food."

A waiter with a large Zapata mustache pushed his way between the tables and set plates in front of Jack and Erika. She stared down at the multicolored concoctions arranged on hers. "I had no idea there was a Mexican restaurant in Charlottenburg."

Lassiter did Groucho eyebrows at her, as if to say, "Stick with me kid, you'll learn a lot."

"What's the thing in the center that looks like an upturned hairbrush?"

"Cerviche, little white fish set in bread. They don't cook them, just marinate them in lime juice and peppers overnight. They have an unusual taste. But this food is as much about textures and temperatures as it is flavors. Like the heat of the refried beans and burrito against the cold of the salsa verde and the sour cream."

Erika took a little of each onto her fork and tasted the mixture. "All right."

Lassiter ordered golden tequila with sangria chasers and waited for the combination to kick in.

"Criminals who find themselves in foreign countries often use local currency to make themselves less conspicuous. Rinsers are the most methodical of them all. If that's their regular policy—and it seems it was our man's—they'll apply it rigidly, from day one. The currency of St. Stephen is the Netherlands Antilles guilder. They're not marketed, so you can't buy them abroad." He carved a four-lane highway through his refried beans with his fork and took it to the outskirts of the city of Cerviche. "Our man arrives at the airport. He needs to change or draw money, there's no bureau de change there, because I checked. He takes a cab into the city. He has to pass the bank on his way, so he stops, draws out the cash he needs in local currency, and goes on."

Lassiter tipped back in his chair and started to wind down. "So the date of each withdrawal would be the same as the date he flew in." He poured a little of the tequila onto the fish and tried it. "If we can get to immigration records—a big 'if'—and we can match landing card data and identify a guy who entered the country on all three days, we can maybe find a face and a real name."

"Can I ask you something, Jack?" Erika toyed with her food. "This case, you talk like it really matters to you. I mean, don't get me wrong, but this isn't your country. The issues don't affect you either way. Why do you care?"

Lassiter pondered the question for a moment. "You know what finally screws you in this job? The feeling that you can bust your butt for as long as you like, but you'll never really change anything, never really make a difference. I knew ten years ago I'd gone about as far as I could in the department. The obvious move was to the DEA. But I'd been around those guys too long. I know how that one goes. You spend a chunk of lifetime trying to take a trafficker or dealer out of the system. Screw up your health, every decent relationship you've ever had, to get a conviction, and a day later, another trafficker'll be working the same run, another dealer selling from the same pitch. It's soul-destroying. I wasn't gonna get sucked down into that. Then in '85, the Wringers were formed."

"The Wringers?"

"Our part of the investigations unit was called that from the beginning. It's slang, tied in with the idea of 'laundering' money, I guess. We put the squeeze on the 'rinsers,' so that makes us 'wringers.' The unit was formed on the basis that all money recovered would go into the Federal Drug Rehabilitation Program. I don't think many of us had any idea how much some of these convicted drug barons had salted away. We started clawing back tens of millions of dollars. One day, they took us out to see this new detoxification center they'd just finished in Miami. It was a kind of a PR thing really, a booster for the boys. But I remember feeling good about myself that day. I really felt we were achieving something."

Two boys with guitars had started to pick their way through a José Feliciano tune. The strain of the day was beginning to tell on Lassiter now. The music was too loud for talk, so he paid the bill and they moved out into the narrow street. "The Wringers had been going about three years when I heard that some senate committee was going to make a lot of changes. In future, most of the money we recovered would be going to the Treasury Department, as part of the drive to balance the deficit or something. I got stonewalled when I tried to check it out. I didn't say too much to the guys I was working with because I didn't want to undermine morale. But to me it was the ultimate sellout. I was thinking of quitting altogether. And then the unit got expanded to include an OpReGo office—Operations against Renegade Governments. I got assigned to the Noriega case. Turned out he had cash stowed away everywhere, nearly four billion dollars hidden in eleven banks. At least most of that found its way back to Panama. A lot of it went to building homes for refugees."

In the shadows ahead of them, kids were spraying graffiti onto a wall. As the couple drew closer they ran off.

"You think that will happen with the Mielke money?" Erika asked.

"I really don't know. I have to find it first. But I'll tell you this, if I go back to the department now, it means starting work on another Pensacola case, or something like it. And my heart isn't in that any more."

"I wish I could believe that Mielke money would be used for something positive." The garbage bags were crammed so close along this stretch of road they had to walk some distance before they could find a place to cross. "It must be hard for you to understand what's happening in this country," Erika said. "It's hard for us, believe me. Unification was a fine dream. In the mid-Eighties, it seemed that's all it would ever be. Few people really sat down and thought the likely repercussions through. What was the point? And then wham! The Soviets pull out of territories they've occupied since the war, down comes the Wall; chaos. Our boundaries are open to refugees, as part of our 'Sorry For World War Two' policy. Suddenly: flood tide."

They turned off the street into the parking lot. Erika shone her flashlight ahead. "Germans were frightened already. Look around; how many German cars do you see? Not too many. My father was a child when the war ended. It was his generation whose energies helped rebuild this country from the ashes. He worked for Porsche, one of the great success stories of the Seventies and Eighties, until the Japanese got in on the act. He was made redundant three years ago. At his age, he's unlikely to find work again. People like him feel very aggrieved when they see jobs they might have had going to immigrants. To them, it's like when the house guest steals the Sunday lunch. I'm not saying for a minute he wants to behave like those Nazi thugs we saw tonight—they don't give a shit about the issues, they're just looking for faces to break—but people in his position are pretty vocal on the subject, I can tell you."

They got into the car and drove out onto a northbound street. Here, the doorways were crammed with sleeping homeless. Boxes, crates, shelters of every kind, spilled out onto the sidewalk. "The immigrants are only a part of the story," Erika continued. "But they're everywhere you look so they get more than their fair share of the blame. For other Germans, this strike is the outlet. They see Europe and the industrialized nations of the East changing at the speed of light around them but they won't accept that Germany has to change too. All they know is they have the highest salaries and the longest holidays in Europe—as far as they're concerned, they've earned them and they deserve them—and they're going to put up a hell of a fight before they let all they've struggled for slip away again. The misery of the early postwar years is all too fresh in their minds for that. They feel to give an inch, to agree to lower pay rises, longer hours, is the beginning of the rot."

"And what is this?" Lassiter said, gesturing at the chaos in the street around them.

"Unless we learn to change . . . a glimpse of things to come."

Erika stretched out under the sheets of her bed and focused her attention on the short verse being read aloud to her. Lassiter paused, plumped up his pillows, then continued,

" . . . *Mei Freund, des is a Mann von Tat. Wia jetzt sei Frau a Kind kriagt hat, na war mei allererste Frag: 'A Bua oder a Madl, sag?' 'Ja, du bist guat,' moant der, 'ja mei, da mischn mir uns doch net drei. Ob Bua, ob Madl muass beizeiten as Kinderl ganz alloa entscheiden'?*" He laughed, delighting in the wide peasanty dialect of the German south. "See what I mean?"

"No. Still sounds like gobbledegook to me." She turned and kissed his naked stomach.

"So much for my one-man mission to bring the pleasures of Bayrisch to the Prussians."

"Try something less rustic, more romantic," Erika said, settling back into the crook of his arm.

Lassiter closed the book in his hand, reciting from memory a troubadour's song:

Unter den Linden	*(*Under the Lime trees
an der Heide	on the heath
da unser zweier Bette was,	there, we made our bed,
da mugt ir vinden	there you'll find,
schone beide	beautiful together,
gebrochen Blumen unde Gras.	broken flowers and grasses,
vor dem Walde ein Tal,	and before the wood a vale,
Tandaradei	Tandaradei,
Schone sang die Nachtigal.	How sweetly sang the
	nightingale.*)*

She sighed. "How long will you be gone?"

Lassiter shifted uncomfortably. "Three weeks at the most. Let's not think about it now."

The heavy-lidded brown eyes narrowed. "No, let's not." She reached under the bedclothes and ran her hand down his stomach. She was surprised to find him erect. "I thought your mind was on the poetry."

He drew her face to his and kissed her. "It was. That was the whole point." His hand slid between her legs and their bodies moved together. He knew the way he read, the timbre of his voice, excited her, that his fingers would slip effortlessly into her now. In these moments, as her breathing slowed and deepened, when the act of love seemed inevitable, he'd think of Marianne. For the first two months he and Erika had been sleeping together, the woman he'd married, been captivated by, for more than four years, had invaded his mind. The nights he and Marianne had spent locked in each other's arms were still too fresh in his memory for their echoes to bring anything but a deep sense of loss. Then, as Erika's own softness and vulnerability began to touch him, Marianne had faded, into a disquieting shadow. Until the phone call from Washington, recalling him for the Pensacola hearing. As he began to adjust to the idea of going home, Marianne's face had taken shape again.

Erika kicked back the bedclothes and wrapped her white legs around him as he entered her. Marianne was there now: as Erika's body arched and twisted beneath him, it was her face he could feel pressed against his. Again, he shook the image away. Erika eyes opened, muscles relaxed. "What's the problem?" she asked.

"Nothing. Really. I'm just finding it hard to unwind."

She knows, damn it, he thought. He lifted her shoulders off the bed and rolled back until he was in a sitting position, so that she was straddling him. Her own bodyweight drove him deep into her. She came alight instantly, thrusting downward on him. He lay back on the bed and watched her hips move rhythmically against his. He made no attempt to hold back. Let it happen. Let it happen now. With it will come sleep. Peace.

The anguished cry that broke from Lassiter's lips echoed through the stillness of the bedroom. His stomach muscles spasmed, jackknifing his torso until his head almost touched his knees. Erika was wrenched from sleep. "Sweet Jesus, what's happened?" She threw back the bedclothes and sat up. Jack's wide open eyes stared vacantly ahead. A low moan rose from within him. Sweat dripped from his eyebrows and his whole body began to shake.

She put her fingers gently to his face. "Darling, wake up, please." He seized her by the shoulders, his fingers digging into her flesh. Gradually, the unblinking eyes began to focus. With a gasp of relief, he pulled her to his chest.

"Darling, what on earth did you dream?"

He swallowed and tried to find his voice. "Oh God . . . The subway thing. I was back there. It was just like it was."

"What subway thing?"

He let her go and ran his fingers though his wet hair. "When I was ten, when we lived in New York . . . We were going to Coney Island, Mel and I . . . " He got out of bed and put on his robe. "A maniac got into the rail car and shot a lot of people," he blurted out and made for the living room.

Air. I must have air. His mind raced as he struggled with the window that looked out over the tiny garden behind the flat. He cursed and hammered at the frame. Must get rid of the stink. His eyes were streaming again. He fought for breath. He felt a blast of cold air hit his face and drew it into his lungs as though his life depended on it. Still the acrid stink clung to the back of his throat.

Now he was fully awake, aware of Erika standing silently behind him. She reached forward and passed him a glass of brandy. He held it to his nose and drew in the scented aroma. Slowly the chemical odor faded.

Teargas. That was what he could smell. Police had pumped it into the rail car through the ventilation system. When options ran out, they'd taken the only choice left. The man in the motorbike leathers had shot three hostages already. He and Mel had cowered in the corner of the car with a dozen adults for almost seven hours. Screaming women, ashen-faced men waited to know who would die next. Police marksmen lurked behind makeshift barricades along the eastbound platform of the station, powerless. The man had killed so many now he had nothing to lose . . . Each mind screamed the same prayer: for pity's sake let them give him the money, let him go. Let him let us go . . . Then suddenly the hostages began to choke. The stench of human feces and blood was masked by another. Their eyes streamed with tears as Lassiter's streamed now. The carriage had filled with gray vapor. The gunman broke cover. He stood upright, clear of the seats. A volley of gunfire hit from all directions. He turned from man to a bloody carcass in a second. He pitched forward onto the sopping floor, two feet from where Jack and Mel lay, numb with fear. His face was shattered like a china doll's. Broken faces . . . all around them. Pieces . . . That's what Lassiter could see now.

" . . . The few ounces of flesh and gristle that make the human face . . . "

He shook the image away and tried again to focus on Erika. "It was the smell of the teargas . . . the riot we saw today. It triggered something in my subconscious. Something I badly want to forget."

At the third urging, Erika returned to bed. Lassiter sat alone by the window and waited for the brandy to kill the crippling ache in his gut. It had been there that night in the subway too, and for many months afterward. Not just from fear, but from shame. Irrational as it was, he felt deep inside someone should have done something to stop the man. *He* should have done something.

Tonight, maybe he'd take a pill, the hell with it. If he woke up feeling like he'd been whacked on the head with a shovel, then okay.

He flicked through the TV channels, then switched off the set. The prospect of another empty night alone stretched out in front of him. Of many nights to come. Self-hypnosis, therapy, relaxation tapes; he'd tried them all. *Abnegate the need to sleep.* Call someone. At least being on the other side of the world to most of one's friends and family meant they'd still be awake too. There was that about it. Who should he call? He knew then there was only one voice he wanted to hear.

Marianne Lassiter closed the bedroom door, then stood and listened, waiting for the cascade of notes that announced Brahms' First Piano Concerto. There it was. Why he always played that same CD when they were about to make love, she would never know. Mitch probably didn't even know himself. It had just got programed in there somewhere, like so many other things. That kind of predictability would be hard to live with all the time, she thought as she crossed to the bathroom. But then that wasn't likely to be her problem. The relationship was fine for now. That was all she knew. She stripped and stepped into the shower. Better not to think these things through too far.

She toweled herself dry in front of the full-length mirror. It was funny, whilst half the women she knew could spend a year fighting to shed eight to ten pounds, she had struggled for as long to regain all the weight she'd lost since the split with Jack. The bust that had surprised no one more than her, when it first swelled her blouses when she was fourteen, was back again. The perfect arc described by the small of her back and her buttocks had returned. She tended to think of herself primarily as a creative force, a questioning, intuitive animal. It had come as a shock a year ago to find how much of her self-confidence was rooted in the way she looked. Perhaps because she'd always taken it for granted.

"Are you gonna be in there all night?" His voice was barely audible over the sound of the music and the air-conditioning.

"Just give me a minute." It would be good tonight, she could tell. Until a year ago, she'd always felt confident, stripping in front of a lover, always enjoyed the level of arousal it seemed to create in them. Not that there had been so many, but enough for her to be sure of the kind of reaction she could expect. Then suddenly she was this shapeless, bony woman, alone and the wrong side of thirty. Much of the pleasure of sex had gone with that realization. But now, at last, that too seemed to be part of the past. The strain on her face had gone too. She studied her erect nipples in the mirror as she dried herself between her legs. The feeling she felt there was hard to describe. Not exactly an itching, not quite an ache. Yes, it would be good tonight. She applied her lipstick carefully, crossed to the closet drawer and began to look through her lingerie.

The phone rang. Let it, she thought, and slipped on a lacy camisole. There's nothing that can't wait a couple of hours. She heard the answer machine kick in. Suddenly there was Jack's voice.

"Hi, Marianne. Listen I'm leaving Berlin Friday. I'll be in Washington at the weekend. I may only be in town for ten days or so. I'd love it if we could meet. Just for lunch, if you can't make dinner. We really should talk, you know? Tuesday or Wednesday would be good. Look forward to seeing you, Babe. Bye."

As the machine switched off, Marianne rolled on hold-up stockings and stepped into a pair of high heels. She closed the door and checked herself in the mirror and tried to pretend that the feeling she'd felt two minutes before was still the same.

FIVE

"I don't think we have a choice here, Lowell. The order has to stand." Political adviser Vincent Krofft stopped making patterns in the stubs and ash that filled the glass tray in front of him. "Proposition Twenty-Six: Edrich qualifies on every count. Premeditation, homicide for financial gain . . ."

Lowell Vandenberg spun around. "Okay fellas, it's a wrap. Give me an hour and I'll call you all at home."

The boss's face was pale and drawn and experience told the three men in the room that he needed to be alone. Clearly, the decision whether to reprieve the first man to be executed in the state in seven years was one the governor meant to make on his own. Vandenberg stood by the French doors and stared into space, soaking up the first silence in the room for more than two hours.

He'd always found his official office, on the second floor of the residence in Richmond, Virginia, a cheerless place, so much of the real business of his governorship was done in the light airy space overlooking the grounds, known as "the garden room." Memorabilia from his days at Princeton and Oxford lined the walls. Pennants that hung from the wooden cornices came from the eras in his life when rowing and sailing were his passions. Three sofas upholstered in bright Mexican crewelwork surrounded a low walnut coffee table that, for all the polishing of the resident cleaning staff, was obviously destined to be stained with the marks of countless coffee cups and beer cans till the end of its functional life.

Each Tuesday and Friday morning he and his advisers met here to decide the role the state's chief executive would play in its future life. Vincent Krofft had been chief administrator from Vandenberg's first week as governor. Vernon Lacy had joined the team a year later as press secretary. Walt McDermott had too many functions, some indefinable, to have an official title, but had been head-hunted as a political strategist in the governor's third year in office. These three men formed Vandenberg's think tank. When decisions justified it, other experts were shipped in, but this was his kitchen cabinet.

Normally the discussions were toned with a lighthearted camaraderie, the banter often no more guarded or subtle than in the average bar. But this Tuesday, the mood was as grave as any in seven years. Now they gathered their papers quickly, muttered words of support and left. Vandenberg looked up. His wife stood in the doorway. Her arms hung limply at her sides. Her eyes sparkled, close to tears. "This is about Louis Edrich, isn't it?"

Vandenberg stared at her for a moment and nodded.

"You're going to let him die?"

"Stella . . . " He walked toward her.

"You're gonna let them kill him in the electric chair."

Vandenberg's voice softened. "Sweetheart, come here." He reached forward for her. She pulled away. He drew a long breath and he sank onto the sofa.

She dropped forward onto her knees and put her hands together. "In all these years I've never begged for anything, Lowell. But please, for the love of God, don't do this . . . "

In twelve years of marriage, Stella Vandenberg had never attempted to influence her husband's decision-making unasked. Even human rights issues, about which she felt passionately, were debated outside the home at the offices of 'Freedom To Live', of which she was a founding member. But an act of capital punishment, an obscenity her husband would ordain? It would not pass without her being heard.

"This man is insane, Lowell. He talks to himself in some made-up language . . . He has the IQ of . . . "

"I've read the reports."

"Lock him away, yes, for the rest of his life. But don't let them kill him. We don't have that right."

Seeing her in this act of supplication stunned him.

"Dear God, Stella . . . don't. Get up off your knees . . . " He tried to lift her, upward and toward him. She held firm.

"What purpose will it serve? What possible good will killing him achieve?"

He leaned forward and cradled the woman in his arms, finally lifting her to her feet and walking her to the window. "Listen to me." His voice was no more than a whisper. "Edrich planned to kill his neighbor for weeks. This was no sudden act of passion. He did it for gain, for money. That was his sole motive. He left the guy to die in agony. Three doctors say that he can clearly differentiate between right and wrong. That's what's at issue here. Proposition Twenty-Six . . . "

"Fuck Proposition Twenty-Six." It was almost a shriek.

"The laws of the State are clear. I love you Stella . . . " His voice cracked. "My God, you know that. If there was any way I could change this, don't you think I would? But I don't have one solid argument to justify stopping it." Her head fell onto his shoulder. "Okay, you're right. Killing Edrich doesn't achieve one damn thing. But that's just what I think. What we think. But right now, no one's asking me what *I* think. They're asking the governor of this state." He drew her close to him and ran his hand through her hair. "And as the governor of this state, I have to let the order stand. Stella, I have no other choice."

She sighed. For a moment the gray eyes locked with his. She saw only bleak resignation. At last she forced a weary smile, turned and left the office without a word.

The phone on Vandenberg's desk rang. It was Ches Chesterfield, his campaign manager. As usual, he sounded as though he was running late. "Have you looked through next week's schedule?"

"It's fine," said Vandenberg. "Except for Tuesday. I don't want to be taking questions from a room full of farmers at the end of a day's campaigning. Paterson's brief on the proposed subsidies is full of figures, Ches. I want to have them in my head when I speak with those guys, so I'm better doing it first thing. That way, I can look the report over during breakfast."

"Okay, I'll have them switch it around. And Edrich?"

Vandenberg shrugged. "The order stands. It'll be carried out tomorrow morning."

"I don't think you really had a choice, Lowell. I'll call you tonight."

Vandenberg took out a comb and ran it through his ruffled hair. I've taken enough simpering crap this morning to last a lifetime, he thought. The law-and-order lobby wants heads; I'll give them Edrich's. That should put the message on capital crime across clearly enough. The pupils of his eyes contracted in the bright morning sunlight. He burns; I win a primary? Sounds like a deal to me.

Soon after sun-up the next morning, Louis Edrich became the first man to die in the death house of the newly completed Williamsburg State Penitentiary. By tradition, Governor Vandenberg spent the morning working quietly in his office. Two nights later, for the first time in a month, he went home.

Home was a hundred miles north, in Mclean—a wealthy enclave bordering Washington D.C. Hague House, a vast rambling mansion in fifteen acres of ground, had been designed for his great-grandfather in the 1890s by the same architect who'd created magnificent properties for the Rockefellers and the Vanderbilts a decade earlier. The formal diningroom was intended, like the rest of the place, to say much about the family, which traced its billionaire status back to the Dutch East India Trading Company. Like most of their homes, it was formal, heavy and essentially European in style. The dining room would have been cold and cheerless by modern standards, but for the fact that the areas between the marble Palladian-style pillars that lined the walls were hung with a warm terracotta-colored silk. Each space was further brightened by a large oil on canvas landscape. Lit by candles and table lamps, the room was surprisingly hospitable.

Tonight there was a special guest, the only surviving member of Lowell's family on his mother's side. Aunt Helga had been her half-sister, and had only come out of World War Two alive because of her marriage to a Swiss banker in 1938. At the time of the German invasion of her native Holland, she had been living with him in Zurich, in neutral Switzerland. By the time she was able to return to her homeland in late 1945, every member of her family except Lowell was dead. He owed much to his aunt. But for her, he too would have perished. It had been to Helga and her husband that the Red Cross entrusted the thirteen-month-old baby in 1941. Knowing only that he'd been smuggled out of Germany to Switzerland in great secrecy, they had brought him here, to the safety of his grandfather's home in America, a year later. When it became clear that his expatriate father and Dutch mother had both died in concentration camps, his father's brother, Walter, had adopted the child.

Now Aunt Helga was in her late seventies, a small, bent woman with lively eyes. Vandenberg pushed his soufflé around his plate as Stella attempted to explain the significance of the primaries to the old lady.

"I don't know a great deal about what's happening here," she said at last, "but I know what's going on all over Europe. Tell me, Lowell, if you were the president of the U.S., would you send troops to Moldavia and try and stop the civil war there?"

His eyes creased into a smile. "Oh, so I'm back on the hustings, am I?" He thought for a moment. "I might, as part of a UN initiative. People in this country are terrified of another Vietnam or another Korea. No one wants to take men away from their families and draft them to fight in a foreign war again. So, what's important to get across with issues like Moldavia is that UN initiatives only involve professional soldiers. No one's saying that putting them at risk is any less concerning, but men who volunteer . . . "

Aunt Helga dabbed her mouth with a napkin. "Every man who comes home in a body bag will still be somebody's son, somebody's brother . . . "

The phone on the sideboard rang. Stella threw down her fork. "Oh really, they could at least leave us alone during dinner."

Lowell got up and shrugged. "It'll only be like this for a while, I promise you."

The caller was Ches Chesterfield. "Listen, we're all agreed about the new TV campaign. It doesn't punch the messages home nearly strongly enough. Not for what it's gonna cost. To re-do your stuff would take at least two days that we can't afford to lose out of the Florida schedule. My feeling is, we should stay with what we've got, till we have something new worth selling."

"Well, the director told me they could reshoot all my stuff Tuesday before we leave." Vandenberg poured himself cognac from a decanter. "They could have a rough cut for us tomorrow week."

There was silence at the other end of the line. Then Chesterfield sighed and said, "All right, I'll level with you. Even if the new campaign was a killer, we'd still have to hold off. The simple truth is, an air offensive on that scale would knock close to a million and a half out of the fund. You know how much we're committed to across the board already. Writing a check like that . . . "

Vandenberg sounded shaken. "I thought the fund was building well."

"Yeah, it's building. But it's still nowhere near where it needs to be."

"You're still getting: "Why doesn't he just write a check himself and have the nomination sent around?'"

"Yeah, we get some of that. So did Ross Perot at the beginning. When he started to look like a contender, the money came in quick enough."

"And I don't look like a contender?"

"At fourth in the race, no, not yet. That's what you're paying me for. You have the best, most experienced team in the game. It'll all turn around, believe me."

"And the Marcus factor?"

"Well, that's hurting us too. But we always knew that was gonna be an issue. People hear Vandenberg, they think of your cousin, goofing it up in '88. That'll pass, no staying power. I wouldn't be running this if I didn't have faith, you know that. It's early days. I don't have all the answers but I can tell you this: every time you speak, people believe.

They change their views. They commit their votes and their money. And that's the most powerful asset we could have. Listen, relax, get a good night's sleep and we'll speak in the morning."

Vandenberg hung up and walked back to his seat. Marcus had a lot to answer for. It was impossible to know how badly his own cousin's disastrous bid for the Presidency in the late Eighties, and the revelations about his private life that followed it, would damage Lowell's credibility. It was Marcus's animosity that had resulted in Lowell inheriting such a small part of the family fortune. He was certainly in no position to write a check for the better part of the twenty million dollars that still needed to be raised, as many in the media had hinted he could. He studied the picture above the fireplace and wondered just how was he going to convince the electorate of that.

The painting was of John F. Kennedy. Papa Joe had given it to Lowell's uncle, the year his son had taken office. As a young man, Lowell had followed the Kennedy years with a keen interest. Seeing how the nation fawned on a couple who seemed to many to come as close to a monarchy as America would ever want to get. He was certain they would go for that glamour again, given a chance. And he was convinced that he had both the personal charisma and the patrician heritage the American people longed for in a leader.

But in Kennedy's day, the agencies of government could insulate and sanitize a President's private life. The public knew only what the White House wanted them to know. All that was long gone. Vandenberg was very clear that these were times when a puritan facade was a piece of public equipment that you couldn't afford to be without, as vital as a bullet-proof vest. To make the long journey from candidate to nominee, to reach the Oval Office and hold on to it for eight years, you needed, above all, to have an unimpeachable past. And Vandenberg had lived his life obsessively conscious of the fact. Now this little tramp from Manila was threatening everything he had worked for. The next four months would push his mental energies to the limit. She could not be allowed to distract him, could not be left free to torment him in the years that lay ahead. He checked his watch. She would call in an hour, then perhaps he would get a trace on her.

When the ladies retired to the living room for coffee Vandenberg excused himself and walked through the house to the "new" east wing which had been completed in the early Eighties. The upper floor was given over to offices. The ground floor housed his art gallery and screening room.

Vandenberg's fascination with the moving image had begun in a more traditional context. With the inheritance of Hague House had come a small but fine collection of paintings and *objets d'art*. When his appreciation of these led him to add to the collection, his tastes had begun to broaden toward less representational styles. He turned from one modernist form to another, looking for some different vision. The gallery that dominated the ground floor was the showplace for his growing acquisitions. Video art was his current passion. A collector could pay hundreds of thousands of dollars for a one-off cassette and have the satisfaction of knowing he could view the continuous loop of animated surreal or abstract forms, often combined with photographic images, as an exclusive experience. The creators of these precious black boxes of acetate tape usually insisted that the buyer view their work in a specified environment. Creating a room of predetermined proportions, painted entirely in black, had been just one of the conditions Vandenberg had been obliged to fulfill in order to be allowed to acquire a work by one of the accepted masters.

Taken together with his lifelong fascination with archive footage and current affairs, it was not unnatural that this new passion should express itself in his building a screening theater and compiling the vast video library that was housed beneath the southwest corner of the gallery.

Vandenberg threaded his way through statues and installations, now bizarre and unsettling shapes in the late evening light. The screening room was lined on every surface with dark gray short-piled carpet. Although four large armchairs dominated the interior space, only one, set apart at the back, was ever used. For this room, with its large, high-definition central screen, ringed by a dozen regular video monitors, was Lowell Vandenberg's private sanctum, the birthing bed of his dreams.

To his right was a computer screen and keyboard onto which his fingers fell naturally when he settled back into the leather armchair. Vandenberg's fingers skittered over it, punching index codes that would access all the latest media coverage given to his rivals, plus updates on their campaign strategy, fund-raising activities and current poll ratings. Anything and everything that might be relevant to his improving his position in the race for the Democratic nomination in July. He marshalled his thoughts while state-of-the-art

technology that linked a computer program to a
racking and loading system, sought out the tapes
he'd selected from a constantly updated video
archive, stored in what had been the old wine cellar.

On the central screen now was footage of
Senator Edgar Hersh, standing on a vintage fire
engine, waving to a large crowd of supporters. A
caption at the bottom of the frame, added by one of
his full-time librarians, told him that the tape was
from a local TV station in Georgia and had been
shown by a dozen others during the day.

A screen to the upper left, displaying key polls,
still showed Hersh as Democratic front-runner. He'd
been a senator for nine years. Most of his education
had been gained on the hoof, as an army officer
with a list of foreign campaigns to his credit. He was
manly rather than handsome. Vandenberg's media
analysts reported that Hersh had shed at least
thirty pounds off his six foot three frame and had
his hairline taken up a quarter of an inch to give his
forehead greater height and presumably the
impression of greater intelligence. Nothing could
hide his Slavic peasant origins, Vandenberg thought
now.

Hersh's power base was broad, his campaign
well funded and efficiently organized. Screens to the
right listed his team: campaign president, fund
manager, media director, political strategists, spin
doctors and speech writers. The screen below gave
the text of his latest speech. To Vandenberg, the
bulk of his offering was a warmed-over mishmash of
programs aimed at re-restructuring taxes, health
care and law enforcement, based on thinking that
was dated and unrealistic. But his plans to lower
unemployment, to retrain and relocate the trained,

were more impressive than any of his rivals, and it was that, more than anything, that was gaining him support.

Vandenberg's fingers tapped into the keyboard again. Gradually images of Hersh faded and the face of Illinois Governor Bradley Mandel replaced them. According to most polls, Mandel was running second in the race. He was an Ivy Leaguer, middle-class background, Harvard MBA. His latest TV commercial and radio sound bites displayed a boyish charm, but he spoke in a flat Midwestern drawl that seemed to take the edge off even the most trenchant rhetoric. He was underfunded and, most importantly from Vandenberg's point of view, he was a practicing Catholic. It had taken the Mafia to deliver the crucial votes that gave America's first Catholic President, John F. Kennedy, a slender majority in 1960. For Mandel, there would be no Mafia. To Vandenberg it was obvious that Baptists, Episcopalians, and all the other brands of Protestants that formed the mainstream of voters registered to the party, would mark their cards elsewhere.

Third in the race was Gene Bravington, acknowledged as the most credible black candidate ever fielded. Born in the L.A. ghetto, he'd gained higher education at night school and had been called to the American bar when he was almost thirty. Vandenberg turned up the sound and listened to a speech he'd given that morning to factory workers in Detroit.

"I'm not taking the black vote. I'm creating a black vote! In the last election, less than one in five blacks voted. There's millions of worthwhile Americans out there who just say to themselves:

'What's the point in voting for any of these guys? What are they gonna do for me and my family? What's really gonna change?' Well I believe I can get these voters to care this time. To trust what I promise and vote for what I mean to do. And that's gonna change one heck of a lot. Not just for them, but for anyone in this country who asks themselves each day: 'Why don't I own a home? Why don't I have a job?' I tell you, I know how that feels. I didn't want to be there, so why should they?"

Bravington could unquestionably find support in the inner cities that the other candidates could not. All the same, no political analyst seriously believed he could become America's first black president—the country wasn't ready for that. But with Bravington running as the nominee for vice president? It would be a dream ticket for any of the candidates. Many of them had had representatives open up lines of communication with Bravington's camp, within weeks of him declaring as a runner. Vandenberg knew that he, himself, would have to be showing a lot higher in the polls before Bravington paid serious mind to anything his people had to say.

Fourth in the race for the presidential nomination was Vandenberg himself. A screen to the left gave his CV: " . . . graduated from West Point in '63 . . . Tour of duty in Vietnam, honorable discharge with rank of captain . . . entered Harvard Law School. Called to the Bar in '68. Joined the law firm of Forbisher, Caulfield, Bowers the following year . . . joined the main board in '74. Elected to the House as the representative of the Fourteenth District of Virginia two years later . . . "

He watched impassively as a montage of his TV commercials played through. Still fourth, he thought. There were just four months to change that. He could not beef up his poll rating without increased exposure, and Chesterfield insisted that required more money. And the money would only come with an improved credibility rating. A vicious circle. And the upcoming "Super Tuesday Primaries"—the elections amongst the party's registered voters, predominantly in the southern states including the populous Florida and Texas—seemed unlikely to improve his fortunes.

The mobile phone rang. Vandenberg's heart missed a beat. He checked his watch. She was five minutes early. The heavily accented English left him in no doubt as to who his caller was. "I don't want to make trouble for you. I don't want to make trouble for anyone. I just want to go back to Luzon. I need enough money to buy a home and start a new life there. Three hundred thousand will do it. Then you'll never hear from me again, I swear."

Vandenberg turned to the computer in front of him, cued a program, and typed into the keyboard. He held the mobile phone to the speaker as a synthesized voice asked, "How can I be certain of that?"

"I was twelve years old the last time you saw me, Mr. Vandenberg. I'm now twenty-seven. But some things don't change. I'm still a girl from a little village outside Manila. I saw how things happen in the Philippines, how they happen here. Where I come from you learn: if you get a break, don't push your luck. Take the money and run."

Vandenberg typed again. "How will I get the money to you?"

"There's too much at stake for you to play games with me, we both know that. I have opened a bank account specially for this." She gave him the account number. "You can transfer the money there any way you want. The minute I have it, I'll send the negative of the film to any address you give me." Teresa rang off.

Vandenberg poured himself more cognac and sat down. His one slip in almost thirty years of calculation was going to cost him dear. He'd met Teresa only once, when he'd been part of a trade delegation to the Philippines in the early Eighties. Ferdinand Marcos had gone to great lengths to ensure that his valued guests had everything they needed to make them comfortable, so Vandenberg was not surprised when Teresa turned up at the door of his hotel suite in Manila with a bottle of Cristal champagne. What shook him was how young she was, no more than a child. He was entranced.

Just why such a nymphet should fascinate him, he'd never fully understood. He only knew that, once you had broken the greatest of all taboos and taken human life, the others held few mysteries that defied examination. The youth, the vitality, the purity; it was as though he might draw some of it into himself through such an encounter. Was that why he still had Stella play out a teenage fantasy?

As taken with Teresa as he was that night, he hadn't dared risk making love to her in the hotel. Instead she agreed to meet him at daybreak outside the town. They would drive to a beach of his choosing and make love there. Six thousand miles from home, who would ever know? For more than two hours, they had lain on the sand in each others arms, with only the sound of the breakers and seabirds circling above them. Two days later Vandenberg returned to the U.S.

Fifteen years on, he was to learn that someone, probably also in the pay of Marcos, had taken shots of the whole episode using a 35mm camera fitted with a telephoto lens. Just how the Marcos régime had intended to make use of it would never be known. He and his spendthrift wife, Imelda, had been forced to flee the country in 1986. But Vandenberg had few doubts what Teresa would do with it, if her demands were not met.

She may not be an educated woman, he reasoned as he canceled the synthesizer program. But she will have lodged the negative of the film and some kind of a statement with someone for safekeeping. Probably a lawyer. I may be able to get a trace on her through her banking data, then I can have her watched, have her phone tapped. There's only one man I can trust to handle this. He'll have to be redeployed for a day or two. Then all Teresa will have to do is contact the attorney once and I'll know who, and what to do.

Now he dialed the number of a computer hacker in Chicago who'd proved useful to him in the past. Hacking into bank databases, he knew, formed a routine part of the man's day. When there was a time problem, a little "social engineering" was sometimes necessary to procure an entry code. That might require a sweetener or two. But the man's rates were never unreasonable . . .

The hacker answered warily. As they talked, Vandenberg's fingers moved over the computer keyboard again. The images on the center screen gave way to footage of a lanky man in a white T-shirt and loose-fitting cotton pants, being led into an overlit room. There was no tone in his movement. He planted his feet heavily, reacted to the glare of the light sluggishly, as if he was drugged. The camera panned, following the shambling figure as he was conducted through lines of somberly dressed men to a solidly made wooden chair on a low rostrum. Two attendants lowered him onto it and strapped him in. For a moment, as he sat whilst metal contacts were attached to his head and ankles, he resembled some enthroned potentate facing his court. The attendants withdrew. Seconds later, a man standing to the far right of frame, lowered his hand. The blindfolded man in the chair seemed to spring to life like some ghastly marionette. Every muscle in his body was thrown into spasm. His fingers reached forward through the straps as though in a frenzied attempt to grasp something beyond their reach. The tongue thrust out of a silent howl, vibrating like the tail of a rattlesnake. The white blindfold was suddenly stained with two patches of dark sizzling blood. Louis Edrich's head fell forward onto his chest.

Vandenberg put down the phone and sat watching the images. "What purpose does killing this man serve?" Stella had asked. In politics, there were few ill winds, he thought. Every death brought its benefits.

SIX

"**Have you ever come across the stone tapes**
theory?" Fraenkel's voice resonated through the
vast empty shed.

Lassiter looked around him and thought for a
moment. "No, I think that one slipped by me."

"It's based on the idea that exceptionally
traumatic events may generate energies so violent
they actually record themselves into the fabric of
the buildings and the rooms where they happen?"

Lassiter had never heard Fraenkel talk about
anything so fanciful, or less connected with their
professional concerns. "I suppose if you can get
materials like plastic and celluloid to retain a
replayable image, you can't rule out stone or brick,"
he said.

Fraenkel turned and began to walk along the east
wall, inspecting the indentations, the rusting metal
rings protruding from it. "I don't know if I believe in
the theory or not. But if there's any place in Berlin
that has stone tape energy it should be here."

"This was the Counter-Dissident Block, I take it?"

Fraenkel leaned against a heavy steel door at the end of the room and they moved out into the main corridor. "For a nation that was able to put the first satellite into orbit, the Soviets didn't stretch their imaginations too far when it came to updating their interrogation techniques. They seem to have been content to muddle through with the usual cattle prods and chainsaws. Surprising really." He lit a cigarette. "We think there could be anything up to five thousand bodies buried out there under where the executive car park is now."

Fraenkel's face caught Lassiter's attention. For a fleeting second it seemed as though the irises of his eyes were rimmed with white. The nostrils dilated, the man swallowed. Fear.

"It's only a matter of time before we have to start digging the whole thing up."

Lassiter had put Fraenkel in his mid-fifties, with that gray hair and heavily lined face, but now it occurred to him that he might be younger. Perhaps late forties. He checked the man's hands. The skin was smooth, free of liver spots. He studied his neck and his eyes. Fraenkel probably wasn't a day over forty-two.

The geography of the Stasi complex was still a complete mystery to Lassiter. It was only the long gallery lined with busts of Lenin, that told him he was back in the main administration block. "Do you mind if I ask you something, Herr Fraenkel? Why do you go there?"

Fraenkel stopped and faced him. "I can't help myself. Is that a good enough reason?"

"Yes." I have stepped inside his grief, Lassiter thought. It's a private place where only he goes. I was wrong to ask.

"So you want us to hunt out every picture of Mielke ever taken?" Fraenkel said.

"Taken since late teenage."

"And then what?"

"I want you to put together a team from some of the old staffers you have here. Have them go through every photograph and see if they can find a face. I should have a shot of the gentleman I want a match on by this time tomorrow."

Lassiter explained that the man he suspected was Mielke's rinser had made withdrawals from a bank account he had in St. Stephen on three dates in 1984. His theory was that they were also the dates the man had entered the country. It had taken pressure and good luck to obtain copies of the landing cards handed in by those entering the country on the given days. Pressure from three U.S. departments on the immigration authorities in St. Stephen to release the detailing. Luck because the records they needed were over ten years old and might have been junked long before.

Fraenkel unlocked the office that had once been Mielke's and checked through the messages on his desk. "So what did they tell you?"

"The name the man used on his Berlin account was Otto Krause. We know that was an alias and I wasn't surprised to find no landing card bearing that name on the days in question. No one person with the same name and passport number flew to St. Stephen on all three dates. Three men came in on two of them. One turned out to be a pilot for American Airlines, another was a local hotelier. We discounted them both. The third man was a different story. The Swiss passport office say no papers correlating with the data we faxed them were ever issued."

"So Number Three's a phoney."

"Has to be. But is he our phoney? I hope to know that for certain by tonight."

"Does Interpol have anything on him?"

"Nothing. And there was no way St. Stephen would have had an IDM system then, probably doesn't even have one now . . . "

"A what system?"

"IDM—Immigration Data Microfiching. You must have noticed, an immigration officer usually puts your passport under a desk light to read it. Well, it isn't just a light. It holds a concealed camera that works automatically."

"Oh, I see. You thought you might get a look at the man's passport photograph that way."

"Well, that was the general idea. The St. Stephen's landing card filled out by Number Three, shows he'd come in from Amsterdam via Miami. All transit passengers have to go through immigration in Miami, regardless of where their final destination is, and the authorities there have operated an IDM system since the early Eighties. Still, after such a passage of time, tracing the records we needed was no easy matter."

"I can imagine."

"The shot Miami eventually sent us was of very poor quality. I'm having some work done on it. But at least we now have a face. There's only one way I can think of pushing things on any further and that is to take a leaf out of the CIA's book. Put together a file of every picture taken of Mielke since he first put on long pants. See what company he kept over the years. If we could find Number Three's face in just one of them, we've got our connection . . . "

☆   ☆   ☆

The Berlin Police Photographic Unit was in a cul-de-sac off Stendalerstrasse. Lassiter flicked on the flashlight and negotiated his way through the inevitable mountain of trash bags. Raw sewage spewed out of a crack in the rickety paving stones, soaking his shoes. He gave his name to the security officer on the door and was taken to a laboratory on the sixth floor.

Max Gehrhart listened to the squelch of Lassiter's shoes as he approached. "I see you found the sewage pipe."

"Jesus Christ, Max, isn't this city ever gonna function normally again?" Lassiter had fully expected to see Number Three's face on the computer screen at Gehrhart's terminal. Instead he was greeted by a photograph of his own.

"If you're going to sit near me, Lassiter, do me the favor of passing over that aerosol . . . Thanks." Max sprayed around himself liberally with air freshener. He took a gulp from a tarnished silver hip flask and wiped his mouth. "Right, what you see on the screen is a computer graphic, sampled from the full-face photograph we took of you yesterday." He turned up the color a little. "The quality of the image has been enhanced to make the analysis easier. The computer program has a hundred and eighty thousand different faces in its data bank. Using what it's learned about them, it can scan this graphic a pixel at a time. To do what we want it to do, it'll take particular interest in the slightly shaded areas, see, that little shadow under your cheek. The dark area around the bridge of your nose. The whole process takes about five hours to complete. Then this is what you get."

He typed into the keyboard, and the flat two-dimensional image of Lassiter's head began to rotate, showing a three-quarter view of his face and then his full profile. Lassiter stared at it transfixed.

"Keep still Jack." Max produced the Polaroid camera again and took a shot of Lassiter's face in profile. As the image slowly formed on the card, he held it up to the screen. "The simulation has got your chin a little too pointed, but apart from that . . . "

"It's a pretty accurate system."

"Oh, this is only for starters. Want to see what you'll look like in twenty years?"

"No thanks. I think I can live without that at the moment."

Max changed the software and his own face came up on the screen again. "Here's how the simulation reckons I looked at the age of eighteen." As the image began to alter, like the picture of Dorian Gray in reverse, Max rummaged through the drawer of his desk and finally found a buff-colored envelope, from which he slid a black and white print obviously taken with a box camera. "Here's a picture of me at nearly twenty." He held it up to the screen so that Lassiter could make a comparison.

The Customs agent nodded slowly. "Extraordinary."

"But the important one is this picture of my father and mother. Oh, and here's one of my brother." He pulled out some sheets of computer printout. "These are profiles I've written on all three of them. All I know or could remember. Their dietary and drinking habits, hobbies, exercise routines. I also have on file their medical reports and their DNA profiles showing hereditary defects and traits. All this data affects the way one ages. This program will take it into account. Okay, hold your breath. Here's how I'll look in twenty years when I'm sixty."

As Lassiter watched, the three-dimensional graphic of Max's face began to age. The hairline receded. Lines appeared on the forehead, wrinkles below the eyes. The nose blunted a little and the jawline sagged. Max reacted as though it was the first time he'd seen it.

"God in heaven, what a prospect!"

"I had no idea the technology had come so far. I've been fascinated with faces all my life . . . "

"Why do you think I'm bothering to show you all this? Hoffman told me all about you. About the state of your living room."

"Yeah, but that's amateur stuff."

"Not necessarily. You can't beat the human eye. Or the human nose. Pass the aerosol again will you?" Max changed the software again. "Okay, here's the computer-enhanced version of Number Three." Lassiter stared at the new, sharp, colorized version of the passport photograph. It showed the gaunt, humorless face of a man in his late sixties or early seventies. "That's a vast improvement."

"Cheerful-looking fella, isn't he? I bet he's fun at parties."

"Rotate the head through three hundred and sixty degrees." Lassiter sat transfixed as the head revolved. "Could you give me a printout of how he looks at each thirty degrees of turn and an aerial view?"

There was one area of wallpaper, above the freezer in Lassiter's kitchen, that had yet to give way to the Rogues's Gallery. It had remained unblemished for months, as though he was planning something special for it. Lassiter stood in the doorway and studied the space, like a fresco artist sizing up a wall he was about to paint. He checked the cooker clock—4:10 A.M.—and yawned as he tied his bathrobe. Long experience told him that he would not sleep again that night. He brought the desk lamp through from the living room, plugged it in above the freezer and adjusted it until the area was fully lit. Then he laid out in front of him the thirteen prints showing Number Three's head in various positions.

"You're a phoney, Number Three. But are you my phoney?" Slowly he began to pin the pictures to the wall. As each simulation fell into line, it was as though the head turned in slow motion. Lassiter began to assess it, to break it down feature by feature. The basic structure was ectomorphic— triangular, dominated by a large crown. Number Three was essentially a cerebral beast. Now, as the head revolved to show the profile, he could see that there was a bony protuberance along the lower part of the forehead, like a rounded ledge above the eyebrows—a super orbital margin. Number Three was methodical, meticulous. He could carry a secret to the grave.

He pinned up another print. It was clear that the ears were set almost on the center line of the skull and there was an unusually large area of cranium behind them. Three was solid, quiet, the "Rock of Gibraltar" type. Criticism seldom phased him. He could work well alone, seeking no praise, only the satisfaction of a job well done.

For each print, he made a note. The last one showed the head from an aerial position. Lassiter checked it against the full-face shot. The face grew steadily wider as it went back from the mouth to the ears. Number Three was probably skilled in management, in handling money. He had an acquisitive nature.

By 5:30 A.M., Lassiter had completed a three-page profile on the man. By daybreak he had compared it to those of a dozen others, selected from the databases of the principal law enforcement agencies. As the shabby little kitchen began to fill with sunlight, he started to shape his conclusions. The photograph that had been behind the simulations had come from a fake passport. Number Three was a crook. But he was also one smart cookie, the kind who could have turned his hand successfully to any area of legitimate business that interested him. So whatever racket he was involved in had to offer huge rewards to make it worth his while. And the only racket that would pay that kind of money would be something so specialized that only a man of his expertise could pull it all together. Number Three was a loner. And possibly, that rarest of things in a crook, trustworthy. Only one job specification required all these skills, all these qualities, and Number Three was born to it. Master rinser.

Lassiter examined the landing card again. The man had given his nationality as Dutch—a not uncommon cover for German crooks to use. To the untutored ear the two accents could sound much alike. Even if he was genuinely Dutch he would almost certainly speak some German. Mielke preferred to speak little else. So at least these two would have been able to communicate.

So what did he have? A German-speaking rinser

who'd had a *per diem* account in St. Stephen . . . funded from an account in Berlin . . . that received 120 thousand D-marks a month throughout the mid-Eighties from one Erich Mielke.

Master rinser. Mielke's rinser. Number Three had to be the man.

By breakfast time, Lassiter's elation had begun to ebb. He put fresh bread into the toaster and laid a dinner plate on the black plastic handle to hold it down. Suddenly the photo-matching process seemed the longest shot in the world. If Mielke and his rinser were such a secret association, was it likely the Stasi chief would risk their being photographed together? Or was there just a chance they'd known each other in earlier days, that they'd served in the same Soviet-trained unit? Maybe there'd be a group shot . . .

It took three attempts to produce a piece of toast that was edible. Even the third slice was almost as black as the coffee he carried over to the computer. He bit into it and keyed the access code to Interpol's central database at St. Cloud. Once on line, he typed in Number Three's various pseudonyms. As before, there was nothing listed under the names. Now that would be changed. From his notes, he began to put together a file containing everything he had on the man he believed to be Mielke's rinser. Max would add the new photographic data himself. Lassiter then copied the file into the FIRU section of the database. The acronym stood for "Further Information Required Urgently." He'd just have to hope that someone, somewhere, would have reason to pick up on it. For now, there was no more he could do.

Lassiter yawned. He could sleep now, he knew

it. He switched off the computer and turned for the bedroom. As his head hit the pillow, Max's parting shot of the night before came back to him. "The point of all this is to find out who the guy is and where he is, right? Well, it may sound like a damn fool question, but why don't you ask the Chief Pig himself?"

SEVEN

"Look me in the face, Barrett."

The man with his back to Craddock seemed not to hear. But several in the party gathered around him shot the intruder nervous glances.

"Look me in the face, Barrett . . . Oh, excuse me. I mean Mayor Barrett." He bowed exaggeratedly, making a ridiculous sweeping gesture with his arm. "Tell me it wasn't rigged, the whole shebang . . . You can't!" He looked at the ground and shook his head slowly. "Your family have stuffed more ballot boxes than mine have turkeys. No, I don't suppose your family eats too much turkey." He rubbed at his chin. "No, at your place, my guess is it's chicken all the way."

The barrel-chested man turned around and faced the intruder. "Look, Craddock, I'm here to have a quiet evening with my friends. But if you can't keep that ugly mouth of yours closed, I'm gonna have to come over there and give you a little help."

Craddock moved his hands away from his body in a gesture that said, "any time you want." Dead silence descended over the crowd gathered in Sullivan's small town square. Those with children gathered them up and hurried away. The two men moved slowly around each other. Craddock edged out into the center of the street.

Barrett saw Craddock's hand go down. He dropped to the ground and spun over on his side, fanning the hammer of his revolver as he did. Craddock stood and stared at him for a minute, tried to take a step forward and pole-axed onto his face.

Applause broke out around the square. Kevin Mackay, artistic director of Sullivan's community theater group hurried forward. "Craddock" scrambled to his feet and examined the split seam of his jacket. "Sorry, Kev."

"That's nothing. If you have to rip a seam or two to die well, go for it. Do the knee pads help?"

"Yeah, they do. Do they show through the pants?"

"Nah." Mackay turned to his company and clapped his hands. "Okay, thank you very much everyone. That's a wrap. Don't forget. Everyone must be in their places, in costume by five."

Thirty people in late nineteenth-century costume began to disperse across the square of the small south Texas town, which now looked much as it had a hundred years before.

Photographs of Sullivan, circa 1870, on sale at the Old Fire House Cafe, showed white clapboard houses and shops with elegant façades clustering a tree-filled square. Other yellowing views commemorated the old colonial-style portico of the town hall, the mayor's house with a balcony enclosed by fine wrought-iron work, and the steeple of St. James Baptist Church rising through the apple blossom.

By 1980, all that remained of this idyllic picture of nineteenth-century rural life was the church, though not the blossom. Where the town hall had stood, there was a gas station. The mayor's house had been replaced by a supermarket built of concrete and glass. The once flourishing canning industry had long since collapsed, reducing Sullivan to little more than a dormitory town. Property prices were falling and the feeling amongst many was that the town was dying.

The establishment in 1985 of a trading estate, five minutes' drive from the town center, was the breakthrough descendants of the town fathers and other environmentally conscious citizens had been waiting for. The supermarket, looking for more parking space, was the first to move out to it. The filling station the last. Finally, after a campaign that had lasted more than forty years, the Sullivan Main Street Society found the way clear to recreate the town center their great grandfathers had known.

Old plans were located, old photographs blown up and studied, architects and craftsmen consulted. As fund-raising activities got under way, tenders were examined and decisions taken. In the next five years the town and the main street leading east-west through it, moved almost imperceptibly back into the slower, quieter world of the nineteenth century. Time after time funds dried up. With the onset of economic recession, donation fatigue set in with a will and hopes of ever completing the project began to fade.

Ches Chesterfield had noticed how the Sullivan scheme had caught the imagination of the state's media, and, ever the master of the vote-catching gesture, had brought the issue to Lowell Vandenberg's attention while his decision to stand as a Democratic candidate was still known to very few.

"Let's face it, Lowell, the Texas primary is gonna be a bitch for us. Write these folks a check. No need to go crazy. Call it an investment in the future. You invest in them right now, when they need it most, they'll invest in you when you need them. And there's a couple of fat fish down there I'm anxious to net. This is a fine opportunity to get close to them."

Local archivists had scoured the town records for a historical hook to hang the opening event on. Sullivan's only documented gunfight seemed to have all the right ingredients. The broad facts of the incident were pure Zane Grey. There had been a fair in the town square a hundred years before. The local election was over. The new mayor and his family were amongst the revelers. The local bad man, Jack Craddock, who'd run against him and lost, appeared on Main Street, shouting that the election had been rigged and that the matter should be settled between them, there and then. In a duel John Ford would have been proud of, Craddock was gunned down.

Later editions of the *Sullivan Clarion* made it clear that Craddock was in fact little more than the town drunk with delusions of grandeur. Seemingly, he'd had the hots for the new mayor's daughter and a public announcement of that fact, containing some colorful speculations on her capabilities as a lover, had resulted in his being shot stone-dead where he stood. These later versions of the story were hastily removed from the public library. And the edition of the paper carrying the earlier, more sensational version, with the headline "Sullivan: A Safe Town At Last," was reproduced in facsimile as a giveaway on the great day.

With the gunfight dress rehearsal over, an army of volunteers began to move seats into position in rows, facing the canopied podium at the west edge of the square. Vandenberg was to have been guest of honor at the evening celebrations, with the re-enactment as its high point. But a $5000-a-plate fund-raiser had already been scheduled in for Houston that night. An additional ceremony was hastily arranged in the town square for noon, when the governor would switch on the new fountain "as a symbolic gesture of rebirth."

Leland Daker, Lowell Vandenberg's field security adviser, finished his coffee and moved out into the center of the square, followed by five men in dark suits carrying rifle bags. He turned a ground plan around in his hands and located the landmarks in relationship to it. The party made their way across the square to a gift shop fixed up to look like an old-fashioned general store. A painter was putting a final coat on the architrave of the door as Daker and one of the men walked across the bare boards into the empty building. They climbed the three flights to the flat roof and walked to the front. Through the cut-work of the ornate façade, there was a clear view of the podium. Daker agreed positioning with his man and passed him a labeled key. "When you've checked everything out, lock yourself in." He hurried back down the stairs. "How long are you going to be?" he asked the painter.

"One hour, tops." He studied Daker's identity badge. "What's the hurry? Ain't nothing happening for a coupla hours yet."

"As soon as my man's checked the building out, he's sealing it. It's standard security procedure."

The man shrugged. "I can only do what I can do."

Daker stifled a yawn and walked back to the four men waiting in the square. It was going to be a long hard day.

Lowell Vandenberg braced himself against the wind and crossed the narrow runway to a gray stretch limo. Marianne and his bodyguard loaded attaché cases and two small valises into the trunk and they headed northwest.

"We should be in Sullivan in about fifteen minutes," Marianne announced as they pulled off onto a winding country road. Vandenberg wasn't listening. His eyes had locked on to a sign on the highway and he swiveled around in his seat as they sped past it, then pressed a button in the armrest. The glass partition between him and the driver began to slide down. "Make a left at the next junction, will you." He turned to Marianne. "I want to make a detour. We'll be on time, don't worry about it."

The road sign on the right as they made the turn, "Apeldoorn Place," looked as though it had been freshly painted. A minute later they were level with high steel gates that stood at the entrance of the property. "Pull on around," Vandenberg said. To the left, amongst willow trees, stood an old colonial-style mansion. Marcus Vandenberg's place.

The limo began to pull up a steep hill. At the top, the governor signaled the driver to stop. He got out and walked to the edge and looked down. Marcus's property was stretched out beneath him. Visible now was the swimming pool, tennis courts and various outbuildings. A man lay on a sunlounger reading a newspaper. Vandenberg sniffed the air. It was clean and good. Some pieces of newly cut grass floated up on the light northwesterly wind and settled on Vandenberg's suit. He brushed them off and studied the figure way below.

Oh Marcus, we should have been friends you and I, he thought. Good friends. Way, way back at the beginning we were.

Lowell's first recollection of his cousin came from when he, himself, was three and the shy ten-year-old had finally, on sufferance, let the child into his bedroom to see his model car collection. Such fond memories were few. Walter Vandenberg had done the best he could to make a home for his orphaned nephew. Neither he nor his wife Connie had ever been "hands-on" parents. Their own children had been raised by a succession of nannies. Marcus, the only boy, the longed-for heir, had been over-indulged from the beginning. He saw the adoptee growing up in his father's home, playing with his cast-off toys, vying for his mother's affections, as a usurper, to be discredited and plotted against at every opportunity. On

Lowell's fifth birthday, he finally received a fuller answer to the question, "Why don't I call you Mother and Father like Marcus does?" Inevitably, Lowell asked himself, if these people aren't my parents, did they only take me in because there was no one else? Do they really love me? It was soon clear to the child that Marcus didn't. Not without enterprise even at that age, Lowell tried everything to beguile his cousin, but a child's aversion is a powerful force. That failure focused his attention on the whole family. At thirteen, Lowell entered St. Anthony's School in Boston in the clear knowledge that he was unloved. As the years went by, his desire to be valued by those around him became obsessional. All activities, in and out of school, were subsumed to that aim. Those who thwarted him, did so at their peril.

When Walter Vandenberg died twenty years on, Marcus relished his newfound authority. Lowell was in his third year of law practice. Uncle Walter had made few provisions in his will for his brother's boy, holding till the end that, "His father's money will turn up someday." When it was clear that apart from some real estate in Holland and a modest sum that had been paid by the West German government as reparation for all that had been lost, his cousin stood to inherit little more than a small stockholding in the family's companies, Marcus decided to make some adjustments. The bequest of Hague House and most of its contents was the result. Marcus had always loathed the place. With three other homes in which to stretch his carcass he would hardly miss it. It was just the sop he needed.

"This place is yours now," he told Lowell. "With

this and your shares you should be able to live in comfort for the rest of your days. Be happy, Lowell. Be anything you want. But be it away from me. Away from us and Vandenberg International."

Lowell had never analyzed the needs that drove him forward, but he knew now, as he stood on the rim of the hill above his cousin's home, that the course of both their lives might have run very differently if they had been allies instead of enemies.

"What now, Governor?" The chauffeur's voice broke through his reverie.

"Move on around the property. See if you can find a way back to the road."

To their left they could see wide corrals, stabling for maybe fifty horses. Marcus had started work on the property the year he had run for the Democratic nomination in the 1988 race. Being seriously rich had rarely proved a handicap to acceptance as a Presidential candidate. To the electorate, a self-made millionaire running for the nation's highest office was an affirmation of the American dream. What was more difficult for voters to swallow was the candidate who dared to reach for the presidency on the strength of "old money." No one had pulled that one off since Franklin D. Roosevelt. To those who remembered Papa Joe, even JFK, for all his family's aristocratic pretensions, was no more than the son of a prohibition bootlegger: a self-made man.

Marcus Vandenberg's credibility problems had in no way been helped by his decision to run on the "Too Rich To Cheat" ticket. Like those who were to follow, he was soon accused of trying to buy the nomination. His TV campaign alone, paid for out of his own pocket, accounted for more air-time than all the other Democratic candidates put together. Amongst registered voters in the early primaries that year, Marcus soon became the "Too Rich To Care" candidate. The Republican front-runner tore into him when he and Marcus debated on network TV. "Seventeen percent of Americans live below the poverty line. Meat on the table more than a couple of times a week is simply beyond their means. How a man who spends two thousand dollars a month on dining out can claim to identify with their needs is completely beyond me."

Marcus hastily denied that he spent anything like that amount on restaurants and added that a recent survey published by the Food and Drug Administration showed that most families on welfare had at least one high-protein meal every day. "'Pure Texas' meatloaf is by far and away the most popular brand product," he told viewers. "On average, two pounds of it is eaten by each family every week."

The Republican pounced. "Now that about says it all! You see, anyone who had the first understanding about how the rest of his countrymen live, would know that 'Pure Texas' is meat analog. It's made entirely from soya bean yarn, Mr. Vandenberg, with a little meat flavoring added. But then I don't expect that's something your family would know a whole lot about."

That small gaffe put a big hole in Marcus's bid for the presidency. The media played it for all it was worth. But it was not the last of "Meatloaf Marcus's" bloopers. His fate seemed settled, when a leggy brunette in her twenties sold the steamy love letters she had received from him over a period of five years, to *Star* magazine. Many voters in the upcoming primary wrote on their ballot papers what most of the nation was now thinking. A month later Marcus announced his withdrawal from the race.

Lowell settled back into the plush leather seating of the limo. Only Marcus would have been insensitive enough to build himself a home so close to a town that had openly booed and ridiculed him when he'd campaigned there, he thought. Now that'll be redressed.

At 11:30 A.M. exactly the mayor of Sullivan and the committee of the Main Street Society mounted the steps at the back of the podium to the strains of "America the Beautiful," to be greeted by a roar of approval from the people of the town. The voice of a large contralto in a wide-brimmed straw hat echoed across the square for ninety seconds as press photographers positioned themselves, crouching low, so as not to obscure the mayor as he moved up to the lectern to the right of the podium. A man strapped into a Steady Cam harness moved down the center aisle in the audience, to capture the moment live for local TV.

The mayor's voice echoed through the square.

" . . . Probably the most important moment in this town's history . . . a legacy for our children and their children to come . . . none of what you see would have been possible without the continued support of so many . . . " The mayor glanced at the new town hall clock. "This project could not have been completed without the help of one man.

Thanks to his generosity, our dream has finally been realized. He's here today to celebrate with us all. Ladies and gentlemen, I give you the man I believe will be the next president of the United of States of America, Governor Lowell C. Vandenberg."

Vandenberg strode onto the podium and up to the lectern to strong if restrained applause. He held up his hands. Not until there was silence did he look around him and smile broadly at his audience. "What a beautiful town! What a wonderful job you folks have done." More applause, and this time a few cheers. "I can't tell you how proud I am to be a small part of this. I want to tell you why I got involved. When I heard just what it was you folks were trying to do here, it instantly struck a chord with me. I can't tell you the number of streets I've walked down in this country and thought, now this must have been a nice little place once, a good place to live in. But look at what they did to it!" He gestured around him and his voice changed to dynamic. "When they could have done . . . this." Over more cheers he said, "Do you know what you did? Do you? You gave Sullivan back it's soul!"

He hit the last word hard. Pandemonium from the audience. "You've given us back a sense of the old values. Values that made this country the finest in the world. Values that as a nation we need to find again. This place speaks of a time when the lessons our parents taught us, the guidance they gave us, really counted for something. When women and children could walk down the street in safety. When maybe the world was a little more about people and a lot less about things." His eyes picked out black faces in the audience. "Oh, the past wasn't perfect. Far from it. That's why this project is so important. It gives us all a chance to relive the best of the past . . . with the best of the present."

By now, most of the audience had realized Vandenberg was working without a script. He seemed to be speaking his thoughts as they came to him. "This project took a lot of tenacity, and dedication. But most of all, it took good old-fashioned hard work. The people of this country are good at that. Everywhere I go they say to me, "Just give us the chance, Mr. Vandenberg. Get us back to work. We'll show you." I look around me now and I get a glimpse of what this country could be if they were given that chance." He drew the heavily scented air into his lungs. "I tell you this, never in my life have I felt more strongly that the best of the future is just around the corner. And we can get there, believe me. Let's do it together." Vandenberg pressed the button in front of him and the fountain in the center of the square cascaded into life. A flock of pigeons, roosting in the willow trees, took to the air in a flurry.

"Sullivan; the best of the future begins here," Vandenberg said solemnly.

The brass band in the corner struck up, barely audible above the hubbub of cheers and applause. Vandenberg moved from behind the lectern and waved, clearly surprised by the reception he was getting.

The crack of a gunshot resonated through the wooden buildings around the square like a string snapping inside a piano. Splinters of wood spun into the light, a foot from where Vandenberg stood. He seemed to freeze. An audible intake of breath rose from the crowd. In an instant, the second shot pierced the warm air. Vandenberg was thrown back across the podium. He slumped to his knees, his head almost touching the stage. Then slowly rolled over onto his side.

The screaming began. The sound that rose from people's throats was almost unearthly. Some men flung themselves and their wives to the floor, covering their bodies with their own. Others gathered up their families and darted for cover at the perimeter. A few sat immobile, unable to accept what was happening. Many heads turned. Across the square, a little pall of smoke hung around the open third floor window of the west side of a department store.

The nearest marksman to it was Leland Daker himself. From his position on top of the cinema, he raced across the flat roof and jumped the six-foot gap between it and the department store. Police and security moved in on the building, some rushing to the back to close off the obvious line of escape. Though no gunman could be seen, a barrage of small arms fire was loosed off at the window.

Bodyguards began to carry Vandenberg off the stage to safer ground behind it. "Don't move him!" a women screamed. "For pity's sake, you'll kill him!" But Vandenberg was clearly still conscious. His face was ashen, drenched in sweat. A doctor pushed forward through the crush. As the guards pulled away, it was clear that Vandenberg had been hit in the chest. There was a bullet hole under the pocket on the left side of his shirt, but not a trace of blood. The governor seemed to be trying to scramble to his feet. The doctor laid him gently on his back, spread the jacket open and ripped the shirt apart.

There was a ragged crater in the bullet-proof vest it had concealed. Vandenberg sat up slowly while the body armour was cut off him. There was a livid purple bruise the diameter of a baseball on the left side of his chest. He looked down at himself. "My God . . . my God . . . " was all he seemed to be able to say.

Meantime, Daker appeared at the front of the department store roof, having clearly failed to find an access point to the stairs. He climbed over the lowest section of the wooden façade and, clinging to the guttering, swung his body away from the locked window beneath him. As he swung back he threw his legs forward, kicking the window inward. He reached through the frame with one hand, and in seconds was inside.

"Hold your fire!" Police Chief Calloway bellowed through the pandemonium. "We don't wanna hit our own man."

Police who had reached the back door of the department store and found it locked from the inside, were smashing it with gunfire. Now more gunfire could be heard from within the building itself. A short burst, followed almost immediately by the repeated smack of a large-caliber handgun. Suddenly one of Vandenberg's own security guards jammed his head to his shortwave radio, then screamed across the square: "I'm getting Daker! He says he's got him . . . neutralized . . . He says he's gonna unlock the back door."

Minutes later when Daker swung open the doors to the parking lot, the police who poured in found a man, a Caucasian, about thirty years old, lying upside down on his back on the first flight of stairs. A rifle lay on the landing above him. His body was soaked with blood, but there was no mistaking the security badge pinned to his lapel. Chief Calloway lifted open the blood-spattered jacket and started to go through the pockets. Daker lay back against the wall and searched for a cigarette. "Don't bother. I can tell you who he is." Calloway turned around to look at him. "He's a security guard. One of five I took on for today. Ex-Secret Service marksman. He was supplied by the Lambton Agency in Houston. I checked his credentials myself."

"Nothing on him but the badge." Calloway skewed around to read it. "Meldrum. Arthur S."

"I was gonna make for the room at the west end of the third floor, where the shots came from," Daker explained as he and Calloway retraced his movements from the minute he'd swung into the building through the window. "I got to here at the end of the corridor and I saw movement on the stairs. I shouted 'Freeze'." Daker pointed to bullet holes in the door behind him. "That was his answer. I came in at floor level and let him have it with the Magnum. That's all there is to tell."

Calloway looked down at his shirt. His face creased with irritation. "Look at that. Blood on my new uniform. Jesus Henry! New on today. Where did you see this Meldrum last, I mean before the shooting?"

"Around ten thirty. When I assigned him to this position. It had a clear view of the podium. It seemed ideal." Calloway's large face was beginning to resemble a bull frog's. "Look, there was no way . . . "

"Ideal. I'll say it was!" Calloway stomped off down the stairs. "Those biological powders take half the color out. Jesus. Fuckin' amateurs! Make me sick."

EIGHT

"So, do you think he's wacko?"

The prison officer seemed not to hear. He examined the pass the governor of Ploetzensee Prison Hospital had given Lassiter ten minutes earlier, and punched the code at the top of it into the computer on his desk and waited. The massive shoulders squeezed upward into a shrug. "Why ask me?"

"Well, you've been watching him for the better part of a year."

Data flickered on the screen and the man seemed to relax a little. His small eyes swiveled up to the U.S. Customs agent. "He heard the outer door open when you came in. It's not due to open till six when he gets his dinner. The doctors aren't due here again until Friday. Since his wife divorced him, nobody else comes. So he knows he has an unscheduled visitor." He gave out the information as if he was reciting flight departures from Newark. "Either he's wacko or real smart." The guard pulled himself out of his seat and punched a code into a small panel to the right of the heavy grillwork door that was the only other exit from his office.

Lassiter hesitated. "So you're saying I've blown it already?"

"You should have come at a mealtime." Again the shrug. "I don't know. Who knows what real difference it would have made?" The door slid silently back. "Walk on the balls of your feet." The guard settled down to study the sports pages of *Bild Zeitung*.

The corridor ahead was utterly featureless except for two doors to the left and one on the right, at the far end. In that room languished the man who had once held the power of life and death over seventeen million East Germans, Alone and apparently forgotten even by the few that had ever loved him.

Lassiter moved soundlessly down the corridor, stopped ten feet from the door and listened.

A clipped, guttural voice.

" . . . not my problem. How clear do I have to make myself? You stay on this as long as it takes . . . Well, make him go through it again . . . "

Lassiter moved forward. He peered cautiously through the tiny window in the upper left-hand corner of the door. Who the hell's he speaking to? Himself? Mielke had his back halfturned to the door. He was smaller than Lassiter had imagined. A squat man with a monkey face. He held the receiver of a telephone to his right ear. He has a telephone? They give him a fucking telephone in jail? He could be speaking with his rinser right now.

" . . . If you don't know how important this is . . .

Let me worry about that, you just take care of your end. Just come through . . . "

There was a brief electronic buzz, a clicking sound and the white-enameled door swung ajar. Lassiter pushed it gently open and Mielke turned. The small hazel eyes studied the Customs agent. There was no curiosity in them. Whoever this man was, he would bring no good news. Another specialist here to study some new aspect of the prize specimen's psyche.

Lassiter sensed none of this. He was transfixed by what Mielke held in his hand. The telephone was about three quarters the size of a normal one. It was made of bright orange plastic. There was no lead extending from it. Dominating the large old-fashioned dial, with its childishly large numbers, was the faded image of Minnie Mouse.

The old woman aimed the luggage trolley at the line of passengers, standing meekly at the Lufthansa check-in desk, as though she was on some kind of kamikaze mission. Lassiter pulled Erika toward him to let her pass through. "Will you see Marianne?" she asked.

"I may." He took his ticket and boarding pass and they began to walk toward the passport control barrier in the international terminal of Tempelhof Airport. "There's still a lot of stuff to sort out." She put her hand on his shoulder. Her watch slid forward on her wrist. Lassiter noticed she was wearing a rubber band around it. "What on earth is that for?"

She looked a little embarrassed. "Oh, it's silly really. Something left over from childhood. When I want to stop myself thinking about something, I pull it out and let go. It's like a slap on the wrist."

"I should have been wearing one for years." They joined the line of passengers. "Look, if you've got it into your head that I'm going back with Marianne, forget it. She's caught up with some trial attorney. I'm part of the past."

She put her head on one side and crossed her arms. "God, you're so vain. It has nothing to do with you, as a matter of fact. I was going to say that I also wear it to remind myself of things. Like remembering to take the pill."

"Ah."

"Will you call me when you get in?"

"Of course."

"You know where to get me for the next couple of weeks. I'll be at the lab till late, most nights. It's going to be the wonderful world of blood, spit and semen for me."

"Well, for Christ's sake don't lose the rubber band!"

She let out one of her wonderful dirty laughs. "I should be so lucky. I sometimes wonder how anyone ever got a rape or murder conviction before they discovered DNA. If you don't come back to Berlin, I shall find a Museum of Natural History somewhere that'll have me, and devote my life to dinosaurs. At least whoever killed them will have been dead for sixty million years."

"I shall come back."

"Good. I love you, Jack." She kissed him once, long and hard, turned and hurried toward the parking lot.

Lassiter watched her go, felt an emptiness open up inside him. But, as the long transatlantic flight carried him inexorably closer to his homeland, thoughts of Marianne seemed to push Erika further from his mind.

He thought about the way they'd met, at his parents' house, the day of that last Thanksgiving party, five years before. She'd come with her father, Senator Cattell, and had sat in the corner of the living room making practiced small talk with the purple-haired ladies and obese, tartan-jacketed men. Lassiter had worked hard that afternoon. He'd made her laugh with tales of the villains he encountered, fired her up with some of his views on modern art and music, racked his brain for anything he might say or do to make himself attractive to her. Whether she was attracted to him, he couldn't tell, but subconsciously he knew he wouldn't rest until she had fallen in love with him.

The more rarefied Lassiter's casework became, the more of a one-man band it seemed to make him. By the weekends, he was usually heartily sick of his own company and, no matter who he might be dating, was happiest in a roomful of friends. But Marianne soon occupied a unique place in his life. He found he was content to spend much of his free time alone with her. She stimulated him, fulfilled a need that no one else ever had. After they made love, he felt a oneness with her he'd never known before. Perhaps it had been too intense, he thought now. They had shared too much, too many anxieties, too many secret fears. They had allowed the real issue to become clouded: they had a rare relationship, the kind that neither was likely to find again. Had too much been said and done for them to turn the clock back? he wondered as the plane began to make its descent.

His arrival at Dulles International Airport evoked a dozen others, when his eyes had singled out her face from the crowd that gathered on the concourse.

At 6 P.M.—five hours after the attempt on Lowell Vandenberg's life in Sullivan—the taxi pulled up at the family home in Rockville. The place smelled of disinfectant and polish. The note on the kitchen table from the cleaning woman gave details of what she'd spent on stocking up the freezer and the drinks cabinet. There were "welcome home" messages on the answering machine from his father, calling from the retirement home, and his sister in Milwaukee. And three of a less cordial nature from the assistant manager of the First Interstate Bank, Rockville.

What do they think, I'm going to leave the country forever for a lousy twelve thousand dollars? Lassiter thought as he carried his bags to the guest room, which he'd used as his from the day he'd moved out of the downtown apartment. Then he poured himself a large scotch and walked out to the garage.

The Jaguar XJS had had fifty thousand on the clock when he'd bought it. The bodywork and interior trim had been in such good shape that it had been hard to believe the car was almost seven years old, even then. He'd had to buy it on hire purchase and the repayments were knocking a big chunk out of his monthly pay packet, but it was worth it. When Marianne went, his outgoings had dropped. His heart was on the floor and he'd felt, "Well, what the hell."

The sleek blue car stood much as he'd left it. The Eddows' boy, from a couple of blocks up, had polished it and turned the engine over once a week. Lassiter slipped in the ignition key. The engine started immediately, a deep low growl. A V-12 made a sound like no other. He savored it for a moment, then checked the fuel gauge. Hell, the kid had filled it with gas too! Around eight he'd stop by the Eddows' place and settle up with him.

He went back up to the bedroom and started to unpack. Soon the silence was unbearable. There should have been the clink of pans in the kitchen as his mother began to fix dinner, the steady thump of his sister's feet in the attic above him as she practiced her pirouettes. Family noise. He switched on the radio. A news correspondent was winding up a report on a shooting incident in some hick town in south Texas.

" . . . For the people of Sullivan, this was always going to be a day to remember, but no one here could have foreseen that it would live in the town's history as the day Presidential Candidate Lowell Vandenberg was almost shot to death."

Marianne.

The newscast moved on to another story. Lassiter switched on the TV at the foot of the bed and flicked through the channels. Nothing. He checked his watch. 6:45 P.M. The Hague House office would know where she was. There was no point in calling the main number, the switchboard would be jammed. He tried Marianne's private line. To his surprise she answered immediately.

"I just got in from Berlin. I heard on the radio. Are you okay?"

"Yeah, Pretty shaken up. I'm still in one piece."

"I don't know what happened. I only caught the end of the newscast."

"Some maniac tried to kill Lowell. He was wearing body armor, it saved his life." Marianne sounded exhausted. The twang of her Georgia accent, smoothed by her years in Washington, came through as it always did when she was tired.

"Look, it's a madhouse here. I have to go. It was sweet of you to call."

"I want to see you."

"I can't think ahead at the moment. The whole schedule's screwed up. Everything's haywire. Are you at your folks' place?"

"Uhuh."

"I'll call you later tonight."

She hung up. Lassiter downed the scotch and worked on steadying his breathing. He took his copies of the Mielke files through to the walnut veneer desk that had stood against the wall in his parents' bedroom for as long as he could remember. His stomach still churned. What the hell had happened out there in Sullivan?

The drawers were still crammed with his father's papers. He'd been putting off clearing the desk out ever since the old man had moved into the home. He took a cardboard box from the kitchen and began emptying the top left-hand drawer. Folded in four, at the back, was a letter he'd written to his parents from summer camp almost twenty years before. There were character studies on the other boys who shared his tent, and a description of his first attempts at cooking. The writing was good. The sharp observations showed a natural feeling for words.

He poured himself another drink, then opened

the kitchen door and sat on the stoop. How strange things had turned out. His father had been a newspaper man all his life, editor of the *Washington Tribune* for more than twenty years. Until the "subway thing" it had always been assumed that his only son would follow him into the business. By now, I might have made editor, Lassiter thought, had my own column on a big city paper.

He looked down the garden to where the raspberry canes had once stood. Until his mother's death from a stroke in 1986, there had been ten rows of them, each with about a dozen six-foot bamboo canes in each. The raspberries, grown originally from saplings brought over by his English grandparents, had grown tall and lush here, turning the plot that they covered into a jungle that was a children's paradise. Protected by netting to keep out the birds, it became an entirely separate world, a maze of green where he, his sister and his cousins had disappeared for an hour before dinner, ostensibly to gather the tiny ripe red fruit for a salad or pie, and acted out their fantasies. The elder children would return to the kitchen with china bowls heaped to the brim. The younger ones would emerge guiltily at the third calling, with a token offering of berries, their mouths smudged all around with red, their tongues stained purple.

Here on this stoop, Jack had sat with his mother and shelled the peas that tasted like no others he'd eaten. Here the world of literature that had enraptured her life had gradually begun to filter into his. She'd encouraged him to keep a journal, to put his feelings down in words. "Once you've expressed your fears on paper, they're there to look at whenever you want them. So there's no need to have them rattling around your head all night."

After her first stroke, the peas she served were canned, sweetened with a little sugar. Jack no longer noticed. The "subway thing," which his father was certain had induced the stroke, had shut his mind to such details.

So much that he'd taken as necessary began to seem utterly futile after the incident. "When ten more minutes of existence seems too much to hope for," he'd written in his journal, "how much does all the rest really matter?" He now found it impossible to relate to the inconsequential little stories that were the lifeblood of his father's business, and all plans to join him on the newspaper were dropped. His parents didn't understand—how could they? A chasm had opened up between him and them. He'd been asked to grow up too quickly. Flung suddenly into a world few adults ever experienced, his childhood had been snatched away. If they loved him, why had they let that happen? By now he understood as well as he ever would why he had cut himself off from them. But at the time . . .

In recent years, he'd refound his father to an extent. Joe came from a generation that found it hard to express love, to hold, to kiss. When his wife had died, the old man had been able to show it, just for a few months. Then things had gone back the way they were.

The Wringers unit, the detox center, the Noriega project that had funded new homes for refugees, the squeeze on Saddam that the Pentagon was certain had helped to contain him, these had mattered. If they mattered, and he had helped to make them happen, then it followed that he mattered. Gradually, Jack Lassiter had begun to find strength in the inner core that he had not dared to look at and, with it, a measure of peace.

And when the Mielke case was over, what then? Lassiter asked himself. Could he write now? Was it way too late to think about the newspaper business? Was one day in the tenth year of his life destined to change every one that was to follow?

"I don't know that this is the best idea." Stella Vandenberg studied her husband's face as CNN cut to footage of the assassination attempt that morning. Much of her husband's natural color had returned. But the green eyes, normally bright and animated, were flat, ringed with dark shadows. A dozen or so people—family and senior campaign staffers—had gathered in the large reception area of the Vandenberg home, known since his grandfather's time as the Music Room. They fell silent as the sequence began.

Vandenberg squeezed his wife's hand. "Hey, I'm okay. I'm here . . . They screwed it up."

There was a collective intake of breath as the second shot was shown hitting Vandenberg. "The governor, who was wearing body armor, escaped unhurt," the newscaster stated. "However, immediately following the firing of the second shot, the *Texas Constitution,* the state's principle newspaper, received a fax from an organization calling itself the National League of America, which claimed responsibility for what it termed as 'the execution of the candidate'." Part of the text of the statement was shown on the screen.

" . . . As a U.S. President, Lowell Vandenberg

would have built his cabinet from Jews and Blacks and other races who threaten the fabric of American Society . . . " The newscaster added that this was the first time this particular extreme right-wing organization had been heard from.

Someone switched off the newscast. A gasping sob broke from Stella's lips. Vandenberg cradled her head to his chest. Marianne Lassiter took the initiative. She walked to the fireplace. "Folks, I think the governor and his wife have had about all they can handle today. Let's give them a little time to themselves."

There was a muttering of assent and people began to take their leave. Vandenberg stood up uncertainly. "Before you go, there's one thing I need to say. I'm only here now because of one person. Seeing that footage, I know that, had it not been for her, I would be lying in the city morgue." He beckoned to Marianne to come to him. "But for this lady, I'd have walked onto that podium without the vest." He put his arms around her. "I owe her my life." The gathering applauded loudly. "I know I'm a pig-headed sonofabitch a lot of the time, Marianne . . . "

She put her finger to his lips "You're worth it."

"Thank you for my husband's life, Mrs. Lassiter," Stella said softly, biting back tears.

Marianne looked embarrassed by the sudden attention. "I don't know what to say. I was just doing . . . what seemed sensible."

"His family are glad you did."

As Marianne crossed the entrance hall, Arlen Lydell, Vandenberg's security chief, called to her from the door that led to the administration wing. He closed it behind them. His forehead was bathed in sweat. "I've got the FBI in my office." He swallowed. "They're saying Meldrum was a patsy."

"What do you mean?"

"He couldn't have fired at the governor. Someone shot him full of sodium pentothal at least two hours before the hit. He had to be out cold at the time."

"So how did Daker see him running down the stairs?"

"If we could find Daker we could ask him." Marianne had noticed that whenever Lydell was tense, he'd turn a gold ring he wore, round and round as though looking for some secret combination. Right now, it looked like his future peace of mind rested on his unscrewing the pinkie of his left hand.

"He's probably . . . "

"He's gone, Marianne. The Feds went into his apartment an hour ago. Everything of his has been cleared out. He's taken off."

Suddenly the full implications of what he was saying sunk in. "Oh, my God . . . Do they think he fired the shots?"

Lydell peered down the corridor behind her. "Keep your voice down. They don't know. Their ballistics people say the shots definitely came from the department store, from the gun found on the stairs. So it's hard to see how he could've. Look, let's deal with our end of this. I hired Daker, I'm not disputing that. But I seem to recall I got his name off a short list you gave me."

"Yes, I have it. I got it from the Central Security Agency."

"Do you still have it?"

"Absolutely."

Lydell lay back against the wall and breathed out slowly. "Thank God for that, at least."

"They can call them . . . "

"They've already rechecked Daker's references. They just wanted to know our end of it."

"You mean they think . . . "

"They're feds, Marianne. Who the hell knows what they think? My guess is they just want to eliminate us from their enquiries." He started to walk purposefully down the corridor. "We're clean. Right this minute, that's all I care about."

Agent Collison flicked through Daker's file. "Kinda long in the tooth for this game, this Daker, wasn't he?"

Lydell shrugged. "We didn't feel so. As we saw it Daker was the most experienced man on the team. I remember the governor and I were particularly impressed with the job he'd done on the Don Blythe campaign in the '88 race. You know how that one went. For a while there, it seemed like half the country wanted to tear Blythe's head off. The fact that he came through it all without a scratch seemed to say a lot about Daker."

"Maybe."

"Yeah, he was in his late forties, but he seemed to be right up to date with all the latest techniques and technology. I'd already been contracted to run the main security team, but we needed a real experienced advance man to work a day or two ahead of the main group, checking out upcoming venues. Someone who could assess our security needs, assign men and hire outside people where necessary."

Agent Collison flicked through Daker's file. "So what was he doing on the roof of the movie theatre?"

"Daker said you couldn't run rooftop surveillance from the street. In a high-risk scenario, he said it was better to be up where the action was, where you could get the same perspective as the marksman. It made sense, as we already had my team on the ground. And, hell, the guy had a list of NRA awards from here to September."

"Well, this seems to be one target he missed."

"But you said he couldn't have fired the shots . . ." Marianne cut in. The smug look on Collison's face faded a little. "You said yourself they both came from the department store. And everyone in the square saw Daker on the roof of the movie theater—we just saw the tape ourselves on TV."

"We don't have the answer to that," Collison said. "There has to have been another man."

"But obviously not Meldrum." Marianne was taking notes now. "Why was he shot full of pentothal?"

"Daker and . . . whoever, had to have Meldrum on ice to play fall guy, I guess. As far as we can tell the man's clean. Ex-Secret Service. Divorced guy, nothing special. Just picked off a list by the Lambton Security Agency for the assignment this morning. The other marksmen say he was the last man to be positioned. My guess is, as soon as Daker got him to the department store, he shot him up with the pentothal to keep him quiet till they needed him."

"Why didn't they just kill him then?"

"For Daker's story to be believable, Meldrum's body had to be warm and it had to bleed. He couldn't be killed till the last minute."

Lydell had had enough of being made to look like the number one asshole in all this. "So how come it took so long to figure all this out?"

"It only showed up in the autopsy. Unfortunately the senior pathologist was on vacation and it took some hours to track him down."

Marianne, too, was starting to feel a whole lot better. "By which time Daker was long gone. Which, I take it, was the whole object of the exercise."

"It bought Daker almost six hours." Lydell lit a cigarette. "He could be almost anywhere in the world by now."

Lowell Vandenberg rested for two hours in his bedroom and then, despite his wife's protests, visited his viewing theater to catch up on his rivals' progress in the race for the Democratic nomination. Mail selected by Marianne was laid out on the console, in front of the seat he always used. Only one package was marked "By Hand. Private and Confidential." Vandenberg opened it. Another envelope inside was marked "For the Governor's Eyes Only." He tore off the top, pulled out a document and turned the pages, reading carefully. Then he tipped back in his seat and made a sucking sound through his teeth. His breathing slowed and he read the surveillance report again.

The hacker Vandenberg had employed had Federal Expressed a report to him, thirty-six hours before. He had used information he'd obtained from the database of the bank where Teresa had opened a new account to access stuff on her from state records, TRW bureaus and other sources. Vandenberg now knew that his blackmailer was born Teresa Lucana. She'd been twenty-two when she married a U.S. Navy officer, many years her senior, whom she'd met, it seemed fair to assume, when he was serving on the Navy's base in Manila. When he retired a few years later, she'd gone to live with him in his hometown of St. Louis. He'd divorced her two years later, citing a building contractor as co-respondent, and she'd been living on welfare at an address in the city ever since.

As soon as he'd received the hacker report, Vandenberg had deployed a trusted member of his staff to run surveillance on her. It was that report the governor had in front of him now.

Teresa Lucana had turned out to be every bit as resourceful as he'd suspected. The transcript of a telephone conversation she had that week made it clear that she had gone to the St. Louis offices of the law firm Knight, Drew, Mather earlier in the month, and left a package with an attorney there containing the negative of the film taken fifteen years before—by her brother who had since died, Vandenberg now learned. It seemed from the transcript that Teresa had just completed an account of her relationship with the Governor and wished to come in and have it notarized.

Knight, Drew, Mather. That's Bryce Mather, Vandenberg thought. He graduated from Harvard the year before me . . .

The governor went to the safe in his study and took out a box of disks. He loaded one into the computer on his desk and typed in the name. There was no file on the man as such but, using the hypertext, he located a reference to him in a document marked simply "Leverage Data: 217."

Vandenberg's talent for being able to relate

seemingly unconnected pieces of information or hearsay to uncover a truth that had escaped the keenest eyes had been developed over many years. It now seemed to have borne its greatest fruit. The author of document "217" was a judge, a family man, respected for his forward thinking. When he had sat in Vandenberg's office a little more than two years ago, the governor had found it hard to equate the august figure he remembered from his days as a lawyer with the shivering wreck of a man in front of him.

Reading the document again now, Vandenberg thought he'd been charitible in the circumstances. Even solicitous. He had no desire to hurt the judge, he'd explained then. How he chose to fill his spare time was of no interest to the governor. But the identities of those who shared his proclivities, well, they might prove to be a different matter. Full and frank disclosure was the only course. Always the best way. An anonymous communiqué. The judge need not allude to his own activities and if Vandenberg was pleased with what he read, he was certain he would have to bother the man no more. And Vandenberg had been pleased. He was certain the document would prove invaluable in the course of time. And now that time had come.

Vandenberg printed out the judge's account and put a circle round the name listed seventh. He remembered Bryce Mather clearly now. He'd been a partner with the law firm referred to in the private detective's report, from the beginning. Vandenberg had seen him at meetings of the Washington Law Society, his expression always alternating between smug and supercilious. He was a fastidious little man, forever fidgeting with the knot of his tie,

picking microscopic particles of dust off his jacket.
What did psychotherapists say? Those who
continually fuss over their outward appearance do
so in the hopes the inside will come right too.
Vandenberg turned the pages of the document. Mr.
Mather was a real mess on the inside. A guilty, dirty
little man who just couldn't be honest with himself.
Hell, thought Vandenberg, facing him with this will
be doing him a downright favor.

NINE

As Lassiter turned around in his seat, he caught sight of his face in the heavily framed mirror on the restaurant wall beside him. For a split second, he fancied he saw himself as Max Gehrhart's gizmo would have pictured him at plus-ten years. The few strands of graying hair behind the temple became a silver lock. The lines under the eyes deepened and spread into the bridge of the nose. God, I look beat, he thought.

He glanced at the door again. Washington's Connecticut Avenue was crowded with lunchtime shoppers. Marianne, dressed in a tight-fitting, rust-colored jacket, stooped to pay off a cab and crossed the sidewalk to the restaurant. She was on time. He watched her weave rhythmically through the lines of tables.

The way Marianne looked was an essential part of his fascination with her. To pretend otherwise would be ridiculous. She was an accomplished, intelligent woman. She stimulated him. He felt complete with her. And when the talking was done, there was the loving. The physical and the metaphysical were mixed in one heady cocktail— one part champagne, five parts adrenaline. As he watched her now, he knew that whether they stayed together or apart, she was in his bloodstream.

Three words. That's all it would take. He could say them now, almost as soon as she sat down. Okay, there was this married fella she was seeing, but instinct told Lassiter that he was just a bit player in her life. He could say them now, he knew, and things would be as they had been. So simple. And yet to say them would mean lying to them both.

He took her shoulder gently and kissed her cheek. She smelled good. Eau de Marianne was one of the planet's ten great smells.

She sat down and studied his face. "A few wisps of gray. Hmm, very distinguished. I approve."

"You want an aperitif?"

"I'll have a spritzer." He watched her check her makeup in the mirror. "Wow, this is the first lunch I've had off the campaign trail in a month."

"So, do they know any more?"

"Only what you've read. The guy they found shot couldn't have done it. And our field security guy's disappeared, so your guess is as good as mine. Lowell's been ordered to rest till Monday. The whole campaign's on hold."

"Well, seems like Space Boy's got himself all the press coverage he needs right now." Marianne's composure faded. She was in no mood for the brand of sarcasm her husband reserved for her boss. Lassiter cut in quickly. "I'm sorry. I know you've been through it. You know what I think of

Vandenberg but I've no wish to see him get his head blown off."

"That's big of you." She began to look through the menu, her eyes moving nervously from item to item. She looked around her. "Can you ask for my drink, Jack?" He stood up and made signals at a waiter. Her voice softened. "Hey, I didn't come here to talk about Lowell."

"Neither did I." A waiter came over and Lassiter ordered drinks. "It's good to see you, Marianne."

She squeezed his hands and smiled. "You too. Have you seen your father yet, how is he?"

"I'm seeing him Thursday."

There was silence for a moment as they scanned the menu. Marianne studied him in her peripheral vision. Any time now, he was going to settle down and choose something to eat. She could tell what he was doing even without looking up—he'd be checking out the fire exits. When they'd first started dating she had thought it was some relic of the army years. But she'd quickly discovered that the ritual had very different origins. Marianne watched Lassiter close his eyes, then, with a barely noticeable shake of the head, return to uncluttered thought. She knew it was part of a self-invented thought-stopping process by which he kept his fears at bay.

"The old problem?" Marianne asked.

"Uhuh."

"How long?"

Lassiter studied the wine list. "Couple of weeks."

"What set it off?"

"Who knows for certain . . . There was one of those race riots in Berlin . . . the smell of tear gas probably got to me. How did you know?"

"It had to be around four in the morning your time when you left that message on my answering machine, so I knew you weren't sleeping."

Lassiter shrugged. "It happens. I'll just have to let it work it's way through, that's all." He tried to catch the eye of the maître d'. "Still seeing . . . the married fella? Sorry, I can never remember his name."

Sure, Marianne thought. He was really gonna forget the name of the guy who was screwing his wife. Perhaps keeping him nameless was another part of the protection mechanism. Play it right down. He must have someone in his life by now. God knows, I don't want to hear any more about her than I have to. "I see him when it suits him," she said. The maître d's interruption was not unwelcome. After they'd ordered she said, "When do you have to check in to the office?"

"After the weekend. The Pensacola hearing starts Tuesday."

"How much rests on your testimony?"

"Well, I'm the only witness who saw the key defendant pass the bank manager the money at the airport."

"Jesus, Jack. Shouldn't you have a bodyguard or something?" Strange, she thought, when they were together he would never have laid that on her so casually. He'd have shielded her from the truth. Perhaps "wives in obeyance" no longer had that right.

He took her hand. "Customs agents don't get bodyguards. Relax. I'm not worth a hit at this late stage."

"Look, I don't want to get into this now. I just want to have a quiet lunch with you, talk. But I care very much for you, Jack. I always will. And this shooting's really shaken me. One minute you're standing there, next minute some crazy's blasting away at you. Take care of yourself. Promise me you will."

He pulled open the left side of his jacket to reveal a Glock 9mm automatic in a shoulder holster.

An hour later, Lassiter settled the check and they crossed the parking lot to his car. "Let me split this with you," Marianne said.

"No way,"

"You won the state lottery or something?"

"You pay next time." Lassiter unlocked the car and turned around. "That's if there's gonna be a next time."

"Of course there is."

She watched the Jaguar pull away and began to walk down Connecticut Avenue. She hadn't seen her husband look so beat in years. He was coming unglued again, she was certain. The insomnia was a sure sign. The nightmares and behavioral problems had started soon after the "subway thing." The violent feelings toward the killer that Jack dared not show had often come out in the years that were to follow. His mother had said the symptoms were only relieved when he joined the Marines. But his posting to Bavaria in the mid-Eighties had been the re-making of him. The breathless tranquility of the mountains and the gentle peasant warmth of the people appealed to him instantly. Soon, the trapped energy of his traumatized mind was devouring every aspect of the language and culture.

When his mother had her second stroke, he'd transferred home and taken a position in the U.S.

Customs Service. Lack of any clear objective soon began to wear on him. In therapy, another legacy of the trauma emerged. Guilt. Guilt over the fact that he'd just lain there with his fingers in his ears while people died. Consciously, he was clear enough that no one expected a boy of ten to intervene. Subconsciously, he blamed himself. His promotion into the Wringers unit had seemed like a lifeline. The prospect that his efforts could enable millions of dollars to be pumped into the federal drug rehabilitation program seemed to fulfill something in her new husband. For four years he had been at peace with himself. Then a senate sub-committee changed it all. As part of another program to cut the federal deficit, the money recovered by the unit would now be diverted to the Treasury.

The immediate effect was that Jack turned more and more to his home life to find some sense of worth. Except that now his wife was working for a state governor who had an eye on the Presidency. When Vandenberg was at Hague House, the Lassiters saw something of each other, but when the entourage moved to the official residence, a hundred and forty miles away, Jack felt deserted. At these times, he began to drink; desertion became betrayal. "But I only took the job in the first place because you were working all hours," Marianne would argue, in one late-night phone call after another. "It was the only way I could think of keeping the marriage together. How could I know your needs would change?"

There was a solution. One that would bring peace back to the marriage, for a time at least. But as she watched her husband tear himself apart she began to wonder whether it was all too late.

Three days later, Marianne stood on a street corner in Scranton, Pennsylvania, and watched a carnival float slowly manuver into a narrow street off the main boulevard. Lowell Vandenberg, seated on a thronelike chair next to his wife atop a pyramid of flowers, began to massage his face. He was not the first politician to find that two hours of continual smiling could be physically painful. A ladder was laid in place and the Vandenbergs climbed down. Marianne crossed the sidewalk and handed them both bottles of mineral water. His was Aqua Libre mixed with Perrier and a little dry white wine.

They climbed into the stretch limo and moved off toward the freeway. Vandenberg took hot towels from the vacuum-sealed box on the seat and applied them to his face.

"Okay, what's next?"

Vernon Lacy, Vandenberg's press secretary, handed him an updated timetable and notes. "The meeting with the machine toolmakers at the convention center in Louisville. I can run through the brief with you when we get there. We should have at least half an hour."

"Calls?"

Marianne, seated next to Lacy, passed him a list.

"Okay, get me Den Temperton first."

She dialed the lawyer's number and passed the governor the phone when he came on the line.

"Den? It's Lowell. I'm sorry I've been so slow in getting back to you."

"Jesus! With your schedule I should be the one apologizing. How you doing?"

Vandenberg took another gulp of the Aqua Libre mix. "My wife says that having a baby robs you of every last dignity. I think this must be the male equivalent."

"It'll be worth it, you'll see."

"It'd better be."

"Listen, I'll tell you why I called. This is a real strange one . . . " For a second, Temperton seemed uncertain how to proceed. "It's a real roundabout thing. I have a colleague in a law practice in Hamburg, Germany. He has a client who wants to meet with you while he's in Washington. It's a personal matter. The guy won't get into any detail, but it seems he was in the same concentration camp as your father in the war. Knew him real well."

"You're kidding."

"No. Dietrich checked some documents he had. Seems like the guy's on the level."

It was just possible, Vandenberg thought, but it smelled like there had to be a catch. "Do you think he's looking for a handout or something?"

"No. As a matter of fact it seems like it's the other way around. He says he has something he wants to give you."

"Have him drop me a line, Den."

Three nights later, the seventy-six members of the "Vandenberg For President" team and attendant journalists set up temporary headquarters at the Hyatt Hotel in Portland, Oregon, to begin campaigning for the primary there. Ches Chesterfield worked with speech-writers till two, rose at seven and swam fifty lengths of the indoor swimming pool. He was halfway through a breakfast of corned beef hash and potatoes when Marianne let herself into the suite and moved into the chair opposite him. Open below her chin was the center spread of the *National Examiner*. The headline ran: "Vandenberg: The Silent Killer . . . "The Lowell I Knew" by Corporal Bill Pentecost." Dominating the layout was a shot of two GIs in their early twenties in Vietnam combat dress. The man on the left had Vandenberg's head shape but, as far as Chesterfield could see, that was about it. His mouth, set to receive a mouthful of hash, closed slowly. He shot Marianne a withering look and put down the fork. "Thanks. You sure know how to make a guy's morning."

Marianne poured herself orange juice. "Everyone set?"

"Uhuh. Let me see that." Marianne passed him the paper. "Is the governor dressing?"

"Last time I checked."

Chesterfield skim-read the piece. "I know about a lot of this stuff. Lowell told me about it himself. But . . . well, his version was a lot lower-key. This picture here . . . this fellow with the smashed nose . . . That can't be the governor. Not a chance." The man with his arm around Corporal William S. Pentecost—now apparently an ice-cream sales representative in Duluth—had dark brown or black hair and thick dark eyebrows. The distinctive forehead might have been Vandenberg's but for the hairline which began lower. The nose was smashed and the nostrils spread. The mouth . . . it was hard to tell, but the teeth were large and uneven.

"Killing came naturally to Lowell," stated Pentecost, who claimed to have fought at

Lieutenant Vandenberg's side on half a dozen missions in the late Sixties. "He could move like a cat. Cut a VC's throat with a commando knife so quick, the guy'd never know what hit him. He got his nose smashed in a hand to hand. Before they could reset it, he got an abscess of the septum. After his tour of duty was over, he had it fixed in L.A. They put in a silicon implant and did some work on his chin while they were at it too . . .

"Some of the guys kept in touch with him. I never did. The truth was, he used to scare the hell out of me. You could never tell what he was thinking, or what he'd do next. He had guts, I'll give him that. But he took risks, crazy risks, when there were easier options. Almost like he got a kick out of the whole thing. Like his men's lives were his last concern."

"The lying sonofabitch bastard." Vandenberg's face was crimson with anger. "He was my driver, Ches, my fucking driver. For all of six months. That's where all the detail comes from. All the rest is bullshit."

"And the picture?" Chesterfield asked.

"What do you think?"

"It isn't you."

"Of course it isn't me."

Vernon Lacy put down the telephone and crossed the hotel suite to where his boss was slumped on a sofa. "Phil's seen it. Says we should hit them for twenty-five mill at least. Libel, defamation, infringement of civil rights."

Vandenberg calmed a little. "I don't know if I want Phil on this. We need a killer. Bryce Mather took these bastards on last year, didn't he? See if you can get him out here, will you, Vern?"

"Jesus, I thought you loathed the guy," Chesterfield said.

"What's that got to do with anything? He took the *Examiner* for almost five mill, didn't he?"

"Phil reamed them too, a couple of years back. On the Congressman Kaye case."

"Well . . . let me just talk it through with Mather anyway."

Bryce Mather stepped out of the Bell helicopter and hurried across the parking lot on the west side of the Hyatt Hotel. His mind was still in hyperdrive. Only two weeks before, Vandenberg had referred to him obliquely, in a speech to the Washington branch of the American Law Society, as being "a trial attorney, whose talent for self-advertisement could be more suitably employed in the trailer home business." Now suddenly this man, who many believed could be the next president, had turned to him for help. What could have brought about this sudden change of heart?

Vernon Lacy was waiting at the rear entrance of the building to usher him in. "Thanks for coming at such short notice, Mr. Mather."

The tanned face broke into a smile. "Just glad I could be of use."

"Have you seen the *Examiner* piece?"

"Uhuh. I have to say I'm surprised. Most of what they print is at least rooted in truth. This bunch of crap seems to be out there on its own."

As the elevator carried them to the seventh floor, Mather stared into the mirrored wall and pulled down a lower eyelid to examine the state of his blood vessels. He noticed a hair on his coat lapel and flicked it away. Lacy led the way to Vandenberg's suite.

The governor stood in the doorway in his shirtsleeves. He took the lawyer's hand with unaccustomed warmth. "Mather, good to see you."

The lawyer was shown into a sittingroom that had obviously been used during the day by the governor's team as a temporary center of operations. Vandenberg crossed to a drinks cabinet and poured himself a cognac. "I take it you ate on the plane?"

"Yes."

"Can I interest you in a brandy? Or maybe you'd just like some coffee?"

"A small brandy will do just fine."

"I understand you only got back from Europe yesterday."

"That's right. So tell me, how's the campaign going?"

Vandenberg yawned. "It's going."

Suddenly, uneasy at being alone with a man he'd thought of until that afternoon as an enemy, Mather took his copy of the *National Examiner* out of his attaché case and launched into his opening patter again. "I have to say I'm surprised, Governor. Most of what these people print is at least rooted in truth. But this bunch of crap seems . . . "

"What people?" Vandenberg asked, his back still to the lawyer.

"The, er . . . *Examiner.*"

Vandenberg turned. "If you're referring to the piece in this week's edition purporting to be about me, that matter is being dealt with by my attorney, Phil Calder."

Mather took a step backward. "But I thought . . . I was told . . . "

"Then you thought wrong." Vandenberg turned. His face broke into a resigned kind of smile.

Mather was dumbfounded. "You mean you didn't need me to come out here at all?"

"Oh no, I needed to see you urgently." Vandenberg took a file from his own case and handed it to Mather. "I needed you to see this."

Vandenberg never ceased to marvel at the range of tonal variations the human face could undergo. The natural ruddy color began to drain out of the lawyer's cheeks as he leafed through the file, reducing the flesh to a mottled gray, then the features appeared to take a distinctly greenish hue. For a minute, Vandenberg thought Mather was going to faint. "You know, in your position, you really should take more care." He took the document from the lawyer's shaking hands. "A senator, two congressman, a judge, seven trial attorneys . . . all boys together, huh? Tell me, do you take a piece of the action yourself, or do you just like to watch?"

Mather's face gained color again, reddening to medium rare. His voice shook when he spoke. "What do you intend to do with this information?"

"I'm quite certain I won't have to do anything." Vandenberg studied the lawyer for a minute, then he said, "I believe a young attorney called Kravitz has recently joined your St. Louis office."

"Er . . . I really couldn't say."

"A client of his, a Miss Teresa Lucana, has lodged a package with him. I would be most grateful if you could have it sent to me."

Mather put his head in his hands. "How on earth can I do that?"

"I'm sure you understand the internal workings of your firm better than I." Vandenberg shrugged. "You're a senior partner. Go to St. Louis and just take it out of the safe." He threw up his hands in mock exasperation. "Say it was stolen, I don't know. That's something you're going to have to figure out." The green eyes flecked with brown bore into the lawyer's. "I shall expect to hear from you by the end of the week. Do I make myself clear?"

"Very."

"The helicopter will take you back to the airport."

Mather got up and, with some difficulty, made his way to the door. "How did you . . . "

"By pure accident. A gentleman I was talking to on another matter entirely, put this file together for me. To tell you the truth, I was very surprised to find your name in it."

When the lawyer had left, Vandenberg crossed to the bathroom, unbuttoned his shirt and ran hot water into the basin. *Every day this matter is left to rest I'm at risk. If Mather comes through, the way will be clear. The minute I have the package, Teresa Lucana can be airbrushed out of the picture.*

He rinsed his face and hands and walked back into the living room. Lying on the floor was Mather's copy of the *National Examiner,* open at the pictures taken in Vietnam. Pentecost's shot his bolt, Vandenberg thought. What's done is done. I'll have Phil Calder—I'll tell the team I decided on him after all—hit the *Examiner* hard enough to rattle them, have them kill off any plans for follow-up pieces. Without corroboration, Pentecost's views will count for shit in the long run. He's the least of my problems.

*In a high-risk scenario: balance the probabilities;
gradually eliminate as many potential variables as
possible, estimate what might be achieved and at
what human cost . . .*

The old military doctrine was refreshingly
uncluttered, Vandenberg thought. It followed that if
the objective was great enough, then no one human
life was sacrosanct. He could hear the distant hack
of the helicopter, returning Mather to the airport. In
other words, a risk always has to be calculable—the
odds must be stacked in your favor. For him, the big
question was always the same: what chance do I
have of coming out intact? Can I get away with it?

Can I get away with it? The first time he'd asked
himself that, the hack of a helicopter had been
directly above him. Captain Kopyc, a sergeant and
three grunts had been pushing on into the jungle
ahead. Kopyc had graduated in the first hundred
out of West Point in '63, ten ahead of Vandenberg
himself. Lowell had seen little of him during the first
months of their tour of duty in 'Nam. He only knew
that, by the end of the Spring offensive of 1964, the
young Polish-American captain and his unit had
built a reputation as a ruthlessly efficient and
intrepid fighting force.

"Dear John" letters affected those who received
them in a variety of ways. Vandenberg remembered
seeing men built like linebackers crying like
children, walking around in a stupor for months.
Others trawled the brothels of Saigon in a desperate
attempt to rebuild their self-esteem. A few, like
Kopyc, vented their anger and frustration on the
enemy. Within weeks of hearing that his fiancee,
back home in Pittsburgh, was to marry her boss, he
seemed to transform into a one-man killing

machine. He began to volunteer his unit for high-risk assignments. Week after week he'd push himself and those he commanded to the limit. His objective accomplished, he'd often return to base with no more than a handful of men. The scale of his achievement always seemed to outweigh concern over his own losses, and he was given an open ticket to select new men from other units. The word was soon out around the messes of the marine battalions: Kopyc was the wrong man to impress if you planned to see out your tour of duty in one piece.

Vandenberg had been no underachiever himself. He'd looked on his transfer to Kopyc's unit cooly enough. The man himself was still intact, he'd argued, so he must be doing something right.

The Iron Triangle was a Viet Cong stronghold twenty miles northwest of Saigon. On the 16th of February 1966, 8,000 U.S. troops were deployed to destroy it, in the biggest American offensive of the war so far. The area, riddled with tunnels, was pounded by B-52 bombers and artillery before the troops went in. Reconnaissance aircraft had photographed a concrete emplacement near the heart of the stronghold and identified it as an ammunition dump. The dump had proved to be too deep to be penetrated by concrete piercing bombs, so Kopyc's unit was assigned to destroy it in a land operation.

The company of twenty-five men came under heavy attack almost immediately. Five had been lost by the time Kopyc discovered that bombing had opened up a hole in the main tunnel and there was a chance they could reach the emplacement through it. He left half his force to hold the position and moved into it with Vandenberg and the rest. The retreating Viet Cong had booby-trapped the stretch a mile ahead. Half the detachment steered around the mines. Then one man, laden with charges intended for use against the emplacement, snagged his pack on a root that projected from the tunnel wall and lost his footing. A massive explosion killed the rest of his squad and blew in the tunnel above them, cutting off the survivors from the rest.

Vandenberg and a sergeant propped a mortally wounded boy of about eighteen against some backpacks and tried to get some morphine into him. Kopyc gave the five survivors a minute to gather their wits, then ordered them to push on. The kid had nothing to lose now by saying what he was certain the others all felt. "What's the big hurry? The gelignite's gone, Kopyc. What do you think you're gonna do when you get there, huff and puff and blow the thing in?"

"We'll pick you up on the way back," was all Kopyc would say.

"You won't make it, Kopyc. None of you will. Not a chance."

The officer spun around. "Shut up! Just shut the fuck up! We're going on and that's it."

Soon the sergeant moved up to Vandenberg's side. "I need a better reason to die than a psycho Polack who can't handle failure."

Vandenberg and the sergeant had lifted themselves out of the tunnel system into the fading daylight by a camouflaged exit. They were watching Kopyc, thirty yards ahead, hacking his way through the undergrowth with a bayonet. "I know what they do with mad dogs in my town," the sergeant muttered as he waited for the three GIs to lift themselves clear.

Helicopters, moving out of the battle zone, passed over, high above them. There are still six of us left, he thought. We still have our radio. But for Kopyc . . . one man . . . He began figuring the odds.

Can I get away with it?

They pushed on toward the emplacement. In a clearing, they came upon enemy dead. As they stripped them of their Russian-made hand grenades, Vandenberg asked Kopyc if he could speak with him alone. "There's nothing to discuss," the captain snapped back.

Twenty minutes later, they came under attack from a Viet Cong position about fifty yards southeast of them. Kopyc and the three GIs were pinned down. Vandenberg and the sergeant were forced to move west. The VCs started to rake the undergrowth with fire. Two bullets caught the sergeant, he went down and Vandenberg was suddenly alone. Night was beginning to fall. In the half-light, he saw Kopyc about twenty yards from him, watched him silently break cover. He cupped his hand to shout and then thought again.

Whether Kopyc was right or wrong, a good man or a bad, was no longer the issue. All that was relevant was that, left to function as he was, he and three other men would die needlessly. He pulled the Russian-made automatic he'd taken off the dead VC, from his combat blouse. He was clear now what he was going to do. He checked his position and tried to steady his breathing. The bullet would hit Kopyc from the southeast, from the same direction as Charlie's fire. If U.S. troops ever recovered the body, if doubts were ever raised, if the slug didn't pass clean through him and they dug it out, it would be Russian-made. Vandenberg saw the officer gesture at his men to move on, then gripped the gun with both hands and leveled the sights at Kopyc's head. The man was moving into the brush again. He had seconds to act. A surge of excitement flooded through his whole body. His penis began to stiffen in his pants. He held his breath and tried to hold the gun steady. Sweat dripped into his eyes. The heavy scent of the pawlowma leaves around him, was starting to make his head swim. The only sound now was the distant cackle of a *koel* bird. He squeezed the trigger.

The gun kicked more than he'd expected. There was a dull bap-bap-bap. Across the clearing, he saw Kopyc's body jerk forward and a chunk of his cranium spin off into the brush. Vandenberg laid low as the GIs returned fire, raking an area a little to his left, waited till one of them crept forward and checked the body. "Lieutenant!" the soldier called softly. After a moment, Vandenberg showed himself. "Kopyc's bought it." Bending low, he walked over to where the captain lay. He didn't have to check his pulse to know Kopyc was dead.

"I'm taking command of this operation," Vandenberg said. "We turn back for base right now." An extraordinary feeling of elation gripped him, a thrill that seemed to emanate from a profound sense of dominance. He was in control. He had the power . . .

Vandenberg folded the copy of the *National Examiner,* crossed the bedroom and switched on the TV. Even after all these years that elation had never given way to remorse. Left to Kopyc, he thought, I would have died in agony, face downward in the mud, like so many others I saw. Left to Kopyc, America would have been denied its greatest president. I survived Vietnam. I survived the death camp at Dachau. And I've come too far to be obliterated by a little tramp from Manila.

TEN

The receptionist with the Ronald McDonald rinse pointed to the elevator. "Mr. Caldicott? Mr. Dawlish is waiting for you in the Wentworth suite. You'll find it on the third floor."

The two British CID officers crossed the lobby of the Royal George Hotel, Tunbridge Wells, and made for the ancient lift. The elderly man standing beside them glanced at his watch.

"If you're in a hurry, it's quicker to walk," he informed them. "They've been promising to replace these lifts for twenty years. People leave the gates open when they get out, that's the problem."

Caldicott shrugged. They were ten minutes early. "There's no rush."

No rush. He'd been sifting through the files on Gregor Tanyuk and a dozen others like him for almost two years. They'd waited this long to face him up. What was another five minutes?

Caldicott's transfer to Braithwaite's unit, as it was generally referred to, in the Spring of '93 had not been without its benefits. Early promotion to inspector had given him another hundred and twenty pounds a week. For the first time in his career, his hours were regular. The unit was based in Sheffield, Yorkshire, half an hour's drive from his parents, two brothers and their families. The house they'd rented for him in the town was bigger than his own in Ealing and had better views. But when he'd first walked up the steps of the anonymous-looking offices behind the Woolwich Building Society in West Street, he knew his heart wasn't in the assignment.

"Braithwaite's Unit" had been formed in the spring of 1986, when the royal assent to the War Crimes Act had opened the way for alleged war criminals living in the United Kingdom to be brought to trial. A specially constituted police unit, led by Detective Chief Superintendent Bobby Braithwaite and consisting of three inspectors, a sergeant and three constables, was given access to the Crown Prosecution Service, historians and translators to enable them to begin putting cases together against the principal suspects.

Caldicott was uniquely valuable to the team. His father had met his Ukrainian mother soon after she arrived in England with her parents in 1947, as part of the Foreign Labor Drive, when she came to work at the same shoe factory, near Bolton. They had married in 1950. In the evening, when father was home, the family spoke English, but during the day, after school, they spoke Ukrainian. It had been no small task to reach back into his past for the skills he'd learned in childhood, but Braithwaite's unit was operating on a tight budget. The clear policy was that no outsiders should be hired if there were members of the force who could perform the same functions. Caldicott was the only CID officer in Britain who spoke the same language as four of the potential defendants. He could assess which of the documents, out of the crateloads that were beginning to arrive from what had once been Soviet archives, might be useful enough to the prosecution to justify the expense of being translated.

Few bills this century had been debated more passionately, had divided the two houses of government more deeply, than the War Crimes Act. Thrown out after a second reading by the House of Lords, it became only the second bill ever to require the implementation of the Parliamentary Act of 1922 to make it law. Caldicott said to his wife the morning he started work for the unit, "What's really going to be achieved by prosecuting a bunch of geriatrics, fifty years after the event? This is not what I joined the police to do."

Inevitably perhaps, Caldicott's view changed. In 1989, he'd been on the team that tracked down the child-killer, Norman Cairns. Evidence given at his trial was so appalling that many of those involved, including police and jurors, had to be given counseling for months afterward. But nothing had prepared Caldicott for the deluge of human suffering that was to swamp him for the next eight months. As he waded through thousands of pages of evidence, he began to get a measure of the routine cruelty that had been meted out to hundreds of thousands of concentration camp prisoners and slave laborers by the eleven men they were investigating.

The old lift creaked as it winched the men to the third floor. Until now they've been faceless, he thought. Now at least one will have substance, human form.

No, hardly that.

In the first weeks, he'd been moved. Then he became numb. At night, he would pace the kitchen floor, morose. As he withdrew further into himself, his wife and those who worked with him became increasingly concerned. It must have been clear enough to Braithwaite that Caldicott was the wrong man for the job. Surely it was only a matter of time before he'd be transferred back to his old unit? But the matter was left to rest. It was then that Caldicott began to suspect his transfer was not just to do with his language skills. Word reached him through his Ukrainian relatives that highly placed émigrés had complained to their MPs that these war crimes investigations might turn into a witchhunt against the whole Ukrainian community. Caldicott was certain that his assignment to Braithwaite's unit was a political sop, aimed at taking the heat out of a delicate situation.

So there was no transfer. Instead, Braithwaite declared, "We need to get you out in the field more. Get you back in the firing line."

Let you see the enemy, that's what he means, Caldicott told himself as he slid back the black wrought-iron doors of the lift. Get things back in proportion.

Dawlish was one of those guys who are born as solicitors. His hair was white-blond, his face bloodless. He looked as if he needed coloring in. "Right on time. My client will be with us presently." He smiled. At least, Caldicott took it for a smile. It was a cold, cheerless thing. "Shall I order some tea?"

"No. No thank you."

The two policemen stood awkwardly in the small living room of the suite while Dawlish called room service.

The old man from the lobby, who'd come up in the lift with them, stood in the doorway breathing hard. "I'm sorry, I can't move very fast these days."

Caldicott was certain his own face registered utter surprise. This tiny, emaciated old man was Gregor Tanyuk?

"Ah, there you are Steven. Gentlemen, this is Steven Preston." For a second, there was total silence. "Er, that is his legal name. He changed it in 1954."

Caldicott looked into the watery eyes. "Steven Preston. Formerly Gregor Tanyuk."

Dawlish held up a finger. "Gentlemen, I do need to establish with you from the outset that this meeting is . . . "

"Held without prejudice. That's what was agreed. Nothing said here can be used in evidence against your client."

"Well, to that end I've taken the liberty of bringing a tape recorder." Dawlish produced a cassette machine, switched it on and placed it on the table. Then, in a steady voice, he recorded the date, time and place of the meeting, noting those present.

"Yes, I was born Gregor Tanyuk," the old man said at last. "It is not an uncommon name in the Lvov."

Gregor, Tanyuk, Lvov—they were pronounced as a Ukrainian would pronounce them. But the rest of what he had said . . . there was no hint that he'd been born anywhere other than the south of

England. As the detective sergeant checked routine stuff, age, address and so on, Caldicott studied the old man. Outside, there was the familiar drone of buses, the distant hammering of a pneumatic drill— the sounds of ordinary life filtered into a shabby suite, in a provincial English town. It seemed impossible to make a connection between this old man and the acts of unspeakable barbarism he was accused of.

"You asked for a fuller medical report on my client," Dawlish said at last. "I hope this covers the points."

" . . . all tests indicate that the swelling in the patient's pancreas is a malignant tumor. If it maintains its current rate of growth he will live a further eight to ten months." Caldicott put down the letter and looked up. Now, Tanyuk was studying him.

"So you see, Inspector Caldicott, I won't be alive to stand trial, let alone serve a prison sentence."

"I can't comment on that. My concern is solely to provide the Crown Prosecution Service with as complete a picture as I can of your activities during World War Two in as much as they relate to others under investigation by this unit. Where they take it from there is entirely up to them."

"Well, even if Mr. Preston is the same Tanyuk you're interested in, I assure you he will tell you nothing without a deal. As I said in my letter, he can provide you with crucial evidence regarding the wartime activities of Peter Vasilkov, whom I know you're also interested in. It concerns events of which you cannot have knowledge at present. In return . . . " Dawlish took a sheet of paper from his breast pocket. " . . . he wants immunity from prosecution on any charges relating to his own wartime activities together with an undertaking that his name will not be publicly linked with any of those events. His family is to remain unaware of any allegations in that regard. They must be left in peace."

"First of all, I am not in the position to strike any kind of a deal, as you put it. That would be a matter for the DPP alone. I can only make recommendations. To do that I'd have to be satisfied that Mr. Tanyuk's testimony would prove of material value to our investigations."

"So I take it you are interested in Vasilkov?"

Caldicott nodded. "Yes."

"I'm given to believe he's top of your list."

"I've said, we're interested in him."

Tanyuk leaned forward. Caldicott had to strain to hear what he was saying. "I can tell of . . . events that go beyond anything you have on file. Acts of slaughter instigated by Vasilkov to which I am the only living witness."

"Were no other SS men involved?"

"Yes. All Ukrainians. All killed by Vasilkov and a handful of Germans. Of them, only I survived. By right, I too should be dead."

In different ways, both policemen thought, I'll drink to that.

"When did these incidents take place?" Caldicott asked.

Tanyuk looked at the floor. Dawlish took his cue. "You have our terms."

"How will I know there's any substance to what your client's going to tell me?"

"Call the Simon Wiesenthal Center," Tanyuk said. "Ask them for their file on Horst Rathenau. He was Vasilkov's commanding officer for much of the war. Most of what he did was by Rathenau's order. That will give you part of the story. I can tell you the rest. Oh, in later years, Rathenau also used the name Otto Krause. You might check under that name too."

ELEVEN

Lassiter crossed the visitors' parking lot and walked slowly down the gravel path that led to the complex of buildings ahead. To his left, two smartly dressed couples in their late seventies sat taking English tea under a large parasol. Ahead, four old ladies, their coiffeur immaculate, sipped aperitifs as they played bridge. Well, if I have to end my days, Lassiter thought, not for the first time, then please God, let it be in a place like this.

At the beginning, Joe Lassiter had coped with retirement well, viewing it as an opportunity to work freelance for all the newspapers he'd never been able to write for. While his legend in Washington still burned brightly, he was as busy as he'd ever been. But as it inevitably dimmed, spaces opened up in his day. And then his week. Too often alone in the house in Rockville, he began to drink. That period of his life had ended on a bend of the Capital Beltway at 4:00 one morning with the police cutting him out of what remained of his car.

The facial injuries and the punctured lung could be repaired. The spinal cord, severed just above the pelvis, could not. After the initial shock had subsided, Joe began to rebuild his life with surprising vigor, but the Rockville house proved to be an impractical home for a man in a wheelchair, and private nursing care a heavy drain on his resources. Joe had seen for himself that a retirement home was the only answer.

Jack Lassiter walked down the side of a long two-story building and swung open a glass door. Who was the old man's *bête noire* the last time I saw him? he wondered, as he rapped loudly on the door of Room 221. Governor Caulfield, yeah, that's the one . . .

The reply came immediately. "I'm here, where else would I be?"

Lassiter pushed the door and walked in. His father was propped up on pillows, tapping away at the ancient Remington typewriter that always sat on the invalid table that straddled the bed. Joe Lassiter peered over his spectacles, as his son had seen him do since he could first remember.

"Hi kid. Jesus, you look like you could use a decent meal. There's nothin' of you." His son kissed his forehead. "It's great to see you. Give me just a minute here, will you? I have to get this to the *Herald* before close of business."

Lassiter sat down and waited. A stranger coming into Joe Lassiter's room for the first time would've found it hard to believe that the old man had been retired for almost a decade. Central to the room, in the midst of the personal items of furniture and objets d'art that gave the place its character, stood a shelf of TV monitors wired into the major news services. Beneath it, fax, video and photocopying machines had all been installed. This room had been Joe's world for close to six years. Here, he was still a hot-shot newspaper editor. The news stories, features and editorials that had spiced the pages of the *Tribune* through the Sixties and Seventies still spilled out of his typewriter ceaselessly—the word processor his son had bought him sat under its dust cover where he'd set it down three years ago, a disturbing icon of the present.

Jack had no doubt that the piece his father was hurrying to finish would reach the *Tribune* on time. He was also pretty certain that no one would be waiting for it, or had the slightest idea that it was coming. It was an even bet it would end up in a drawer with the several hundred others that had arrived in the same way over the last three years. The occasional piece still appeared in the local paper. As few as they were, they kept alive the fragile illusion that Joe Lassiter was still a force in the industry he'd loved all his life.

"So how was Germany? A lot like '31, from what I hear." Joe's eyes never left the typewriter. "If those punks ever get themselves organized . . . "

"I bought you cigars, Pop. Shall I put them in the drawer?"

"Yeah, thanks."

"So tell me, what's the latest on Bill Caulfield?"

The old man looked up, then shrugged. "Still stinkin' up the governor's residence in Sacramento, I guess. I'm doing a series of profiles on the presidential candidates. I don't suppose you've been able to follow much of it from over there."

"Sure I have." His father's hair was a little whiter but, otherwise, he looked much the same.

"This one's on Edgar Hersh."

"Worse guys have run."

"That's for sure. Myself, I doubt whether he's got the intellect to do more than maintain the status quo."

"How bad! You should try living in Germany right now."

"The shape of things to come, my boy."

Joe rolled the sheet out of the Remington. "The next one's on Lowell Vandenberg." The old man shook his head. "What a choice of candidates. Yeesh! Bring us your uninspired. Bring us those without vision or wisdom, and let us lift them up and make them great in the eyes of men . . . "

"Who said that?"

"Me . . . in this." He wrapped the manuscript with his hand. "It's the system that's wrong. That's why creeps like these can get as far as they have. Now Grant Tollson, he has what it takes," the old man went on. "Integrity, insight. He really cares about people, about issues. He came by a couple of weeks back. I asked him why he wasn't in the race. He said, "I want the job, Joe. But the thing is, I want my family more. I don't want every detail of our lives held up to the spotlight. It's not fair to them.'"

"Yeah, I'll bet."

"He's got nothing to hide—no more than you or me, anyhow. It's just that the good guys don't want any part of the process any more—seen the families of too many colleagues hurt. Once the opposition and the press start digging into your past. I tell you, there are no winners in those things. That's how we end up with creeps like Vandenberg in the race."

"You better write your piece on him quick. Might be more useful as an obituary."

"He ain't going no place." Joe pressed the remote control on the VCR. The chiseled features of Lowell Vandenberg filled the monitor. A news report showed him speaking seconds before he was shot. Joe moved the footage forward almost a frame at a time. "Look at this . . . " He gestured to his son. "He moves out from behind the lectern . . . and then, blam! It doesn't add up."

"What do you mean?"

"I'll show you what I mean." Joe moved the tape back again and jabbed a finger at the screen. "There's the gunman's target, right there. Vandenberg's head. Jesus, the guy was a sitting duck for almost fifteen minutes. Why would the gunman wait till he moved to shoot him?"

Lassiter shrugged. "A head's a pretty small target over that distance."

"They got Kennedy in the head over the same distance and he was in a goddam car! This should have been a piece of piss for a professional. And this had to be a professional job. So how come the gunman blew it? I'll tell you why. Cos those were his orders."

"You mean the gunman meant to miss?"

Joe's face was glowing. "No. He meant to hit him all right. But in the chest. In the body armor. See, this wasn't a screwup." He pushed out his cheek with his tongue the way he always did when he thought he was on to something good. "It was a setup."

Lassiter allowed himself a smile and shook his head. The old man seemed to get screwier every time he saw him. "What are you saying here? Vandenberg set himself up to be shot at? Sure."

Joe rapped on the invalid table. A rap for each

word. "Why else did the gunman wait? Because he knew damn well that Vandenberg would be wearing that vest. Pass me those cuttings, kid, will you?"

Lassiter reached for a stack of newspaper cuttings lying on a chest of drawers and passed them to his father. "Christ, Dad, Marianne was there! She says . . . "

"According to Vandenberg she saved his life." Joe ran his finger down a cutting from the *Post*. "Persuaded him at the last minute to put the vest on . . . "

"You know Marianne. I'm sure she did."

"Vandenberg knows her too, Jack. He was relying on her to do just that, to make the thing look like a miracle escape, not some scam."

It's the old problem, Lassiter thought. He just has too much time on his hands. "C'mon Pop, why would anyone fake up a thing like that?"

"Maybe because they're desperate. Because they'll go to any lengths to get noticed, to get where they want to be." Joe slid over a bunch of clippings held together with a wire pipe cleaner. "Ask yourself, who gained the most out of this? Look at this stuff! Vandenberg's miraculous escape! These two printed the text of that wacko fascist group's letter in full on the front page. But who are these people? Even other leaders of extreme right groups have never heard of them. But it had exactly the right effect. Overnight, it's Vandenberg, hero of the minorities! Vandenberg the martyr, champion of the downtrodden! Horseshit, Jack. Remember when Reagan survived that assassination attempt? His popularity rating went through the roof." The old man fixed his son with his gaze. "I've been in this business forty years. I can sniff out Vandenbergs downwind of a fish cannery. I'm telling you, Jack, this was a setup."

The sequence on Vandenberg had finished. The tape ran on into a news report on the latest outbreak of violence in Moldavia. Further footage showed violent demonstrations on the streets of Minsk in Belorussia. The two men watched it in silence for a moment. "What was the Soviet Union? Hundreds of ethnic groups, who'd loathed each other's guts for centuries, forced for seventy years to unite against a common foe . . . " Jack Lassiter studied his father's face. Where was the old man's mind now? "It was a case of 'mine enemy's enemy is my friend.' But when the Russians pulled out, there was nothing left to bind them together. The old hatreds surfaced again. And that's what's driving them now.

"I tell you, some day soon, you'll see the same kind of divisions open up here, in this country." The old man took off his glasses. "It's going to take a very special man in the White House to hold all that hate in. A breed of man we haven't had running this country in a long time." He stared out across the lawn. "God help us all, if we put in someone like Lowell Vandenberg."

That evening, Lassiter moved back into the apartment that he'd shared with Marianne for four years, in preparation for the Pensacola Drug Ring hearing—the Rockville house was more than an hour's drive from the Criminal Court Buildings in the city; her place, less than fifteen minutes. Marianne was on the campaign trail with Vandenberg for the week, and as the apartment was technically still half his, she could raise little objection to his using it.

He watered her miserable-looking plants as promised—Marianne always referred to him as the "Doctor Mengele of Plant Life"—and moved wistfully around the room, remembering ornaments they'd bought together, pictures, mementoes from a time when it seemed they would be together forever.

His mobile phone rang. It was Fraenkel. "Nothing on the photo search so far, I'm afraid. There turned out to be fewer of them than we thought. It seems Mielke was kind of touchy about having his picture taken. There's no sign of Number Three in the ones we've checked."

"So what happens now?" Lassiter said almost to himself.

"Well, it looks like we may have had a breakthrough on another front. We've had an answer to your FIRU call, the one you left on file in the Interpol database."

"Who picked up on it?"

"Some inspector in the British police. It seems he's interested in the same guy you are. I've got his number here. It's probably better if he fills you in himself."

It was late evening in Sheffield. Caldicott was making cocoa for himself and his wife when Lassiter called. They introduced themselves and got straight to it. "I understand you're interested in Otto Krause," Caldicott began. "Krause is an a.k.a., but then you know that." Caldicott stirred milk into the mugs. There was a pause on the transatlantic line. "The man's real name is Horst Rathenau. He's seventy-nine now, lives somewhere near Leipzig, in what was East Germany . . . "

"Hold it, will you?" Lassiter searched around for something to write on. He opened the top drawer of Marianne's desk. Inside were sheets of old typescripts; most had a line in ink scribbled across them. He took some out and turned them over to write on. "Okay."

"During the war he was Sturmbannführer Rathenau. You'll find a file on him at the Simon Wiesenthal Center. Or I can fax you what I have here."

"This guy was a Nazi?"

"A big wheel in the SS."

"It can't be the guy I'm interested in. My man's a lifelong communist."

Immediately after Lassiter said it, a question sparked in his mind. What evidence do I have that makes me so certain of that? Just because he handled stuff for Mielke doesn't make him a communist. And even if he was, couldn't he have still been a Nazi, a fascist, whatever, during the war? Didn't the *Finanzamt* file say that Premier Honecker himself had shopped his communist comrades to the Gestapo? If he could change allegiances so easily, why not this Rathenau?

Caldicott was talking. Lassiter had missed most of it. "I'm sorry, what were you saying?"

"This old Ukrainian, Gregor Tanyuk, we've been debriefing seems to know quite a bit about Rathenau. I don't think much of it's relevant to our enquiries, so if you want any more on this man, you better get over here and speak to him yourself."

Caldicott's file on Rathenau, including the stuff put together by the Wiesenthal Center in Los Angeles, began to pump out of Lassiter's fax machine minutes later. Rathenau had been wanted

in connection with cases arising from the fate of
tens of thousands of slave laborers put to work in
underground factories in World War Two. Like so
many war criminals, he'd never actually been
indicted. The file on him was made up of affidavits
from survivors who'd suffered at his hands, and
some inter-office correspondence, salvaged from
the thousands of documents that had been
destroyed during the last days of the Third Reich, in
1945. A note made it clear that Rathenau's SS file
had never been located and no photograph of him
ever found. A sketchy profile on him had been
produced by Wiesenthal's own people. But it gave
Lassiter enough to be certain that a search for
Rathenau, or those that had known him, in his
native Germany, could be implemented at once.

In his first weeks as Lassiter's assistant, Claus
Hoffman had begun to feel that the Mielke case
might be the career-maker he had been looking for
ever since his graduation to the *Zollfahndung* two
years earlier. But lack of any real progress in recent
weeks had put a dent in his optimism. Lassiter's
abortive meeting with the "Chief Pig" had, for him,
marked a new low point in the investigation. The
call from his boss at 1 A.M.—Hoffman had been half-
asleep in front of the television, an empty can of pils
held at his crutch like a metal phallus—did much to
revive his enthusiasm.

   This was the kind of assignment at which he
excelled. The clipped delivery that marked his
speech patterns whenever his mind was totally
focused was audible when he called Lassiter back
the following evening.

"I'm certain Rathenau could never have lived in East or West Germany under his own name after the war. I can find no trace of him. If he died on us, he didn't do it in the EC. Nothing's registered."

"Nor in the U.S.," Lassiter said. "So I'd say there's a fair chance he's still around. Does he have any relatives in Germany?"

"He had a brother and a cousin who died in the late Eighties. There's a nephew in his forties living in Dusseldorf who swears he's never met him and was surprised to hear he might still be alive. I ran down some of Rathenau's cronies from the war years."

"SS?"

"So their files say. You can imagine how forthcoming they were! Same crap: 'Haven't seen him since the war' . . . 'I never knew him.' Waste of time."

"Did he marry?"

"Yup." Hoffman was obviously consulting notes. "He married a Krista Gerstein in 1940. She was killed in a bombing raid on Essen in '41. Her sister's still around though. I spoke with her an hour ago. She hasn't had anything to do with him any more recently than the rest. But you should see her though. You never know what she might have."

"Fly back to Germany for that? Sure."

"Who said anything about Germany? She lives in Brooklyn, New York."

The following morning Lassiter drove the five blocks to Dewey's Spoon, on the corner of Colby Avenue and ate a breakfast of corn beef hash, eggs and coffee, then returned to the house to collect an overnight bag, go through the mail and lock up.

There was another letter from the bank and

three bills. He slung them into the growing pile in the corner of the kitchen and checked his watch. If he left now he could make the mid-morning American Airlines' flight to New York. He set the burglar alarm and carried his bag out to the car.

A black male, about thirty, sat in the driver's seat of the Jag. There was a grinding of metal as he engaged first gear and the car began to move away from the curb. Lassiter dropped his bag and ran down to the road. He pulled the Glock 9mm automatic from his shoulder holster and screamed, "Stop the vehicle!" The guy in the car could only hear the radio; his head bobbed in time to the music. Lassiter screamed again and flung himself into the path of the car, leveling the gun at the man's head. There was a screeching of brakes and the Jag shuddered to a halt. Lassiter fell forward onto the hood. The man wound down the window and chewed on his gum for a moment. "You better have a damn good reason for pointing that at me."

Lassiter groped in his pockets and finally managed to extract his badge. "I'm a federal Customs agent and I'm the owner of the car. Is that good enough, shithead?"

"Who you calling a shithead? This vehicle is owned by Courtland Financing and you owe four months' payments on it."

Lassiter, his face crimson with fury, stabbed the air with the gun. "What the hell is it to you?"

The man held up a sheaf of papers. "Cos I'm the repo man, that's why. Now, are you gonna move your bod?"

Lassiter clapped his hand over his forehead. "Jesus!" He put away the gun and tried to catch his breath. "Look, if that's all it is, I'll write you a check, okay?" He began to fumble in his pockets again. The man sniffed the air, sulkily like a child. "Look, I'm sorry I called you a shithead, all right?" Lassiter tried.

"I can't take no checks. Cash or nothing." There was another grinding of metal as he put the car into gear.

Lassiter winced. "Give me ten minutes, I can get the cash."

The man began to roll up the window. "I don't have ten minutes."

Lassiter tried to catch the door as the Jag began to move. "Well, let me ride with you, we pass my bank on the way."

The man shouted through the space above the window, "Speak to them down at the office, pal."

Lassiter remembered the travelers checks left over from Germany. He began to run alongside the car. "Look, I have these, they're as good as cash." He banged on the window as the car gathered speed. "Look!" He pulled out a pen and began to scribble on them. "Take these, for Christ's sakes . . . I have a plane to catch."

There was a spectacular scraping sound from the gear box as the repo man changed up. Lassiter stopped and put his fingers in his ears. "Give it more clutch, you sonofabitch!" He kicked furiously at a mail bin and began to walk back to the house. "Jesus Christ."

The corridor in the basement of the apartment building, three blocks from the Brooklyn Bridge, was so dark that Lassiter could barely make out the number on the door. A man with a beer belly and wearing a postman's uniform answered the bell and stood eyeing the Customs agent suspiciously.

"I'm here to see Mrs. Hofle. I called yesterday." The postman bit into a clumsily-made pastrami sandwich, then, without a word, led Lassiter to a room at the back.

Mrs. Hofle, a tiny birdlike woman, with what appeared to be the early stages of Parkinson's disease, had gamely tried to cram most of the treasured contents of her own home into a room barely twelve feet square. She pointed to a diningroom chair squeezed between a hallstand and a dressing table, and Lassiter sat down.

"It's very good of you to see me, Mrs. Hofle."

"Will you have coffee?" The remnants of a Southern German accent were unmistakable.

"No thanks."

"You want to know about Horst Rathenau, is that it?" she asked, one eye still on the game show winding to a finish on the TV in the corner.

"I know that you haven't seen him since your sister was killed in 1941. It's a lifetime ago, I can appreciate that. But I wondered if you could give me any background detail on him."

She shrugged. After what seemed an age, she said, "Krista brought him to the house for the New Year celebrations in 1938." Her head shook almost imperceptibly as she tried to remember. Across the room Beer Belly lolled against the window and chewed lazily on his sandwich like a bear on a locust. "Yes, 1938." Her mouth turned down at the corner. "He was very charming of course. My sister went for that type. He impressed my father because his family was always in the papers, announcing some big new business deal or something."

"What kind of business?"

"Oh you know, city stuff, high finance. Horst had already made something of a name for himself in all that, before the war. He loved my sister, I guess, but I never took to him. Too stiff, too cold. She liked to laugh. You know, enjoy herself. But he . . . "

"Do you by any chance have a photograph of him?"

The old woman got up and crossed uncertainly to the sideboard, stacked with magazines and newspapers. She took a battered photograph album from the drawer and began to turn the pages. Lassiter's pulse quickened. "This is her on her wedding day."

Lassiter took the proffered album as though he was receiving the Holy Grail. He was barely conscious of the tall, pretty girl who stood on the left, in the faded black and white photograph. His attention was riveted to the man in the uniform of an SS officer. The face was thinner, the jawline tauter, but the man staring back at him was the same one Lassiter had first seen on the computer simulation. Mentally crossing his fingers, he asked, "Do you have a shot of your brother-in-law I might borrow?"

She shrugged again. "There used to be some loose ones at the back." Lassiter searched for them as the woman rummaged in the drawer. "Here she is in her trousseau." He gave the hand-tinted picture in the oval silver frame a polite glance. "That's a lock of her hair I put round the edge. They took it from her after she was killed."

"Yes, tell me about that," Lassiter said distractedly, turning various small snapshots to the light.

The old lady took the framed picture back to her seat, cradling it to her chest. "She was with Rudy, at our mother's house in Essen . . . the Allied bombers came . . . the house took a direct hit in the first minutes. Horst was given compassionate leave. He came on May 27. It was the last time we saw him. I always remember the date because it was the day they sank the *Bismarck* . . ."

After a few moments, Beer Belly eased himself off the window, muttered something to his mother and swaggered out of the door. On the corner of the street he ducked into a bar and made his way over to a pay phone. He dialed and waited.

TWELVE

Vandenberg's fingers moved quickly over the keyboard. Then he sat silently in the gloom of the screening room for the cassette he'd selected to load. Key polls showing the relative positions of the candidates in the Democratic race for the presidency flashed onto the secondary screens.

The central screen showed a poll of polls. Voters registered to the party, it seemed, still considered Edgar Hersh the man most likely to take the nomination at the Democratic convention in July. But Bradley Mandel's muddleheaded campaign platform was costing him dear. Instead of second, he now showed fourth. In his place, was Gene Bravington, the black lawyer from Watts, California. Third was Vandenberg himself. For ten days the media had given him saturation coverage. Some marked improvement in his overall position was to be expected.

Vandenberg checked out the latest footage on Bravington's campaign. The black senator was a fine orator, he thought, but as far as the nomination was concerned, the runes were cast against him. He punched another index code and Hersh's face filled the central screen. He pulled it into close-up and studied it. There must be a way, he thought, as he walked through the gallery to his study.

On the desk was the letter from the man, Vollman, who claimed that he had been Lowell's father's closest friend in Schrobenhausen concentration camp. It had come that morning, through the lawyer in Leipzig. He read the second page again:

I had been a member of the Communist Party since 1933. Many German communists fled when Hitler came to power three years later. Young and idealistic, I stayed on, believing I still had a mission to fulfill. I was rounded up with many communists, Jews and other undesirables and interned in Schrobenhausen concentration camp in the spring of 1939. Your father arrived there a year later. Perhaps surprisingly, we had much in common. I believe our friendship helped sustain us through appalling conditions.

As I'm sure you know, he died of pneumonia the following winter. I was with him. He entrusted me with a number of letters. Correspondence between himself and your mother concerning arrangements to get you to Switzerland. A letter from the Red Cross confirming your safe arrival. Perhaps most significantly, I have details of certain arrangements your father made regarding his business affairs in the weeks before the invasion of Holland. You will no doubt wonder why it has taken me so many years to make all this known to you. The truth is, that to keep these documents safe I had to hide them. The fortunes of war, the twists and turns of my own story and the momentous changes that have come to my country in recent years, resulted in my being able to retrieve these documents only very recently.

As I shall be visiting America for the first time very soon, I thought this a good opportunity to return to you what should have been yours years ago. Be very clear, Governor Vandenberg. I want nothing from you. Except perhaps to spend a few hours with the son of a man I respected and cared a great deal for.

The letter was signed, "Conrad Vollman." Vandenberg held the photocopy the German had enclosed up to the art deco lamp on his desk. The text on the battered sheet of paper shown in it was so faded it was almost impossible to make out. But the signature was remarkably like his father's.

" . . . details of certain arrangements your father made regarding his business affairs . . . "

Vandenberg turned the words over in his mind. *The money.* The millions of guilders his father had hidden in Swiss bank accounts before the war. His money. What else could Vollman be referring to? Uncle Walter had always said it was all there somewhere, though years of detective work had failed to locate it. Even if Vollman had the key to only part of it . . . Was it possible after more than half a century . . . ?

Vandenberg crossed to the small marquetry

table in the bay window and picked up the framed photograph of his father. Paul Vandenberg was pictured beside the huge liner that had been the pride of the family shipping line, at the docks in Amsterdam. Ironic to think of him being marched away from that same dockyard by SS officers only five years later.

He turned to the picture of his mother. It had been taken on the day of her engagement. She looked pretty and coltish in her big floral print dress, her fair hair swept back off her forehead in one of those huge "bangs" that had been the height of fashion. There was nothing Semitic in the face. It was hardly surprising no one ever took him to be Jewish.

He looked out across the wide sweeping lawn to the tennis courts. His teenage children were playing doubles with two schoolfriends as five generations of Vandenbergs had before them.

He had been seventeen when he'd first visited his mother's homeland. Apart from some distant cousins, the only member of her family to survive the holocaust had been his Aunt Helga, with whom he'd stayed in Amsterdam that summer. Family friends had been able to satisfy some of his curiosity about his parents, fill in some of the gaps that the Vandenberg side of the family could not. Gradually he was able to paint a picture of the couple that equated with the image of them he'd held in his mind for so long. It had been from retired employees of the family business there that he'd learned of the frantic last trips to Switzerland his father had made in the month before the German invasion. Exactly what he accomplished there was never established, but then the secrecy that surrounded so much of what he did fitted with all that his Uncle Walter had told him.

What was certain though, was that Lowell Vandenberg's mother Anna had returned to Washington, months before the invasion of Holland, to have her child. The plan had been for Paul to go with her, but there was still some work to do on transferring the family's funds to Switzerland so she had made the trip without him. But for the fact that both parents felt it was essential in all the circumstances that their child should be born in America and kept in safety there, she would have canceled the crossing. From all accounts, she'd pleaded with her parents to come with her until the day she left. Her Dutch father, the owner of a large and successful jewelry business, had refused to believe rumors of an imminent German offensive, and made it clear he had no intentions of leaving all that he'd built up. His wife had felt duty bound to stay at his side.

Paul Vandenberg had been somewhere in Zurich the night his son was born. Within days, reports began to reach the Washington office of the Vandenberg Shipping Line that German troops were mobilizing for the invasion. For thirty-six hours, Anna tried every means possible to contact her husband and her parents, but communications were closing down all across Europe. Anna was alone in a strange country, in a house of cold, formal people who showed her no affection and made no attempt to understand the terrible helplessness she felt.

At 2 A.M., some nights later, the Vandenberg household in Washington was awakened by a hysterical child nurse, with cries that her month-old charge had been kidnapped. Only when it was clear that the mother had gone too, and that the Vandenberg freighter that had left the New York docks that night was bound for Amsterdam, did the family realize what had happened. Later that morning, the captain of the vessel confirmed by radio that Anna Vandenberg and her son were indeed aboard.

Nine days later, they arrived in Holland. Anna was under the impression that as the wife of an American—a citizen of a neutral country—she was at little risk herself. She was determined to talk her parents into leaving immediately, gather up her husband, and catch the next boat out of Amsterdam. If the worse came to the worst, she told friends on her arrival, the U.S. Embassy would get all four of them out.

The Dutch army was in full retreat by the time an American Embassy official told Paul that there could be no certainty of obtaining exit visas for his Jewish parents-in-law. Things were not much helped when Paul called him an anti-Semitic German sympathizer! He knew his wife would never leave Holland again without her parents. Amsterdam hummed with reports that the SS were already rounding up Jews for deportation to concentration camps. He knew too, that since he'd married into a prominent Jewish family the Germans would have a file on him. Now the Vandenberg name too was a liability.

Finally, he managed to buy papers on the black market, made out for the family in a different name. They arrived at the docks to take the ship for New York in early June, 1940. When the Nazi official on duty saw their papers, he immediately summoned a superior and the family were held for questioning.

Friends learned later that the maker of the documents had been arrested by the Gestapo only two nights before, and had given them the numbers of all the passports he had forged. No more was heard of the Vandenbergs until Lowell was handed to the Red Cross eleven months later.

A cheer went up from the tennis court. Vandenberg's fifteen-year-old son, Grant, punched the air. Lowell glanced at the photocopy again and lifted the phone on his desk. "See if you can reach a Conrad Vollman at the Park Lane Hotel in New York, will you?"

"Yes, Governor." Then the secretary said, "The package you were expecting has arrived. Do you want me to have it brought down?"

The sealed envelope inside was marked "The property of Miss Teresa C. Lucana." It contained a four-page notorized handwritten statement and a roll of 35mm film negative. Vandenberg read the statement once, took down some details from it, then put everything into a metal trash bin and burned it. After he had stirred the ashes to a powder, he dialed a number in Cyprus.

THIRTEEN

Jack Lassiter caught the mid-evening shuttle from La Guardia, NYC, and arrived at Washington National Airport just after ten. There was a message on the answering machine at the Rockville house instructing him to report to his Washington office immediately. It was close to midnight when he arrived at the U.S. Customs Service offices at 1301, Constitution Avenue.

Agent-in-Charge Capriotti greeted him wearily and pushed a ten-by-eight photograph across the imitation leather desktop. Lassiter turned it around. It showed the body of a man lying flat on his back on the sidewalk. If he'd had both sides of his face, he'd probably have looked like Marshak, the bank manager whose testimony was pivotal to the federal case against the Pensacola Drug Ring.

"He gave the DEA the slip around midnight. He was shot at four fifteen this morning as he was leaving his mistress's place." Capriotti's long sigh said, "Don't ask me where we go from here." It added, "The chances of getting a conviction on Kawoski now are remote in the extreme."

"Look, I'm not just saying this to make you feel better, Enzo," Lassiter said, "but I think Marshak was gonna be a crap witness, plea bargain or no pleabargain. With Kawoski sitting there across the courtroom from him, it would have been the John Gotti syndrome all over again. He'd have fallen apart quicker than it would have taken Kawoski to scratch his ear. The fact they shot him when they did means he was important, that what he had to say would have counted for something. The jury is gonna read that."

"Thank you for sharing that with me, Jack." Capriotti smacked the heel of his hand into his forehead. "Geesh!"

"We still have my testimony. I'm not chopped liver, you know. I saw the money passed at the airport. And we have the audiotapes of what they said."

"Yeah, with all that background noise. They've been back to the lab three times. The two of them still sound like they're talking through a mattress." Capriotti eased his butt off the radiator. "That hokesy-folksy fuck defending Kawoski is gonna tear the transcript to pieces. He's gonna have that jury believing they were talking about any other damn thing than what they were. Apart from your stuff, all we've really got to work with now are the accounts. You know what they show; I know what they show. How many times have we had this before? With a scam this complex, I don't think we have a prayer of getting the jury to understand it."

Lassiter snapped. His hand slammed onto the desk. "And that, Enzo, that fucking attitude, is why

I'm gonna leave this department, the minute the Germans are through with me." He spun around. "I don't know who the hell you think you're saying this to. I've studied these degenerates till I know more about them and their methods than they do. When the rest of the world is asleep and dreaming, I'm climbing around inside these guys' heads. Marshak gets shoved in the dumper and suddenly I'm no more use! Well, fuck that!" He threw up his arms in disgust. "We don't need Marshak to win this case. Not for a New York second! If you ask me nicely," he hit the first word hard, "I'll deliver Kawoski to you, all on my own. I'll take that jury through the stuff, element by element—no technical shit, no jargon—I'll show them how each piece fits logically and irrefutably into the next. I'll relate to things in their own lives. Stuff a seventh-grade dropout would understand." He turned for the door. "If between now and Monday the spirit of Thomas Jefferson reaches down and rewrites the constitution so that we only get MBAs on juries let me know. Otherwise, I am your best shot, Enzo. Stop treating me like I've got beans between my ears and you might just get lucky." He picked up his coat.

"I had three hours' sleep last night, Jack. It's Friday, so that makes about ten this week. I've had this case in my life so long, my daughter has dolls named after the defendants. Morale here is at an all-time low. The way I feel this minute, if the Almighty burnt your evidence into the wall of Court Room One at noon on Monday, that sonofabitch would still walk free. It has nothing to do with your capabilities; it's called battle fatigue, okay?"

Capriotti's thyroid condition was worse, that was for sure. Even six months ago it'd looked like his eyeballs belonged in a bigger skull. He took off his tinted glasses and rubbed the bridge of his nose. Poor bastard, Lassiter thought. It was hard to tell what his boss's face was registering now. Whatever the rest of it seemed to say, those great poppy eyes seemed to carry a perpetual look of astonishment.

Lassiter said more gently, "If the underlying truth is that we can beat our brains out all the way to Christmas, but we'll never get Duane C. Average to cope with the concepts, then what are we here for, Enzo?"

Capriotti managed a weary smile. "To re-educate the suckers, I guess. Come on, it's late. Let's get out of here." He switched out the lights and they moved out into the hallway. "You gonna be coming in from Rockville while the hearing's on?"

"No, Marianne's out of town, so I've moved back into our old apartment for a bit. Why are you asking? You think they could still make a try for me?"

Capriotti shrugged as though he'd been asked whether he thought it would rain. "I'd be a lot happier if you were in a safe house."

"I've been in Europe for six months, Enzo. I've been visible around this town for five days already. If they were gonna try for me, they'd have done it."

They walked toward the stairs. "Is your car fitted with an ATS system? No it can't be. You were in Germany when that directive went through."

Lassiter pieced together the acronym. "Anti-Terrorist Security system."

"Yeah, originally developed by the Brits for their security forces in Northern Ireland. At least it'll stop some sonofabitch sticking a bomb under your car."

Daker's eyes snapped open. Gunfire. Shotgun. He strained to see through the haze of blistering heat that rose from the sand. A man stood in the stern of a cruiser about a hundred yards offshore, shooting skeet. Clays rose into the air, breaking up almost instantly as shots hit them. Daker picked up the binoculars he'd bought the day before and focused on the man. How'd you like that, he thought. I spend three hundred bucks a day to get peace and quiet and they let this guy shoot skeet!

Truth to tell, the peace and quiet was beginning to get to Daker now. In the three weeks he'd been in Cyprus, he'd seen all of Famagusta and the surrounding region he wanted to see. He was ready to move on.

Blam!

Hah, missed it. Daker allowed himself a little smile. He sipped his ouzo and moved back farther under the sun umbrella.

Blam!

He's lost it. Too stiff. Isn't swinging from the waist.

Blam!

Vandenberg's face. Daker closed his eyes. As long as I live I'll never forget that. The two of us standing there like dummies in that field. Just for that split second I had him, Daker thought. I lowered the gun and blasted him in the chest. With only half the charge in the cartridge, the noise was kinda dull. No whipcrack. It opened up a good hole in the body armor and that was the main thing. But it was the second before, before I fired, that I'll remember. I looked down the sights of the Remington and there was fear in that face. For one split second, he thought I was gonna let him have it right in the puss!

Vandenberg had blinked and moved his head almost imperceptibly to the left. Like it was really gonna make a difference. There was pure fear in those eyes. I waited a long time to see that. Those four days in the jungle, north of Saigon, I started to wonder whether the fella had any feelings at all. Then Vandenberg had relaxed. He knew. Knew I was kidding. Hey, no Vandenberg, no pension fund, right?

He'd helped to shuck off the shirt and the vest. The red bruise on Vandenberg's chest was already beginning to rise.

"Couple of hours, that'll be a honey," Daker assured him. The sun was beginning to come up, but it was cold in that paddock. Vandenberg had folded the shirt and the bullet-proof vest, re-dressed himself in fresh clothes, and the two men had headed back to the cars in silence. Vandenberg swung into his Merc.

"Daker."

"Yeah."

"Don't screw up."

"You do your part, Lieutenant, I'll do mine."

Vandenberg thought for a second and nodded. Then he'd slammed the door and hightailed it back to the city.

Blam!

Swing from the waist, sucker.

Blam! That's better. Roll with it. Daker watched

the waiter begin to lay up lunch. Better stay on the fish, he thought, stay in shape.

The owner of the cafe appeared at the kitchen door. "Are you Mr. Dawson?" Daker shouted back that he was. "I have a call for you."

That better be Vandenberg, Daker thought. Not another living soul has that name and this number.

"I know I'm calling two days earlier than planned." Vandenberg sounded calm. "But I needed to speak with you."

"Something gone wrong?"

"No, nothing. Everything worked fine."

Daker began to breathe again. "How much have they pieced together?"

"Nothing like enough. They've got a dozen theories. Most of them way off the mark."

"Naturally. It was a masterpiece. No one else in the country could have rigged those shots, figured out all the ballistics."

"Yeah, you did well. Did the rest of the money come through?" Vandenberg asked.

"Uhuh."

"Okay, so we're square on that one."

"Yeah. So long as you keep to your side of things."

"Oh, so who am I going to tell, huh? Listen, I've got another job for you."

"What're you talking? You know I can't come back to the States again."

"You won't have to."

"Well I'm bored out of my fucking skull already, so what have you got in mind?"

"I need a follow-up on that surveillance thing, that Filipina woman you watched for me."

"Lucana. Teresa Lucana."

"Yeah. You'll need to fly to Manila. There's no extradition there, I've checked. I want you to locate Teresa Lucana. Have you got some paper there? There's some stuff you're gonna need to write down."

Not surprisingly, there was no direct flight from Famagusta in Cyprus to Manila in the Philippines. Daker went through his notes carefully and established that Egypt would be a safe stopover before booking to fly via Cairo. He then returned to the beach to enjoy the last full day of his holiday in peace. For two weeks he'd half expected to see a couple of CIA agents striding down the boardwalk toward him. Now he could relax and stop looking over shoulder. The Vandenberg job had ensured that, if he was reasonably sensible, he would never have to work again. This new assignment was bonus time. He returned to his table at the beach cafe and ordered another ouzo. So they still hadn't figured out how the gun was rigged.

When Vandenberg had first broached the subject of what he referred to as the "project," Daker had genuinely thought the governor had flipped out.

"You and I go back a long way, Daker. But when you think about it, I mean, about the way our paths crossed in the jungle in 'Nam, who could know about that? One chance in a million. If I had you taken on as our advance security man, as far as anyone would know you would just be another hired gun."

It was like Vandenberg was talking to himself. "I don't follow you," Daker had said. They were sitting drinking beer in the Governor's beach house, the previous fall.

"You and I got to know each other's strengths and weaknesses in a way people seldom do. Going through all that hell together gave us that opportunity. Christ, we were alive, really alive then! Sure we were scared shitless, but maybe that was part of it. I want to use that bond we forged again. I know that you need this job real bad. And we both know you're too old for it, Daker. But I can fix that. You see, down the line I've got plans for you and me. Plans that could see you set up for life."

Gradually, Daker began to examine the draft scenario Vandenberg had sketched out for him. If the governor wanted him to blast a slug into his body armor to make it look like he'd been hired to hit him but blown it, well if that's what the fella had set his heart on, then for the kind of pay-off he was promising, it had to be worth thinking about.

Daker would be almost fifty by the time the Vandenberg presidential campaign was over. As far as his professional services were concerned—apart from a brief stint as a boxing promoter in the late Sixties, he'd been in the security business all his working life—the phone was unlikely to ring again. As things stood, he was faced with getting some kind of job in office security, roaming empty tower blocks in the small hours. Or retiring altogether. He'd put a little money by, so there didn't seem to be a decision to make. His plan was to sell up and ship out to somewhere that had warm winters and cool beer—maybe start a little charter business. The Vandenberg project offered a far brighter future. Pull it off and he could retire in style. Buy himself a smart apartment, a fishing boat, one of those nice little Jap sports cars.

The downside was that he would never be able to return to the States or safely go anywhere again that had an extradition treaty with the U.S. But Daker was a loner, had been all his life. His only marriage, to a small-time actress, had lasted four years and ended in divorce in 1983. His sister Eunice, who was eight years his senior, had married a reader in physics and had gone with him to Toronto when he was offered a chair there. Daker had stayed with them a few times, but had felt uncomfortable in their world. He was never encouraged to visit and contact had been reduced to an exchange of birthday cards. Who would he miss? Who would miss him? The truth was, no one.

The deal Vandenberg was offering was certainly a once in a lifetime shot. The number one problem was to make a clean getaway afterward, to enjoy the fruits of his labor. He thought about cars, motorbikes, even a helicopter. Then he realized he was looking at the problem from the wrong perspective. It wasn't the means that was crucial. It was the time, the getaway time, that really counted. If he could buy himself a day, just half a day's clear running, then it would work.

Meetings between Daker and the governor were kept to a minimum. Vandenberg didn't want them seen alone together. Nevertheless, they had met shortly after Christmas at the beach house to discuss the problem.

"The only way to take the heat off you long enough for you to get out of the country is to use a fall guy," Vandenberg announced.

"You mean some kind of Oswald scenario? Forget it. Way too risky."

"No. Maybe just a body. Something to keep the police occupied for a while."

"And who do you have in mind for that role?"

Vandenberg shrugged. "It has to be someone who would have been able to get close to me with a gun."

Daker laughed. "That's what you're paying a crack team to prevent!"

Vandenberg's green eyes had met Daker's. "Well, then maybe we set one of them up. Maybe one of the hired marksmen we use for the high-risk venues."

Daker was never sure what his face had registered at that moment. He only knew that he now had a measure of how badly Vandenberg wanted to be president.

"If you have a better idea, I'd like to hear it," the governor had said at last.

Daker didn't. Furthermore, given the seeds of a plan, his mind seemed to go to work almost involuntarily on solving the problems it raised. The shots would have to be seen to have come from where the patsy was positioned, he reasoned, and the ballistics would have to match. Daker himself would be in charge of positioning the marksman anyway. Vandenberg was right, the only effective fall guy was a dead one. He couldn't kill the man ahead of time, or the police doctor would be examining a cold, stiff corpse. Somehow, the guy would have to be kept alive until he was needed. Maybe sodium pentothal was the answer. Fall Guy could be knocked out and the drug injected.

Daker finished his ouzo and watched the skeet

shooter giving his kid a lesson in how to hit clays. That guy shouldn't be allowed anywhere near a gun, he thought.

The next problem Daker confronted was the hardest: how to get Fall Guy's gun to fire accurately and reliably with minimal human intervention. Certain that that could not be attempted without considerable danger to the governor, he'd hit on a more subtle plan. The slug could be shot into the bullet-proof vest earlier in the day. It would produce the required bruising, but it could be achieved safely, in a controlled environment. The governor could change back into the vest and shirt minutes before he went onstage to speak. A hole in the linen the size of a cigarette burn wouldn't be too hard to hide if it was positioned right.

Daker would have to rig up some system by which a couple of live rounds could be fired from the patsy's gun, followed by one blank round that would be Vandenberg's cue to take a dive. It took him no more than a week to build a remote-control firing mechanism. He was good with his hands. He'd trained as a motor mechanic in his teens, before he was drafted. The mechanism was built from a motor and worm-and-pinion gears, taken from a windshield-wiper system and a tiny piece of the camshaft from a Honda. The whole thing fitted into a metal box no larger than a Lucky Strike pack, and could be clamped against the trigger of a high-velocity hunting rifle. When the radio control switch was operated by a remote unit (bought from a hobby shop) the electric motor rotated the cam till it bore down on the trigger, firing the gun and then instantly moved away again to allow the trigger to click forward for the next shot.

It was then that Daker had hit his first major problem. To draw attention to Fall Guy—and away from himself—the plan had been for the gun to fire several live rounds before the blank. But Daker found that, no matter how solidly he clamped the rifle into position, only the first shot fired could be counted on to go anywhere near its intended target. The kick of the rifle, although minimal, was designed to be absorbed into the shoulder of the firer. Without that cushion, the gun shook fractionally out of position when it was fired. Rather than turn a calculated risk into a needless bloodbath, he decided that only one live round would be fired from the rifle, aimed at the podium on which Vandenberg would be standing, for maximum effect. The second shot would be the blank.

Checking out the security details for the Sullivan Main Street Society opening gave Daker the solution to the last major problem—how to erase any trace of his own involvement. It was clear that the renovation work would not be finished in time. Half-refurbished buildings around the town square would all have to be sealed. The carpenter's bench in the room above the department store set Daker's mind working. At least five extra marksmen would be required for this venue. It would be easy to drag the bench well inside the window, and clamp the rifle and firing mechanism into the carpenter's vice with a clear view of the podium in the square, during his early morning check on the building. He could zap Fall Guy when he positioned him an hour before the ceremony, get his fingerprints on the stock of the gun and pull him to the bottom of the stairs. No one else could enter the building: it would be standard security procedure for Daker himself to seal it. And as it would also be Daker who took charge of radio contact with the marksmen, he would simply see to it that Fall Guy never got called.

Two days before the ceremony, he checked out every last detail. He'd position himself so that, after the phony hit, he'd be the first one into the building. Freeing the rifle from the vice would also release the firing mechanism, which he'd stow in his jacket pocket. Then he'd run down the stairs to the comatose man, fire the rifle several times back at the door through which he'd just come, and then drop it on the stairs. Back in the room, he'd pump two shots from his own handgun into Fall Guy's chest, knowing there would be a good show of fresh blood.

By now, police and security men would be on the roof and pounding away at the street-level door. But all Daker needed would be two minutes and, as soon as he radioed in that the would-be assassin was dead, the pressure would be off. He'd hand the sheriff the heroic bodyguard stuff and slip out over the roof the way he'd come in, to ensure that press close-ups of him were kept to a minimum.

Blam! The skeet shooter'd missed again. Daker sipped his ouzo. Fucking amateur, he thought.

FOURTEEN

"How serious is it with the married fella?"

Marianne Lassiter stopped and looked at her husband. Way in the distance, the Lincoln Memorial dominated the hazy skyline. "You do that on purpose, don't you? He does have a name." A light breeze caught the hem of the floral dress she was wearing, but she made no move to hold it in place, letting him see her long tanned legs for the first time since he'd been home.

"Yes, but for some reason you don't often use it." Lassiter grinned.

"Mitch," she said purposefully. "Mitch Cameron is a helluva guy. He makes me laugh. We talk the same language."

Lassiter watched the children play on the swings and slides around them. "That's not what I asked you." She was silent. He couldn't tell if she was thinking or just clamming up on him. "Well, how is he in the sack?"

That got a reaction. "None of your goddamn

business." Her eyes flared. "Look Jack, you promised me that . . . " But now she could see the hurt in his eyes, the hurt that said how could you sleep with another man, after all that we meant to one another? After feeling so much? He's touching you, touching parts of you I never dreamed another man would touch again. And the knowledge of it kills me. Still kills me after all this time. Always will. Her eyes held his. "Not as wonderful as you," she said softly.

Three words. He was certain that all he had to do was say them. Right now, as they stood on the pathway in the park. And the clock would be turned back. The chemistry was still there. Probably always would be. But to say the words would be to begin to live a lie again.

She put her arm in his and they walked on. To their left, a massive construction of wooden joists, tires and ropes swarmed with small children. Suddenly a girl of about four lost her footing on a walkway and fell six feet into the cork chippings that covered the ground beneath. She landed badly and winded herself. Although probably more frightened than hurt, it was a full five seconds before a piercing cry broke from her lips. Marianne ran forward, cleared the low fence that surrounded the playground area and lifted the little girl, cradling her in her arms. She took a wad of tissues from her purse and dabbed gently at the child's grazed forehead. A moment later a flustered mother carrying a new baby came scurrying over to the sobbing child.

Lassiter watched from the pathway. Well I'll be damned, he thought.

☆   ☆   ☆

There was a glorious familiarity in the way she felt to him, the way her body fitted against his as they kissed. Eau de Marianne. Shared intimacies that were second nature. She caught her breath and pulled away, unbuttoning, unzipping. Free of her clothes she stood before him in the half-light of the bedroom they'd shared for four years. Marianne was one of those rare women who are as confident naked as clothed. She turned, so that every contour of her body caught the light. It was as though there should have been music. She's done this for Cameron, he thought.

They have music.

He shut the thought away. She'd lost weight. The narrow hips contrasted even more with the wide sweep of the shoulders. The slender waist needed his arm around it. Her buttocks pressed hard into his hand as he pulled her to him. Soon the hand was trapped against the bedcover as it sought to hold her still, to lift her upward to meet him, twisting in his grasp . . . the taste of her . . . and then the heat within her . . . he'd forgotten. How was that possible? Her back arched and a cry broke from her lips and he felt her tighten on him. For some seconds it was as though he'd lost her. To herself. But it was he who'd made it happen. She blinked at him. At the unreality of seeing his face above her. Had she forgotten too? He pressed deep into her now, changing dynamics till her breathing was deep and rhythmic. Her eyes closed, her face, distorted in pleasure, was still beautiful.

Now.

Does she feel this with him? Lassiter thought. Please God, don't let that be.

☆　　☆　　☆

Lassiter was suddenly awake. His heart pounded in his ears, his face was bathed in sweat. For a moment, it was as though he'd woken from one dream into another—Marianne asleep at his side . . . the bedroom they'd shared for so long . . .

The subway thing. Only this time the safety mechanism that had surely saved his sanity over the years was beginning to kick in again. It was as though someone had switched off the projector in the middle of the film. As the dreadful images faded, a face was caught in freeze-frame. A man's face.

Jeff's face. Lassiter hadn't thought about him in years. " . . . My name's Jeff . . . I have boys of my own . . . stand behind me, you'll be all right . . . "

"Shut up! No talking!"

The terrible smell of death. He and Mel, two small kids in the center of a huddle of tall strangers, being herded to one end of a rail car. The seconds ticking away. Who would the madman kill next?

Jeff pressed the boys' faces into the small of his back.

Where was the policeman with the bullhorn? If he didn't speak soon . . .

"Time's up. You, come with me."

Both boys felt Jeff's body jolt. Felt his hands slip from the back of their heads as he moved forward.

Don't take him! Every nerve, every instinct in Jack's mind had screamed. But no sound came out. "Okay, kid . . . I'll take you." Was that what he wanted the madman to say?

And so they'd let him take Jeff. Seven men and five women stood there, most staring at their feet, no doubt thanking God it wasn't them. Why didn't someone do something? Jack's mind had demanded. For pity's sake, the man could only have three bullets left in that gun. If everyone rushed him, how many could he really kill? Jeff turned for a second as the man in the motorcycle leathers forced him down the rail car. His eyes pleaded.

The gunman made him kneel . . . Around then, Mel did it in his pants . . .

Lassiter shook away the image. He slipped from the bed, crossed soundlessly into the kitchen and took a beer from the fridge. He stared at the can for a moment. To hell with Budweiser. This one called for serious liquor. There used to be a bottle of seven-star Metaxa in the living room. Vaphiadis, in the office, had given it to him a couple of Christmases back. If the married jerk hadn't already seen it off, it should still be there.

He poured himself another shot. Three fingers this time. Marianne's earrings lay on the table. Small diamonds in elaborate Victorian settings. A first anniversary present. She'd scolded him, but not unkindly, for his extravagance even then. Hell, it was only money. Some other crazy could get on a train someday soon, and then what would it be worth?

Square One. It was like a year, the toughest year of his life had just evaporated. Like it never happened. He was back in the apartment Marianne and he had bought four years ago. She was asleep, wet, filled with his life fluid. But it was going nowhere. Some chemical—or however those fucking pills worked—was killing it. Killing all it could bring. Why did that matter so much to him? But it did. Every time he passed Schwartz toyshop in N.Y.C., every time he passed a playground or spent the weekend with his sister and her family. Family noise. Jesus Christ, what was so wrong with it?

Had Marianne's little routine in the playground been some kind of subconscious message that he was meant to have picked up on? He wasn't about to ask. Back to Square One. A "no" from her now and that's exactly where he'd be.

Three words. A couple of hours in the bedroom with her had told him that he could say them and that would . . . well, maybe not fix everything for her, but it would go a hell of a long way to. Three words: "Okay. No kids."

He wasn't about to make that promise. Every fight they'd had seemed to bring with it some new justification for her decision. Until today, it had never occurred to him that a year apart could make a difference.

How could it be that you could love someone so intensely, know them so intimately, and yet not have the slightest idea what they were thinking?

Lowell held the faded sheet of paper alongside a known sample of Paul Vandenberg's handwriting—a page of a letter he'd written to a relative in America in 1937.

"The writing certainly seems to be my father's."

The old man opposite him sat patiently, sipping his Perrier water.

"Of course I'm no expert on this stuff," Lowell said at last. He turned the sheet over. The photocopy that this Vollman character had sent with his letter had shown only the front of the sheet. Now Vandenberg read the rest of the letter for the first time. All but the last paragraph spoke of the arrangements his father had made to have his tiny son taken to Switzerland. The last few lines were a personal message to his wife.

" . . . If it be God's will that we shall not see each other again, know that I shall love you as I have always loved you, with a tenderness and devotion that I have felt for no other living soul and that the memory of the all too short time we had together will be in my thoughts as my last breath leaves my body . . . " Vandenberg felt the back of his throat tighten and tears well into his eyes. He walked to the window. Beneath his father's signature was faded writing in another hand.

"The paragraph added at the end is from your mother," Vollman said. "It's her reply."

Vandenberg turned his back as he read it. "Your son is well. He looks more like you with every day that passes, my darling. At least, perhaps now he will have a life . . . " For a moment, Vandenberg lost his composure. His hand moved to stifle a cry. Who were you? What did you talk about when you were alone together? What did you believe in? What dreams did you have for me? Dear God, why did life deal me such a blow? Why are you not here now, to see all that I've become?

Vollman struggled to his feet. "I'm certain you'd rather be alone."

Vandenberg spun around and wiped his eyes with the back of his hand. "No, it's quite all right. Please stay."

"It must be a great shock to be confronted with this after so many years."

"Yes it is. But I'm very much indebted to you. I think there'll be many questions I shall have for you in the next few days." Vandenberg studied the letter again. "Why do you suppose my mother's reply was written on the back of my father's letter?"

The old man shrugged. "I have wondered about that too. Perhaps she had no paper of her own. Whoever got you out of Dachau took an enormous risk. Perhaps they were being extra careful. Having your mother write her reply on the back of your father's letter ensured that it would go back to him and there would be nothing that could be found amongst her possessions to incriminate those involved with your rescue. Believe me, that was the way minds worked in those places. Whatever the reason, at least you have your mother's reply too."

The old German seemed to speak English well enough, but was having trouble articulating the sounds. One side of his face seemed to have dropped and sunken into the skull. Evidence of a stroke, Vandenberg thought. The German was studying him intently now, his head tilted back, as though he was staring through an invisible set of pince-nez.

"And you have no idea who my mother handed me over to, or who it was that got me to Switzerland?"

The German laughed humorlessly. "I didn't even know Paul had a son until hours before he died. After a year in that place one has few secrets left, believe me. But this one secret he kept till last. Who was involved in the plan, he never told me. He gave me the letter you have and the letter from the Red Cross in Switzerland acknowledging your safe arrival. I would imagine that tallies with one your relatives were given here."

"Yes it does." Vandenberg slid a letter from the

Red Cross taken from his own file across the desk to stand by the one Vollman had given him.

"Your father gave me one thing more." Vollman took a folded sheet of paper from his jacket pocket and placed it on the desk between them. "This."

Vandenberg took it and unfolded it. It contained two columns of six-digit numbers in his father's handwriting. "I take it these are numbered accounts."

"Eighteen of them. Eleven at banks in Zurich, seven in Geneva. They are your father's personal deposit accounts."

"Are? You mean they still hold funds?"

"Oh yes. All but three."

"Do you know how much is in them?"

Time switched to its slowest tempo as Vandenberg watched Vollman produce a typewritten sheet from his suitcase.

"I checked with the banks concerned before I left Germany. The balances are shown in dollars. They are as close an estimate as can be made, given that most of what the banks hold is in diamonds."

Vandenberg was barely listening. His eyes moved down the columns of figures, totaling them as he went. For more than two minutes there was almost total silence in the room. The only sound was the labored breathing of the old man. At last Vollman said, "You can see now why I thought it important to meet with you in person."

"Why . . . why has it taken you so long to seek me out?" Vandenberg's voice was barely audible. When he looked up, the strongest color in his face was the flecks of brown in the green eyes.

"There is no quick or simple answer to that. Only I knew that your father was Paul Vandenberg.

The papers he had on him when he was arrested were in another name. To the guards in the camp, he became just a number, like the rest of us. Before your father died, I promised him that if I survived the war, I would see that the details of these accounts reached his son. But afterward, I became very frightened. Can you imagine what these papers were worth to the Third Reich? I decided to hide them, in the hope I could retrieve them after the war. Then quite suddenly, some months later, many of us were moved to Zwickau in what became East Germany. There was no time to retrieve the papers."

Vollman was clearly tiring. He grasped the arms of his chair and tried to ease the pressure on his back.

"I was one of the very few who lived to see the Allied victory. Our camp was liberated by Soviet troops in May 1945. I needn't tell you the difficulties I faced in getting back to West Germany! It took nine years and much negotiation with the authorities. I barely recognized the town of Schrobenhausen. So much had been rebuilt. And the hiding place? It was now quite unreachable. And it remained so until the area was redeveloped a few months ago. Only then was I able to have the papers recovered for me by a trusted friend."

Vandenberg leaned back in his chair and ran his fingers through his hair like a comb. "Were you never tempted to keep the money for yourself?"

Vollman laughed easily for the first time. It was a harsh, rasping sound, little more than a rhythmic cough. He threw his arms upward. "And do what with it? I'm seventy-eight years old! I have no family. I have a pension that keeps me very comfortably . . . " He pondered the question for a minute. "My life has . . .

not been easy. It has been soured by many things. If I had recovered the money twenty years ago . . . maybe I would have sweetened it a little. But now . . . I took the price of my air fare and my hotel out of it. It didn't seem like an unreasonable expense in the circumstances."

"In the circumstances, Herr Vollman, I think that's probably the greatest understatement I've ever heard."

Jack Lassiter stepped out of the elevator at Marianne's apartment building into the underground parking lot and walked toward the Jaguar. It felt good to have it back. It had cost him most of a month's salary to pay off what he owed, but it was worth it. Five yards off he pressed the plastic remote-control unit in his hand to deactivate the main security alarm. Now he could unlock the driver's door. Once inside, he inserted a small chrome key into the black metal box that had been fitted to the underside of the dashboard. As the mechanic who'd installed it the day before had pointed out, even the most sophisticated security systems only cover the bodywork and windows of a vehicle. As there's no point of entry underneath a car that's usually left unprotected. A magnetic bomb can be attached to it in seconds. But with an ATS system fitted, a flat, drum-shaped sensor welded under the gearbox creates a photo-electric field that will set off an alarm if so much as a tennis ball rolls under the car.

With ATS now also deactivated, Lassiter started the engine and moved out toward the narrow exit ramp that would take him to street level. The metal grillwork at the entrance lifted to allow him through. Only now he could see that a white Audi stood at the top of the ramp blocking his way. A balding red-haired man appeared to be trying to get the thing re-started. Judging by the sound of the starter motor, the Audi was going nowhere without outside help.

Lassiter felt his heart miss a beat. Here we go, he thought. He glanced into his mirror, fully expecting another car to move up behind him, sandwiching him in. He waited. None came. Red in the Audi slammed his hand into the dashboard. Scarlet-faced and still cursing, he got out of the car and walked down toward the Customs agent.

"Fuckin' thing. That's twice it's done this to me in a month." His white business shirt was soaked with sweat. He put his weight against the trunk of the car and began to heave. The rear end of the Audi was still on the incline of the ramp and resolutely refused to budge. Lassiter switched off the engine, pulled on the handbrake and got out. "Thanks pal," Red grunted. "Pain in the ass. Turn the wheel right, will you? We'll move her up to the verge."

With his hand on the butt of the Glock 9mm, Lassiter checked the inside of the Audi carefully. Red and he were alone. He opened the door and turned the wheel, pushing against the windshield pillar as he did. The car moved slowly toward the verge. Lassiter hurried back to his own car. "Normally I'd give you a jump start, but I'm real pushed this morning," he shouted back as he swung into his seat.

"Don't worry about it. There's a place on Woodley Road. The walk'll do me good."

Lassiter moved off toward the freeway. Even

three blocks from it, he could see that traffic on the elevated carriageway was virtually stationary. Cars and trucks on the "on-ramp" were backed up solid. Accident, had to be. Why today of all days? If he was called to the stand first . . .

He checked his watch. He could still make it. He made a tight U-turn and headed back the way he'd come, toward Wisconsin Avenue—it would be the quickest way now. He passed his apartment house. It was two seconds before he realized the Audi was gone. The possibilities tumbled over one another in his mind. Red had managed to start it somehow. How could he? The battery was flat. Someone had given him a jump start. Impossible in the time. Maybe the battery just *sounded* flat. Maybe he was carrying two and could switch between them. Suddenly every instinct in Lassiter's body told him something was very wrong.

He swung left, south onto Wisconsin, desperately rerunning the events of the last five minutes in his head. He'd got out to help . . . Red had said steer the car . . . Lassiter had moved forward. There was the Audi three blocks ahead. Red was easing it through the traffic like he had somewhere he needed to be real bad. The truth hit Lassiter like the smack of a baseball bat. He fumbled for the chrome key in his pants pocket. Red had had a magnetic bomb stuck under the trunk of the Audi. As Lassiter had moved forward to steer and push it, Red had disconnected it from his own car, reached behind him and shoved it under the front of the Jaguar parked right behind him. The ATS was designed to protect an unoccupied parked vehicle, not one being driven down a road in broad daylight. Or parked for a few seconds in full view of the driver . . .

His fingers closed round the key and he felt for the lock under the dash. He had begun to close the distance between him and Red. He eased the key into the lock and turned it. His whole body shook as the piercing howl of the ATS alarm filled the air.

His first conscious reaction was, I'm a dead man. If the bomb's on a timer, my life ends any second. He fought to remember what the mechanic had said. " . . . Most of the IRA devices are detonated by remote control."

The truck in front hung a left and Lassiter found himself ten feet behind the Audi. The rational part of his mind said, the likelihood is that the man in the Audi simply has to press a button on a short-wave transmitter and I'm blown to pieces.

Now he saw Red look in his mirror. Even from here, he could read the look on the man's face. It confirmed everything he needed to know. Instantly Lassiter moved up to within three feet of the car in front. It was the only move he had to play. Okay, Red, you press away, he thought. The bomb's under my radiator. So long as I can stay here, right on your ass, you're only about eight feet farther away from it than I am. Press away and blast us both to hell.

Red seemed to have thought all that through for himself, because he suddenly swung the Audi right, slicing through the front wing of a Volkswagen pulling out of a supermarket. A woman with a child in a buggy pulled back with inches to spare. A man in a bright green tracksuit beyond her was less lucky. He was thrown up onto the hood and off to the side, leaving a bloody smear down the windshield. Lassiter had overshot the turn. For a second the Audi seemed to go out of control. Long enough for him to pull the Jag up tight behind it again. *Lose him, for four seconds, let fifteen feet open up between us, and I'm dog chow.*

Red was dead ahead again. Lassiter felt for the Glock 9mm in his shoulder holster. I could shoot the fucker in the back of the head right now. Yeah, and he presses the button anyway. Or ploughs into the crowd. Or he stops dead in the road and I rear-end him, and the bomb detonates on impact.

The Audi was moving close to sixty through the busy street. The wail of the ATS from the car on its tail seemed to have a galvanizing effect. Cars swerved left and right to avoid them as they sped by.

The cross street coming up on the right was 45th. It was unusually wide. Lassiter saw Red's right elbow lift to make the turn. He looked right. The corner was a vacant lot. The sidewalk ahead had been crushed to road level by the bulldozers that had cleared it. *It's my only chance.*

Lassiter slung the wheel right and the Jag shuddered onto the lot. The bomb must've cleared the curb because Lassiter knew he was still breathing. He stepped hard on the gas, hitting the cruise control, under the steering wheel, almost instantly. Then he opened the door, buried his face in his jacket and rolled out. The broken, rubble-strewn earth came up to meet him. As he hit the ground, a stab of pain shot up his back and he felt something in his shoulder give. He bounced, hit again, and rolled over a couple of times. He lifted his head in time to see his car smash into Red's. The Jaguar seemed to cut through the Audi as if it was made of playdough. Lassiter curled up into a ball and braced himself. There was a flash, a searing wall of heat, and a blast that lifted him off the ground and threw him into a heap of trash. Blood poured into his eyes. To his left, there was a dull thud. A large chunk of dashboard and other debris thumped into the earth around him.

Lassiter put his hand to his head and felt another stab of pain as he gashed his finger. A shard of steel about two inches long was embedded in his head. Without really giving the matter much thought, he eased it out of his cranium, with a slight grating of bone, then tore off his shirtsleeve to stem the gush of blood. It was then he realized that the blackened stump of a thing that lay in the dirt in front of him was Red's head. The eyes stared at him balefully and then slowly blinked, as if the sunlight was too bright. They tried to blink again, but whatever was moving them ran out of steam, and they seized up midway.

FIFTEEN

Leland Daker could only see the policeman in peripheral vision. The man lay back against a faded Fiat, staring across the beach. Daker turned the pages of the newspaper and tried to breathe evenly. Behind him, young voices chattered nervously in Turkish. The faintest whiff of hashish hung in the warm air. Now he was certain that the cop was looking beyond him, at the teenagers sitting in a group on the rocks. At last, the man spat into the gutter and moved on. Daker took a deep breath. Was this how it would be for the rest of his life? he wondered. Probably.

He closed that morning's edition of the *Hurriyet,* the largest-selling Turkish newspaper, and laid it with the rest. Though he spoke no Turkish, with the aid of a dictionary, he had identified key words he needed. Neither *Time* nor *Newsweek* had carried follow-up pieces on the attempted Vandenberg assassination, so it was hardly surprising there was nothing more on it in the international sections of the local press.

Before he got involved, Daker had spent a long time assessing the implications his role in the affair might have for him, from a foreign standpoint. Although the governor would come out of it unscathed, the patsy would have to die to buy him running time. Interpol would move quickly, but the reality of the situation was that Vandenberg was still an outsider in the race. If it was a slow news day, CNN would make a lot of noise about it for twenty-four hours at the most. Major newspapers, certainly in the West, would give it some coverage, probably on an inside page, for the same length of time. From the media angle, forty-eight hours on, the story would be dead. Immigration officers at international airports would be reminded to keep a lookout for him from time to time, but provided he kept to countries that had no extradition treaties with the U.S., the probability was that he would be able to live out the rest of his life, move freely between a wide range of places, with little risk of arrest.

From what he'd read, it seemed he'd been halfway to Famagusta when the district pathologist discovered the pentothal in the patsy's blood. And he had been drinking in the bar of Ammakhostos Hotel for almost an hour when FBI agents had broken into his apartment in Washington. He had entered Cyprus using the first of his new identities. Now it was time to leave, he would utilize the second set of papers.

Obtaining new identity papers had proved to be less of a problem than he had imagined. Finding a reliable source was usually the greatest hurdle, but Daker had friends in low places and that difficulty was quickly overcome. The second hurdle was quite simply money. In a country where you can have

almost anyone, apart from an active law
enforcement officer, whacked for less than twenty-
five thousand dollars, even two new passports,
Daker discovered, wouldn't set you back more than
the cost of a '94 Chevy.

He crossed to the counter of the little cafe, paid
for his breakfast and headed back to the room he'd
rented in a lodging house, just west of Ammakhostos.
Inside, he inspected his face in the mirror above the
chipped, enamel basin. Given his current
circumstances, it had to be said that life had dealt
him one or two aces. His face was square, his eyes
small, his jaw on the heavy side. The overall effect
was unremarkable. He propped the second of his
new passports on the shelf and studied the
photograph sealed under plastic on the second page.
Then he compared it with his reflection. The most
distinctive feature of his face, the provider of the
passport had assured him, were his eyebrows. They
were thick and bushy, and almost hid the upper lids
of his eyes. The forger had expertly airbrushed over
the eyebrows in the photograph, reducing them to
less than half the width, and in such a way that they
tilted downward toward the nose. Even Daker had
been surprised by the effect the first time he'd seen
it. It seemed to change the shape of his forehead and
his eyes at a single stroke. Now he set to work with
tweezers, plucking out hairs until his eyebrows
matched the ones in the shot.

Thirty hours later, Daker crossed the concourse of
the international terminal of Manila airport and
hired a car. Then he drove to the eastern edge of
the city and booked into a small hotel. At dusk, he

set off on the road to Apostolou. About a mile from the address Vandenberg had given him, he parked and walked the rest of the way on foot.

He had been crouching behind a low wall that still supported part of the frame of a greenhouse for almost two hours when a Filipina woman of about thirty came out of the front door of the bungalow he'd been watching, locked it behind her and crossed to a Toyota parked near by. He trained the binoculars on her, then rechecked the photograph Vandenberg had sent him. The woman's face was a little fatter, but it was Teresa Lucana all right. He waited till the car was out of sight and, keeping to the trees that flanked the field in front of him, made for the house. In the fading light he went to work on the lock of the kitchen door. It took him a little more than a minute to let himself into the place.

The house was clearly a furnished let. Two partly packed designer leather suitcases lay on the bed in the master bedroom, but otherwise it appeared that Lucana had yet to make her mark on the place. Silently and methodically he began his search. An hour later, satisfied that no duplicates of the papers Vandenberg had described were in the house, he began to plan his next move.

Bringing a gun into the country had never been an option. Getting one here quickly, even a sporting gun, was, given the current political situation, apparently a very long shot. Daker was no trained assassin with a whole selection of killing skills to draw on, but 'Nam had taught him how to use both a gun and a knife. He'd kicked around from job to job after the war, but he knew that he had never been better at anything than the relatively simple business of killing other human beings. He and the lieutenant had been a great team. Hell, the man had saved his life. Daker had felt comfortable taking orders from him. He felt comfortable now. For the first time in a long time his life had some meaning, some order. Now he cooly took the only option he had.

The drawers in the kitchen were filled with the usual ill-matched assortment of utensils found in cheap furnished lets. The carving knife had been sharpened so many times that it now had a concave cutting edge. One more time wouldn't hurt, Daker thought.

The locked room at the end of the main corridor was marked "Owner's Storeroom." Daker forced it and closed it behind him. He sat on a packing case and waited. It must be almost thirty years since he used a knife, he thought. April. Sixty-six? Yeah, the tenth, the same day he'd met Lowell Vandenberg.

Daker had been a sergeant in the 17th Airborne, one of six thousand troops dropped into a battle zone, forty miles north of Saigon, in the biggest push of the war so far. Four of his platoon had been shot up before they'd hit the ground. When the rest tried to regroup, they came under heavy machine-gun fire. His memory of what happened next was still hazy. He'd taken a bullet in the muscle of the left thigh and gone down. When the VC unit finally moved off, Daker had strapped up his leg and limped over to the crater where the rest of his men had taken cover. He'd tried to count bodies. Then he counted pairs of legs. He'd pumped morphine into the wound with a one-shot syringe, checked his compass and set off into the jungle, alone. By dusk, he could go no farther. The leg had swollen up and he'd lost a great deal of blood. He'd eaten cookies and glucose tablets and hidden in the undergrowth, sleeping fitfully, till first light.

"Sergeant!" The word broke through deep, dreamless sleep. Daker had woken with a start. His eyes focused for the first time on Lowell Vandenberg's face. The hair had been dark brown then, the skin around the cold green eyes, smooth and unlined. "I'm Lieutenant Vandenberg. With the Nineteenth. The chopper I was in got hit early this morning." He'd looked around him. "I'm the only survivor as far as I know. So, where's your platoon, Sergeant?"

"All dead," Daker said vacantly.

It took four days for them to get back to base. Days of endless, agonizing torment. How they'd come through it, he still didn't know. Twice they ran into Gooks. The first time they caught one end of some kind of dragnet. A line of V.C., spaced out every ten yards or so, sweeping an area of jungle for pockets of U.S. troops. He and Vandenberg just lay in the undergrowth watching them come closer. "If we can take out this guy ahead of us quietly, we can cut through," Vandenberg had whispered. "Leave him to me. Just move when I say."

Vandenberg had crawled off into the brush and was gone. Within a minute, a Gook with a rifle was no more than ten feet from Daker. Somehow the V.C.'s eyes seemed drawn instinctively toward him, frozen there in the brush like a trapped rabbit. He saw the man open his mouth to shout. He never got a sound out through the ruined tissues where Vandenberg's commando knife sliced across his throat in one fluid movement. The man jerked his gun backward hard, smashing the butt of it into Vandenberg's face. Then he staggered. Blood had pumped out of him in steady spurts, in time with his heartbeat, but somehow, enough was still getting through to his brain to keep him conscious. Not till Daker threw himself forward and opened up the man's ribcage with a bayonet did he topple backward to be caught and lowered by Vandenberg. There was a shout from the next man in the dragnet. By the time he found the body, Daker and his companion were fifty yards behind the V.C. line.

When the lieutenant finally stopped pounding his way through the jungle and turned around, Daker got a shock. His nose was completely smashed, his face a mask of blood.

A second encounter with the enemy, a day later, was no less bloody. One thing was for certain: by the time the two men finally reached base, they had developed a profound respect for one another.

They'd only met once more during the war, by accident in a bar the night before Vandenberg's tour of duty was up. His nose was still a mess. He told the sergeant he was going to have some cosmetic work done on it stateside. They shook hands and Daker said he'd call Vandenberg when he got back in the fall. He called him in the fall. Twenty-two years later.

Now Daker was sitting waiting for a woman the lieutenant wanted killed. The objectives had changed, but for Vandenberg, it seemed, the war was still on.

At around eight, Daker heard the sound of a car drawing up outside, followed by keys in the door and muffled conversation. Damn it, she's not alone, he thought. He put his ear to the door of the storeroom and tried to catch the words. Soon, the talk gave way to the sound of the TV. Then he heard

the front door open and close again. There was just
the clatter of crockery in the kitchen. Was she alone
now?

Daker moved out into the passageway and,
walking on the balls of his feet, made his way
down to the kitchen. He held his breath and
moved his head to the edge of the doorway that
led into the dining area. A peninsula of cabinets
divided the area from the kitchen. Through them,
Daker could see Teresa Lucana. Pretty woman, he
thought. Pity. She turned away now, exposing her
back. She was pouring something into a glass.
Without a sound, he crossed the room. He could
reach through and . . .

"I'm watching you," Teresa Lucana said.

Daker froze. His mind blanked, his whole body
shuddered. Had he imagined it? Christ, it was a
clear enough statement! Still she didn't look at him.

"Do you hear me?"

Daker was about to speak when she half turned,
a glass of orange juice in her hand. "If I let you have
this in the living room, you must promise not to
spill it."

It was 11 P.M., U.S. Eastern Standard Time, when
Lowell Vandenberg answered the private line in his
screening room. He waited for a cassette, nine
thousand miles away, to play the opening bars of
Mahler's First Symphony. When he heard that he
could relax. The job would be done. Instead there
was silence. Then Daker's voice on the line.

"She's got a fucking kid! A daughter, about three.
You never said anything about a child, Vandenberg."

The governor held the phone a little farther

from his ear. "I didn't know about the child," he said cooly. There was a pause. "It can't be with her all the time. There must be . . . "

"There isn't. I've been as close to her as I can get for twenty-four hours. The kid hardly leaves her side. It's insecure or something, I don't know."

Vandenberg could feel his stomach starting to cramp. Daker was losing his nerve. He was going to blow it, annihilate everything. Years of planning . . .

"Say something," Daker snapped.

"Look, I don't want to have this conversation over the phone."

"Well there's no other fucking way we can have it. I don't want this job. I don't like how it's panning out. I have to cut the woman, I don't have another way. It's messy and it can be noisy . . . "

"Two hundred thousand."

"What?"

Vandenberg's face had drained of color. "I'm prepared to pay another two hundred thousand."

There was a quality in his voice that Daker had never heard before. Kind of unearthly . . . like he was on something . . .

"What are you saying?"

"Kill them both, Daker. Kill the child too."

At 3:15 A.M., the phone rang again. Vandenberg grabbed it. For a minute, there was only the crackle of static. Then the dissonant opening of the Mahler symphony blared down the line. The instant the sound registered, he slammed down the receiver as though what he was hearing was a siren call, one that might draw him in, down to the very gates of hell.

SIXTEEN

Normally the traffic noise from the street below Capriotti's office was barely audible through the double-glazed windows. Now the low rumble, combined with the steady chug of a computer printer in the next room, made Lassiter's ears ring with pain. He put his bandaged head in his hands and tried to concentrate on what his boss was saying.

"Apart from the head, there isn't enough of your friend, Red, left to fill a shoe box. All the pathology boys will say for sure is that he was taken out by one big mother of a bomb."

Lassiter turned in his seat, trying to find a more comfortable position to sit in. "They're telling me this?"

Capriotti turned the pages of the report, straining to read the type through the tinted glasses he wore to hide his thyroid condition. "Ballistics are fairly certain the device was built in California. The fragments they have match one used in San Diego only a month ago." He studied the battered, bandaged man in front of him. "Well, at least it didn't break your collarbone right through. That's a bitch of a fracture to fix. It could have been a lot worse."

"Yeah, like it could have been your collarbone. Don't tell me how lucky I am, Enzo. There isn't a part of me that doesn't hurt like hell right now. I have a continual ringing in my ears. And I'm seeing double of everything. Which in your case takes some dealing with." Capriotti blanched. "I'm sorry, I didn't mean that. I just feel like shit, you know?"

"Then why the hell did you discharge yourself from the hospital?"

"Because they said that all I needed now was rest. And when I'm finished here, that's exactly what I intend to get."

"Well, do you want to hear the rest of this report or not?"

"What do you think?"

Capriotti sighed. "About the only thing they're all agreed on is that Red was an import."

"How so?"

"The dental work is European, some of it recent. There wasn't enough skin left on the face to make a mug shot, so they haven't been able to take that much further. But the MO Red was using doesn't fit anything we've seen in this country before."

"Why, where else was it tried?"

Capriotti's bulging eyes scanned a roll of fax printout. "The almost identical MO was used successfully in a hit in 1986. In Germany. Seems like a . . ."

"East or West?"

"What's the difference! East Germany. I already said that. Didn't I?"

"No. Who was hit?"

"I was about to tell you. Rainer Schacht. Is that how you pronounce it? He was some heavyweight with the State Security."

Lassiter turned around slowly. "The Stasi? Who was he in the Stasi? What did he do?"

"Jesus Christ, Jack, what does it matter?" He checked the fax again. "It doesn't say. Listen, in '86, it was something that the East Germans even admitted he was with State Security." He studied Lassiter's face. "I take it this is ringing bells that I can't hear."

"Yeah, you could say." Lassiter rubbed cautiously around the stitched area in his head. "I don't think this hit was anything to do with the Pensacola case. Whoever set it up just used the hearing as a cover. To give us an obvious motive and place to point the finger."

"Are you saying this is tied in to this case you're working on in Germany?"

"That's what my gut tells me. The head man at the Stasi was creaming millions of D-marks off their federal budget for more than twenty years. Maybe this Schacht got wind of it and got himself killed." By now Lassiter was almost talking to himself. "Maybe remnants of the same element are trying to get me."

"That's some leap isn't it?"

Lassiter was no longer listening. Why me? he wondered. A whole department had been working on this case for months. What can only I know that's so dangerous to them?

Lassiter said nothing of his theory about the attempt on his life, two days later, when he took the stand to give evidence in the Pensacola Drug Ring hearing. Bruised and still heavily bandaged around the head and chest, he answered the questions put to him in a clear, steady voice. The Federal Prosecutor took him through the crucial encounter at Dulles Airport, where the agent had seen the alleged leader of the ring, Lester Kawoski, pass the murdered bank manager, Carl Marshak, a case containing 1.5 million dollars. He then played the recording made of the conversation between them, picked up by a body mike that had been taped to Marshak's chest.

It had been Lassiter's own suggestion that the first reference to Marshak's murder should come from him. There was no hard evidence to link either of the recent attacks to the defendants, but from a circumstantial point of view, the chronology spoke for itself. Lassiter was certain that, looking the way he did and speaking as a survivor of one of the hits, he could make the most impact on the jury.

With infinite care, he then went through the procedures the defendants had used to launder the income generated from the ring's activities. He was cross-examined by the three defense counsels and re-examined by the prosecutor. At noon, feeling confident that Kawoski and his co-defendants were set to spend serious time making license plates, he headed for the out-patients' wing of the Navy Hospital in Bethesda. With the strapping on his shoulder streamlined to allow him to wear his shirt and jacket normally, and the head bandage replaced with a plaster, he returned to his apartment.

There was a fax from Caldicott. He had received the copy of the photograph Lassiter had got from Rathenau's sister-in-law. Gregor Tanyuk had identified the man in the picture as the same

Rathenau who'd been his commanding officer at Schrobenhausen in World War Two.

Lassiter dialed American Airlines and booked a flight to London.

The plane hit more turbulence. The Customs agent dug the white plastic spoon into the microscopic portion of beef casserole on the tray in front of him and went back over the report on Gregor Tanyuk that the English police inspector had faxed him.

Tanyuk had been born and raised in Kovno in the Western Ukraine. He'd been eighteen in 1939, an apprentice optician, when Soviet forces invaded. In '41 he joined the partisans to drive them out. The Jews, who welcomed communist rule, were now thought of as collaborators. When Hitler's invasion force swept into Russia and the Baltic states, the Nazi *Einsatzgruppen,* "action groups," seen as liberators and fellow anti-Semites, recruited Tanyuk and thousands like him, into an "auxiliary police force" assigned to the task of destroying communists and Jews.

Later they were organized into seventy battalions of what came to be called *Schultzmannschaften* or *Schumas.* Tanyuk had risen to prominence in the Kovno ghetto, during the liquidation of all Jews there. Soon he and thousands of Ukrainians, Latvians and Estonians were sent to the Polish ghettos and to the extermination camps established at Sobibor, Belzec, Chelmno, Maidanek and Treblinka, as guards. As the tide of war turned and the SS began to take heavy loses, Tanyuk's *Schuma* was absorbed into what became the 14th Waffen-SS Volunteer Division *Galizien.* He became a camp guard at Belzec, and it

was here that he came under the command of
Sturmbannführer Horst Rathenau.

Lassiter pushed the casserole to one side and
began to peel the covering off a dry fragment of
fruit mousse.

Not surprisingly, Tanyuk had initially been less
than forthcoming about the details of his own
activities in these years. In accordance with the
immunity deal struck with the Crown Prosecution
Service he was therefore faced with the affidavits of
a number of witnesses to his crimes, to help refresh
his memory. In this sense, the Tanyuk Report
proved to be a rare document indeed. Most alleged
war criminals pleaded "higher orders," failing
memory, or claimed to be anywhere but where the
crimes had taken place, knowing that to plead
otherwise brought the risk of life imprisonment that
much closer. But Tanyuk knew that he would die too
soon for any such fate to have any relevance for
him, and that to come clean was his only guarantee
that his family would never know the secret he'd
kept for so long.

And so, after some initial coaxing, he told of the
mass shootings he'd taken part in and later ordered:
of the systematic slaughter of thousands of slave
laborers in his charge. But Caldicott's report had
made it clear that the British investigation was now
centered on the wartime activities of a Peter
Vasilkov, apparently the number one war criminal
on their list. Tanyuk needed little persuading to tell
all he knew about the Ukrainian who'd once been a
fellow partisan. For fifty years he had stood guard
on his memories of systematic rapes, the ritualized
smashing of children's skulls against the walls of
synagogues, the disemboweling of pregnant

mothers, the amputation of the hands, feet and genitals of men picked at random from the lines of those waiting to die. Caldicott was an unexpected gift, a safe pair of ears. Tanyuk could hardly stop talking.

Much of what he had said tied in with the known facts on the Horst Rathenau file compiled by the Simon Wiesenthal Center in Los Angeles. Rathenau was wanted in connection with war crimes relating to the deaths of more than thirty thousand slave laborers. As far as could be established, he had been in all the places Tanyuk placed him in the early Forties. Like the vast majority of Nazi war criminals, he had managed to escape prosecution after the war and had lived in West Germany till at least 1982. There appeared to be no serious intention to bring him to trial at any time in the future.

The Wiesenthal file made only passing reference to the Vasilkov that the British authorities were so interested in, but as soon as Tanyuk made it clear that the Ukrainian's wartime activities were closely connected with Rathenau's, Caldicott had checked his file against Vasilkov's as part of the unit's standard procedure. The hope was that it might provide a common link to further living witnesses to Vasilkov's crimes. As Caldicott pointed out in his report, none of the witnesses they had were under seventy-four years old. Two crucial ones had died in the last three months. Subpoenaing Rathenau himself to testify was close to impossible. Prosecuting him fell outside the British remit—his only relevance to their case being his association with a Ukrainian war criminal who was now a British national.

But if Vasilkov's fate had continued to be linked with Rathenau's after Schrobenhausen, there could still be living witnesses to crimes committed by both. That had yet to be seriously examined.

Lassiter read little of the last dozen pages of the report. He had no direct interest in Vasilkov. His sole reason for flying three thousand miles to England was to obtain from the old Ukrainian what information he could regarding the postwar activities and whereabouts of Mielke's rinser, Otto Krause, a.k.a. Horst Rathenau.

Like all those involved with law enforcement, Lassiter had learned long ago that the evil of those convicted of the most heinous crimes often proved etched into their souls rather than displayed on their faces. For all that, he'd subconsciously expected more of the Ukrainian. After the passage of more than half a century, it was impossible to connect this tiny, frail man, slumped in the corner of a suite in an English provincial hotel, with the appalling acts he had confessed to. As Caldicott checked notes he'd made during the previous day's interview, Lassiter studied the man. He needed, as Caldicott had, to establish that link. Lassiter studied the grainy photograph clipped to the file from the Wiesenthal Center. It showed a man in SS uniform in the company of three others, standing in front of a large gateway. The picture had clearly been taken with a cheap box camera. The face, in three-quarter view, was thin with high cheek bones. The note on the back of the shot said "Believed to be Gregor Tanyuk, taken in 1943. In the background is the entrance to Schrobenhausen Labor Camp." He studied the picture again. The gateway wasn't the kind you could mistake—two uneven, Germanic "onion towers" rose on each side of it. He looked back at the emaciated figure hunched in the armchair opposite him, at the man who now called himself Preston, who had been an optician in Tunbridge Wells for as long as anyone could remember. Who had married the daughter of a local printer, and fathered two children, one of whom was an estate agent in the local high street. Half a century had blunted and stretched his features. Whatever the eyes had once conveyed, now they showed only weariness and pain.

The mouth. There was the key to the man's character. It was small, so thin-lipped that it was no more than an opening in the flesh. Like he's taken a whack in the face with a machete at some point in his life. Compassion, forgiveness—it was hard to imagine they had ever disturbed its grim composure. From the mouth, Lassiter began to reconstruct his features the way they might have looked more than fifty years before. Somewhere in there was Tanyuk, the ripper of pregnant women, the render of children . . .

Traveling east was hell. Lassiter shook away the desperate desire to sleep and tried to focus his mind on what the man was saying.

" . . . In 1943, our *Schuma* was posted to Schrobenhausen. As I have said, these camps were run by twenty to thirty SS personnel, overseeing a *Schuma* unit of several hundred men, trained at a special camp in Trawniki. My unit was in charge of about five hundred slave laborers of various nationalities. They were worked in shifts in an underground plant to produce parts for tank engines. Vasilkov spoke fluent German and was well educated. Rathenau treated him like one of his own SS. He gave him assignments even his own men might have questioned. To them the laborers were subhuman life, unworthy of even a decent exit from the world."

"And what were they to you?" Caldicott asked.

Tanyuk was silent for a while, then he said, "It's hard to put into a modern context . . . " He motioned to the window. " . . . here in a hotel room in Tunbridge Wells, in England, in the 1990s. You British are an island people. The sea is a natural boundary that separates you from your neighbors. In Ukraine, the country I grew up in, all but one of the boundaries are merely lines marked on a map. In reality, a road here, a river there, a fence at the end of a field. Even the name means "borderland." Invasion has been a part of our existence for two thousand years. When I first came to this country, I used to hear old women say to their grandchildren, "Look out, or the bogyman will get you!" When I was a child, the Jews, the Soviets were our bogymen. Killing them was right. Killing them would free our country, I was told. I killed many. Thousands. Looking back now over fifty years, it seems an extraordinary thing to have done. But I did it. I killed them as decently and cleanly as I could. We dehumanized them. Killing them dehumanized us. If we became beasts . . . " The old man shook his head. "What then were Vasilkov and Rathenau?"

Tanyuk ground out his cigarette and lit another. "They drew pleasure from what they did. To them, the laborers were so much condemned meat on the hoof, to be slaughtered and burnt as soon as was expedient. Each volley of gunfire, each pyre of bodies, for them was a cleansing process."

He drew deeply on his cigarette, his hands perfectly steady. "Some prisoners, ones Rathenau was certain had hidden their assets away before the war, he would interrogate himself. He'd torture them until they coughed up. But there were others—Vasilkov used to call them Rathenau's "pets"—he did deals with. I have no idea what kind of deals, but I'm certain money changed hands and it didn't go to the Third Reich. In the last months of the war, the plant was shut down and dismantled. The underground site became a store for Nazi loot. Gold, art treasures . . . a couple of hundred of the workforce were kept on to move the stuff in and out. Rathenau had been in big business before the war. He was in his element. Especially as it brought him closer to the Nazi big wheels in Berlin. In the final days of the war, the main entrance was blocked and filled in with reinforced concrete. Afterward, the ground surrounding it was bombed by the Luftwaffe to make it look much the same as the rest of the terrain. A smaller entrance, the only one left, was concealed.

"Then Rathenau gave the orders for us to shoot all the prisoners. No one was to be left alive to talk." Tanyuk paused for breath. "We made them dig a pit in the forest, then they were lined up and shot. Once, through the head, with pistols. As the last few fell, it suddenly occurred to me that there were still fifty left who knew what was hidden in the underground factory—we Ukrainians. Rathenau's timing was perfect. I was opening my mouth to shout a warning when about a dozen SS armed with automatic weapons stepped out from the forest and rounded us up, all of us except Vasilkov. He took his place at a machine gun and helped to mow us down. I was half covered with the earth they threw over us before I realized I was still alive. Two bullets had gone clean through me."

Tanyuk watched Lassiter shift uncomfortably in his seat. "The story of my survival is irrelevant to these proceedings. Suffice it to say that I joined some thousands of other displaced persons in Rimini and was brought to Sheffield, here in England, as part of the Foreign Labor Drive in 1947."

"Were any checks made to establish your role in the war?" Caldicott asked.

"None. All that seemed to matter was whether I was fit to work."

"Do you mind if I ask a question?" Lassiter intervened. Caldicott nodded and switched off the cassette machine. Lassiter leaned forward and massaged his aching collarbone. "You stated in the interview on the tenth, that you saw Rathenau after the war."

"Not I. A good friend of mine. A reliable man. You see, through the community of Ukrainians I met here, I learned that Vasilkov too had come to England. When I informed them about the *Schuma* unit massacre, I can tell you there were some who wanted to kill him. But that might have made trouble for us here, so we decided just to keep track of him. Some years later, Vasilkov was seen in Brussels with Rathenau and two high-ranking members of the East German government. I don't know where he fitted into it all . . . "

"When was this sighting exactly?" Lassiter asked.

"It would have been the spring of '67."

"What was your guess about Rathenau's connection with the Soviets? Do you think he told them what was hidden in the underground factory at Schrobenhausen?"

Tanyuk shrugged. "It was a great card to play in 1945, if you didn't want to end up against a wall."

"And you're certain that this Rathenau is still alive?"

"If he'd died, I'm sure we would have heard."

"Do you know where I can find him?"

Tanyuk thought for a moment. "Let me make some calls tonight."

As Caldicott's car pulled out into the rush-hour traffic, Lassiter began to turn over in his mind all that the Ukrainian had said. Rathenau had been receiving a salary from an account in Switzerland known to have belonged to Mielke eighteen years after the Brussels sighting. The Nazi loot would have been long gone by then. Maybe the East Germans, maybe Mielke himself, hung on to Rathenau because of his financial expertise. If a group as paranoid as the Nazi hierarchy trusted the man enough to appoint him to hide their spoils of war, who better to handle a deal as sensitive as the Mielke scam?

The woman with the Ronald McDonald rinse consulted the guest book. "You're the first to arrive, Mr. Lassiter. Do you want to go to the suite?"

The American looked at his watch. He was early. "No, I'll wait in the bar."

"It's up the stairs at the back."

He walked through the shabby lobby of the Royal George, Tunbridge Wells, to where the flock wallpaper still held some traces of its original acid green and ordered a beer at a small bar. To his surprise, it came chilled. He sat on a chesterfield that was leaking horse hair from a split in the seating and studied the oil painting that dominated that end of the lobby—one of those "After the Hunt" epics, with dead rabbits and pheasant, trussed up and hanging from a hook.

Please God, Caldicott was right, Lassiter thought. The inspector had spoken with Tanyuk late the night before. He'd said that that old man was still playing his cards close to his chest, but he was pretty sure he'd come up with what the U.S. Customs agent so badly needed—Rathenau's current address. It was almost too much to hope for.

From where he sat, he had a clear view of the main entrance when a taxi pulled up and Gregor Tanyuk got out. Lassiter drained his beer glass, his eyes fixed on the Ukrainian. Tanyuk searched his pocket for change, paid off the cab and began to cross the pavement. The taxi pulled away. The crack of gunfire echoed against the high stone buildings. Tanyuk's body jerked each time he was hit, but somehow he remained standing. By the time Lassiter reached the entrance, he was staggering slowly out into the road. A Rover saloon on the opposite side of the street moved off at speed. Lassiter threw himself forward, diving to pull Tanyuk out of the path of an oncoming bus. In the same instant, the bus driver jammed on the brakes. There was a triple crunch of glass and grinding metal as three cars behind it piled into one another. A fourth car swung violently right to avoid hitting

the vehicle in front and rammed the oncoming
Rover head on. The impact drove the gunman
halfway through the windshield. For a second he lay
in a pool of blood on the bonnet, then he shook
himself, pulled the lower half of his body gingerly
through the glass and took off with a loping gait
between two lines of stationary traffic.

Blood was coming out of Tanyuk from more
places than Lassiter could count. He searched the
man's neck for a pulse. When he could find none, he
lowered the Ukrainian to the ground and ran after
the gunman.

The man twenty yards ahead of him was limping
badly now. His thick brown curly hair was matted
with blood. The bandages wrapped tight around
Lassiter's chest and shoulders restricted his
movement drastically. I don't know who's in worse
shape, pal, you or me, he thought as he tried to
close the distance between them.

The gunman skidded to a halt, breathing hard.
He turned to face Lassiter, pulling an automatic
from his waistband. Lassiter was unarmed. He too
slid to a halt, lifting his arms away from his body in
a gesture that said: "Okay pal, you made your
point." Hell, he thought, Tanyuk wasn't worth dying
over. It was then he noticed the man's face. It was
smeared with blood, much of it drying into the deep
lines that spread from the forehead to the neck.
Tanyuk's killer was an old man. In his sixties or
early seventies. The thick curly hair that had made
him look younger from behind was clearly a wig.
The gun shook in the man's hand. He looked
nervously around, searching for an escape route.
Could this be Vasilkov? Lassiter thought.

The chaos ahead had stopped both lanes of

traffic heading into the town. The gunman began to edge backward through a narrow gap between two cars in the line to his right. Lassiter took a step forward. The gun snapped back into position, leveled at his chest. The cars began to move up. The gap behind the gunman widened for a second and he took his chance and slid through.

The tow-rope connecting the cars had been lying slack on the road. It tightened as the car ahead took the strain and the taut line caught the man behind the ankles, throwing him violently backward into the fast-moving traffic in the next lane. There was a screeching of brakes. Cars skidded left and right. The gunman's body was flung into the air, then crushed between a truck and a battered delivery van.

SEVENTEEN

Senator Edgar Hersh potted the black, leaned back and tried to get the crick out of his neck. "Well, Marty, that makes three hundred dollars you owe me."

Marty Machette, with his shock of dark, wavy hair and tight waistline, had looked to be about thirty-five until he bent forward to reset the pool table. The glaring lights above it did his skin no favors. Hersh put him around his own age—mid-forties.

The door opened and Hersh's host for the weekend, Elizabeth Randolfi, sailed into the room. The restrained laughter of Fort Lauderdale's finest filtered in after her. "Oh, so here you are, Eddie. We can't have our star guest hiding himself away."

Hersh chalked up his cue. "Now, Elizabeth, you promised me you'd let me do my own thing this weekend."

Elizabeth put her arm around her lover's waist and beamed at Hersh. "Has Marty been looking after you?"

Machette laughed. "If Marty looks after him any better, he's gonna be on welfare."

"Eddie, darling, at least let me give you one little toast before everyone starts to leave." She wrinkled up her nose, as though she was talking to the Mexican hairless dog that seemed to live the better part of its waking life cemented to her left armpit. Hersh couldn't stomach her when she did "cute." All the plastic surgery and liposuction in the world could no longer disguise the fact that Elizabeth Randolfi was now drifting haplessly toward that great barrier reef she described as the "Big Six Zero." Cute didn't cut it anymore.

She watched irritably as the men began another game. When they had been young, Lizzie Lieberman from White Plains as she then was, had watched for a while as her prettier contemporaries attempted to climb the social ladder, one rung at a time, then she'd swept into the express elevator and pressed "penthouse." Three husbands had signed on, cried off and paid out, to give her the lifestyle she now enjoyed. Hersh could be certain that a party at Elizabeth's would include fat checks for his campaign fund, so if his position as Democratic frontrunner was to be maintained, it seemed sensible to include a weekend at the ten-bedroom mansion she always referred to as the "beach house" in his itinerary. It had taken all his powers of persuasion to talk her out of presenting her spectacular donation in front of the gathered company that night. On balance, Hersh thought now, she'd been crossed enough. He put down his cue and kissed her on the forehead. "Okay, Elizabeth. I know when I'm licked."

She threw up her arms like a child. "Wonderful!" Machette followed them through to the living room. "Tell me, Senator, do you like deep-sea fishing?"

"As a matter of fact, there's nothing I like better."

"Well, I have a Hatteras 60 and we're taking her out tomorrow. I wondered if you'd care to join us."

Hersh looked at his host. "Can I go, Ma?"

"Not so much of the "Ma." You will be back for bridge at five, now won't you, Marty?"

"For sure."

She sighed, clearly disappointed at not having either of them around to show off to her friends all the next day too. "You will take care of the senator?"

"No, Elizabeth. I shall throw him in chains and sell him to Chinese pirates."

"Wait in line, buddy," Hersh said. "That's already scheduled in. It's called the Democratic Convention in June."

The giant black marlin was running toward deep water now. As it turned, the line slackened for a fraction of a second, and Edgar Hersh, harnessed tightly into the teak and stainless steel fighting chair in the cockpit of Machette's sixty-foot sportsfisher, reeled in again. The fish was still moving close to 30 m.p.h., but Hersh could sense it was tiring. Machette and Hersh's bodyguard Bruckman stood by, gaff, wire cutters and tag pole at the ready. The marlin arched high above the water, its head shaking violently in the shimmering light. At the same moment, Hersh tried to reel in a few more feet of line. It was a judgment made by a man wearied from two hours of playing a fish weighing close to 300 lbs. The line broke instantly and he was thrown back into the seat.

He unbuttoned the harness and struggled to his feet. "Goddamn it! I had that sonofabitch mounted on the wall of my den an hour ago."

Machette shrugged. "Well, he seems to have had other ideas." He passed him suntan oil. "It's gonna be too hot to fish for the next couple of hours."

"Well, break out the beer and let's play a little poker."

"To hell with beer!" Machette said. "I have Dom Perignon in the icebox, and smoked salmon in the fridge."

"Well, get the champagne out before it explodes."

The senator and Machette moved forward to the galley. The engines were shut down and the anchor dropped. A short, slightly-built man with deepset eyes called Leahy, who had been acting as helmsman, swung down the ladder from the flying bridge and joined the others.

Machette's luck with cards squared with his eye for pool. After losing his fourth hand of poker, he went down to his stateroom and returned carrying an underwater camera. "I've been itching to use this sucker ever since I bought it."

Bruckman threw his cards on the table and stood up. "Well, that water looks good to me too."

"Oh, yes!" Leahy bent down and slipped off his trainers. "The scuba gear and tanks are in the forward hold."

Only Hersh stayed where he was. "I have a busted eardrum, happened when I was a kid. It's too hot to just swim, so I'll have to, er . . . bow out of this."

Machette scratched his chin. "Jesus. That's a tough break."

Bruckman sat down again. "Well, I'll stay here and play cards with the senator."

"The hell with that." Hersh poured himself more champagne. "You've run around after me all month, Glen. This underwater stuff is right up your street. Get in there, go on."

Bruckman looked uneasy. "I don't know if that's the right thing to do. Are you sure, Senator?"

"How are the Chinese pirates today, Marty?"

Machette studied the horizon. "Becalmed, forty leagues to our north," he said in his best Robert Newton. "We'll not see those blackguards afore dawn tomorrow, sir."

"I'll stay," Leahy announced. "I spend half my life in the water, but I don't get to play cards with a senator too often."

Hersh smiled. "It's not a memorable experience, I can promise you, but I'd be glad of your company."

"Okay!" Bruckman let out a boyish whoop. "Let's go."

Ten minutes later, Hersh and Leahy watched Machette and Bruckman disappear over the stern of the boat into the clear, viridian water and settled down to a game of gin rummy. After about twenty minutes, Leahy said, "Jesus, this champagne gives you one hell of headache. I'm gonna get myself some Perrier."

Hersh shuffled the cards. "Good idea. Get me some too, will you?"

When he returned, he looked distinctly unsteady on his feet. "What's the matter?" Hersh asked.

Leahy took his baseball hat from where it lay

under the table, and pulled it down hard on his head. "I think I just had too much sun. Do you mind if we play inside?"

"Not at all." They gathered up the cards and moved into the saloon. As they were clearing the coffee table to make space, Leahy let out a low moan and pitched forward onto the floor.

"Good God, man, what's the problem?" Hersh ran to Leahy and turned him over to see a gaping mouth and eyes rolled up in a way he didn't like. The man was barely conscious. Hersh took off his T-shirt, soaked it with Perrier and wound it around the man's head, then grabbed at a cushion and lowered his head onto it. Leahy started shaking, gradually curling into a fetal position.

Hersh began to scour the boat for a first-aid kit. There was a clip on the wall near the navigation equipment, where it should have been, but no kit. He put his hand to Leahy's head. It felt like he was burning up. Hersh began cursing out loud. He ran out and round the deck, desperate for a glimpse of the others. "Of all the irresponsible . . . "

Leahy was calling from inside. Hersh dashed in. "I can't breathe . . . do something . . . for God's sake."

He laid Leahy out flat on his back, his arms at his sides. Crouching alongside him now, he pulled the man's mouth open, pinched his nostrils together, took a deep breath and pressed his mouth to Leahy's.

There was a voice behind him. "What's going on?"

Hersh twisted around. Machette was standing in the doorway.

☆   ☆   ☆

This time there were no kids with stones at the entrance of Normannenstrasse. Instead, two armed soldiers patrolled the littered wasteground. They watched sullenly as Lassiter swung the BMW into the Stasi complex. With the first police strike Berlin had ever known moving into its third week, they had become a common sight in troublespots all across the city. "Maybe Greta makes it home at night these days," Lassiter speculated. The parking lot to the right of the Counter Dissident Department was cordoned off. Lassiter parked on the roadside and walked through to the crowds that had gathered around the site. Then he saw Fraenkel standing alone. The wind had caught his long white hair, giving him a strange, wild look. Lassiter moved up to his side. "Herr Fraenkel, good morning. What's happening here?"

Fraenkel did not look round. He simply said, "This was woodland till about eight years ago. Then Mielke had it turned into a parking lot. We're finally digging it up. We expect to find up to a thousand bodies."

Two JCBs tore at the tarmac. Men and women, some little more than children, others old enough to be their grandparents, worked with all manner of tools to break up the clay beneath. "Who are these people?" Lassiter asked.

"Relatives, friends, workmates of the "Disappeared." The authorities wouldn't finance the project, so in the end they got permission to do it themselves."

"How on earth will they be able to identify the remains after all this time?"

"They'll find ways."

"Aren't they simply going to add to their anguish?"

"The agony of the truth passes. The pain of uncertainty . . . that has no end. I know." Fraenkel turned to face him. "You see, Mr. Lassiter, somewhere down in that mud they're going to find the body of my son. He would have been twenty-seven this year if he'd lived. Herr Mielke saw to it that he didn't."

They walked back to the administration block in silence. Then Lassiter asked, "What was your son accused of?"

"We don't know for sure. There's no file on him here. We could get no information out of the police at the time he was arrested. We believe it was because he was involved with a dissident newspaper at college. But so were many others. They were amongst the voices that were heard in the end, those that helped drive out Honecker and the rest. My son was a little before his time, I suppose . . . "

Lassiter thought for a minute. "Look I don't know if this is any help, but the lady I'm dating works for the forensic unit of the Berlin police. She's an expert on DNA profiling. If the diggers do turn up a body that you believe might be your son's . . . Well, I'm sure I could get Erika to run some DNA comparisons."

Fraenkel stopped and faced him and put one arm on his shoulder. "That's extremely good of you. If that should happen, my wife and I would be most grateful for your help." The wound in Lassiter's head was still visible, and Fraenkel noticed now that he moved with difficulty. "I've checked the file on the Stasi officer who was blown up in '84. The MO was remarkably similar to that used in the attempt to kill you. There's evidence to suggest that the man

who died was not working for Mielke, but for
President Honecker."

"You think Honecker was checking Mielke out?"

"It's certainly a possibility."

"Well, whoever was used to close down that
little operation, seems to have gotten the call to
deal with me."

"Perhaps. We may not have Rathenau yet, but
we seem to have him, or someone close to him,
pretty rattled."

"So we must be doing something right."

They walked through to Fraenkel's office and he
began to make coffee. "Have the British police
finished going through Tanyuk's things?"

"Yes. If he did have Rathenau's address, he must
have memorized it. There's nothing written down."

"Do they have any more on the hit man?"

"He doesn't connect to the Mielke case. They're
fairly certain he's a man called Vasilkov. It seems he
was trying to stop Tanyuk ratting on him to the
British authorities." Lassiter took his coffee. "You
know, the more I read about this Mielke, the more I
realize that the thing that drove him above any
other was paranoia. He must have started salting
Stasi money away in the mid-Sixties, at the height of
the Cold War. The Soviet régime was probably the
most powerful state apparatus in the world at the
time. We could take the view he started creaming
off the cash because he was, quite simply, a crook. I
don't buy that. It doesn't match with what we know
of him. My view is that it was his getaway fund, his
insurance against the whole system caving in. Now,
given the times and his position, that's paranoia!
Then I ask myself, would a man like this take on
someone like Rathenau to handle an issue as

sensitive as this, just because he'd come in useful in the war? Hardly. He'd have had him checked every which way first."

"You mean you think there might be a file on him here? Good Lord, it never even occurred to me."

"Nor me, till last night."

Lassiter completed his second shave of the day and inspected his raw face in the mirror. "I saw Kyung Wha Chung play the Brahms Violin Concerto in New York in 1990. I've never forgotten it."

Erika ran the shower on her hair. "I've only ever heard her on record. I always thought she was extraordinary."

"When you see her tonight, you'll see what I'm talking about. She stands there with her legs apart—it's a very Eastern kind of a pose—and she attacks the rhythmic sections with an energy I've never heard anyone else produce." He dabbed on aftershave. "And then, just when you think that's all she's about, she'll glide into a legato section with such sweetness, such delicacy, it's hard to believe you're listening to the same player."

Erika put a towel around her hair and stepped out of the shower. "Well, that's why I like to sit front row, center. All my dates complain about being made to sit so close, go on about not getting a good orchestra balance unless you're further back. But I like to be almost inside the orchestra itself, right in the middle of the spit and rosin."

"So what's changed?"

She laughed. "You're right."

"Well, with a player like Chung, that's where the thrill is."

Spit and rosin. Lassiter watched Erika put on her makeup. That was Erika all over. Organic, visceral. She was confident, analytical, very much her own woman. But there was a femininity, a joyous spontaneity here too. She was a captivating woman.

What, then, was Marianne? The first thing Lassiter always sensed, whenever he saw her again after a passage of time, was the presence she had about her. More than just in her physical appearance, it was something she radiated, a sense of order, calm, intelligence, mixed with a suppressed sensuality. But Lassiter knew much of it was a façade. Underneath, Marianne had little real sense of her own identity. He was sure that, during the years she had worked for her father, she had seen herself as an extension of him—a perception he, no doubt, encouraged. In the early years of their marriage, Lassiter believed that to some extent he had inherited the father's role. Then he too had begun to lose sight of himself. No doubt sensing that the most stable element in her life was slipping away, she'd transferred her focus to her new boss. Lassiter knew now that he'd been subconsciously aware of it and, in the strangest of ways, even resented it.

Marianne's outer polish and inner fragility— whatever its causes—had been one of the things that had drawn him to her in the first place. In different ways, both women fulfilled needs in him. What, he wondered, if anything, do I fulfill in them? The force that drove Lassiter, the inner element, had been switched to slow burn for so long that it was hard to believe either woman had a proper measure of him. *Something has to change.*

The phone rang in the bedroom. "Get that for me will you, Jack?"

It was Fraenkel. "It's for me," Lassiter hollered back.

"Well, you were right. There is an index card on a Horst Rathenau," Fraenkel said.

"Thank the Lord for the bureaucrats."

"He's also shown as a.k.a Conrad Vollman. That's not a name we have, is it?"

"We do now."

"And there's an address."

"An address!" Lassiter searched for a pencil.

"Don't get too excited. The street doesn't exist anymore."

"Does the index card show a file?"

"Yes, but so far we haven't located it. We've searched under both names, but you've seen this place, the state it's in. It could take days, months to check properly. I've deployed as many people on this as I can."

"It gives us another start point, though," Lassiter said. "We need to comb government records again, this time for the name Vollman at that address. See where he moved to, what tax he paid. Everything."

"That's right. We'll make a start in the morning. It has to be said though, that in view of Rathenau's role in Meilke's life, it's pretty unlikely he stayed put after reunification. Any address we'll find this way will almost certainly have been vacated by '89. Anyway, I'll call you later if we turn anything up."

"Okay. Good hunting."

Lassiter left Erika to dress and slumped on the sofa in the living room. It struck him now that if nothing broke soon on this case, Fraenkel would

pack him back off to Washington and the affair with
her would be over for good. He began to turn over
in his mind what life without Erika in some part of it
would be like. Some part of it . . . which part, where?
Should he ask her to come back to the States with
him? he wondered. Would she come if he did?

He turned on the TV and flicked through the
channels. NTV was running a series of nightly
reports on the forthcoming American election.
Tonight, it seemed, they were profiling Lowell
Vandenberg. There was no getting away from the
man. Maybe when Marianne is done traipsing
around after him, there'll still be a chance for us,
Lassiter thought. He turned up the sound. There
was a taped interview with a woman, now in her
seventies, who had worked for the Red Cross center
in Switzerland in World War Two. She told of the
night the baby who had turned out to be a
Vandenberg heir was brought in, and how she had
arranged for the child to be passed on to relatives
in Zurich. Then there were shots of a young
Vandenberg with frail survivors of a death camp
walking with heads bowed between the mass graves
where it was believed their friends and relatives
had been buried. The anchor man was saying
something about Paul Vandenberg dying from
pneumonia in '42 . . .

Lassiter watched and wondered idly whether
the governor of Virginia was really as dangerous as
his father was insisting. Once the old man gets his
teeth around something . . .

Suddenly he sat forward, In the footage on the
screen, the mourners were shown grouped around
the entrance of the deathcamp. Clearly it had been
preserved after the war, as so many had, as a

reminder of all that had been done in the name of the Third Reich. But this gateway was unmistakable. It rose with two onion towers, one on each side; the one to the left was half the size of the other.

"Schrobenhausen!" Lassiter shouted. The picture of Gregor Tanyuk from the Wiesenthal Center, taken during the war—the gate behind him, in the photograph, had been the same one. Lassiter ran to get the case notes from his attaché case, his mind racing. Paul Vandenberg had been a prisoner at the concentration camp where Rathenau had been commandant. Now he cursed that he had not seen the TV report from the beginning. Marianne had talked about all this stuff when she had first taken the job with the governor. He put his head in his hands and tried to remember what she'd told him.

It was 3 A.M. Berlin time, when Lassiter finally got through to his wife in Washington. He was back in his own apartment now, a carefully written list of questions laid out on the desk in front of him. "I know this is a bit off the wall, but I need you to help me with something. When you first went to work for Vandenberg, you told me about his start in life, about his family."

"Did I?"

"Yup. Do you remember which concentration camp his father died in?"

"Good Lord! What on earth do you need to know that for?"

"The governor may be able to help fill in some background stuff on that period, information I need urgently."

There was silence on the line for a moment. "No, I haven't a clue. I know he went over there to some kind of memorial thing in Germany. His father had transferred all his funds to Switzerland before the war, because I know Lowell spent some time there after that trip, trying to locate them."

"That's it! That's what I remember you telling me." He set off through the thought processes again. Tanyuk had said that, as commandant of the camp at Schrobenhausen, Rathenau had had what the Ukrainian called "pet prisoners," those he interrogated himself: prisoners he was certain had hidden their assets away before the war. Paul Vandenberg had been one of the wealthiest men in Europe. He would have been a prime target for Rathenau. If the funds had disappeared they could well have gone to him. The Vandenbergs would have used the most sophisticated resources to scour Europe for their money after the war. What might they know of the whereabouts of the man who had, in another life, become Mielke's rinser?

At the other end of the line, Marianne was running on about how the entire media was convinced that her boss had millions salted away, and how unfair it all was. Then suddenly she became wary. "The governor's not under some kind of investigation by your department is he?"

She was so protective of the man there were times when Lassiter wanted to shake her. "No, of course he isn't. But his people may have tried to trace a man I very much need to speak to. I want you to set up a meeting with the governor for me."

"You're not serious."

"I'm very serious."

"The man's in the middle of a presidential campaign, Jack."

"And I'm in the middle of an extremely

important investigation . . . " Then he had an idea. "Look, if I can move forward on this, I may be able to tell the governor a lot more about his father's killer, even about what happened to his money."

Marianne at least seemed to be considering the matter now. "You're putting me in a very difficult position, you know that don't you?"

"Uhuh."

"And you're certain it's just some background stuff you need?"

"Certain."

There was a long sigh. "Are you intending to fly back here specially for this?"

"I shall have to."

She sighed. "Well, call me this time Monday, and I'll see what I can put together."

At seven that morning Lassiter was awakened by another call from Fraenkel. It took a moment before he recognized his voice.

"I'm sorry to call so early. I've been up all night, you see . . . " Then Fraenkel began to sob.

Lassiter shook himself awake. "What on earth's happened?"

"Oh . . . it has nothing to do with the case. It's my boy. You see I . . . I think they've found his body."

EIGHTEEN

A telephone, ringing in the dead of night; for Edgar
Hersh there was no more chilling a sound. His heart
slammed in his chest as he reached for the light
switch. No one calls with good news at 4 A.M., he
told himself as he lifted the receiver. His campaign
manager's anguished voice broke through the
silence. "Ed, it's Blake. Switch on CNN. Right now."

Hersh had never heard him sound so shaken
up. "Is someone dead?"

"Turn on CNN."

Hersh's wife Kate sat up beside her husband
and shielded her eyes from the light. "What's
happened?"

Hersh reached for the remote control. The TV at
the end of the bed came on. Hersh switched to the
news channel.

" . . . Leahy's affidavit is still being studied by
Miami police. But a statement is expected from
them shortly . . . "

"What the hell are they talking about, Blake?" Hersh could hear him take a slug of something.

"That fishing trip you went on. The helmsman, or whatever the fuck he was meant to be, he was a rent boy. Or according to him, an ex-rent boy . . . I don't know how to tell you this . . . Christ, you're godfather to my son, I'd trust you with . . . "

"Say it!" Hersh screamed.

Again, a gulp. A good hard one this time. "He said the minute you came on board, you recognized him from somewhere. You contrived to get him alone, and then you propositioned him . . . "

"I did what?" Hersh's wife was by the window now, and shouting something. He put his hand over his other ear to hear more clearly.

"They haven't said exactly. But, according to him, you wouldn't take no for an answer. He alleges you tried to rape him and that the other guy, Machette, caught you in the act."

"Oh my God!" His wife was shaking him now, trying to drag him to the window. "You don't believe . . . "

"I'm not even gonna honor that with a reply. The first thing we gotta do . . . "

Kate's impassioned plea broke through the haze of shock that was beginning to close in all around Edgar Hersh. *"Ed, what's happening to us? The street outside is full of cameramen."*

Duane Appleton, Hersh's attorney, put down a long length of fax printout and rubbed at his stubbled chin. Then his large head swiveled in the direction of his client. "You got yourself set up, Ed. There's no more to it than that. They saw you coming, hooked you good, and reeled you in. Now we have to find a way of cutting you free." He perched his horn-rimmed glasses back on his nose and squinted at the text again. "What's your answer to Leahy's claim that you said, 'I recognized you the minute I saw you again. Once a rent boy, always a rent boy.'"

"A goddam lie."

"And Machette saying, 'As I walked up the deck I could see the senator, wearing only his shorts, sitting on Leahy, trying to kiss him'?"

Hersh combed his fingers through his hair. "I never touched the man, I never suggested anything, I never offered him anything. We played some cards . . . He got a little faint because of the heat. I got him some water. Then Machette showed up. That was it."

"Nobody in this room—hell, nobody that knows you—doubts that for minute, Senator." Appleton eased his considerable bulk off the sofa in Hersh's office, rose unsteadily to his feet, walked over and put his arm around his client. He was a man who moved himself with great reluctance, even as far as his own drinks cabinet, and so the gesture took on an added poignance. "The people we have to convince are the other ninety-nine percent, the ones who we hope are gonna vote for you in November." He seated himself on the corner of the senator's desk, which creaked in protest, and turned his attention to the campaign manager. "The first thing we have to do is issue a statement. We have to give the clearest possible picture of what happened on that boat from the minute the senator came on board till the minute he left. You tell me that the bodyguard's testimony isn't going to be overly helpful?"

Blake poured himself more coffee. "Bruckman has to drive in from Bedford Park. He should be here any time. From the little I got over the phone, it seems he didn't come back on board till twenty minutes after Machette. By which time, they claim, Leahy had gone to his cabin."

Hersh put his head in his hands. "They had every part of it figured out, Duane. Machette lent Bruckman a real high-powered spear-gun to play around with. I'm surprised he came back when he did."

"The key stuff they had to know for this to work was all out there," Blake said. "Your passion for fishing has been in every profile you've done. The thing about the busted eardrum came up in that interview you did for *People*. That ensured that if everybody else went scuba diving, you'd have to stay behind."

Hersh stood up and began to pace. "We need to dig up everything we can get on these scuzzballs. This was too professional a scam to have come out of nowhere. They'll have a list of 'priors' from here to Lake Michigan, I'll stake my life on it."

Appleton looked down and realized that he'd dressed in such haste he'd forgotten to change out of his bedroom slippers. "Leahy admits he's an ex-pillow-biter, so there may be some history on that, but so what? Unless we can show that these guys are habitual liars or perjurers, in a case like this, their 'priors' don't matter. It is not a crime for men with records to ask a senator to go fishing with them. And Leahy's civil rights can be violated like anyone else's. I mean there's no extortion here. No one's come to us for money. And neither will they, now."

"What makes you so sure of that?" Hersh asked.

"Because this isn't about payoffs, Senator. This is about power, surely you see that." Appleton looked his client hard in the face. "This is a well-staged smear job designed to take you out of the race, nothing else. If we play it straight, all the way down the line, we'll expose it as just that."

Radio coverage of Hersh's press conference that afternoon was so extensive that finally his chauffeur had to tune to a local music station to avoid it. The boss had clearly had enough. He sat slumped in the corner of the blue stretch limo, lost in thought as members of his campaign team worked on his schedule, and wondered just how effective Appleton could really be. Blake, seated in front of him, took a call on the car phone then passed it to Hersh. Appleton's voice bellowed down the line. "I said to you, Ed, I told you, if you play it straight down the line I can make this thing go away. But you couldn't do that, could you?"

Hersh sat forward. "What are you saying?"

"You didn't level with me, and so now we got real trouble. Tell me, Ed, what would Machette have seen when he climbed back on board? I really need to know."

There was a long silence, then Hersh sighed and said, "Leahy had passed out, at least that's what I thought. I thought he was going to die on me. I . . . I tried to give him the kiss of life. I didn't say anything because, in the circumstances, I could see how it could be made to look."

"Well, it would have looked one fuck of a sight better in the statement we issued this morning than it's gonna look now."

"What's happened? For God's sake tell me."

"Ask yourself, Ed. What was Machette carrying when he came back aboard?"

Suddenly, time lost significance for Hersh as his memory zoomed to the scene. He caught his breath. "An underwater camera," he whispered. "They have a photograph."

"Yup. A doozie. It was waiting for me with an affidavit when I got back to the office. The way they've set things up, they're gonna make it look like we have something to hide."

"What happens now?"

"We meet right away and we do a lot of talking."

"I'm on my way to a fund-raiser."

There was a humorless laugh at the other end of the line. "If we can't turn this around, Ed, the only funds you're gonna need are for legal fees."

The little Chinese girl could have been no older than ten, but she threw herself into the game of table tennis with the governor of Virginia with a confidence and skill that astonished the crowd gathered in the assembly room of a San Francisco School. For ten minutes—twice the time scheduled—the tiny white plastic ball click-clacked back and forth across the green trestle table. Vandenberg seemed to play as though his life depended on it. Then the girl took a breath, stepped forward and sent the ball diagonally across the net like a spark from a crackling fire. Vandenberg dived for it, missed, and almost toppled into the crowd. A score of cameras caught his exaggerated look of surprise: the jaw dropped, the eyes staring in disbelief. Then he ran to her and swept her up into

his arms. When the laughter and applause had died
down, he asked, "Who taught you to play like that?"

"My grandfather," she replied in a clear voice.

"How old is he?"

"Seventy-nine. And he beats me every time."

Another gale of laughter. Vandenberg turned to
parents, town dignitaries and members of his own
local campaign team. "This kid is incredible. She
thrashed me!" He signaled to a small man in an
obvious wig—a textile magnate who had just
donated twenty thousand dollars to his campaign
fund—to join him and the child, as the press closed
around them. He sought out the cameramen from
the TV networks and turned the three of them in
their direction, beaming and chatting easily to both.

Chesterfield pulled Vernon Lacy to him. "This is
my fourth presidential campaign, you know that?
But I've never had an operator like this one. He
never misses a trick." Chesterfield waited till the
press were done, caught his client's eye and rubbed
the left side of his nose—their signal for him to
wind things up.

Vandenberg turned to the crowd. "Folks, I have
some nurses waiting for me at a hospital in
Sacramento . . . " Laughter and catcalls. " . . . so I'm
gonna have to leave you, but I want to thank you for
all your kindness, your generosity and, most of all,
your support. And I'll tell you this. When I make the
White House, the first thing I'm gonna do is have
the Olympic Selection Committee take a good look
at this little lady." Spirited cheers and applause.

"They don't have table tennis in the Olympics,"
someone piped. "Sure they do," another hollered.
No one seemed to know for sure whether they did
or not. Vandenberg, determined not to have his

parting shot ruined, shrugged amiably and, surrounded by his security team, moved through the crowd toward the door, shaking the many hands that were thrust toward him as he went. Over the heads of schoolchildren standing at the back, he could see Marianne running down the corridor toward him. Judging by the expression on her face, she had something of importance to report. He watched her push her way to Chesterfield and whisper in his ear, saw the man's eyes widen and then turn to meet his own. At the door, their paths converged. "We have to get to a TV set," Chesterfield called.

A mystified janitor moved out into the hallway as seven tall men in gray suits and one well-groomed woman squeezed into his tiny office to follow the newcast on the TV, perched on a filing cabinet in the corner. Edgar Hersh's face looked pale and drawn, but his voice was firm enough.

" . . . I will not dignify the accusations made against me with a fuller reply. The place for that is in a court of law. I have thought long and hard about the months that lie ahead, and it is very clear to me that I could not continue to run for the Democratic Party nomination with this issue unresolved. It would be unfair to my party, my supporters, my campaign team and, most importantly, my family." Now his voice began to falter. " . . . I believe it is in everyone's best interests, therefore, if I step down as a candidate. I needn't tell you what a hard decision this has . . . "

Vandenberg shook his head. "Someone pinch me."

Chesterfield slung an arm around him. "Lowell, my boy, you just moved into history. The nomination's all but in the bag." A yelp of excitement went up. Vandenberg turned from one face to another. A smile played around his lips but no other reaction seemed to register. The group linked arms and watched the rest of the newcast in silence. "Poor sonofabitch," Vandenberg said at last, and they walked out into the sunlight.

It was almost midnight when Vandenberg finally got a chance to return his wife's call. Five months of campaigning had taken its toll on all of them, but tonight the scheduling and planning that often filled the early hours was called off, and Vandenberg and his team had celebrated. "I wish you could be with us," he told her. "This is the first time I've seen Chesterfield let his hair down. It's quite a sight."

Stella sighed. "I wish I could be there too. *Women's World* had a team here all day, taking pictures. NBC is here tomorrow. I'm certain my fudge brownies recipe is the same as the one used by ten million other American women, but the magazine people seem to think it's special." She laughed. "Three years at UCLA and that's what I'm going to be famous for."

"You're gonna be famous as the most accomplished and elegant First Lady since Jackie Kennedy," Vandenberg said gently.

"Maybe. All I can think about at the moment is poor Ed Hersh. He's a sweet, good man. My father thought the world of him. God knows what his wife must be going through."

"I want the nomination more than anything, you know that. But not like this."

"I miss you," she said.

"I'm sorry to put you through all this hoopla, but it'll be worth it, I promise."

"Don't drink too much, you know how you are in the morning."

He hung up and began to change out of his suit into jeans and a sweater. She makes it easy, he told himself. In that respect, she's as smart as hell and I admire her for it. But politics is a blood sport. Her grasp of the subject was like her grasp of most other things in the real world—tenuous.

Vandenberg had fallen in love with a fellow law student when he was twenty-two. When, out of the blue, she married a distant cousin three years later, he'd told himself he could never feel the same way about any woman again. By the time Stella Cornel-Stuart walked into his life, four years later, he was a much changed man. He knew what he wanted in a wife, and in most ways Stella seemed to supply it. Like him, she could trace her family back through generations of wealth. She was a capable host and would no doubt prove a loving mother. The perfect photogenic partner. But she was, Vandenberg knew, a woman of limited intelligence. He had always equated intellect with curiosity, and in that respect Stella seemed to live most of her life sublimely undistracted. Not that she was particularly self-obsessed. She was just content to run her husband's homes, bring up his family, serve on her charitable committees and do whatever was necessary to keep the press aware that Lowell Vandenberg had a beautiful, capable spouse who might, if she was ever given the chance to prove it, be a memorable First Lady.

Stella was a great asset now. He had always known she would be. It had been one of the many reasons he'd selected her in the first place. That she stimulated him not a whit intellectually was something he was prepared to live with. She had the kind of body that was impossible to ignore. She worked hard to keep their sex life fresh. And when the poverty of her conversation wearied him, began to scrape on his nerves, he'd lose himself in the pleasures of her body. The marriage worked. It would never be more than it was, and he would live with that.

Vandenberg walked back into the living room of the hotel suite. Only Chesterfield and Marianne were still partying. Although they had eaten well at a dinner staged by a local mayor, some hours before, since then they had drunk so much Bollinger that both had had an attack of the munchies and were now working their way through a plate of smoked salmon sandwiches.

"Come on Lowell, eat." Chesterfield's speech was slurred. "It'll help soak up the booze."

The only outward sign that Marianne was less than sober was a hint of red in her eyes. "I hate to be the party pooper here, but we do have to figure out Friday's schedule." She looked at her watch. "Unless I get it on a fax in the next hour, we're gonna miss them in L.A."

Chesterfield staggered to his feet. "You've got my draft, so I'll leave you to it." He turned to Vandenberg. "If you think you can do the Silicon Valley people and the Napa Valley folk back to back, then we're cooking on gas." He bowed uncertainly, and blew Marianne a kiss, then studied her for a moment. "My God, if I was twenty years younger . . . I could make a damn fool of myself over you."

Marianne reddened and Vandenberg moved to

close the door. "You're making a damn fool of yourself right now, Ches. Go to bed."

"Well, that's the first time I've seen him unfreeze," Marianne said when he'd gone.

Vandenberg chuckled. "You had that effect on every other man on the team the first day. It just takes ol' Ches a little time to come around."

She put her head on one side. "I wasn't claiming credit."

He topped up her glass and poured another for himself. "Listen, you're a lovely looking woman. At the risk of sounding like Father Time, my advice is, enjoy it. It doesn't last forever."

"It's not easy for me, working in a team like this. A lot of the time I have to keep myself a little . . . Well, at arm's length."

"My guys breathing all over you, huh?"

She did her "Oh, please" look. "Most men find me threatening, so I'm told. And a lot of the rest find the way I look too . . . obvious."

The green eyes, flecked with brown, caught hers. "Then they must be blind or stupid or both." He moved his face an inch closer to hers. There was silence. She tried to look away but their eyes connected again. After a long moment, she smiled and said softy, "This may not be exactly what you wanted to hear me say right now, but will you be able to address members of the domestic wine industry and computer software firms in the space of four hours, this coming Friday?" They both laughed at the utter incongruity of the statement.

"Give me words, and I'll speak 'em. Go to bed, Marianne, I'll see you in the morning."

Her bedroom was hot. She turned up the air-conditioning, stripped and slipped into bed. I've been around this man for seven years, she thought. I probably know him better in some ways than his own wife. He's flirted with me now and again, he has with most of the women on his staff at one time or another. Innocent enough stuff. But tonight . . . There was something else there, I could have sworn it. He's climbing to new heights, his whole world is changing . . . Could it be possible that he wants me to be some part of it? She laughed out loud and set her alarm clock. It was unthinkable. Why would he consider taking such a risk, at this of all times? Surely he hadn't consciously thought it through. But . . . even if his behavior was circumscribed, where was it written that he couldn't feel?

In the darkness of her bedroom there was no reality. In the privacy of her own imagination there were no taboos, only feelings. So she parted her legs a little and began to imagine what it might be like to be loved by Lowell Vandenberg.

NINETEEN

Chaos theory suggests that maybe a sneeze in St. Kitts can set up a chain that leads to a hurricane in New Orleans. Lowell C. Vandenberg had laid his plans to take the presidency with infinite care, but nothing could have allowed for a sneeze on a warm spring evening in Miami's Little Havana.

Police patrolman Ray Froggat leaned back in the driver's seat of the battered Ford and studied the girl in tight shorts striding lazily across the street in front of him.

"Will yer look at those buns. They're a federal case, I'm here to tell you." Hers must have been the fifth ass he'd found worthy of comment in the last hour.

Howie Crane sucked on the straw in his iced coffee till the cup made a slurping sound. "What's the matter, Bulf? You not getting any at home these days?"

"No, not since the baby. Says she's too tired. To tell the truth, I'm not pushing her either. That neat little waist she had. Those tight little jugs . . . "

"Ah, it'll all come back. After our second kid I remember . . . "

Bulf's eyes hooked on to another shapely female. "I don't know right now whether I care if it does or not, you know that?"

A brand-new black Mercedes slid by and he locked on to it instinctively. "That's the ride, Howie, my boy." He reached for the ignition key and moved the Ford out, winding the wheel with the palm of his hand.

Crane spat his gum out the window. "What are we doing, Bulf?"

"That's Huerta's new ride."

"What happened to the 911 Turbo?" Crane asked.

"Totaled a month ago."

With a surname like Froggat and a head built on a barrel chest without the intervention of a neck, "Bull" or "Bulf" had been an inevitable nickname. Froggat was black, born in the ghetto. Much of his information on the life within it came from his own network of contacts. Crane, a white "blow in" from Baton Rouge, had been his partner for seven years. He tapped the number of the Merc's licence plate, now three cars in front of them, into the Ford's onboard computer. Seconds later, the name of the registered owner flashed on the screen.

"Am I right or am I right?" Froggat snorted.

"That sonofabitch changes his cars like most people change their shorts."

Huerta was a drug dealer. But then so were eleven percent of the kids in the burg. But Huerta was different. He was one of the candyman elite. He dealt in heroin, cocaine, crack, ecstasy, LSD tabs, amphetamine sulphate, paradise poppers. If it took away the feeling of not being worth dog wham, deadened the fear of being unemployed your whole working life, it had a street value. But then a Smith and Wesson .38 could do that for you. And Huerta dealt in those too. Huerta was a Cuban ghetto rat, one of the few who could drive safely through the black enclave—since the recent crackdowns, too many brothers relied on him to keep them supplied. He was more than street smart. Like all the main movers, he used others to take the big risks. He played the streets like a virtuoso.

"Is Huerta driving?" Crane asked.

"Damned if I can see, all that tinted glass."

The Merc hung a right and moved through a rubble wasteland. Since the Thirties, the shacks and tenement buildings that jostled for space here had provided a boundary line between the black and the Cuban ghettos, a thin no-man's-land that separated the two most feared gangs in the city, the Bloods and the Flames. In a district with fifty percent unemployment, gangs flourished. Black and Cuban kids took up the mantles of their fathers and grandfathers and pledged themselves to the brotherhoods as part of their natural right. Black and Hispanic cops found themselves on the wrong side of no-man's-land, or what was now left of it, at their peril.

Urban renewal—inner city redevelopment—had been a vote-catcher for a long time. It had taken the L.A. riots of '91 to turn any of the programs into reality. Renewing this district was listed as an "A" priority. That spring, a wrecker's ball had torn into the timber frames and old brick and the skyline began to change. For the first time in three generations the Flames and the Bloods faced each other across open ground.

The Merc rolled over the uneven road surface, torn up by the excavators, and crossed the boundary into the Cuban quarter. It swung left, and three blocks down pulled up at the gates of a derelict factory. A block behind, the brown Ford turned off the street and out of sight.

"That place has been locked up for ten years. What can Huerta want with it?" Bulf said.

Crane chewed gum nervously. "What's it to us? Tenth Precinct can handle it. This side of Opa-locka . . . "

Froggat gestured around him. "What fucking Opa-locka? Look around, pal, it ain't here no more. Just a big hole in the ground." He remembered that factory five years before. It had used a lot of cheap local labor. The yard had been busy with delivery vans stacked with polyester leisure suits, destined for the major thrift stores. As any cop knew, for most of the years since it had been a shadowy haven for derelicts, hookers, rent boys and dealers. Now two steel gates sealed the only entrance.

Bulf watched Huerta's driver get out of the Merc, unlock the gates and swing them open. "How yer like that! They got keys." The car eased through. The chauffeur hurried back to close the gates behind it.

"He must be paying off the security company. He's making a pickup, I'm certain of it."

"Jesus! Let the 10th handle it, Bulf." Crane reached for the radio.

Froggat turned angrily in his seat and snatched the mike out of his hand. "Chill, will yer. If you think I'm gonna pass up a chance like this, you outta your mind." He got out of the car and buttoned his denim jacket over his shoulder holster. "Huerta's head'd look just fine on my belt. Oh, yes sir. Call in and say we're checking out a possible 618. Do it!"

Crane sighed and radioed in. Then he got out too. "Why would Huerta chance a pickup on the old Durolene lot? Come on, that's not his style."

"It's been sealed for how many years? Three at least. It's the last place those 10th Precinct spickballs'd think to check. I'm not letting them have this, Howie. To hell with 'em."

The policemen edged their way across the street to the factory entrance. Bulf got down on his stomach and peered under the lefthand side of the gate. "Just the Merc. Lights on inside." The gate swung a little as he scrambled to his feet. He realized it was still unlocked. "Come on, we're in." In a second, he was through the gate and moving for cover amongst some outbuildings. Most of the yard was in darkness. Crane thought for a moment, then eased himself through.

The interior lights of the Merc were too dim to make out how many were in the car. Crane and Froggat sat staring at it for the better part of twenty minutes. Crane, his ear cocked to his shortwave radio, seemed to be willing them to get called out. At last Froggat said, "Maybe he ain't making a pickup. Could be he's making a drop. That Cubano could have fifty grand's worth of crack in that car."

Without waiting to hear Crane's thoughts on the matter, Froggat moved out into the center of the yard. What the hell's he playing at? Crane thought, as he unclipped the strap that held his .38 in place and took up a position behind and slightly to the right of his partner. This seems like a real good way to get killed.

Police procedure called for Froggat to shine his

flashlight into the car and verbally caution those inside to lift their arms to where they could be plainly seen and get out of the vehicle. But those tinted windows were spooking Bulf now. Here in the center of the yard, where the lights of the elevated freeway, a block down, illuminated the asphalt, he knew he was clearly visible. Whoever was in that car was either asleep or too busy snorting nose powder to notice him. Or could be they were watching him. Huerta could have a shotgun leveled at his gut. Bulf pulled his gun from its shoulder holster and moved slowly up to the driver's-side door. There was no one in the front of the car. There'd be two of them in the back seat snortin', Bulf was certain. The door locks were in the up position. Screw procedure, he thought. Let's nail this son of a bitch. To Crane's astonishment, Froggat leveled his gun at the offside rear door and with the other hand, wrenched it open. Then he grabbed for his badge and hollered, "Police!"

A naked man was kneeling across the back seat with his head down and his ass in the air. Two slim, dusky legs were drawn up under his armpits. The man's head jerked up and he rolled onto the floor. The naked girl beneath him froze. For a split second, Froggat had a clear view of her open vulva, the dark pubic hair plastered back against her thighs. Then she recovered herself and curled into the fetal position to hide her nakedness. The man reached for his clothes in the front seat.

"Freeze!" Froggat screamed, instinctively taking up the firing position. "Lift your hands to where I can see them and move out of the vehicle." The man was Hispanic, about twenty. He was slightly built and as naked as the day he was born. His penis stuck out in front of him, still half erect. Crane, who was now breathing a lot easier, moved up to cover the man. Froggat started to go through the clothes.

"What do you want?" the trembling girl shouted. "What the hell are you doing?" Her Cuban accent was pronounced.

"What does it look like I'm doing?"

"Let me have my dress."

"Not till I've checked it out," Froggat said, enjoying himself.

Suddenly her lover broke free and made a run for it. Froggat spun around and leveled the .38 at the back of his left leg. Then he realized there was no way you could shoot at a naked man and get away with it. He put his hands on his hips and watched his partner clatter up a fire escape in pursuit. For a second he could see the kid on the roof and then he was gone. Froggat began to search the backseat. Again, the girl tried to reach for her dress. Froggat slapped her across the face. She let out a howl. "You're making a big mistake, you dumb . . . "

Froggat stopped searching and put his face an inch from hers. "Dumb what?" His voice was low and menacing. No fucking guinea whore got to call him a nigger. He could smell the sweat on her now. It was sweet. "Where's the keys . . . the keys to the trunk? Nah, why would a twenty-buck hooker know?" She was shaking now. She didn't like the look on his face.

Crane held his breath and waited. Suddenly he heard the slap of bare feet on concrete. He spun around, moved out from behind the water tank and switched on his flashlight. The man looked sullenly down the barrel of the Smith and Wesson and skidded to a halt. Crane cuffed his hands behind him as he bent over and tried to catch his breath. Five minutes later they were back in the yard. Froggat was going through the trunk of the car. The girl in the backseat was sobbing. Suddenly her small face appeared at the window. The minute she saw the boy she began screaming.

"He raped me. The bastard raped me."

Froggat showed no reaction. The trunk of the Merc was proving a disappointment. "Oh yeah, sure. Nothing I like more than Flagler Street bangtail," he muttered.

"She's no whore, Bulf," Crane said. "She's Huerta's kid sister. This creep's her boyfriend. They come here to screw."

Froggat turned. "What shit is this?"

"What did you do to her?" the kid screamed. *"If you touched her . . . "*

"You'll what?" Froggat spat back. "You mind your mouth."

Froggat didn't like the way this was going. He turned his back to his partner, unbuttoned his shirt and reached for the small packet he kept taped under his arm. Times like this, it was good to have "Plan B." Both kids were still hollering. Froggat timed his moment, then turned back, and picked up the girl's totebag and produced a clear plastic packet from it, about the size of a teabag. "Okay, chill, both of you. I want to know what this is. That's what I want to know." He tried to hand the packet to the girl. She backed away instinctively.

"What kind of dummy do you think I am? You're not getting my prints on that."

Froggat reached for her angrily. The girl was

about all in. She let out a hysterical yell. *"Naaah! You're gonna be sorry . . . Oh yes, you're gonna be sorry!"*

Froggat didn't like the way his partner just stood there. He began to move toward her. "Look, shut up or, so help me, I'll smack you all over this . . . "

Suddenly the yard was filled with hard white light. A police car rolled in through the entrance, its spotlights glaring. The doors swung open and two cops got out. Froggat watched them come. They were Cuban cops. The girl began to scream again.

"Now you'll see! Now you'll see, you black sonofabitch!"

"Bulf" Froggat threw back his head and took a deep breath. "Thank God for that! Thanks for letting me know." He put down the phone and punched the air with his fist. "Yes!" He crossed the living room of the police safe house in Olympia Heights and poured himself another bourbon. "That was the captain," he called out. "They've got the medical examiner's report. No evidence of rape. None." There was silence from the bedroom.

He walked through. His wife was taking the last of her clothes from a bag and hanging them in a closet. "Have they dropped the case?" she asked at last.

"Not yet. But it'll just be a matter of . . . "

She turned her sullen face to him for the first time that day. "So we're still stuck here?"

He looked at his shoes. "Yup, I guess. But it'll only be for a day or two. Still . . . it's great news."

She shrugged and went back to hanging her clothes.

Froggat put his hands on his hips and shook his head. "I don't believe this."

"What do you want from me, Ray, a round of applause?" she snapped.

"You still think . . . Don't you know . . . "

"I'll tell you what I know. I know that you haven't been near me since I had the baby. And this was a man who couldn't keep his hands off me a year ago. I don't know where all that sexual energy's going, but it sure ain't coming my way." She began to cry. "I know that I'm stuck out here, away from my family and friends, and I can't walk down the street without feeling the whole world's staring at me."

The door to the yard slammed. Froggat stormed off down the sidewalk to the liquor store. What the hell does a guy have to do to get his ass out of a sling these days? he asked himself again. The forced inactivity was driving him crazy. How long were they gonna keep him cooped in this geriatric wasteland?

He didn't like the way the man in the liquor store looked at him, hadn't from the first day. How could the man know who he was? He hadn't used a credit card, he'd paid cash intentionally. Christ, the man looked terrified. What the hell was going down here? But the man was looking beyond Froggat, to people in the line behind him. Froggat turned around. At the door stood two men in ski masks. Both carried shotguns. Their skin was olive brown. Cubans.

The liquor store owner began to move away. The gunmen let him. Then Froggat understood. *They're here for me,* was his last thought. The first blast hit him full in the face, obliterating his features. A chunk of his brain came out the back of his head and broke up against the bottles that lined the shelves behind him. He was already dead when the second blast tore open his chest, driving his body against the counter and onto the floor.

Froggat's killing got substantial media coverage. Two nights later, three detachments of Bloods crossed no-man's-land from the black ghetto into the Cuban. For the next two hours, they torched shops and homes, and attacked those unlucky enough to be found on the streets. Police cars dispatched to the area were raked with gunfire, petrol-bombed and set alight. Seven police were injured but none killed.

Later that night, Officer Elaine Brody turned the sheets of the updated missing persons list. By early evening most of the citizens of Dade County—which takes in the city of Miami—listed as missing the night before had usually shown up somewhere. Tonight was not one of those nights. She'd worked the late shift at the Police Department headquarters building on 25th Street since her marriage had broken up three years before. One of her regular duties was to compile the missing persons list and to circulate it to police precincts across the county.

Eighty percent of persons listed as missing in the county fell into a handful of categories. Their apparent disappearance was due to a domestic spat or a transport problem. They were invariably debtors on the run, traumatized fired employees, epileptics, diabetics, drunks or drug users. Most of those would turn up somewhere within hours. The rest were, variously, victims of serious illness, motor-related or domestic accidents, or violent crime. On a normal night the names and details of the "no shows"—those missing for more than eight hours—generally ran to nine or ten pages. Tonight the list was almost double that.

Elaine was tired now. The words on the screen began to swim in front of her. She fought to pull her mind to the subject in hand. Many of those listed were Hispanic—almost certainly Cubans given their addresses. She turned the pages slowly, remembering names from the night before. Some of the "no shows" lived within blocks of one another. She sat pensively at the terminal for a minute. The computer listed names alphabetically. She leafed her way through the printout, copying the Hispanic names into a separate list. Fifteen minutes later, she was satisfied that the sudden upswing in missing persons was due entirely to the disappearance of over a hundred and fifty Cubans.

Her initial reaction was that the size of the list was directly related to the violence that had broken out in Little Havana. But when she checked it more thoroughly, she found that all the Cubans in question had been reported as missing for eight hours or more, before the first signs of trouble.

She found her superior, a gaunt-looking police captain, at the elevator. "Excuse me, sir, do you have a minute to look at this?"

The weary face turned to her. "Can't this wait till I've had breakfast?"

"I thought you should see the 'no show' list before I sent it out. There's something very odd about it. For a start, we've had almost double the usual number reported, mostly Cubans from districts covered by the Eighth, Ninth and Eleventh Precincts . . . "

The captain jabbed irritatedly at the elevator call button. "What the hell do you expect? They took off because of all the violence."

"Well, I thought that too, at first. But most of these people had been missing for hours before the firebombings and stuff even started."

He threw up his shoulders in a shrug. "Maybe they got word there was trouble coming. They took off, Ellie, that's all there is to it."

"Without telling husbands, wives, parents? I don't buy that."

The elevator arrived at last. The captain lay back against the wall and sighed. Brody held out the list. "I really think you should take a look."

As first light broke over Miami, young Cubans began gathering at the perimeter of their ghetto and, under the leadership of Flame gang members, began to cordon it off from the rest of the world. All along no-man's-land the line was three deep. Most of the youths, aged between fifteen and twenty-five, were armed with baseball bats, metal bars and other makeshift weapons. Many others obviously carried concealed firearms. Police moved in and disarmed as many as they dared, but otherwise tried to keep a low profile.

A hundred yards across the open ground, black youths began to form their own battle lines. As the day wore on, numbers swelled. Police met with various local leaders in an attempt to get the mobs to disperse, but by late afternoon it was clear they intended staying right where they were.

At 5:50 P.M. National Guard transporters began to rumble into the streets.

The incumbent president's announcement in the fall of the previous year, that he would not stand for a second term, due to reasons of health, had caught the electorate by surprise. In the early Republican primarys the vice president had shown as the clear front runner, but less-than-full answers to questions concerning his personal life and a number of erstwhile business deals, soon cut into his poll rating. Backed by an expensive and well organized campaign, Florida Governor Matt Travanion moved quickly to steal the advantage, and soon after the California primary it was clear that he'd gained enough support to win the Republican nomination at the first ballot at the party's convention in August.

If voters needed further proof that they were looking at a presidential nominee-in-waiting, it came in the shape of a network TV debate with his nearest rival, industrialist Patrick O'Farrell. Travanion seemed to bristle with ideas; audiences watched as O'Farrell blathered and blustered his way into political obscurity.

Travanion was on the road campaigning when news of the situation in the ghettos came in. When Miami Mayor Cal Cochran called for the third time that day to give him the update position, the candidate sounded anything but presidential. Cochran heard him out, and then said simply, "We got a lot of trouble here, Matt, I can't pretend we haven't."

"I just saw the CNN report. The National Guard still looks thin on the ground down there."

"Well, we've got two thousand men deployed. They're maintaining the status quo."

"That's not good enough, Cal. In two hours I have to go on network TV and make it damn clear I have this situation under control. I can't do that with four thousand ethnics drawn up in battle lines, itching to tear each other's throats out. I want them cleared off the street."

"I think any such move could be disastrous." Cochran sat forward in his chair. "These people are good and mad, sure. But most of them have been out there for the better part of fourteen hours. They've gone off the boil. If they were gonna make a move they'd have made it by now. I know how these things go. We've made a lot of studies of these kind of scenarios. And there's some very disturbing side issues here . . . I say side issues, I'm not certain yet whether they're related or not. We have close to a hundred and fifty missing people reported in the area . . . "

"I'm not surprised! It's a war zone down there."

"I think there's more to it than that. Look, these demonstrators, vigilantes, whatever you want to call them, they're getting tired and hungry, Matt. And there's the Mike Tyson comeback fight on TV in ninety minutes . . . "

Travanion gave a cough of derision.

"My people tell me that could be a real factor. If we can just maintain the status quo another hour or so, this thing'll diffuse by itself."

"I can't take that risk."

Cochran stood up and started to pace. "Well, we start trying to push these people around, we're asking for a bloodbath. To tell the honest truth, I'd sooner they smashed a few more windows, looted a couple more stores—Jesus, I'm not saying this is the way it should be—but better that than anybody else gets hurt."

Travanion lowered his voice as though someone might be listening. "You know the position I'm in. I'm not just concerned about what happens in Miami, I'm concerned with how this goes over in the wider community . . ."

I'll bet you are, Cochran thought.

" . . . Unless I can show people at home those streets cleared, things settled back to normal, we could have a full-scale race war on our hands by tomorrow morning. Cal, we have to contain this thing at all costs. I'm ordering the guards to move in right now. I want bars closed and a curfew in place until six tomorrow morning in all relevant areas."

TWENTY

Few septuagenarians regard birthdays as anything more than a stark reminder of their own mortality, to be faced with foreboding or, at the very least, a numb sense of resignation. Joe Lassiter was not one of those people. To him, birthdays meant going home. So did the Fourth of July, Thanksgiving and Christmas. He knew that on such occasions his son or daughter or both, would put the Rockville house in order, stock up the freezer and collect him from the retirement home. It seemed this birthday, his seventy-fourth, would be celebrated with his daughter's family alone. Then, two nights before, Jack had called from Germany to say he was returning to the States for a few days and would catch the party after all.

Now, Joe sat in the diningroom of the house he loved, soaking up his family, the sound of them, the look of them, the smell of them, savoring it, bottling it up to be savored again when there would be only silence. Around them were the remnants of a fine meal. Talk, inevitably, turned to the coming election.

"People living today are the most politicized in history," Joe said. "They're bombarded with facts, news and opinions, every waking hour. They've gotten a lot smarter. The old rhetoric no longer inspires, the old lies no longer convince. They're skeptics in a post-heroic age." He sipped his wine, clearly enjoying himself. "When it comes to their leaders, they've run out of trust, they've run out of patience. We're seeing the consequences of that right across the Free World."

Jack Lassiter poured himself more coffee. "When I think back to the Watergate Scandal, it wasn't all the stuff about 'break-ins' and 'cover-ups' that really shook me. It was those Oval Offices tapes, hearing a U.S. president cursing like a stevedore, hearing the open contempt in his voice. For a lot of people in this country, I think it confirmed their worst fears about how officialdom really regards them."

Joe took out the cigars his son had given him and offered them round. "I think it's gonna be a helluva long time before people here believe in their leaders again. It's gonna take a man in the White House who recognizes the difficulties, who has what it takes to put back the bridges."

"I think Ed Hersh might have been that man," Joe's son-in-law Phil said.

The old man drew on his cigar. "Nah, he'd have been a caretaker president at best. I tell you, the only decent candidate amongst the lot of them is Gene Bravington. I didn't really take too much notice of him until Hersh dropped out of the picture. I dug up some articles Bravington wrote five or six years back when people first started taking notice of him. He's got damn good ideas. He's got a whole new slant on how to build 'transitional communities' in the inner cities, places where residents can be temporarily rehoused while their own homes are redeveloped. He's figured out a whole new template for urban renewal, down-to-earth solutions to grass-roots problems. He's pretty impressive on a whole range of issues, as a matter of fact."

"But the reality is, surely, that Vandenberg will take the nomination now," Jack said.

His father blew out smoke and sighed. "Well, I hope I'm dead and buried by the time they swear in that sonofabitch."

"What bothers you so much about the guy?"

"He has no vision, Jack, and not one ounce of humanity. Inside, he's a cold, soulless thing. He has no grasp of the social upheavals that are taking place in the world, because people's needs don't interest him. In another time in history we might have survived a Vandenberg presidency, but not now. Look at all this trouble in Miami. That's just the beginning, a mirror of what's happening across the rest of the world. Someone like Bravington, someone from the streets who really identifies with the issues, he's the kind of man we need at the top now."

"And if Vandenberg does get in?"

Joe wiped his mouth with his napkin. "He's a pariah. What's inside him is like a cancer and it'll grow, and some day it'll break out. In my view, putting Vandenberg in the Oval Office will be striking the first blow for global anarchy." He looked at the grave faces around the table. "Hey, come on, this is my birthday. Let's talk about something else."

"No, let's stay with this a minute longer, it interests me," Phil said. "Let's say for one minute, there was no Vandenberg; I still don't believe the electorate is ready to put a black guy in the Oval Office."

"Well, I'm telling you, they've had it up to here with the dummies and scuzzballs they're being handed. Geriatrics with the intellect of a fruit fly, cut-price Kennedys with terminal zipper-osis . . . It's got to the point where you show 'em a guy with what as far as anyone can tell is a clean slate, a solid marriage and a God-fearing family, he's halfway up the steps of the White House before anyone can shout, "Hey mister, what's the master plan?"'

"Do you know something about Vandenberg the rest of us don't?" Jack asked.

"Uhuh."

"Well . . . what?" his daughter asked.

"Someone opened up to me, oh, ten years back now, some old councillor with nothing left to lose. He told me plenty about Lowell C. About how he strong-armed his opponents, the scare tactics he used, blackmail . . . worse. Stuff to keep you awake at night, believe me. I followed up on it, but his people had covered their tracks real well, and in the end the old boy's testimony was all I had. He died of a coronary before I could sew the thing up, and the story died with him. We had a tape, but the *Tribune*'s publishers got nervous. I mean, you don't take on the Vandenberg family lightly. They'd close ranks over something like that, past differences or not. A dead man's word against their megabucks? Well, Lowell C. wasn't big news at the time, and it didn't seem worth the hell. And, before you ask, it doesn't now."

Later that night, Jack Lassiter began to put together his notes for his meeting the next day with the governor of Virginia. Till now Vandenberg had been little more than his wife's boss, a man who, if he cared to admit it, he resented for occupying so much of her time and, as he often suspected, her thoughts. Now Vandenberg began to take on a different persona. Washington people with reason to know considered Joe Lassiter to be one of the shrewdest political analysts of his generation. He'd had his *bêtes noires* before and some of his concerns about them had proved to be unfounded. But never before had Jack heard his father sound off so vehemently, with such icy clarity, about anyone in public life. Perhaps his father was just getting old, spending too much time in his own head. Or maybe he would be proved right. Tomorrow, thought Lassiter, I might get an insight of my own.

"Clear the streets! Clear the streets and return to your homes!"

Black and Hispanic faces tilted skyward and focused their attention on the police helicopter circling overhead.

Armed National Guardsmen, standing back to back, with only a block between, had separated the youths of the two ghettos for more than fifteen hours. The rubble wasteland between them was crammed with police and riot vehicles. Now, as the voice from the bullhorn droned above them, the guards began to force the gangs farther apart. A sea of soldiers in battle fatigues, armed with automatic weapons, their barrels poised inches above the heads of the mobs, seemed to be having the desired effect. Soon the Cuban youths had been pushed back four blocks. The odd small rock or bottle smacked into the guardsmen's ranks but otherwise the physical resistance was token.

Three storys above the jeering mob, a moon-shaped face peered through the railings of the fire escape. Jerry Cardenas had tired of the new videos his mother had bought him hours before. Although he had been twenty-three last birthday, he still had trouble with clocks, but he was hungry now so he knew it had to be close to dinnertime. He hated work days, hated being alone in the apartment hour after hour with nothing to do but watch TV. In the distance to his right, he could see a large black truck. He had one like it. Just like it. He climbed back through the window into the tiny living room and found the remote control troop carrier his mother had bought him for his birthday.

From his perch on the rusty iron platform, he could see soldiers with guns. The noise from the street was deafening now. Momentarily, the mob beneath him halted. Jerry stared transfixed at the line of guns. His mouth fell open, he looked about him excitedly. This was a good game. The boys farther down the block would never let him play with them. But these were new people. They played the games he liked. He hurried back into the apartment and began to rummage through his bedroom closet. There it was, behind those stupid skates he couldn't even stand up in. He pulled the replica M16 from a pile of toys and dusted it off with his sleeve. When the batteries were new, what a noise it had made! Now he would just have to pretend. It looked as good as the soldiers' guns, he assured himself, and that was the main thing, after all.

National Guardsman Errol Trench had done a lot of growing up in the last seven hours. The emotions he felt as he'd faced the Cuban mob across no-man's-land, had had little to do with those he'd read about in *Soldier of Fortune*. The mercenaries who'd kicked ass in Bosnia and Turkestan had made it sound . . . was glamorous the word? Well, a hell of a sight better crack than selling condominiums, anyway. He'd wanted to kick ass ever since he'd been picked on at school. The first day he'd really felt like someone was the day he'd put on his Guard's uniform. He'd stared at himself in the mirror and thought, "Hell, if those shitheels from Medley High could see me now!" He enjoyed his one night a week training, marching up and down the parade ground at battalion headquarters, cracking away on the shooting range. Drinking with the guys afterward.

Nothing, none of it, had prepared him for this. For the churning nausea he felt in the pit of his stomach now as he stood five feet from a mob of Cubans baying for his blood. His finger tightened on the trigger of the M16. They were too close. The officers behind were forcing his detachment forward too fast. How many shots could he get off before these greaseballs got to him? His gut told him not enough. What was holding up the advance, for Christ's sakes? He looked around him. Movement in his peripheral vision caused him to look upward. Three storys above him, on a fire escape, a man stood leveling an automatic rifle at him.

No thought pattern Trench was conscious of had time to register. He was only aware of lifting the M16 to his shoulder, lining up the sights on the man's chest and squeezing off a couple of rounds. For a second, the only sound in the street was the echo of the gunfire. Jerry Cardenas' chest opened up like the doors of an advent calendar. His body was thrown back against the wall of the tenement building and then toppled forward over the railings to land with a crunch on the sidewalk beneath.

Almost without a word, the mob of Cuban youths that formed their front line fell back. As those that stood behind replaced them, they produced guns. Handguns, sawn-off shotguns, automatic weapons of a dozen varieties were pulled from belts, coat pockets, from under jackets. The exchange of fire that followed sprayed and ricocheted round the street in a volley that could be heard ten miles away. As the mob surged forward the Guard attempted to fall back in good order, then turned and broke into a run. A seething, sweating mass of human life stormed through the streets of the ghetto as though someone had proclaimed Armageddon. Those who faltered or fell, were trampled by a hundred feet. Those wounded or exhausted guardsmen who fell off to the side streets were pursued individually and cut down.

Soon no-man's-land was in sight, empty now except for a few police. The remains of the guardsmen and the mob stumbled across the rubble like stampeding cattle. Within minutes, the guards who were herding the black mob back found themselves trapped between two breeds of humanity bent on ripping out each other's hearts. The black contingent had dwindled, many returning to their homes as the mayor had predicted they would. The force with which the Cuban gangs hit those that remained drove the fight deep into the black ghetto. At point-blank range, guns became counter-productive. Knives cut, slashed and dismembered.

Three or four loud whistles sounded amongst the main body of blacks and they all took flight, running full out to the shopping mall on Franklin Street. Soon the walkways through the vast mall that had, until the recession and the rise of violence in the neighborhood, housed a score of chain stores and other retail outlets, rang to the sound of boots and the roar of the mob. At the far end, in what had once been a branch of J. C. Penney, the black contingent turned and waited. There was no fear, no panic. Within seconds the first of the Cubans skidded into the area and took cover. Soon the entire ground floor was filled with Bloods and Flames. Now there was no noise. The Flames, who made up the core of the Cuban force, stood silently staring ahead. In front of them, in the unoccupied ground between the gangs, were more than a hundred and fifty people, kneeling in a frightened hundle. Old people, women, teenagers. All of them Cubans. In their midst was what appeared to be a pile of explosives.

A black man in his early twenties, a ski-mask pulled over his face, moved out onto the floor. There was total silence as all present strained to hear what he was saying.

"One of these people dies every minute there's a Flame on Blood territory." Without ceremony, he put a magnum to the head of an old man, kneeling in front of him, and shot him. An animal howl went up from the watching Cubans. For several seconds the black killer's life hung in the balance. At the front of the mob, Flame leaders consulted. Then, with barely a word, they and their followers began to pull back.

By the time the Bloods were satisfied that their territories were theirs again, thirty-seven of the hostages were dead.

Chesterfield stopped the cassette machine. For several seconds there was complete silence in the dressing room, as its impact began to sink in. The nucleus of the Vandenberg campaign team were used to early morning starts. They were less used to having to address issues that were certain to change the political map of America for the next four years, before their breakfast. At last Chesterfield said, "How did you come by this?"

Vandenberg's eyes never left the mirror. He ran a comb through his hair. "Cal Cochran called me at home around midnight, said he didn't intend to take the rap for this. He made the recording when Governor Travanion called him that evening."

"Isn't Cochran gonna use it himself?"

"I'm sure he will. But he's got an eye on his future. He's giving me what you might call a head start."

Chesterfield twisted around to the only assistant in the room. "Can you get some coffee and bagels in here?" The man hurried up the corridor that flanked Studio Four of the CBS Building in New York City, to dispatch one of the chauffeurs to a deli. Chesterfield began to talk more freely. "Are we absolutely certain that's Travanion's voice?" he asked Lacy.

"I made a copy of sample phrases only and gave them to Soundtronics two hours ago. I had their chief engineer come in specially, and he ran a comparison test using one of Travanion's own sound bites. He's quite certain it's his voice, and there's no evidence that the tape's been tampered with."

Political adviser Walt MacDermott yawned. "Nobody in the Travanion camp is denying that he and the mayor spoke. But the spin they're putting out is that the governor . . . " He ran his finger down the fax in front of him. "' . . . only acquiesed to Mayor Cochran's call for troops to take peremptory action because it was impressed on him that the mayor had specialist knowledge of this kind of scenario.'"

Chesterfield rocked back in his chair and rubbed his eyes. "Horseshit." He stretched the word for emphasis. "Do CBS know what we have?" he asked Lacy.

"How else do you think I got Lowell on 'This Morning'?"

Chesterfield's face looked as grave as anyone present had ever seen it. "Well, I hope to fuck you know what you're doing."

Lacy looked like he'd just swallowed a canary.

"God knows I don't want to be seen as making political capital out of a catastrophe like this, but Travanion just shot himself in the head, Ches. He's shown himself for what he is, a manic. He's unelectable. And our man got the goods on him. The primaries are over. Unless the Republicans can work some kind of miracle, sell the party on some new killer nominee in about ten minutes flat, they're out of the loop. I don't want to sound complacent but . . . "

Chesterfield got up and made for the door. "I don't want to hear it, Lacy," he snapped. "Not today. Not today, all right?"

Vandenberg eased himself into the chair to the right of the anchor man, taking care to trap the hem of his jacket under his butt, to prevent the collar from bunching around his neck. A makeup girl gave his forehead a final brush over to cut down the reflection of the studio lights and the floor manager chanted the countdown. Vandenberg breathed deeply and evenly, like an athlete limbering up for a race, as the anchor man went straight into the top story—the riots in Miami.

A partially live report included aerial shots of the city. Smoke from hundreds of fires rose in columns from an urban battlefield. Further footage showed firemen being stoned by gangs of youths, looters climbing over piles of debris, bodies lying in lines on a church hall floor.

The director cut back to the studio. "With me is the man many in this country believe will take the Democratic nomination at the party's convention in July, Governor Lowell C. Vandenberg." The anchor man turned to his guest. "This morning the nation is stunned and appalled by the worst violence seen in this country since the Chicago riots, last year. Experts on civil disorder are saying that City Mayor Calvin Cochran mishandled the situation from the beginning . . . "

"I'm very clear that Mayor Cochran did everything in his power to diffuse the situation. The reason that we have a hundred and eighty-six Americans dead this morning is that State Governor Matthew Travanion ordered a totally inexperienced battalion of the National Guard into a very sensitive trouble spot."

"You have evidence to support that?"

"We're talking here about the worst bloodshed on American soil in living memory. I'm not here to muddy the waters, believe me. I have irrefutable evidence to support what I'm telling you. The mayor, I know, made it clear in a telephone call to the governor yesterday evening that he thought that any peremptory action on the part of the National Guard would have disastrous consequences. He also told him that the police were concerned for the safety of a large number of Cuban-Americans who had been reported missing in the area. The plain fact is . . . "

"But Governor Vandenberg . . . "

" . . . The plain fact is that Travanion ignored these concerns and ordered the Guard in. Had he waited for further information on the missing people to come through, he would have learned that they had been taken as hostages, and would have been forced to take a much more considered view."

"But I fail to see . . . "

"Are you aware that because of spending cutbacks made by this administration, the National Guardsmen that were deployed last night had received less than fifty hours' training each, less than five in riot control?"

"It's hard to see how you can lay the blame on

the military, when what you had here was two of the most vicious gangs in the country . . . "

"Only a small percentage of the people identified from police video, taken before the riot, have any previously known gang involvement. The fact is that neither community made any move on the other until troops moved in. It was Mayor Cochran's view, explicitly declared, that this incident would have petered out by itself. I think he was right."

Vandenberg now turned directly to camera. "I believe the terrible loss of life was a direct result of judgment error on the part of the state governor. Seventeen children died last night. If one of them had been mine, I know what I'd be feeling right now."

In Rockville, Jack Lassiter reached forward and turned off the TV. He opened the kitchen door, walked out onto the back porch and took a deep breath. Gradually the churning nausea began to subside.

That night, Vandenberg returned to Hague House for the first time in a week. He ate alone in the family den and called his wife in L.A., where she'd been attending a teachers' convention, to bring her up to date on the day's events. Whilst the political news of the last twenty-four hours replayed on the video wall, he made some calculations. The Hersh offensive had been a very expensive exercise, he concluded. And worth every nickel.

The secret report on the pedophile ring that

had already entrapped Bryce Mather had proved invaluable again. It had led the governor to another lawyer, a man called Samitz, who had, as friends or clients, a number of Hersh's key supporters, one of whom was Elizabeth Randolphi. Satisfied that only Samitz would ever know that he was behind all that would come to pass, and that the lawyer could be relied on to remain silent for fear of being exposed as a pedophile, Vandenberg had him set in motion a chain of blackmail and bribery that had culminated in the scam that had wrecked Hersh's presidential hopes.

The result of that endeavor was reason enough to celebrate. But the riots . . . Every campaign needed a little luck, he thought as he poured himself red wine. And the Miami mess had certainly been that.

The internal phone rang. It was Marianne. "God, are you still here?" he said.

"The press have been blocking the switchboard for six hours. Vernon and his crew are almost on the floor, so I'm just trying to spread the load a little. I need to check the revised schedule with you."

"Bring it down to the viewing theater."

Marianne stood at the door, and looked around a little uncertainly. In all the years she'd worked for Vandenberg, she'd never before been asked into his private sanctum.

"What do you think I have in here, blue movies?"

Marianne looked at the video wall. "Very impressive. I always wondered what those guys in the library under here did all day. Now I know."

Vandenberg poured them both red wine. "At the end of the day, when I just can't absorb any more reports or projections, I use this. The moving image is about the only thing left that still registers."

She leaned back against the door. "I know how you feel. By this time, most nights, I'm brain-dead. Still only another eight months to go, huh?" They both laughed. "I don't suppose presidential assistants have it any easier . . . " She looked embarrassed. "Oh . . . well, that's rather presupposing that you'll want to take me with you . . . I mean, if everything goes the way we think it will."

"I can envisage a whole lot of changes, but I certainly hadn't thought of you as being one of them. God, without you, my whole life would fall apart."

"Oh, come on."

"I picked you, Marianne, because I saw the way you were with your father." He walked across to her and his voice softened. "I saw the way you handled his friends, his enemies, everyone he came in contact with. You wrapped a protective wall around him, of caring and loving . . . I don't know, I just thought to myself, when she's ready . . . I want some of that."

Her eyes looked deeply into his. Her head moved forward and she kissed him. He slipped his hand around her waist and pressed his mouth to hers, locking the door behind them with the other hand. Soon she felt that hand between her legs, her back arched as it pressed deeper.

She struggled out of her underclothes and he tipped her back into the leather chair, opened her with his fingers and began to kiss her.

All she knew in her conscious mind was that she wanted this man, had for a long time. In some

distant part of her, she was clear that in touching
her, kissing her as he did now, he was putting at risk
all he had striven for. But that must mean that he
truly knew who she was, and trusted her implicitly,
and this . . . this was a measure of that trust.

The video wall behind him multiplied the faces
of the bereaved, around them, the wreckage
wrought by the Miami rioters. Cuban women
shrieked and tore at their hair as the broken bodies
of their children were brought out of the rubble.
Their cries, rising into the seemingly airless box of
darkness that encased the couple, mixed with
Vandenberg's own.

TWENTY-ONE

Marianne emerged through the ring of Corinthian columns that dominated the reception hall of Hague House and she greeted her husband coldly. "What's the matter with you?" Lassiter asked as she hurried him down a wide corridor that led into the heart of the house.

"Well, frankly, I don't much relish the prospect of having my boss grilled by my husband."

She feels protective of him. How touching, Lassiter thought. Or maybe she's just embarrassed by the situation. "I'm not grilling anyone, I've told you that. I genuinely need the man's help on an investigation that's running out of steam. That's all there is to it."

"Well, I hope so. This is the governor's first day off in three weeks. If he was to think I've set him up for something . . . "

"Relax."

She put her weight against a set of swing doors and they moved into a kitchen. No scenic route for the U.S. Customs officer, Lassiter thought. Relegated to the staff areas. Someone's told Marianne to keep me out of sight.

The scale and layout of the kitchen belonged more to a hotel than to a private home. Marianne hurried him down a line of stainless-steel units. At the far end, two chefs stood at what looked like a Nineties version of the old-fashioned kitchen range. As Lassiter approached, they turned, and he saw to his astonishment, that the taller of the two was Lowell Vandenberg. Apart from jeans, he was dressed entirely in chef's whites. "Good morning, Jack. This is our chef, Raoul Toller." They shook hands. "I've heard a great deal about you."

"That sounds ominous." Vandenberg was a good deal taller and better built than Lassiter had realized.

"Not in the least." The governor turned back to his saucepans. "Do you cook?" he asked.

"I used to. Used to enjoy it very much."

"Cooking relaxes me. It's one of the few things that does." He turned the gas a little lower. "This is a Polynesian dish, a family favorite. A kind of elaborate chicken curry. This the crucial stage— adding the pineapple to the sauce. If the gas is a fraction too high, it curdles." The chef began to stir as Vandenberg added the fruit. "Poor Raoul, he waits weeks for me to get back here so he can fix me one of his delights, and the first thing I do is put on an apron and cook for myself."

Yup, life's a bitch, Lassiter thought.

Vandenberg tasted the mixture, mused for a moment, then put a wooden spoon into the pan and offered it to Lassiter. "A little light on cumin, what do you think?"

While the agent let the flavor register he wondered whether to mention that to add a little cornflour would remove the risk of curdling. Instead he replied, "It's the ground coriander that's not coming through to me."

Vandenberg checked again, then nodded slowly. He passed his spoon to Raoul. "You know I think he's right." Without waiting for the chef's opinion, he took a glass jar and sprinkled a little of the dark seed into the pot. With that, he took off his apron and white tunic and made for the door, beckoning for Lassiter to follow.

"I know the kind of schedule you must be on, Governor. It's good of you to see me at such short notice."

Vandenberg's arm slapped at the air, as if to say, "Think nothing of it."

"I hope you don't mind me using my wife to get to see you. This is an official matter but it's a German case. My local staff have no involvement in it, so I had to use whatever resources I could."

Vandenberg led him into his office on the second floor of the new wing. "It's not a problem. So, tell me, how can I help?"

Lassiter settled himself into a leather armchair. "I caught a profile on you on German TV at the weekend."

"I hope it was better than the one NBC did this week. Very sloppily put together. They got dates wrong, all kinds of stuff." Vandenberg was clearly in a garrulous mood. "They had me being handed over to the Red Cross in November 1940, instead of May '41. And yet they still used the line about it being the same day the British sank the *Bismarck*. Jesus! You'd think with all those researchers . . . "

As he spoke, Lassiter studied him. The dominant features were unquestionably the eyes. There was something very familiar about them that he couldn't place. "I believe your father was interned at the labor camp at Schrobenhausen," he said at last.

"That's right."

"Well, that was of particular interest to me because I'd just learned that a man who's central to the case I'm working on was the commandant there at that time."

"Rathenau—he must be well over seventy now."

"Late seventies. In his fifties he handled a number of major money-laundering operations for the head of the Stasi—the old East German Security Police. The trouble is, even the most recent of the deals was put in place more than ten years ago, so it's been hard to get a line on him."

"Where do I come into this?"

"According to my source, Rathenau was very adept at getting wealthy prisoners to part with their life savings. I read that details of bank accounts opened by your father in Switzerland, not long before the German occupation of Holland, disappeared later in the war, and it occurred to me you may well have taken a close look at this Rathenau in the course of your own investigations and have valuable information on file." Lassiter held up his hand. "Let me say straightaway that my department has no interest whatever in you or your own finances. My sole reason for being here is that this man has gone to great lengths to keep his past under wraps and we're desperate for any information that could help us to trace him."

Vandenberg settled back into his chair and

thought for a while. Then he said, "Nothing would give me greater pleasure than to see that sonofabitch behind bars, but I'm not at all sure I can be of much help. Most of the detective work was carried out by my late uncle in the Fifties and early Sixties. It's all on file here somewhere. You're welcome to take a look at it, of course. But as for Rathenau, if you're suggesting that he was implicated in the disappearance of my father's money, I can tell you that my uncle looked into that possibility thoroughly."

"I'm sure he did."

"The Simon Wiesenthal Center has the records kept by Adolf Eichmann's office through the whole period, listing property and valuables confiscated from Schrobenhausen prisoners. It's one of the few files of that nature that are reasonably intact. My father's name is not there."

"And your investigations went no further in that direction?"

"Not as I remember."

Lassiter sighed. "Well, then this looks like being a very short meeting."

"Do you know something about Rathenau I don't?" Vandenberg asked.

"Not for certain, no. I have a theory. I think that Rathenau got his hands on your father's money and the reason it doesn't show up in the official records is that he kept it for himself."

Vandenberg frowned. "What makes you believe that?"

"Two weeks ago I interviewed a Ukrainian, now living in England. He was an SS guard at Schrobenhausen at the time your father was a prisoner there. He told me that Rathenau had what he referred to as 'pet prisoners,' ones he suspected had hidden their valuables before their arrest. He extorted their secrets from them and salted away whatever he got his hands on, for himself."

It was immediately clear to the Customs agent that this was the first Vandenberg had heard of any of this. His mouth set into a hard line, his brow into a frown. Then he turned for the door and bellowed down the corridor for coffee. When he turned back to Lassiter, his face was in repose again, but his eyes were as flat as a beached bass. The half-smile that had played around the corner of his mouth throughout the meeting was gone. "And this Ukrainian believes my father was a . . . 'pet prisoner'?"

"I never got a chance to ask him that. The man was killed in a shooting incident shortly after I interviewed him, probably by one of the wartime comrades-in-arms he was busy fingering to the authorities at the time."

Vandenberg nodded slowly. "Well, in the end, we simply came to the conclusion that my father had hidden the numbers of his Swiss bank accounts somewhere or committed them to memory and that the details had died with him. Your theory throws a whole different light on the matter. Is that Rathenau's file?"

"Yes."

"May I see?" Lassiter passed him the buff-colored folder. The governor took it and walked toward the French doors that looked out onto the gardens.

"May I call my office?" Lassiter asked.

"Sure. Use the white phone." Vandenberg opened the file. Clipped to the first page was the photograph taken from Mrs. Hofle's album. Next to it was the computer simulation showing Rathenau as he probably looked now. Vandenberg swayed back, struggling for air. For a second it felt as though someone had rammed a boathook through his ribcage. He steadied himself and took a quick glance over his shoulder. The Customs agent was occupied with his phone call. Vandenberg took a deep breath and returned his attention to the file.

"Is there any chance someone here could hunt out the Rathenau stuff by the weekend?" Lassiter asked, when he'd hung up. "You see, I'm going back to Berlin on Friday."

By now Vandenberg had regained some of his composure. "I'll get someone on to it straightaway. As I've said, I think you'll find what we have very unrewarding. I will say this." He forced a smile. "If you do track him down, my own people would be very interested in talking to him."

When Marianne had seen Lassiter out, Vandenberg locked the office door from the inside. He switched off the phone and slumped back into his chair. How long he sat there in the fading light, he was uncertain, but when he got up to visit his drinks cabinet, the face he caught sight of in the lacquered Chinese mirror that hung above it was drained of color. The light suntan left his skin a pale sepia hue. That's how I'll look when they bury me, he thought absently.

He took a decanter from the cupboard and with shaking hands poured himself a large cognac. How could I have been so naïve? he asked himself. The old man's story was so full of holes it was barely plausible, but I never thought to question it. All I saw was the money. I offered my gratitude to a man who almost certainly sent my father to his grave.

He sipped the brandy. Why has this man come so far, after all these years, to offer me money he stole from my family almost half a century ago? He wants something in return. There can be no other answer.

I could simply lift the phone, call Lassiter, and tell him where to find his precious Herr Rathenau this very minute . . . And put everything I've worked for at risk. The existence of my father's money would be known instantly. Yet if the old German can be believed at all, the whole beauty of those accounts is that not another living soul, other than the banks that hold them, have any concrete knowledge of them.

From the first minute the old man had presented him with details of his father's fortune, Vandenberg had known that every dream he'd had could be fulfilled. With a little ingenuity, sums larger than the whole of his previous budget could be drawn from the accounts and filtered into his flagging campaign without him being implicated in any way. He could mount a TV offensive, take his platform to the American people, on a scale of which even Ross Perot could have only dreamed. And there could be no cries that Billionaire Vandenberg had simply bought the election, he'd told himself, for he alone would know the truth.

But now it was clear that Rathenau had not only lied about his identity, about his whole role in Paul Vandenberg's life and death, but had given his son a totally distorted view of his own financial dealings, no doubt just the part he considered he needed to hear. From what Lassiter had said, there was in fact a third face to this odious old German: he'd been a money launderer for the head of the Stasi—and who knew who else?—involved in a case sufficiently important to the German authorities to justify bringing in a top U.S. Customs agent to help solve it!

Vandenberg sank a little lower into his chair. *If they ever get access to Rathenau's records they could well get a trace on my father's money's too. Even uncover the connection between him and me . . . So the money has to stay where it is.*

"Damnit to hell!" Vandenberg slammed down the brandy glass, breaking the stem. He ground the sharp end into the polished wood of the desk. Then he put his head in his hands. There was a knock at the door.

"Are you okay, Governor?" It was Marianne.

"I'm . . . okay," he called back after a moment. He knew now that even to see the German again was to hazard everything he had worked for. But as that thought crystallized, a resolute voice from that part of his mind where his key decisions had always been taken was urging him to do just that. There were too many questions still unanswered. His thoughts turned back to Lassiter. Was there more to his visit than he had revealed? Although Vandenberg's gut told him that the Customs agent had probably leveled with him, was it safe to assume that he knew nothing about the money in the Swiss banks? Was Lassiter simply waiting for a withdrawal to set a trace in operation?

Daker must watch him. With directional audio surveillance he could tap in to almost any conversation Lassiter had. He checked his watch and began to dial a number in Cairo.

☆   ☆   ☆

There was a fax from Fraenkel waiting for Lassiter at the Rockville house. East German tax records had established that a man called Conrad Vollman—the alias Rathenau had been known to use, according to his Stasi file card—had lived at an address in Leipzig as recently as two years ago. The family now living there had never met the rinser face to face and had no knowledge of his current whereabouts, but thought the law firm they had used in the conveyancing might still have an address for him. The firm had since dissolved but Fraenkel was trying to trace the partner who had handled the sale.

Lassiter screwed up the fax and threw it in the trash. At the same moment, the phone rang. It was Marianne. "How did it go with the governor?" she asked. He sensed the same tension in her voice as before.

"Fine."

"What did you ask him?"

"To hunt out some papers he has on this man Rathenau that I'm looking for."

"You must have said more than that."

"Why?"

"He seems very distracted. I don't know what you . . . "

"Good God, Marianne, what are you, the man's wet nurse?"

"Don't shout at me, Jack."

"If he's looking like someone burst his balloon, it's probably because he's realized that if his investigators had looked a little more thoroughly into Rathenau, thirty-some years ago, he might be sitting on poppa's millions today."

"You don't give a damn if there's a knock-on effect for me here, do you?"

Lassiter sighed. "I don't want to fight with you, Marianne. I want to straighten things out between us. That's why . . . "

"As far you're concerned, my career is just a fucking irritation, isn't it? If you had your way, I'd be pushing a baby carriage around the park all day. Filling my life with shopping catalogues and . . . "

"You make it sound like the worst thing in the world."

"Look, you want to know why I didn't want a child when you did? It was because, at the time, I didn't think our relationship could stand it. And I didn't think you were stable enough to be a father. Okay, I can see now that was probably wrong, it might have sorted out a lot of things for you. But not for me. I've spent my whole adult life running around after people. My father . . . you . . . "

"Vandenberg?"

"Him too. Don't you understand? I need to do something for me now. If the governor becomes president, he means to find some kind of executive position for me, where I count for something in my own right. You always used to say, 'I want to make a difference somehow.' Well, that need isn't exclusive to you. I have a real chance to make something of my life now, and babies are just not . . . "

"Part of the schedule?"

"You make it sound a little cold-blooded but . . . no, not for a long while."

"And neither am I, you're saying. I'm glad we've had this talk, Marianne. I have a lot of decisions to make, and at least now I'm clear about one of them. Leopold is still your attorney, isn't he? I'll have mine call him. I enjoyed loving you, Marianne, more than you'll ever know. Be happy, you deserve it." Lassiter rang off.

The phone rang several times that evening. He didn't take the calls, and the caller left no messages. It had to be Marianne, but he needed time to cool off, to think things through. Why was she so fired up about what I said to her boss? he asked himself. Was she just worried about losing her precious promotion, or was this something far more personal? He drank near his limit and went to bed early. Predictably, the 4 A.M. anxiety attack arrived right on time. Lassiter paced the house and tried to get his thoughts off his wife and back on to the case.

No matter what Vandenberg believed his uncle's papers on Rathenau would show, they could still yield a line on Mielke's rinser. And something the governor had said at the beginning of their meeting was scratching away at the backdoor of his mind, now. Something about the CNN profile. Vandenberg was pissed at them over their sloppy research. " . . . They got dates wrong, all kinds of stuff. Had me being handed over to the Red Cross in November 1940, instead of May '41 . . . " Was that it? What was the last bit? " . . . They still used the line about it being the same day the British sank the *Bismarck* . . . "

Where had he heard that line before? And what possible relevance did it have to the case he was working on?

TWENTY-TWO

For the third time that morning Vandenberg heard a voice on the line announce, "The Cairo Hilton."

"Marlon Gable in 737, please."

Vandenberg waited and was about to hang up the gas station pay phone when a rather breathless voice said, "Gable."

"It's me."

"Oh . . . hold on a minute." A hand was clapped over the phone. Vandenberg could hear Daker trying to convey some kind of instruction.

"Who's with you?

"A two-hundred-dollar hooker, that's who. Can I call you back?"

"This won't take long."

"Well, every second we talk I'm losing expensive cocksucking time."

"Tell her to stop the meter or something."

"Very funny."

"What kind of name is Marlon Gable, for fuck sake?"

"A name I like, that's what."

"Listen, I got another job for you."

The hooker was obviously still plying her trade. There was a pause and some heavy breathing at the other end of the line, then Daker said, "Yeah, if it was anything like the last one, you can keep it. That business with the kid really got to me. Christ I . . . "

"No, it's nothing like that. Straight surveillance . . . I take it the lady with you speaks no English."

There was a dirty laugh. "No, only the language of love. Okay; who, where and how much?"

"A U.S. Customs agent, on secondment to the German treasury."

"Oh, a nice, low risk assignment. I can't go to Germany and you know it. And even if I could, I'm not gonna start messing with those jerks."

Vandenberg was suddenly aware that the balance of power had shifted. Daker was getting rich and lazy. There was no respect in his voice any more. "You don't have to 'mess' with him. I just want him watched." The governor thought for a moment and said, "Have you been following the riots in Miami?"

"Yeah, I caught some of it . . . What's that got to do with anything?"

"The Republican front-runner is out of the loop, Daker. They're screwed. They have no one credible they can field at this late stage. I've got the Democratic nomination pretty much sewn up now. The *Washington Post, Newsweek* and *Time* are predicting a landslide in November . . . "

"Okay, I get the picture. It's Hail to the Chief from here on in."

No respect. "My first appointment would be Barry Macduff as head of the FBI." Daker was unimpressed. "There are a lot of big ifs here, I accept that, but once he's in place he owes me a lot of favors, and we could work something out—take you off the Active file."

Daker wasn't stupid. He knew Vandenberg was winging it. But what the hell, it sounded good.

"Christ, LBJ did it for the Mafia bosses who got him on the ticket with Kennedy in '60. Nixon did it all the time."

"And you're saying I could come back to the States then?"

"Eventually, yes."

"Well, it's a nice idea, but it doesn't get me through German immigration."

"One of the passports you're carrying is Irish isn't it?"

"Uhuh."

"Okay; fly to Barcelona, Spain, using any identity but your own. They have no extradition treaty with the U.S., so even in the unlikely event they pick up on you, going through immigration there is a very low-risk option. Then drive across France to Germany. All three are EC countries; show your Irish passport and they'll just wave you through. No details are taken, no checks are made."

Daker was impressed. "You have been busy. I could still end up spending a couple of hot nights in a Spanish jail."

"For what I'm offering, it'd be a small price to pay."

☆   ☆   ☆

"Are we going to Hague House?"

The swarthy, heavy-set man at the wheel of the shabby Chevrolet glanced at his mirror for the third time in a minute. "No, sir. The governor is at another of his properties today."

The old German gripped the seat in front of him as the car swung left again. Whoever this chauffeur is, he thought, he's certainly taking no chances on being followed. Why is Vandenberg being so careful?

Fifteen minutes later, the car turned onto what appeared at first sight to be a derelict lot. A narrow lane to the right took them into the forecourt of a complex of low buildings. There had once been an electric sign above the doorway. The mark left on the wall by the letters spelled "Fulton Film Services." The chauffeur guided the German inside and took him down a dark winding staircase to the basement. He turned the handle of a heavy door and they moved into an editing suite. Vandenberg sat with his back to them at a Moviola. "Sorry to bring you all the way out here, Herr Vollman," he said. "Tomorrow I'm back on the campaign trail. I have to fly to Wyoming at seven. This is my last opportunity to check out some footage."

The German threw up his arms. "I have all the time in the world. Well, all that God chooses to give me." He looked about him. "What is this place?"

"Till the early Eighties, it was one of the best film libraries in the state, perhaps in the country. It'd been a family business since the Thirties." Vandenberg pulled a length of 35mm footage out from a spool on the machine and began to thread it up. "It'd been losing money for years. Most of the other outfits in the game were transferring everything to video. For these people, that simply wasn't an option. I bought the place about six years ago. Whenever I get a chance, I come down here and run through stuff, try and decide what's worth transferring. You'd be surprised what you can turn up. Like this for example."

Grainy black and white footage of some kind of military convoy filled the small screen on the editing machine. There was a shot of trucks entering a prison camp. Pale skeletal men in loincloths gathered around Red Cross workers. "This is the liberation of the camp at Schrobenhausen. None of the networks here seem to have footage of their own of this. They keep dredging up stuff about my childhood, and using footage of other camps. So I thought I should hunt this out." There was silence as they watched the film together. Soldiers, with handkerchiefs clasped to their faces, picked their way through piles of corpses.

"This must bring back very strange memories for you," Vandenberg said.

The old man studied the faces of a group of survivors as Red Cross workers gently held cups to their mouths. "Yes."

The same men were shown, a few days later, sitting at trestle tables, eating their first full meal in months. Some rolled up the sleeves of their brand-new U.S. fatigues to show journalists their prison number tattooed on their left forearm.

"I suppose some memories must fade after a time, but that mark is a reminder for life."

"It can be removed surgically," the German said.

"Is that what you had done?"

"Yes. But after all . . . "

"Show me."

The old man looked shaken. "What?"

"Show me the scar on your forearm." Vandenberg's face was impassive but the chill in his voice made it clear this was not a request but a demand.

"I . . . "

"If you were in Schrobenhausen with my father, show me." The German just sat there. Vandenberg grabbed his left arm with one hand, and the razor blade, used for editing, with the other, and slit the sleeve of his jacket to the elbow. He ripped back the shirt and turned the man's thin wrist to the light.

The old man wrenched back his arm and pulled himself to his feet. He stood there, swaying uncertainly, trying to catch his breath.

"No tattoo was ever removed from your forearm, Herr Vollman." They stared at one another for a moment. "I daresay you did have a number removed. But from your left armpit. That is where an SS officer has his blood group tattooed, isn't it?"

The old German's eyes flickered and he collapsed into the chair.

"You were no communist, no slave laborer at Schrobenhausen," Vandenberg continued. "You were the commandant at the camp. That's how you came to know my father."

The old man stared at the flickering images on the screen awhile longer and then nodded slowly. He began in a haltering voice. At first Vandenberg had to strain to hear what he was saying.

"Your father and those with him were detained at the docks in Amsterdam on suspicion of carrying false papers. They were using the name 'Sonntag.' Intelligence sources soon established that the papers had been bought on the black market. The real Sonntags were long dead. They all maintained their silence, but German racial experts confirmed that at least three of the group they were holding were Jews. In those days that was all that mattered. They were sent to concentration camps. You and your mother to Dachau, your father to Schrobenhausen. The young fit prisoners at my camp were used as slave labor at an underground factory nearby. I recognized your father the day he arrived. At first I could not put a name to the face, but later I remembered that we had met once briefly, before the war."

The old man seemed almost relieved to be telling the truth at last. "I knew that Paul Vandenberg was an American by birth and one of the richest men in Europe. He knew that to make that admission would positively identify the four arrested with him and expose them to extortion and torture. My first thought was that if your father and his family could fall so easily into German hands, the probability was that his personal fortune was still somewhere in Europe too, almost certainly in numbered bank accounts. I knew that if I could locate the Vandenberg millions for the German Reich, I could advance my own career. I said nothing to my superiors because I wanted this to be my victory alone. I interrogated your father, week after week, but he resolutely refused to say anything. He was a very courageous man, Mr. Vandenberg. For the good of the others . . ."

Vandenberg stood up. "*Save it!* Just tell me what happened."

"As the months went by, I heard nothing from Berlin about handing this man over, and it occurred to me that I alone knew his real identity . . . "

As the old man spoke of events that had taken place more than fifty years before, it was as though some part of his mind had traveled back through the decades to the camp itself . . .

"*Look at me! Look at me when I'm talking to you!* This is a picture of you, I believe." Sturmbannführer Rathenau turned the magazine around and passed it across the bare wooden table. The man with the pale cadaverous face opposite him gave it a cursory look and returned his gaze to the floor. "The Paris Motor Show, 1938—a rare sighting of the great man, yes?" The German softened his voice. "I was there too. The new Mercedes was the star of the event, I seem to remember." Rathenau stared out of the window of the wooden hut that served as his office, and across the compound of the camp. "You are in a fortunate position in one respect alone, Mr. Vandenberg. Currently, it would seem that I am the only member of the Reich that has this information. Were it otherwise, you would have been handed over to the Gestapo long ago, and forced to give them details of your Dutch assets."

A small beetle had appeared from the skirting board of the hut and was making its way across the floor. Prisoner A3709 studied it.

"Failure to comply with the Gestapo would have caused pressure to be exerted on those arrested with you." Rathenau's tone was conversational. The two men might have been bank manager and client. "To identify yourself would have, in turn, identified your father-in-law, a wealthy Jewish jeweler, I understand. I've no doubt the Gestapo would have gone to some lengths to find out what he had hidden away too. Which is precisely why you so resolutely refuse to admit who you are. You are to be admired. But I have some news which may cause you to reconsider your position."

In the far distance, a squad of Ukrainian guards was dragging exhausted prisoners onto the back of an open truck. Rathenau watched them. They could barely stand, much less work; their usefulness to the Reich was over. "I have colleagues at the Dachau camp. I have made discreet enquiries with regard to your wife and child. The boy has typhus. He will last a matter of days unless he receives expert medical care."

Still Prisoner A3709 gave no visible indication that the news had any relevance for him. He continued to study the beetle's progress across the office floor. How shiny and black he was, the man thought. How confident.

"There is a Red Cross center at the Swiss border, near Zurich. My influence in this matter is limited. I can do nothing for your wife and her parents, but I might be able to arrange for the child to be got to safety. It will take money, a very great deal. Only I and one other will be involved. He will know nothing of your real identity."

Slowly the prisoner's head turned. His sunken eyes locked with Rathenau's. There was still great strength in them. In the far distance, there was the rattle of machine-gun fire. The eyes did not flinch. At last he said, "Why should I trust you?" He spoke

German with a Dutch accent. There was no indication that he was American.

Rathenau got up and paced the office. "Write to your wife, explaining that your child will be taken to the Red Cross in Zurich. I will see to it that she gets it and that she is allowed to write a reply."

"That guarantees me nothing."

"It will show that your wife and child are still alive and that I am telling you the truth about his condition. And that I can reach them."

The prisoner's bony shoulders lifted for a second.

"You will then give me details of some of the numbered accounts I know you have, I suspect in Switzerland. When I am certain that the amounts I shall have access to are sufficient, I will put the rest of the plan into action."

Rathenau took a packet of cigarettes from his pocket and offered the prisoner one. He stared at it, took one with shaking fingers and put it to his lips. The commandant lit it with a small gold lighter. "You will write another letter to the senior administrator of the Red Cross in Zurich, identifying your child, with instructions to pass it to whomsoever you wish. I will see to it that they provide you with notification that the baby arrived safely." Now the beetle was moving down the join between two floorboards. The prisoner's eyes never left it. "You will then provide me with details of further account numbers, giving me access to a previously agreed amount."

Silence.

"I don't know if you are familiar with the symptoms of typhus. The first signs . . . "

As Rathenau spoke, the beetle found a knothole

between the floorboards. It slipped through and disappeared from sight. Paul Vandenberg rose to his feet. "Enough . . . Give me some paper . . . "

The old man raised his eyes to look at Lowell Vandenberg. "The letter I gave you the first time we met—your mother's reply—is the one that I brought to your father from Dachau. Later, I also gave him a letter from the Red Cross as promised. Twice, your father sat down and, from memory, produced lists of numbered accounts he held in Switzerland. Of course, they were all I needed to gain access to the funds they contained." Rathenau's eyes glazed over again. "By this time there had been changes in my own life. My wife had been killed in the bombing of Essen . . . my whole attitude to the Nazi cause had begun to change. I no longer believed any good could come from the war. Now, I had no intention of handing the money over to my masters. I knew it must all stay where it was until the war was over, but then I would be a very wealthy man."

Rathenau's voice was beginning to crack. "Is it possible I could have a glass of water?" Vandenberg found a glass, filled it from a basin and gave it to him. He drank for a moment, then he said, "By 1945, the underground site at Schrobenhausen had been turned over to housing art treasures and gold bullion. I spent much of the time in Berlin, organizing shipments. I was given an office in what has become known as Bunker Two. I had put a list of the account numbers into a bank deposit box. But in the closing weeks of the war, when it was certain that the city would fall to the Allies, I feared the end might come too quickly for such measures to be sufficient. I committed as many numbers as possible to memory, then made a coded list and put it, together with other papers, where I knew it would be within reach at all times. My office might have been searched at any point, so I hid the envelope inside the Bunker's main air duct, in the pump room at end of a corridor.

"Soon after that, Berlin fell. In the last moments, the concrete roof of the corridor beyond my office was pierced by a bomb. I was cut off from the pump room by a wall of debris. The Russians were closing in. I had to make a run for it. I went down in the shelling—hit in the back of the head by something not sharp enough to kill me. When I came to, in a Russian internment camp, I didn't know who I was. Gradually, much of my memory returned, but the numbers of the accounts did not.

"All day as I lay there, I could hear the firing squads. They were executing SS and Gestapo. I knew it could not be long before my turn came to die. I thought of the cave at Schrobenhausen with its art treasures and bullion. I decided to trade what I knew with my captors for my life. I even took them to the site and showed them the concealed entrance. How much of the booty they found inside I don't know, but I was spared the firing squad. I was interned in Russia for two years. When they finally released me in 1947, Berlin was a mass of rubble. Nothing remained of the bank where I'd kept my deposit box. A concrete road had been laid over the site of Bunker Two. I gave up hope of ever retrieving my secret envelope. Then, a few years ago, engineers working in the area accidentally broke into one half of the complex. I read everything I could find on the discovery. It was clear that the collapsed corridor, beyond what I was certain was my old office, was still impassable. Later, I believe the whole area was filled in with concrete. Then, six months ago, work started on the Berlin Hassler Hotel, right over the second half of the bunker. When I read that the new building would have underground parking, I knew that sooner or later the pump room would be exposed. I decided that I would be there when it was. I was, of course, too old to retrieve the documents myself. There was a Bosnian I knew, who'd been helpful to me in the past. He went to Berlin and found the envelope. An engineer was killed in an accident in the exposed part of the bunker the following day. From the newspaper report I saw, it seemed unclear as to why he'd gone down there. I wondered for a while if he'd found evidence of the Bosnian's expedition. But there were no comebacks."

It was now dark outside. The only light in the room came from the screen of the old Moviola. Vandenberg sat for a long time staring at his hands. Then he asked, "So what happened to my parents?"

"You must understand, your mother's fate was out of my hands. She went to the gas chambers with thousands of others, weeks after you were taken to Switzerland."

"And you had my father worked to death?"

"Very soon after, he contracted pneumonia. He developed a number of complications . . . "

Vandenberg's eyes connected with Rathenau's for the first time. "And you let him die."

Rathenau looked away and rubbed his forehead with a trembling hand. At last he said, "You see now why I had to invent the story I did. You would never have agreed to see me, to hear me out, had you known any of this."

TWENTY-THREE

Lassiter sat bolt upright in bed, the echo of his shriek still ringing in his ears. The dream again. He put his head in his hands and tried to rerun the last few moments of the nightmare. The face of the killer was usually blurred or turned away from him, but this time it had been clear. Those cruel eyes that had haunted a thousand nights had stared incuriously across at him again. And then they had changed. The look was the same, but now they were Lowell Vandenberg's eyes . . .

The instant Lassiter had come face to face with the man who might soon be president, he had noticed his eyes—green, flecked with brown. Powerful, searing eyes. But there was something at the center . . . something unutterably cold, devoid of humanity, and somehow grimly familiar. Now Lassiter was certain where he'd seen that look before. In a subway car in New York, almost thirty years ago.

He got out of bed, crossed to the bathroom and

ran the cold water. Over the years, Lassiter had developed a profound respect for his own subconscious powers of reasoning. Somehow his inner mind could seize on the most subtle of indicators, minute details that his conscious mind overlooked, sift the data, weigh possibility against probability, and then, when he was least expecting it, present him with a whole new line of thought on a current case.

Over the last few days his subconscious had returned again and again to Vandenberg, to the line about the sinking of the *Bismarck*. Now it was steering him back to it once more. On 27 May 1941, the 42,000 ton "unsinkable" battleship, *Bismarck*, the pride of the German Navy, was sent to the bottom of the Atlantic together with over two thousand of its crew, after one of the biggest naval chases ever mounted. Lassiter was no student of maritime history, but he knew that the event was a landmark in the minds of all those who lived through those times . . . especially Germans . . .

As he splashed water on his face, it came to him where he'd heard the reference before. Mrs. Hofle had used it. Rathenau's sister-in-law. She'd said the day the British sank the *Bismarck* was the last time she ever saw her sister's husband. Vandenberg had said that it was on that day he'd been handed over to the Red Cross. Was it just coincidence or was there a tie-up? And what possible relevance could it have to the Mielke case?

Lassiter was no stranger to the demons of the night. He'd paced away the chill hours before dawn more times than he could remember. He knew all too well how the mind could turn in on itself and begin to gorge on its uncertainties, turning niggling doubt into

breathless panic. But he knew too that, when the
metabolism was at its lowest, thoughts could expand,
become more lateral, force him to look at ideas from
new standpoints. Now it struck him that the *Bismarck*
issue might have no bearing on the Mielke case at all,
that the inner quest that was disturbing his sleep,
distorting his dreams, was bound on an entirely
different course. The more he thought about it, the
more it seemed to him that his subconscious was not
working on the search for Mielke's rinser, or anything
else to do with the case. It was as though it had
identified a new mission of its own.

He began to think through the *Bismarck*
business as an isolated issue. He took his attaché
case from the bedroom closet, turned on the lamp
beside his bed, and hunted out the notes from his
meeting with the Hofle woman. Then he
remembered why it was that Horst Rathenau had
made the journey to the South German town of
Rosenheim that spring day in 1941 . . .

He caught his breath. It was an involuntary
thing, but his whole body seemed to resonate. The
only feasible connection between the two events
struck him like a blast of cold air. He switched off
the light and sat for a long time in the darkness,
turning over other possibilities. Light was beginning
to pierce the shutters when he finally knew that his
first conclusion was the only one. In a moment of
absolute clarity he saw that the search for the
Mielke billions had led him to an issue of far greater
consequence and urgency. He did not believe in fate
or destiny, but when he had recognized the
emotional logic that had dictated the lives of two
families half a century ago, it was as though the
past had reached out and . . . chosen him.

Was it possible that only he had made the crucial connection? If others had that knowledge, why hadn't they spoken up? Why was Lowell Vandenberg being allowed to inch closer to the Oval Office with every day that passed? If others knew, the only answer could be that it was to their advantage to let things stand as they were. Who else could have stumbled on the vital clues? Few, if any. In the distance, beyond the copse of trees that enveloped the garden of the Rockville house, a night bird called. Lassiter didn't know what kind of bird it was, but it was a lonely, unearthly sound.

It's up to me, he thought. Only me. And from here on in, I'm on my own.

"Answer me! Tell me now!" Vandenberg roared. He grasped the old man by the throat and slung him across the room. For a moment, Rathenau lay there in a crumpled heap, his face parchment white. Then he eased himself up a little on his elbows. His body trembled, beads of sweat broke through his eyebrows into his eyes. Vandenberg's face was crimson.

"You swapped the babies, didn't you? As soon as you had the letter to the Red Cross and the identity papers from Ravensbruck, you swapped the babies. The child you took to the Red Cross was your own, wasn't it?"

Rathenau looked very old now, a man close to death. His eyes flickered in Vandenberg's direction and he looked away. At last, he nodded.

Vandenberg took a long breath. "I'm your son. That's why you're here. You wanted to make certain the Vandenberg money would be mine . . . "

With great difficulty, the old man got to his feet and sat back in the chair. "Yes."

"So what happened to the real Lowell Vandenberg? I need to know."

Rathenau's reply was barely audible. "He's buried in the woods near Dachau . . . "

Now he told of the night in May 1941 when he had received a phone call from his sister-in-law. She had said that his wife of a little more than two years had been killed in a bombing raid on the city of Essen.

" . . . Göring had told us that the Fatherland was invincible to air attack, but my wife had never believed the Nazi propaganda. She had slept with our eight-month-old son in the converted cellar of the house we'd bought in the Spring of '39. She must have stayed up reading in the kitchen. When the house took a direct hit she was killed instantly. But the baby, who'd been asleep in his cot in the basement, had been dug out of the ruins alive. He was taken to my sister-in-law's home in Rosenheim in south Germany where it was thought he'd be safe."

Rathenau ran his thin hands up around his face. "But the bombing of Essen changed everything for me. Until then, I had believed that England would fall like Poland, Holland and France, in weeks, to *blitzkrieg*—lightning war. Indeed we had been told only that month that the British were finished, London had been bombed into ruins. But I knew when my wife was killed, blown to pieces on German soil, that Hitler had drastically underestimated the British strength, and if the war with them was now to drag on, perhaps for years, then was it not possible that the Americans would join them as allies as they had in World War One? I began to lose faith in our struggle, to see the deal I'd struck with Vandenberg as a heaven-sent opportunity to get my child away from Germany, to where there would be no bombs, to where food would always be plentiful.

"Lowell Vandenberg was two months younger than you, sick with typhus. He would not have survived anyway. You were thin, but healthy enough. Officially, you didn't exist. The Rathaus, where I would have registered your birth, was a heap of rubble. As soon as I had the letter from Paul Vandenberg and his son's identity papers I went to Rosenheim and took you. I gave you to the Red Cross willingly, knowing that you would have a new life, a better life, in the care of a wealthy American family.

"You are not a Vandenberg," Rathenau looked at his son steadily now. "But you have their name, and now you have their money. And there's not a soul on this earth who can dispute your right to either."

"Are you okay, darling?" Stella asked.

Vandenberg blinked. His mind made the long haul back to the present in the fragment of time it took for his eyelids to move. When he took in the press of people around him, the corners of his mouth lifted and his face regained the fixed look of well-being that public figures learn to affect. Now his head nodded occasionally as though he was taking in what the current speaker was saying. But his wife knew he was still lost in some distant place.

Stella too twisted her face into an expression that could be read as enjoyment and stared around the packed function room. The testimonial dinner for her husband had been planned before he'd announced his decision to run for the Democratic nomination. As it was, the event, attended by friends, relatives, colleagues, well-wishers, representatives of organizations to which Lowell had given either his time or his money, served as a perfect campaign vehicle for a man who was seeking the presidency. A number of media stars, potential fund donors and other notables had been added to the guest list, and the business of celebrating the life of Virginia's most newsworthy son began in earnest.

The host of a daytime TV chat show, his face unknown to a good many of the players present, who had only been allotted speech time because it was rumored he would soon take over the old David Letterman slot, completed his tired "roast" of the guest of honor and returned to his seat. Stella watched her husband's hands come together, saw him rise mechanically to his feet and wave his appreciation, then sink back as the next speaker moved up to the microphone. She had never seen him like this: not in all the years they'd been married had she seen him so distracted. It took a visible effort for his eyes to lock on the man about to talk now, his longtime friend and ally, Gary McClintock.

McClintock, positioned on the top table, four seats from the Vandenbergs, cleared his voice, then pointed to the guest of honor and said, "I've gotten to know this man pretty well over the last ten years. I've had a chance to take a good close look at him. To some of you in the media who've not had that opportunity, I say this: this man is not the man you take him to be . . . "

He knows. Sweet Jesus, he knows!

Vandenberg's body jerked so hard, Stella thought for a second he'd been hit by something. He seemed to be gasping for air. Was he having some kind of attack? A puzzled look spread across the governor's face. Stella looked around the room. Ches Chesterfield had noticed that something was badly wrong, but no one else seemed to register anything untoward. McClintock was holding forth, unawares.

"Some of you would have us believe that he's a dilettante, a complacent fatcat—that, for Lowell Vandenberg, the only issue is the next deal. But I'm here to tell you, the only thing on this man's mind is, how do I deal with the next issue? Unemployment, housing, health care, education . . . "

Stella put a hand on her husband's, which were clasped together. She could feel him fighting to steady them. She watched Chesterfield reach over and slide a slip of paper to the speaker, who glanced at it, and began to hurry his speech to a close. As soon as the applause had subsided, Vandenberg rose to his feet and made for the door to the kitchens, immediately ahead. A waiter with a tray of drinks swerved to avoid him. Stella and Chesterfield hurried past.

Vandenberg crossed the hotel lobby, climbed two flights of stairs and let himself into his suite. He locked the bathroom door and vomited into the basin. The convulsions began to subside but he threw his head back and slammed it into the mirror with enough force to smash it to pieces. Blood oozed from a gash in his head. A long shard of glass lay in the basin. Vandenberg eyed it vacantly for a moment, then dipped his hand into the mess of regurgitated food and fished it out.

Seconds later, Chesterfield darted across the

suite and tried the bathroom door. "Lowell, are you okay?" No answer. He tried to force the lock. Stella came hurrying in behind. He called again and then slammed his shoulder against the architrave.

"I can't break the door in, Lowell. If you can hear me . . . I'm gonna have to go and get help."

There was the sound of movement in the bathroom and then some fumbling with the lock. The door swung open to reveal a pallid-faced Vandenberg stumbling back against the bidet, his right arm swathed in towels.

Stella saw the broken mirror and stifled a cry. Vandenberg's eyes, ringed with white, glistened as though he was on something. "I had a stupid accident . . . That's all," he said at last. There was an eerie detachment in his voice. "Get Doctor Puchatski. He's at a table near the stage."

The doctor was a small, florid-faced man with a mass of white curly hair. His napkin was still tucked into his tuxedo vest when he arrived at the suite. Vandenberg lay on the bed now, towels around his arm scarlet with blood. He indicated that he wanted to be alone with the doctor, and his wife and manager withdrew. Puchatski unwrapped the towels carefully. The inside of the right forearm was slashed in about six places. Most were not deep but they were bleeding profusely. Puchatski was used to describing wounds, he'd been a police doctor for more than twenty years. If he'd had to describe these, he'd have called them a series of straight cuts in a zigzag pattern, The first two, like the letter "L," the second two, the same, only tipped to the left . . . like the letter "L" or "V."

He looked hard at Vandenberg. "This was no accident, Lowell . . . "

"It was an accident. That's exactly what it was. I got sick . . . I fell against the mirror . . . I got cut. End of story."

The doctor shrugged. "Well, whatever happened . . . "

"That's what happened."

" . . . Several of these cuts are going to need stitching."

Vandenberg was clearly in pain. "Can you do that at your surgery?"

"I can, but really you should go to a hospital."

"No way. Take me to your surgery. I could be back here in an hour."

Vandenberg looked drawn and weary when he made a brief appearance in the ballroom an hour and a half later. He held his lapel with his right hand. There was no indication that the arm was encased in a thick dressing. He told his guests that the shock of the Sullivan incident had affected him more than he'd first realized, and had caught up on him that evening. All that was needed was a quiet weekend at home with his family. He thanked them, wished them goodnight, and Stella whisked him away to their car.

Despite having taken a sleeping pill, he was awake again at 5 A.M. He slipped from the double bed in the governor's residence and walked downstairs to the garden room, where he poured himself brandy and stared at the photographs that stood on the desk. All his life, these, and a handful of letters, had been the only mementoes of his parents. Every evening in his childhood, he'd wished them goodnight and said a little prayer that

their souls, at least, had found safe haven. A
thousand times he had looked at them smiling
confidently in their silver frames and wondered
what kind of people they'd been. What was he to
make of them now? They were no longer his to love.
If he was wrong, and there was a hereafter, then to
them he was pariah, a cuckoo in the nest.

The air that seeped though the frames of the
old windows sent shivers up Vandenberg's back.
How could it be this cold in late May? He pulled his
robe around his shoulders. Am I now to regard this
appalling old German, who's tried to buy himself
back into my life, as my father? It was unthinkable.

As rationally as he could, he began to take stock
of the problems he now faced. In civil terms, I'm a
fraud, he thought. I have no rights to my name or
anything that goes with it. Most vital is the fact that
as a German, born in that country—in Essen, so
Rathenau had said—I am not eligible for
presidential office. If my true background were
known, I would be automatically barred as a
candidate. As Henry Kissinger had been for the
same reason in '76. The enormity of that single fact
closed every perspective he had ever had. He
couldn't see past it. Taken at its best, he told
himself, I am the worthless son of a wanted Nazi
war criminal, living off the birthright of the family
my father and his kind destroyed.

Again, he felt resentment burn inside him. He
had orchestrated his rise to power with an
unequaled determination. He had curbed his sexual
appetite, purged himself in every department of his
public and private life solely to ensure that nothing,
nothing, could ever be found against him. To ensure
that he was the perfect candidate, clean and

unimpeachable. Every detail of his presidential campaign had been handled with the utmost care. He had gone to extraordinary lengths to make certain that he would carry the nomination at the Democratic Party convention in ten days' time. And now this. Never in his worst nightmare . . .

"Who the hell am I?" he cried aloud. His right arm began to ache. He took another slug of brandy. Open on the desk in front of him lay the souvenir program from the evening before. The inside page carried a color photograph of a man dressed in a sweater and slacks, standing at the helm of gaff-rigged ketch. The caption beneath read, Governor Lowell C. Vandenberg. He turned the pages. To all of them, I am him, he thought. To everyone, other than my father. The other child died. How can I be anyone else? He worked to steady his pulse; leaned back and took deep breaths. Things can be as they were. Must be as they were.

Only one man knows the truth. Only while he still exists will there be doubt . . .

TWENTY-FOUR

The line of people at the Lufthansa ticket desk moved forward. Lassiter picked up his case, closed the gap in front of him, and asked himself for the tenth time that morning whether he was crazy. I'm a fucking Customs agent, he told himself. What am I doing trekking across the world to try and prove some hare-brained theory about a presidential candidate? He sighed and tried once more to get it straight in his head. Because, if I'm right, the man in question isn't just an impostor, disqualified by birth from taking the nation's highest office; he's the candidate who'll almost certainly take the Democratic nomination at the party convention in six days' time. And, unless the Republicans could perform the fastest credibility turnaround in American political history, that means he's likely to be the next man in the White House. Good enough reason?

He scratched at his scalp. If my father's right and this man is as dangerous as he says, then if I just sit back and do nothing I'm colluding in what follows. If delegates to the convention were to be freed to choose the better man, Bravington, then somehow Lassiter had to make the difference. Was that it? Did he, in some crevice of his mind, see this as the opportunity he'd once been too young to grasp? The face with the merciless eyes in the subway dream had somehow merged in his subconscious with whatever lay behind the political mask of Lowell Vandenberg. Was this one-man mission some bizarre exercise to rid himself of a nightmare, to prove to himself that he could "take charge" of events?

Whatever the reality was, Lassiter had now dropped everything else to develop his theory. The previous morning Fraenkel and Capriotti had both called for assignment updates. He'd bought himself time by playing one off against the other, while he sat with a pot of coffee in the study of the Rockville house and made careful notes on what he knew.

Mrs. Hofle had said that on 27 May 1941, at around noon, Horst Rathenau had arrived at her home in Rosenheim and taken his son, and that she had never seen the child again after that. A woman who had worked at the refugee center on the Swiss border at that time, whom Lassiter had seen interviewed in the German TV profile on Vandenberg, said that on the afternoon of that day a man had arrived with a baby. He had handed her a document identifying it as the son of Paul Vandenberg plus a letter from the father asking for the child to be put into care of relatives in Zurich. If Rathenau had driven direct from Rosenheim, he would have arrived at the Swiss border around the right time. From all the evidence, it was certain that only he could have had possession of those papers at that point. All he had originally cared about was getting what amounted to a receipt for Vandenberg's child from the Red Cross, to convince the father that his son was safe, knowing that in return he'd receive the list of the man's numbered bank accounts in Switzerland.

Lassiter moved up to the ticket desk, presented his credit card and passport and waited while his booking was processed.

But something had changed. Had Rathenau seen that the tide of war would turn against Germany, and that here was an opportunity to get his son to safety? Was it even possible that the real Lowell Vandenberg had died before he could get him to Switzerland and he had simply used his own son to get the receipt from the Red Cross to close the deal with the father? Not likely; he could simply have taken another Jewish baby from the concentration camp if that was all he wanted to achieve.

No; Rathenau had reasoned that all small babies looked much the same to everyone but their parents. Their faces and coloring can change quickly in the first months. So why should he send the child of a Jewish woman to safety, to a life of luxury in America, when he could send his own? This way he could benefit his son and take the money as well. And if he himself survived the war, he could perhaps reclaim him at a future time.

Lassiter had decided that if he could establish that the man who handed the child over to the Red Cross was Rathenau himself, the story moved from the bounds of coincidence into probability. Without that vital link, he had little more than an intriguing piece of conjecture. To share it with anyone in authority as it stood was, at the very least, to invite ridicule and, at worst, to destroy himself professionally and make an enemy of the man who was likely to occupy the most powerful office in the world.

Lassiter had no personal experience of how to prosecute a matter of this kind, so he had put it in terms he could understand. If this was a trial of the type I've been involved with, he reasoned, the case I could bring against the man who is calling himself Vandenberg, would rely on no more than circumstantial evidence at best. The "human" qualities of the story might impress a jury, but to get a conviction, I would have to produce hard evidence; DNA profiles, medical submissions. Without those, a judge would have no choice but to stop the trial on the first day.

And even if I can prove my theory, should I? Legally and morally, I'd be doing the right thing. But, for all my father has said about him, for all my own gut tells me, can I be certain that history will thank me for knocking this man out of the race? Might a Vandenberg presidency prove to be a blessing I'm just too prejudiced to foresee? Down the line, I shall need hard evidence that this man is the pariah I've come to believe he is. But legal and moral issues first. Without evidence to support the first allegation, the second is irrelevant.

His first move, he decided, should be to try and contact the woman in Switzerland. If she could identify Rathenau from the wedding photograph that Frau Hofle had given him, he was on the first rung of the ladder. It had taken five phone calls to track down the researcher at NTV, Berlin, who had worked on the Vandenberg profile. She was fairly sure she had the address of the Red Cross woman on file but had resolutely refused to give it out. Lassiter had been tempted to use his clout as a Customs agent on secondment to the *Finanzamt,* but could see no feasible way he could drag this investigation under the Mielke umbrella. "The best thing you can do is write to me and I'll see that your letter is forwarded on," he was told. The best thing I can do, Lassiter had thought as he hung up, is turn up on your goddamn doorstep.

His next call had been to Erika to tell her that he was coming back to Berlin and wanted her professional advice. "What do you need?" she asked. "A DNA profile on Mielke?" He explained that this had nothing to do with the *Finanzamt* case. He needed her help with an investigation of his own. He couldn't talk about it on the phone, he'd tell her more when he saw her.

He'd dialed Lufthansa without a second thought and begun booking his flight. It was only when the woman had asked for his credit card number that he stopped to think. I'm on my own with this, he reminded himself. I can't reasonably use U.S. Federal resources to fund what any reasonable person would view at this stage as a wacko project. I might get the odd favor out of the Germans, just so long as they didn't get wind of what it was all leading up to. Either way I'm going to have to pay the airfare myself. It was only then that Lassiter got the full measure of his own convictions about the Rathenau-Vandenberg equation. All his instincts told him he was right. They had never yet let him down. The woman on the other end of the line was getting impatient. Lassiter took out his American Express card and read her the number.

In the normal course of events, Lassiter studiously avoided media coverage of Vandenberg's activities—his wife's preoccupation with the man's every move, he felt, was enough for the both of them. But now Lassiter knew that he needed to absorb everything he could on the governor of Virginia. His father had just finished writing a piece on him, and had said that he had a file on him going back to the beginning of his political career. Lassiter called Joe and, an hour later, as the Customs agent was about to leave for the airport, a package arrived by motorbike.

As the plane to Berlin lifted onto its flight path, Lassiter settled down to read. Toward the front of the file were the newspaper reports of the attempted assassination. His eyes settled on the text of the fax sent by the neo-Nazi group that had claimed responsibility for the act. " . . . As a U.S. president, Lowell Vandenberg would have built his cabinet from Jews and Blacks and other subhuman breeds who threaten the fabric of American Society . . . "

Lassiter read the phrase again more carefully. The actual words in the press cutting were, " . . . and other races who threaten . . . " but still Lassiter's brain wanted to read the phrase as, " . . . other *subhuman breeds* . . . " There was almost a compunction to read it substituting the other words. It was as though the alternative term had somehow imprinted itself on his subliminal memory. And yet Lassiter was certain that he'd never read the text of this document before. Perhaps I heard it misquoted on the radio, he told himself.

☆   ☆   ☆

Erika pushed her way through the crowds thronging the international arrivals hall at Tempelhof Airport and ran to Lassiter. "I'm sorry I'm so late, Jack. Everything's in chaos here."

Lassiter was looking stressed and weary. He stepped forward and took her in his arms. He was surprised at the intensity of the emotion that rose inside him. "I was getting worried. I thought something might have happened to you."

"There's a big anti-government demonstration moving north along Mehringdamm. The police have closed the road. I had to leave my car at the canal and walk most of the way. That's why I'm so late." She produced a hair grip and wound her long blonde hair up into a bun at the back. Her brown almond-shaped eyes were filled with concern.

"Walk? Christ, that's miles." He kissed her again. He could feel her heart pounding in her chest. "You poor thing. Why didn't you take the subway?"

She laughed mirthlessly. "What subway? It's been on strike for more than a week. God knows whether we'll get a taxi back or not."

The line of people at the cab rank stretched almost the length of the terminal building. Erika and Lassiter walked down and waited in silence. He took her hand. For the last few days, little but the Vandenberg business had been allowed to invade his thoughts. But now the closeness of her banished the matter from his mind for a few moments. The fight with Marianne had given him a chance to examine his feelings for the German girl more clearheadedly than at any time since he'd known her. When the inevitable question about the nature of his mission did come, he knew that Erika was the one person he could open up to, trust to understand, not only the political implications, but the significance it could have for him personally. He didn't have to wait long.

"So what is this new case you're working on?" she asked.

"It's not a case as such. It's something that's come out of the Mielke investigation, but has nothing to do with him, something I stumbled into. It relates to one of the U.S. presidential candidates." They moved up a few feet. "I made a pact with myself not to get into it with anyone in authority until I have more proof, but I think the man's an impostor, a man who has someone else's identity. In reality he's the son of a wanted Nazi criminal—may even have inherited some of his father's traits. I'm in a unique position. None of it's really my business, except that if I don't act, I don't believe anybody will. And we could up end up with a very dangerous man in the White House."

Erika thought this over for a moment. "Dear God, that's some undertaking, Jack. No wonder you're so tense. And that's why you need to know about DNA profiling procedures."

"Yes, I need a crash course. Come on, for Christ's sakes let's walk." They gathered up his luggage and headed off on foot. "It's strange, I didn't realize how much this whole thing mattered to me until a few days ago. Remember the night we went to the Mexican restaurant? You were talking about the changes happening in Europe. The forces that are tearing societies apart. It's beginning to happen in America, Erika . . . "

"You mean the riots in Miami?"

"Miami is just ground zero, a reflection of how

people feel across a whole continent. I hesitate to call it a country because I'm not certain that it is anymore. All the "one-people-under-one-flag" hype, no one buys that anymore. We're a nation of Hispanic-Americans, Afro-Caribbean Americans, Irish-Americans, Polish-Americans . . . What happened to just 'Americans?' These groups identify with the folk from the old country more than they do with the new. They take their attitudes from them." He gestured around him as they walked. "Systems are breaking down everywhere you look, except one thing has changed since the Sixties. The minority groups of those days are now the mass. When the National Guard opens fire, they're shooting at tomorrow's voter, and they hit the politicians."

Erika struggled to match his pace. "Well, the sages of Washington should take a look at what's happening on this continent and learn from it. Not just to judge the next UN involvement: they need to respect the way whole countries' needs and desires are changing. Because, for all you say, the U.S. is the only superpower now. When it speaks, a lot of the world still listens."

"And that's exactly why the next man in the Oval Office has to be someone who has enough vision to realize the direction the world is going in and command enough respect to be given the chance to reshape it, before it reshapes itself. The man I'm investigating is not that man, Erika. Now I believe I know the truth about him, I realize how vital it is that he's taken out of the race. I have to do that before the party convention in five days' time. That's the only way I can let the right guy come through."

"There is such a man?" Erika did not hide her skepticism.

"Perhaps there isn't, but there may be someone who should have the chance to try. I don't know a great deal about him, but my father is something of an expert. He says that the number two runner in the race, a black candidate called Bravington, has many of the right qualities. But if he misses out next week, we may never know."

Erika signaled for them to cross the road. "There's another taxi rank at the junction with Dudenstrasse. My God, you've certainly set yourself some goal. So tell me, what exactly do you need from me?"

Lassiter was breathing hard now. The injuries he'd sustained in Washington were starting to slow him down. He stopped, dropped to his knees and breathed evenly. "All right, I know that to establish someone's genetic makeup, you need tissue or body fluid samples, from which DNA can be extracted," he said as they walked. "Tell me this, is there any way you can get samples from a suspect without their knowledge?"

"Sure, that's no big deal. If they eat in restaurants or at public dinners, saliva can be taken from a napkin they've used, hair samples collected from a toiletroom floor. A reliable witness has got to be able to vouch that the sample did come from the donor, of course." Erika swung around and waved frantically at a taxi that promptly hung a left and sped out of sight. "As to whether the samples would be admissible as evidence in those circumstances . . ."

"If I can prove what I need to prove, Erika, then I think the issue becomes too important for that to be of concern to the authorities. Okay; difficult to get unofficial samples but not impossible. Now, I need to prove this guy isn't who he says he is, so I would need to get tissue samples from at least one of the people he alleges are his parents as well?"

"Correct."

"The trouble is, his father, his mother and almost all her side of the family, died more than fifty years ago. And from what I've been able to find out, his closest living relative on his father's side is a cousin."

"Well, that presents more of a problem. If you approach him for a control sample you risk him refusing and telling the suspect he's under investigation."

"Fatal." If my father's right about Vandenberg, Lassiter thought, and this thing misfires, how much would my life be worth? "And I know nothing about the cousin's lifestyle. Getting an unofficial sample from him would take way too long to set up."

They turned the corner onto Dudenstrasse. Erika stopped and put her hands on her hips. "I remember one murder case where we had two defendants, but we were pretty certain that only one did the actual killing. We couldn't forensically prove the elder man did it." She was half talking to herself. "But we were able to pressure him into confessing by establishing that the younger man couldn't have. Only this scenario of yours is kind of the opposite way around . . . "

Lassiter saw where she was going. "You're saying I'm looking at the problem from the wrong direction. If I can't get tissue samples that would prove the man is not a Vandenberg, the answer is to prove he *is* a Rathenau. It's a nice idea, but we're back to square one, because we can't find Rathenau. If we could, we'd charge him with rinsing around three billion D-marks, for starters."

"And his wife?"

"She's been dead for more than fifty years too." They could see the taxi rank from here but there was no cab waiting. They turned and pushed on north toward the *Landwehrkanal*. "Do you have this Rathenau's last known address?" Erika asked.

"We may have that in the next few days. Why?"

"Well, even if he's not there, you may be able to pick up some usable samples. If he's already a wanted man, you can safely take anything of that kind you need. One fragment of hair from the lapel of a jacket could do it. Here again . . . "

"Again, my problem is time. Unless I can get something watertight on this in the next four days, a hell of a lot of damage is gonna be done." He stopped and looked at her. "This situation is in a different league from anything I've handled before. It's not even my area. I don't fully understand why it matters to me so much, I just know that it does . . . "

"Well . . . If genetic fingerprinting is a factor, I'll help you all I can. If you turn up a viable sample, I can have it in the lab and back to you with a report in less than twenty-four hours."

They moved off again. "Thanks. Right now, all I have on the man that's worth a damn to this investigation are some photographs of his father. And most of those are computer-generated. Oh, and I have a picture of his wife on their wedding day . . . "

Lassiter fell silent. Max Gehrhart: that computer program of his had produced a three-dimensional image of Rathenau from a photograph; it was able to show how he might look at any stage of his life . . . How much further might it be able to go? If it was set to scan the wife's picture too, maybe Max could get the images of the parents to interact in some way . . . show how a grown son of theirs might look . . . If we could get one that came out looking like Lowell Vandenberg . . .

Erika yelled and waved at a taxi speeding north, which braked and pulled in to the curb. Lassiter was still deep in thought when they got in. Five minutes later they passed a pay phone. He told the driver to stop and he hurried to make a call.

Erika sat in the cab and watched him. This was a very different man from the one she'd met eight months ago on a double date, she thought. She'd found him physically attractive from the beginning. He'd made her laugh. There were nights when it seemed that one lifetime wasn't long enough to say all that there was to say. But there was a cynicism there, a bitterness. The affair had begun almost immediately, but he'd never tried to hide the hurt he felt over the collapse of his marriage, to pretend that he was doing anything more than marking time.

Erika wasn't certain why she'd let things run on as they had, but as she watched him now . . . His was face animated, his eyes bright and alive. There was such enthusiasm here, such passion. Now she knew why she'd held on. There was another man inside the one she'd known, she'd always felt it. But somehow until this case, or whatever it was, he had never been able to let that come through. It was as though it was exorcising something within him, in some way making him whole again. This man she knew she loved deeply. She knew too that he was one she was going to have to learn to live without.

TWENTY-FIVE

The narrow cul-de-sac leading to the Berlin Police Photographic Unit now lay under several inches of raw sewage. Lassiter switched on his flashlight and, for the second time in six hours, picked his way along the series of upturned beer crates that had been put down as stepping stones between the mountains of rotting trash.

Behind him, a blue Renault moved slowly along Stendalerstrasse. Leland Daker wound down the window and watched his progress with some amusement. So much for Europe's showpiece economy, he thought.

Max Gehrhart looked up from his computer screen and peered suspiciously at the man advancing toward him. "Safe passage down Yellow River?" He leveled the can of aerosol in Lassiter's direction.

"Yup. I smell no worse than I usually do."

"That I can handle." Max turned back to his computer screen. "How are you coping?"

"Jet-lagged stupid."

"Well, get your mind in gear, Lassiter, you're gonna need it. I'll give you this: in the eight years I've worked here, I've been asked to do a lot of stuff, but marry two people and give birth to their son? That's a first. I'd be a liar if I told you I wasn't getting a kick out of it." He took off his plastic bifocals and studied the Customs agent's face. "But, without more data it's really educated guess-work."

"How far have you got?" Lassiter asked.

"Well, I've scanned the monochrome of Frau Rathenau from the wedding picture." Max's fingers clattered over the keyboard and the face of a young woman in her mid-twenties filled the screen. She was handsome rather than pretty. The hairstyle placed her firmly in the 1940s. Lassiter fancied he could see something of Lowell Vandenberg in the eyes. "The program reckons she had reddish hair."

Lassiter shrugged. "Who am I to argue?"

"You definitely don't have any shots of her face in profile?"

"No. It's like I told you, I had to do a lot of finessing to get what you have. Maybe down the line I can go back to my source, but not right now."

"Okay, then this is what the computer came up with for that." The head swiveled around to show that Krista Rathenau had a broad face and an almost Roman nose.

"Now the task is to try and devise an algorithm that gets these and her husband's image to interact. The first problem is purely technical. The way the program's set up, scanned images are designed to respond to a database of about 180,000 faces. I want it to respond to just one—Frau Rathenau, right?"

"Right."

"I couldn't think how to do it. So, in the end, I created a new data base with just her face in it. Then it occurred to me that we're assuming that a son's face is purely a product of the two parents."

"You're talking about when facial features miss a generation?"

"Well, take my kid: he has my father's ears, my wife's mother's chin, no question. And the kid's nose . . . She says that's a gift from the Good God in heaven, but then she's got a charitable heart. The 'Good God in heaven factor' I can't simulate. But some of the grandparents' features I perhaps can." He took out the battered photograph that had come from Mrs. Hofle's album. "See these folk to the left here, especially this stuck-up-looking old biddy? And this fat little fuck to the right of her. I'm no geneticist, but I'd say they were his mother and her father. They're easier to see on the enhanced simulations." The image on the screen was replaced by computer graphics of the two in question. "What do you think?"

Lassiter studied the pictures for the best part of a minute. "Max, you're a scholar. I never would have thought of it."

"Of course we're two grandparents short, but it's better than nothing. I added the ones we have to the new database. The next problem's a major one. It's so obvious, I don't know why I didn't think of it at the start. A woman doesn't have only one son with a standard set of looks. Theoretically, she could have as many sons as she has eggs fertilized by male sperms. And all of them could look totally different. Now as far as . . . "

"Stop. Suppose I had some photographs of a man I want a match on."

"Well, now he tells me."

"I've been running around town trying to get better pictures of him. All I have for the minute are these." He produced a buff-colored envelope from his jacket pocket. Inside were photographs of Lowell Vandenberg cut from various publications, including *Newsweek,* as well as a single ten-by-eight glossy he'd obtained from the press office of the American Embassy. He'd removed any captions, any reference to Vandenberg, gambling that Max was a Berliner and a loner by nature. Work, fishing and music—he was the organist at the local Catholic church—were his life. With luck, the face of an American presidential candidate might well not have permeated his ordered little world. Either way, Gehrhart made no comment as he inspected the pictures. Lassiter breathed more easily.

An hour later, a color simulation of Lowell Vandenberg's face gazed back at them from the computer screen. Max then fed each of the family pictures through the scanner and integrated them with his feature-analysis program. Five different screens displayed the five images. On a sixth, carried in from the next office, he put up what he called a "blank-slate face"—an androgynous, hairless human head, with no defined features. The two men watched all the heads rotating eerily for a while, then Lassiter said, "Let's start with the forehead. If we take Frau Rathenau's . . . broaden it a little, with a touch of her mother-in-law's . . . and ship in the hyper-plasia of the super-orbital margin from Rathenau himself . . . "

Max leaned back in his chair and stretched. "While I'm playing Frankenstein, you can get us some cola out of the trunk of my car." He dangled the keys.

"Cola? Can't I have a proper drink?" Lassiter asked.

"This is a real drink all right. Stim-Cola; six times the usual caffeine dose. Programers live on it. We have it imported from your country." He swilled the last of the umber liquid in his glass. "Sleep is for wimps. Prost!"

Lassiter held the cuffs of his suit pants over the sink one last time and rinsed them through. The stench of sewage still clung to them. He sponged them as dry as he could with a small hand towel, sprayed them again with Max's aerosol, and laid them on the window ledge to dry. Max turned to look at him standing forlornly in his undershorts. "In the last month I've been stoned, gassed, shot at and blown up," Lassiter muttered sulkily.

Max shrugged. "So now you've been polluted, soiled and degraded. Welcome to Berlin. What do you think of this?"

The "blank slate head" now had a defined forehead. High, distinguished . . . patrician. Lassiter compared it to the presidential candidate's. It could have been Vandenberg's. "Yes!" Lassiter toasted the screen with the bottle he'd just brought in. "All right! It's working, Max."

"Maybe."

Lassiter poured them both the Stim-Cola and sat down beside Gehrhart. "Let's try for the eyes. Again, let's start with the wife's . . . maybe add a little of her husband's . . ."

Small, greenish blue eyes appeared on the blank head. As Rathenau's were factored in they appeared to change fractionally in width and position. But they were still not Vandenberg's eyes. Max adjusted the eyebrows with a touch of the father-in-law's, which seemed to help. After a number of other changes Lassiter said, "No, we're losing it again. Bleed in a little more of Frau Rathenau's eyes." He drained his glass. Jet lag was really getting to him now. He was having trouble focusing on the screen. "No, that's not doing it either."

"I'm telling you, we're missing too much data." Max yawned and refilled their glasses.

"The subject's eyes are more Frau Rathenau than anybody else . . . And she looks like she has a lot of her father in her. So when we add more of her, we add more of him too. Maybe that's what's screwing things up. Could be we're not getting enough of her mother's side into the face."

"You're getting tired, Lassiter. We don't have a scan of her mother."

Lassiter sat upright. "Max, I've got a screwy idea. Could we subtract Frau Rathenau's father's facial characteristics from her face?"

"Subtract?"

"We agree that Frau R. has a lot of her father in her face: around the mouth, the eyes, the jawline . . . If we could nullify his influence on the way she looks, we should get an idea of what her mother looked like."

"What do you think this is, Lassiter, some kind

of game show? Human genetics doesn't work like that."

"Can you try it?"

Max shrugged wearily. "I really don't know. If you can tell me the parts of her you think owe something to her father . . . It's not a standard feature of this program, but maybe I can improvize some instructions . . . Though we're bound to increase the margin of error here."

As Lassiter talked, Max moved between two keyboards, typing commands into both. Five shots of Stim-Cola later, the simulation of Frau Rathenau's face had changed. The eyes had moved slightly farther apart, the face had lengthened, the jaw had grown more defined. An entirely new mouth had materialized. When the metamorphosis was complete, both men stared at it in silence. "Well, I'll be damned," Max said at last.

Lassiter's eyes moved from the new image to Vandenberg's and back again. "Well there's the mouth we're looking for, right there."

After that had been incorporated into the face under construction, Lassiter had Max replace the Frau Rathenau element in the eyes with those of her simulated mother. Even before the work was complete the agent shouted, "That's the look. That's exactly the look I was searching for."

Sometime after daybreak, other employees began to arrive for a new day's work. They called greetings to the two weary-looking men seated at the bank of computer screens in Max's office as they hurried to their own. Toward late morning, a low moan broke from Lassiter's lips. He and Max peered at the newly constructed profile of the completed face and nursed the last of the cola. The full-face simulation did bear a striking resemblance to the man Lassiter knew to be Vandenberg. But the side view of the face seemed to have precious little in common with the computer-generated profile of the man. "The top half of the head works up to a point," Max said at last. "But the rest . . . the parents and grandparents have real strong noses. The mother's side have Roman jobs, Rathenau's is a beak of a thing. Yet the profile produced from photographs of your man, shows him with a small neat nose. If your man is their progeny, it's hard to see how he could have ended up with such a trim schnoz."

"And it's almost the reverse with the chin," Lassiter said. "Both families have indifferent chins at best. Our man seems to have this strong, jutting jaw."

Max saved the new data and the men meandered down the beer crates that ran the length of the Yellow River to the delicatessen on the corner of Stendalerstrasse.

"It's like I told you when you came to me with the passport photograph of Rathenau, this program is far from perfect. There's a degree of error in the computer-generated profiles especially. And all the profiles we're relying on have been created that way. That's a lot of error." Max stretched his mouth to accommodate a vast pastrami sandwich. "We need a few definites, a few real photographs, to get anything reliable. Can I ask you something? Who is it we have to sell on this?"

Lassiter stared out of the window. A miserable group of soldiers in combat dress were trying to lift a manhole cover in the road. "Me, Max. We have to sell it to me."

☆   ☆   ☆

Lassiter returned to his Berlin apartment and slept deeply for three hours. Then he showered, shaved and dressed in fresh clothes—wellcut jeans, a cream polo neck sweater and a fawn suede jacket.

The only thing in the fridge that still looked edible was the salami and eggs. He fried the eggs and made some sorry-looking sandwiches, which he washed down with strong black coffee. Then he took his wallet from his jacket pocket and emptied out the contents. Receipts, crumpled slips of paper bearing scribbled phone numbers, credit cards for shops and services he had never used, buttons from various shirts and jackets he no longer possessed, business cards and a number of newspaper cuttings piled onto the bedcover. One was a revue of the movie *Apocalypse Now,* showing at a theater in Times Square.

"Christ, I must sort this lot out," he thought as he probed the inner recesses of the wallet. In a small slot at the back, he found what he was looking for, one of his father's old business cards. It named Joe Lassiter as features editor for the *Washington Tribune.* On the back, his father had written various numbers where he could be reached during the day. The card had to have been there for at least twelve years, although sandwiched tightly between two layers of leather, it had hardly yellowed at all. It would provide him with some temporary credentials.

He crossed into the living room to his attaché case, which lay on its side on the floor. He snapped back the catches and lifted it up, only to find that the case had been upside. It's contents spilled out onto the floor. Lassiter cursed, got down on his haunches, and began to replace his papers, turning them right-side-up as he went. For a moment he was confused as to why pages of typescript, annotated in what he instantly recognized as Lowell Vandenberg's hand, should be amongst them. When he turned them over, he remembered that, when Inspector Caldicott had first called from England, he had been staying in Marianne's apartment. Without his own stuff around him, he'd been forced to scramble around in her desk for something to write notes on. Not surprisingly, one of the upper drawers had been stuffed with early drafts of Vandenberg's speeches, covered in his handwritten notes. Lassiter had taken half a dozen pages—then, according to the date on them, more than three months old—and written on the backs of them. Now, he checked through the notes quickly to see if there was anything worth keeping.

At the bottom of one, beneath Lassiter's large, clear hand, was something written by the governor, scrawled hastily across the corner of the page, little more than a doodle . . . Lassiter read it twice and dropped back into a sitting position. He stared at the sheet for a moment longer and then hurried into the bedroom to get his father's file on Vandenberg. He found the newspaper cutting that reproduced the text of the right wing group's statement, in which they claimed responsibility for the assassination attempt, and laid it next to the sheet with Vandenberg scrawl. He read each of them aloud:

" . . . other subhuman breeds who threaten the fabric of U.S. Soc." The writing was clear enough. The text in the clipping ran, " . . . other races who threaten the fabric of American Society." The wording was marginally different—the second was like a later draft of the first, as though the writer had decided to tone it down a little—but the sense was identical.

How, in the name of all that's holy, could Vandenberg have almost exactly prophesied the wording that a bunch of Neo-Nazis would use in a letter to the press in three months' time? He checked the date on the manuscript again. There was only one conceivable answer: because he'd written the letter himself. There was no Neo-Nazi group, never had been.

Lassiter stood up and let out a yelp. Joe was right; Vandenberg had set up the hit himself. Simply to get publicity, to get a sympathy vote, he had arranged for his own security chief to shoot at him, and had had an innocent marksman murdered to use as a patsy. The "Nazi" letter had been intended to spotlight Vandenberg's professed concern for minorities, to promote him as a champion of the downtrodden, almost martyred for their cause. The headlines on the press cuttings in Joe's file showed that, to a large extent, the scam had worked.

At that moment, the impact this revelation might have in a court of law was the least of Lassiter's concern. *I know now,* he told himself. *I know now, for certain, that you are everything my father told me you were. And that somehow you must be stopped.*

Lassiter ran a comb through his wiry, salt and pepper hair and checked himself in the mirror on the wall, opposite the reception desk at NTV. He looked tired, but there was still a sparkle in the dark eyes. Behind him, he could see a slim woman of about thirty swiveling down the corridor toward him.

"Mr. Lassiter?"

He turned and his eyes creased into a smile. "Miss Schochow. It's very good of you to see me."

"Well, when you first called, I hadn't realized you were with the *Washington Tribune*."

He passed her his father's business card. "Well, as I told you, I'm doing a piece on the Vandenberg family. While I was in town, I thought I'd try and fill in some of the blanks surrounding the war years. I thought an interview with the Red Cross woman who took him in as a baby could have a lot of human interest."

She handed him a sheet of paper. "I've put Frau Dressler's address and telephone number down here for you."

"I'm most grateful."

The large blue-gray eyes connected with Lassiter's for a moment. "I would appreciate it if you don't say you got this from me."

Lassiter put a finger to his lips. "Not a word. Look, maybe you could give me some advice. I'm only here a few days and I need a good photo library service?"

"That's really not my field . . . Why don't you try our press office on the second floor? Ask for Claus and tell him I sent you."

Claus turned out to be a tiny man with a Kaiser Wilhelm mustache and side whiskers that extended upward, somewhat incongruously, into a bald pate. He looked like a refugee from a Grimm fairy tale.

Lassiter extended his hand. "Good morning. I'm working on a story about Lowell Vandenberg, the American Democratic presidential nominee." That was quite a mouthful in German and Lassiter had to go over it several times before Claus's glum little face brightened in recognition. "We were wondering what stills you had of him."

Claus looked Lassiter up and down and shook his head. "We don't have much on him at all yet. Stay there, I'll see what's on file."

The folder he produced five minutes later was surprisingly full. While Claus went to check amongst stuff that had just come in, Lassiter went through the contents. One ten-by-eight showed Vandenberg talking with the German foreign minister. His face was shown in profile.

Claus returned with a handful of contact prints a few minutes later. "Some of these might be . . . " He looked around him. The visitor was gone.

Max Gehrhart held the ten-by-eight up to the light. "Well, that explains a whole lot. Our man's had a nose job. Had his septum shaved or something. Could be an implant."

"Are you certain?" Lassiter asked.

Max shot him a look which said "you want to argue with the expert?" "The computer program just isn't sophisticated enough to show it up . . . And he's had something done to his chin too." He lifted his glasses and stared at the photograph more closely. "Could be Walt Lindquist's work. He did John DeLorean." Max began to search around his office for his cola tipple. "So that's why the computer-generated profiles don't match up with the photograph we have. The program's showing us what he would have looked like if he'd left himself alone."

"Well, as he didn't, we're screwed."

"Not necessarily, not if we could get a picture of him before he had all the work done, and match it to our simulation."

Getting a picture won't be easy if he had it done before he entered public life, Lassiter thought. The Vandenberg family have had a high profile in Washington, D.C. for more than a century. Even if I'm right, one of the older newspapers might have something on file. I can't believe the young Lowell C. didn't show up in society pages now and again. "I'll call my father, he has contacts that may be able to come up with something," Lassiter said.

"Do that." Max headed off in the direction of the men's room.

On the screen to Lassiter's right was the "Frankenstein Head," as Max called it, the simulation of Lowell Vandenberg's face they'd constructed themselves. So it's probably accurate after all, Lassiter thought. He stared at it for a while. "So this is what you'd look like if you hadn't screwed around with yourself."

One thing was certain: from a physiognomical viewpoint, the face Lowell Vandenberg was born with was a lot more revealing than the one the world knew. The bridge of his original nose was much higher, making the eyes very deepset, an interesting combination with the high forehead and the ridge above the brow. This man is obsessively secretive, Lassiter intoned to himself. Brooks no opposition, accepts no failure, in himself or others. The tip of the nose slants downward: might normally mean he was a skeptical or suspicious man, but taken with all the other features, especially the shape of the upper lip, it probably means a great deal more. He typed into the keyboard, recalling the keys Max had used, and the head began to rotate. He stopped it and moved it back and forth a few times. The bone structure was such that, when the head was turned as little as ten degrees to the left, the left eye was obscured by the bridge of the nose. Lassiter struggled to recall all that he'd read. Now he checked the placement of the ears, the pitch of the forehead, how much of the brain lay behind the central axis. The Neimann Precept: classic.

"Tell me, what value would these computer simulations have in a court of law?" he asked as Max sidled back in.

"The basic program was first used in the Ivan Demjanjuk case. His conviction was overturned on appeal, but the accuracy of that aspect of it was never challenged. Since then computer-generated image-matching has figured in about seventy successful prosecutions. Defense councils get pretty exercised when this stuff turns up in a case, but the fact is, juries love it. They relate to the visuals, to the hi-tech feel of the process, I guess."

"Yes, I can understand that."

"But God knows what they'd make of this little effort of ours."

"On its own, not much, but this'll just be an appetizer. I still have to come with the entrée, dessert and coffee." Lassiter picked up his attaché case and turned for the door. "You know, Max, our friend Frank here is a real interesting fella. He has a very rare combination of facial traits."

"Oh yeah? What are they telling you?"

Lassiter shrugged. "I don't take this physiognomy stuff as holy writ but . . . it could be he takes after his daddy. I need to dig into a couple of my reference books, check a few things out. But I think ol' Frank's a psychopath."

TWENTY-SIX

Horst Rathenau held the telephone receiver closer to his ear, barely able to believe what he was hearing.

"I've given considerable thought to all you've told me," Lowell Vandenberg was saying. "Clearly, we have a great deal more to say to one another. I'm certain there's much you must want to ask me. This is a little sudden I know, but I have that rarest of things in a presidential candidate's life—a free afternoon. I wondered if you would care to join me for lunch."

Rathenau's voice was barely audible. "I should like that very much indeed."

"Good. I'll send a car for you at noon. Is that too early?"

"No, not at all."

"And we must find you somewhere a little more comfortable to stay, too."

"I'm not uncomfortable here," Rathenau said.

"I'm having our guest house made up for you.

Check out of there, and I'll have you moved in later this afternoon."

Rathenau put down the phone and rubbed his eyes. Over the last sleepless nights, he'd tortured himself with every imaginable outcome of that last terrible meeting. His son's call fitted none of them.

"My son." For the first time in over fifty years he said the words aloud. To think them is to risk saying them. To say them is to risk destroying a future president of the United States, he thought. It was a luxury he must deny himself.

What had changed Lowell's mind? The old man wondered. Once he was beyond anger, had curiosity set in? He'd find out soon enough. At last, he could relax a little. If only the Customs agent was out of the picture. If the bomb had blown Lassiter to pieces, he thought, I could be at peace with the world.

Rathenau's first two weeks in America had drained every ounce of his energy. He'd been in the country less than twenty-four hours when the call from Kurt Hofle, his sister-in-law's boy, had come. Like many of his generation, the boy had been fascinated by the Nazi era. From all accounts, he had started collecting books and memorabilia in his early teens. Anxious not to encourage Kurt further, his mother had said nothing of her brother-in-law's Nazi past. It had been another relative who told him about his dead aunt's husband. The boy, desperate to communicate with a real live SS officer, had traced Rathenau through the family to his then home in Leipzig. The two had secretly been in touch for years. Kurt had traveled to Germany a couple of times to meet his uncle and Rathenau had taken advantage of his nephew's New York base to have him run minor errands from time to time. Now, at last, Hofle was able to prove he could be invaluable to his uncle. The German had barely unpacked in his Washington hotel room, when he learned from Hofle that a U.S. Customs agent had been to Brooklyn to see his sister-in-law. She had told of the day Rathenau had collected his baby son. Even given the man a photograph. It was the one eventuality the old German had never allowed for.

Rathenau had retired as Mielke's rinser in the spring of 1986. The golden handshake he'd received from the Stasi chief had been more than generous. What became of the billions that Mielke had salted away, he neither knew nor cared, as he was by now a very wealthy man in his own right. A year later, the biggest stock market crash since 1929 wiped out 80 percent of his capital. Soon after, the communist régime in East Germany collapsed. Rathenau had had no illusions about the effect that would have on him personally. The arrest of Mielke, the opening of the Stasi files, would lead the authorities to him sooner or later, he was certain.

But years passed and he heard nothing. He'd almost put the whole matter out of his mind. To find that they were investigating him, just when he had established a link to Vandenberg, was a potentially disastrous development.

On the day of Hofle's call, Rathenau had contacted one of the old Stasi staffers, whom he knew was still employed at the complex. He was able to establish that Lassiter was working on the Mielke case for the *Finanzamt*. Clearly it was them that he had been representing when he had gone to the Hofles' place: no American agency was directly involved. At that point, Rathenau had assumed the agent was probably interested only in facts that related directly to the Mielke case. There was no immediate reason why he should have put together the rest of what he'd been told. On that basis, neither would he have passed it on. But the Stasi veteran had stressed that Lassiter was an extremely smart and, worse still, very tenacious operator. How long could it be before he realized what he had?

Rathenau had already seen a TV profile on his son that had covered his extraordinary start in life in detail. He had noted the text: "May 1941, the day the British sank Hitler's greatest warship, the *Bismarck,* a tiny baby is brought to the Red Cross in Switzerland . . . " *Time* Magazine that week had carried a feature on Vandenberg, covering his father's internment in Schrobenhausen. If Rathenau had seen all this, then Lassiter could have too. Only he had spoken to Frau Hofle, only he could make the fatal connection. Every day he was allowed to continue his investigations, the risks redoubled. Rathenau was no longer concerned for himself. What began to haunt his every moment was the fear that his son might be exposed and his bid for the presidency destroyed at a single stroke.

Rathenau's mind was soon made up. While there was still a chance that killing Lassiter would close the book whose subject was his son's true identity, he knew he must act. He would a use a tactic that had worked for him before. He called contacts he'd made in the U.S. underworld during his years as Mielke's rinser, and from them obtained details of Lassiter's whereabouts and the necessary hardware for the scheme he had in mind. The cost of the project cut deeply into the last of his savings, but to be doubly certain that everything would go as planned, he then contacted the trusted Bosnian he'd used to retrieve the documents from the Berlin bunker and had him fly to Washington to carry out the job.

The morning the killing was to take place, Rathenau had sat in his hotel room, anxiously awaiting the killer's call. But no call came, and a short report on the early evening news told Rathenau that the assassination had failed and the Bosnian was dead. He had hurried to the man's hotel, collected his belongings and did what he could to cover his tracks.

My son is just beginning to trust me, Rathenau thought now, as the taxi drove him to Vandenberg's mansion. Perhaps now I shall be respected instead of reviled. Everything I have longed for may come to pass. If I should tell him now of the risks he faces, I shall jeopardize everything.

The same chauffeur who had collected him before was waiting for him in the less-than-immaculate Chevrolet. Again they took what seemed to Rathenau to be a circuitous route to Fulton Film Services. This time there was another car in the parking lot, a black Mercedes sports. The man at the wheel wore a baseball cap and dark glasses. As Rathenau got out of the Chevy he wound down the window and took off the shades. The German saw that it was his son.

"Sorry to drag you out here again," he said. "I had a few things to take care of." Rathenau got in beside him and they headed for the freeway. "I was due to campaign in San Diego today."

"Yes, I heard about the firebombings on CNN."

"Iraqi terrorists, that's the general view. We

should get security clearance later. I may have to head out there tonight and show my face, talk with survivors and so on. Till then the day's my own."

A gray limo that Rathenau had thought was following them, swung off to the left. "You have no . . . bodyguards or anything?" Rathenau asked.

Vandenberg laughed. "Oh yes! Around me every waking moment. Sometimes I just say to hell with it, and tell 'em to take a hike for an afternoon. They go a little crazy but . . . well, while I'm just a candidate I can still do that . . . "

After their last encounter, it seemed strange to Rathenau to be talking so easily with his son.

"If I take the nomination that'll change. So I'm enjoying the little freedom I'm allowed while I can still have it."

When Vandenberg swung the car onto the northbound on-ramp, taking them away from the city, Rathenau asked where they were to lunch.

Vandenberg's eyes never left the road. "I thought you might like to meet my wife and children."

For a moment, Rathenau was too surprised to speak. Then he said, "I should enjoy that very much."

"Well, this weekend they're at our home in the country."

"Who shall I say I am?"

"My father's friend from Schrobenhausen. Why, what did you have in mind?"

The old man didn't like the edge in Vandenberg's voice.

"No, I shall tell them that. That's fine."

Vandenberg seemed to want to concentrate on driving so Rathenau held his peace. The urban sprawl around them soon gave way to open countryside, lush woodland thick with dogwoods and magnolias. This is a beautiful part of the country, the old man thought. Perhaps, if today goes well, I might buy a small house here somewhere. Near my family. My grandchildren. They must never know they are that, of course . . .

Vandenberg dialed a number on his mobile phone. He was clearly talking to his wife. There was a short conversation about lunch arrangements and the guest he was bringing, then he hung up and turned to his passenger. "Do you like picnics?"

"I haven't been on a picnic for thirty years," Rathenau said.

"Well, the kids are going to fix us a barbecue in the woods on our property." Vandenberg glanced at Rathenau's gray business suit. "If I'd known, I'd have said to come in casual clothes. But it's dry enough, you shouldn't get in too much of a mess."

Forty-five minutes later, Vandenberg turned off the road and they sped for a while through a maze of country lanes. Then Vandenberg pulled off the road onto a grass verge, got out of the car and unlocked a high wooden gate that stood at the entrance to a private driveway.

"I bought this property in the recession a few years back," he told Rathenau, as they negotiated the potholes that peppered the road ahead. "The house is little more than a cabin. It's the grounds that are really something. This way takes us to the woods."

Ahead was a wide copse of trees. Vandenberg parked the Merc, helped Rathenau to his feet, and they set off along a narrow, overgrown pathway. "I built the kids a barbecue area up at the house,"

Vandenberg said as he led the way. "But you know kids. Mine like to do it the old-fashioned way with a proper wood fire." As they pushed on, Rathenau strained to hear the sound of children's voices. There was only the crunch of leaves under their feet. Then ahead of them, he saw a column of woodsmoke rising through the trees. The way ahead was blocked by a hanging branch. Vandenberg snapped off some of the greenery and then pulled the bough upward so that Rathenau could pass. The German moved on ahead of him into a clearing. In the center a pile of leaves was smoldering. They were alone.

Vandenberg moved so fast that the old man never knew what hit him. He never saw the commando knife, just felt a hand clamp to his forehead and a sudden rush of cold air hit the inside of his neck. As his face splashed with blood he realized his throat had been cut. He turned slowly, staggering round until, through a column of spurting blood, he saw Vandenberg staring impassively at him.

"I'm not your son," the stranger said softly. "I'm Paul Vandenberg's son. I was brought up to loathe you, and people like you, for all that you did to my parents." Rathenau felt his life force ebbing away. He buckled at the knees and a second later, he lay face downward in the dry earth. "I may have your blood, but I have their son's rage. Their son's everlasting sense of loss. His abiding need for retribution. You can't take that away from me or change that now. No one can. The Lowell Vandenberg that was born to his mother can't punish you for what you did to him, to them. But this one can."

He knelt and dragged the twitching body toward

the bushes. Close by was a freshly dug trench. Vandenberg put his weight against the old man's frame, and the body dropped into the opening with barely a sound. He reached for a spade from where it lay on the ground and worked feverishly to fill the trench in with earth.

After a while Vandenberg stopped, leaned on the spade and looked down. All that was visible now was the German's face. The skin was alabaster white, but the eyes still showed a flicker of life. The labored breathing came in desperate gasps. The gash in his neck had opened, to take in soil and bubble out dark blood. Its ragged edges trembled like the lips of an obscene second mouth, as the lungs fought for air.

"I can kill. Without remorse. Without guilt. For years I wondered how it was I was able to do such a thing. Surely I had not inherited this from them. Now I know where it came from: you—the Butcher of Schrobenhausen. You left that baby to die in the woods under a few feet of wet earth. Perhaps, in a sense, you left me there too. Now you're going to find out how that feels."

Vandenberg closed the grieving eyes with a spade full of earth and hastened to finish his task.

TWENTY-SEVEN

The only indication that Frau Dressler had once been a member of the Red Cross was the faded citation Lassiter noticed above a writing desk to the left of the fireplace. The room was paneled in oak, stained dark by a century of smoke. The arms and backs of the heavy leather furniture were hung with lace antimacassars. The post-war world seemed not to have touched the place at all. The Customs agent paced impatiently, breathing the stale air, till he heard a footfall on the stairs.

Herr Dressler moved with great difficulty, as though every movement caused him pain. "It is as I have said: my wife told all that she remembers of the incident you're interested in to the people from the television company." He handed back the photograph. "It all happened far too long ago."

"Is it possible I could talk with her myself?" Lassiter tried. "I've come to Munich especially to see her. I would only take up a few moments of her time."

"That would be quite out of the question," Dressler said stiffly. "She's recovering from one of her attacks, she's not allowed visitors."

Lassiter picked up his attaché case and crossed the hallway to the front door. "Well, could I at least leave my number? Something may come to her, you never know."

"I think that most unlikely. But you may leave it if you wish."

Lassiter took out one of his business cards and wrote Erika's number and his own in Berlin on the back. As the front door swung open, they heard a voice behind them.

"Wait, Gustav." They turned around. An elderly woman, dressed in a quilted bed jacket, stood on the stairs. Her frail hands shook as they clasped the banister rail. "Herr . . . Lassiter?"

He stared up at her. "Yes."

"I . . . I do remember that man." Her Swiss accent was pronounced.

Gustav hurried over to her. "Isgarde."

"Don't fuss over me so. Just help me . . . " He half-lifted her down the rest of the stairs and eased her into a chair. "I do remember that man. He was the one who brought the Vandenberg baby from Dachau, to the Red Cross Center. Show me the picture again." Lassiter passed it to her. She turned it to the light. "Yes. He was SS, I'm sure. He was in civilian clothes, of course, but you could always tell—the Aryan looks, the deportment . . . " Her filmy eyes looked up into Lassiter's. "The Vandenbergs were a Jewish family, were they not?"

"The child had a Jewish mother. I understand that determines its race."

Frau Dressler nodded slowly. She wrapped a

shawl around her shoulders and stared out the window, her eyes focused on some far distant place. "We were so overworked that day . . . there were so many distraught people . . . But I remember the image clearly now . . . Did I see it in a mirror? Perhaps."

"There were so many children, Isgarde, so many people . . . How can you be sure it was him after all these years?"

"Because of what he did. What he did when he didn't think I was looking." She grabbed Lassiter's arm, her thin fingers urgent on his flesh. "As he was about to leave, he held the baby up . . . and he kissed it. He kissed a Jewish baby . . . "

Lassiter swung the BMW out into the fast lane of the autobahn, heading southwest toward Munich, and accelerated until he heard the automatic gearbox kick into top. His heart hammered in his chest. Of course he kissed the baby! It was his own, for Christ's sakes. He was kissing it good-bye.

"I've almost got you, you sick sonofabitch," Lassiter said out loud. "I knew what you were the first time I saw you. Saw it in your eyes. Because I'd seen eyes like it before. In a subway train when I was ten. I saw that look again in the face we made on Max's computer screen—your true face. I knew the look and it carried me forward, compelled me to hunt until I had something that would prove beyond doubt that you are what you are. And I have that now. I know for certain that what my father told me was right—you had an innocent man killed, just to pull off a publicity stunt. No accident, a premeditated crime you planned for weeks.

"You're not Lowell Vandenberg. Whether you yet know it or not, you are your father's son, the son of Horst Rathenau—a remorseless Nazi killer. The evil that drove him, drives you. And unless I stop you, you could be the most powerful man on earth . . .

"And now I think I can stop you. I can prove that you are who you are. I've got the story from start to finish and every part locks into the next. I've identified motive, means, and opportunity. I've crosschecked the history with the geo-chronology. I've got a fucking airtight scenario.

"Now all I need is one drop of blood, saliva, a hair, a fragment of body tissue or bone, from you and from one of your parents, *and you are out of the loop, pal.*

"So the next time you sit down to a five-thousand-dollar-a-plate fund-raiser, wipe your mouth, comb your hair, remember! Erika or someone like her will be waiting. Then we'll have our sample. *And then, Sweet Jesus, I'll have you . . .* "

The kiss was the key to everything. Rathenau loved the baby son who was all he had left to remind him of the woman who'd borne him. Her killing in Essen completely threw him, probably shook his faith in the Nazi cause. Could be he even foresaw the Americans coming into the war on the side of the Allies later that year—his file at the Wiesenthal Center said that he'd traveled to the U.S. in the mid-Thirties, so he would have known better than most then the kind of war effort we could mobilize if it came down to it. He had begun to see the war as an interminable nightmare, with nothing ahead but deprivation and disgrace. So he'd sent his boy to safety.

But was it conceivable that Rathenau had lived out his whole life without once trying to see the son he loved? Lassiter asked himself now. They must have met. It could be that Vandenberg knew Rathenau well. It was an even bet that he could take me right to Mielke's rinser, Lassiter told himself. But that's down the line. My first priority is the DNA samples.

He put a call in to Normannenstrasse from his mobile phone. Fraenkel sounded stressed. "Christ, Lassiter, I've been trying to reach you all afternoon."

"I'm sorry, I had a lot to go through. I've had my phone switched off."

"Remember the address in Leipzig we traced Rathenau to? The current owners thought the lawyer who handled the conveyancing for them might know where we could find him."

"Yeah, I remember."

"We had a hell of a job tracing the lawyer. He didn't have anything on our man, but the attorney acting for Rathenau, or Vollman as he called himself then, did. Better still, he recognized his client from our photograph. He's given us an address in Würzburg. Hoffman is driving down there right now."

What had Erika said? "Even a hair from a jacket lapel would do . . . "

"The local police are raking through all relevant files." Fraenkel went on. "Where are you now?"

"In Munich . . . checking out a lead of my own," Lassiter said quickly.

"Does it take us anywhere?"

"Don't know yet."

"Well, stay where you are," Fraenkel said. "If you need to, you could drive out to Würzburg in about three hours from there. Nothing new is going to break on this tonight, so I'll give you the number of our local office—they'll arrange accommodation for you there. I'll call you as soon as I get an update." He rang off.

Lassiter smacked his hand against the dashboard. It was all coming together. The next seventy-two hours could be the most pivotal of my life, he told himself. If there's some way I can pull all the threads of the DNA thing together—which, in the circumstances, is still a helluva big "if"—the first thing I'll do is track down Senator O'Sullivan in New York. He'd take a call from me, Lassiter told himself. He was really charged up about my handling of the Saddam operation and he'll remember all the work I did after the Noriega conviction. He loathes Vandenberg's guts. I remember Marianne saying so awhile back. Wouldn't he love it if I laid this on him? And the Democratic Convention is right on his doorstep.

Lassiter took a deep breath. For the first time in years he felt truly alive.

An hour later, he called Erika from the room he'd been assigned in a government-owned apartment building in the center of Munich. He longed to share every part of his discovery with her, but years of discipline said not, so he told her simply that things had turned out better than he could have hoped, and that he was staying where he was, in case there were further developments on the DNA front. If nothing broke in the next forty-eight hours, he would fly straight back to Washington. As she had just walked in through her front door, she said she would call him later when she'd had something to eat and rang off. Lassiter began to update his notes, talking into his dictaphone in a slow clear voice.

Outside, it had started to rain—one of those summer showers that burst for little apparent reason and fall off within minutes. Leland Daker wound up the window of the Renault hire car, leaving a gap of an inch or so, for the directional rifle mike. The rain was pounding on the roof now. He adjusted the headset he was wearing and turned up the monitor level on the cassette recorder. The double-glazing in the windows of Lassiter's room was doing nothing for the clarity of the signal he was getting and the noise of the rain made it hard to hear what the Customs agent was saying. The recording would be hardly broadcast quality, he thought, but, judging from what Lassiter was saying, that would be the very last thing Vandenberg would want to use it for.

The Lear jet banked steeply into the west and began its descent. Ches Chesterfield steadied himself and walked from the partitioned area at the front of the plane to the drinks cabinet amidships. With some difficulty, he collected another bottle of Jim Beam and staggered back to where Vandenberg, Lacy and cattle baron Dale McKendrick were drinking. Six months of relentless campaigning were getting to him now and Dale's presence on the plane was doing little for his resolve to cut down on the booze until his job for his client was done. It had been McKendrick's donation of three-quarters of a million dollars to their campaign fund in January that had enabled the governor of Virginia to enter the New Hampshire primary as a serious contender.

It was his plane Vandenberg and his team were traveling in now. McKendrick liked to come across as a smooth man of the world, but two stiff shots of bourbon and any polish he had acquired over the years was stripped away. He was a good ole boy from Oklahoma, and proud of it. It was his party, his dollar, and his talk set the mood.

" . . . I'm tellin' yer, if the population of this country continues to grow at the present rate, sixty percent of Americans will be fuckin' Hispanic by the end of the century." McKendrick topped up his glass. "It's a fact. There was a piece about it in the *Post* last Saturday."

Vernon Lacy put down his drink. His head was beginning to spin. "Well, if you believe what you read in that rag . . . "

McKendrick jerked his thumb in Vandenberg's direction. "Well, it's something he needs to be aware of if he's gonna be president."

"Gimme me a break, here." Vandenberg laughed and threw up his hands. "I'll airlift in fucking condoms, okay?"

"I'll tell you what we do," said Lacy, who was marginally more sober than the other three. "We get the World Health Organization to establish the concept of 'Non-Proliferation Zones.'"

"And what the fuck are they when they're at home?" McKendrick slurred.

"I'm coming to that. The World Health Organization says the maximum population density we should allow anywhere on the planet is 55,000 people to the square mile. After that people literally die from overcrowding."

Vandenberg tried to get his eyes to focus on the press agent. "That must be a pretty old statistic."

"It is, it was something they came up with in the late Sixties. You never hear zip about the issue now."

"Well, on that basis, most of the cities in this country are environmental deathtraps."

"That's just the point I'm coming to: everyone screaming for us all to be more environmentally conscious. So why not use these people's own figures to have the relevant areas in the U.S. monitored, and once they pass the magic figure, have them closed to further migration."

There were hoots of derisive laughter. Lacy was smiling too. "No, hear me out." He seemed to be having trouble putting his sentences together. "The only way you could move into the neighborhood after that would be if . . . someone else moved out."

"He's got a point, you know," McKendrick managed. "Close the fuckin' cities. That's it! Let's see the wetbacks figure a way round that one!"

"And cite environment issues as the reason? Oh sure, Vern, that's a real vote-catcher." Chesterfield topped up the glasses. "All you'd do is drive 'em into the desert. They breed like fucking gophers as it is. In ten years you'd have the country littered with shanty towns. If we wanna control the birth-rate we should do like the Chinese do."

"What, drown the girl children?" Vandenberg asked.

"Oh please. No, we should tax the Bejesus out of anyone who has more than one child." Again, laughter. "I'm fuckin' serious, Lowell. It's something we should look at."

"They're all on welfare, Ches," Vandenberg said. "You're talking about zilch. No, I'll tell you what we do." His eyes sparkled. "We follow the Russians' example, do what they do in Brazil, Chile and China. Round 'em up, fillet the fuckers and sell off their organs for spare-part surgery." He had to wait for the laughter to subside. "Hell, that's the new growth industry, isn't it?"

"Yeah, that'd fucking slow 'em down a bit," McKendrick said.

"Cash in the treasury, immigrants off the streets. Next question please."

The only other passengers on the plane were Marianne and two bodyguards. The guards were drinking coffee at the back. Marianne, who'd been on the jump since five that morning, was stretched out on a sofa on the other side of the partitioning. Chesterfield's expedition to the booze cupboard had woken her from a deep sleep. She'd lain with her eyes closed listening to all that had been said.

Moments before, hazy with sleep, she'd tried again to make sense of all that had happened in Vandenberg's screening room, that night after the Miami riots. She'd been alone with the governor for no more than a few minutes since. There had been no hint in his treatment of her that anything in their relationship had changed. But then, in the circumstances, she'd reasoned, that was to be expected. Had that outpouring of passion just been the product of one overwhelming moment of euphoria? It was impossible for her to know her own feelings until she had some indication of his . . .

But now, as Vandenberg moved through the plane to the toilet in the rear, she turned her face to the wall. Seven years she'd been with him. In some ways, she'd always felt, she knew him better than anyone. But now, with the "good ole boy" talk still ringing in her ears, it seemed to her that she barely knew him at all.

Twenty minutes later, the Lear landed on the narrow runway that adjoined the governor's residence. Lowell Vandenberg eased himself out of his seat, stepped down and walked unsteadily toward the conservatory entrance at the back of the building. He looked at his watch. Nine hours campaigning had left him with little enthusiasm for the evening "flesh-presser," a dinner he and Stella were set to attend in a little more than an hour's time.

To his surprise, she was at the door to meet him. Her face was carefully composed as though she was bracing herself to impart something painful. She took both his hands in hers as he came in. "I'm afraid I have some very sad news," she said almost immediately. "Aunt Helga died this afternoon at around two. Josef called from Switzerland to tell us."

Her husband crossed the plant-filled conservatory and lowered himself onto the larger of the two sofas that faced into the garden. "Oh, poor Helga . . . "

"Josef said it was very quick. She was there one minute, talking cheerfully about coming back to Washington. And the next minute, she was dead. A massive heart attack, the doctor said." Stella went to the drinks cabinet.

Faced with this news a week ago, Vandenberg would have been devastated. Helga had been the one relative who had shown him love, had, in the vacations he'd spent with her, attempted to provide him with some sense of family life. But what would she have made of him now? Without the answer to that, it was impossible for him to know what to feel. A steel gate had already descended in his mind, separating him from the events in the woods the day before. If he thought at all about yesterday, it was as though someone else had dug and killed and buried, as though he'd been no more than a disembodied witness, dispassionately watching the acts of another. The only residue that was permitted to register openly was the dull ache in his right arm, still stitched and now sore from the recent exertions, and an overall feeling of exhaustion. In the circumstances, the news of Helga's death marked him hardly at all.

Stella brought him a drink. "The funeral's on Friday. I have that 'Freedom to Live' dinner. They're expecting me to speak and I don't see how on earth I can get out of it. It's been in the schedule for seven months."

"No, you shouldn't cancel that." He closed his eyes, leaving the drink untouched. "I can't even think about my schedule, right now . . . "

Stella put her arm around him. "My poor baby. You look exhausted. I know how much Helga meant to you. I'm so terribly sorry . . . I didn't know what you'd want to do about tonight. I had my secretary warn the organizers that we'd had a death in the family . . . "

"I can't cancel at this notice. It wouldn't be right." He kissed her on the neck. "But I think I might lie down for a bit."

Once in his dressing room, Vandenberg loosened his tie and unlocked the far-end closet door. Covered by a blanket was Rathenau's suitcase. He pulled it out, took the German's keys from his pocket and unlocked it. There were clothes and the usual personal items.

The only article of interest was a large faded envelope. He leafed through the yellowed documents it contained—papers relating to a dozen different men. The text was all in German, but Vandenberg was in no doubt that this was the package that had been hidden for so long in the air duct of Bunker Two, in Berlin, and that the papers had been taken from interned Jews, now long dead—documents Rathenau had obviously thought might come in useful, if the tide of the war turned against Germany.

The only other document was a passport, in the name of a Bosnian called Vukan Babic aged forty-two. Vandenberg examined it. Hadn't Rathenau said that he'd used a Bosnian to retrieve the papers from the bunker? How come his passport had ended up in Rathenau's suitcase in Washington? Vandenberg wondered. Clearly, the man had paid a heavy price for sharing his employer's secret. He locked the envelope in a drawer of his dressing-table and returned the suitcase to its hiding place. He would dispose of it tomorrow.

He ran the bath and had begun to undress when there was a knock at the door. He put on a robe and opened it. Marianne looked embarrassed, her eyes no longer met his directly. "I was so sorry to hear about your aunt . . . I was told you were sleeping, but then I heard the bath. There's a call from a man called Gable in Munich. He said it was urgent and that you would want to speak with him. I thought it might be related to your aunt's death or I wouldn't have disturbed you . . . "

Vandenberg's face registered nothing. *What the hell is Daker playing at? He knows the correct procedures. He's risking everything . . .* "Have them put the call through," Vandenberg said as casually as he could. Over the private line in the dressing room Daker sounded cool. "Can you talk?"

"Are you out of your mind? I told you never to call me through the main switchboard."

"Suit yourself. I've been calling the direct line all day and got no reply. I thought you needed an urgent update, and I figured it was worth the risk."

Vandenberg tried to steady his nerves. "Okay, what's come up that's so important?"

"I've run surveillance on your friend the Customs man for three days. It's not been easy, he won't keep still. Right now we're in Munich. I've been able to monitor most of the phone calls he's made. I even know a lot of what he's thinking. See, he dictates stuff to himself, for hours at a time . . . He knows it all, Vandenberg."

He knows it all. For a fragment of a second, the beast rose in Lowell Vandenberg. The demon inside struggled for a voice and then was overcome.

"Go on," he said at last.

"You want me to spell it out on an open line? Well, it's your life." Daker measured his words carefully. "He's real interested in Horst Rathenau's baby boy, how he's turned out . . . you know what I'm saying?"

Lassiter knows it all. So now Daker knows too . . . Vandenberg fought to control the panic in his voice. "Who has he told . . . do you know?"

"No one yet, as far as I can tell. Right now, he's being real cagey. He's said in his notes he doesn't want to commit himself until he has forensic evidence to back up his conclusions. But, if you ask me, he's going to start shooting his mouth off any day now. That's why I thought you should know about this straightaway."

"Yes, you were right to call. Is this an official investigation or what?"

"I'm pretty sure Lassiter's a loose cannon. He's acting purely on his own. You'll have to hear the tape for yourself and make up your own mind. Either way, the sooner he's turned around the better."

Vandenberg's hands were shaking so badly he had to clamp the phone between his jaw and shoulder to be certain of holding on to it. He tried to shake off his exhaustion and the effects of the drink, to bring the full strength of his intellect to bear on the massive problem at hand. But somehow the immensity of it was impossible to grasp.

"You want me to Federal Express the cassettes to you?" Daker asked.

"*No!* For Christ's sakes don't do that! I don't know who else might be . . . watching me." He began to go over his immediate schedule. Then he remembered Aunt Helga's funeral. In Switzerland; the house at Lake Constance. Daker was in Munich . . . no more than an hour and a half's drive. "Look, there might be a way I can get to you . . . Is there somewhere I can call you later?" Daker gave him a number. "Daker, I may need this tidied up in a hurry . . . There'd be a hundred K in it for you."

The laugh from the other end of the line sent a chill down Vandenberg's back. "That's small change, Lieutenant. The way I see it, this guy can cost you the whole farm. With him out of the picture, you're safe enough. So this is what you might call the big one, wouldn't you say?"

Vandenberg's mind raced. Daker was pushing hard. Without him, he said, the faked assassination would never have worked. Without him, Teresa

Lucana would have nailed him as a pedophile. "If you want the guy closed down, it's gonna cost you a million."

There was silence. "Look Daker, I've got a lot to sort out here," Vandenberg said at last. "Stay on his case. I'll call you at around 7 A.M. tomorrow, my time."

Vandenberg hung up. He began to tremble. It began at his knees and resonated up to his shoulders. For the first time in his adult life he was losing control of the situation. *I've risked everything to rid myself of the one man who knew the truth about me, only to find there are now two more . . .*

Vandenberg lowered his shoulders into the soothing heat of the bath water and tried to put his thoughts in order. The key question is, can Daker be trusted to kill Lassiter, knowing what he now knows? If I pay him a million, can I rely on him to do the job and stay silent? He'll be in a position to blackmail me till the end of time. But, hell, he's had that option open to him for months already. Every time he did what I asked of him and went away. If I give him what he's asking now, why should things change? If I pay him half before and half afterward, it at least reduces the risk of him disappearing with the million and leaving Lassiter alive.

But what if Daker keeps his side of the bargain, and then is caught and arrested? What's to stop him opening up to the police, implicating me as part of a plea bargain? Again, that has been a risk I've run all along. But this assignment isn't like the Sullivan deal, a carefully-thought-out thing, with months of planning behind it. Nor is it like the Teresa Lucana business, the straightforward killing of an anonymous Filipina woman, living in the middle of nowhere. This is a high-risk hit, where a million things could go wrong.

Whatever the outcome, Vandenberg decided now, I must find a way to silence Daker for good, and soon. But right now, I need him. First, I have to be as certain as I can be that he's still on track. I can't be that unless I see him face to face.

There was a primitive, Pavlovian element to his relationship with the man he'd met in the Vietnam jungle, always had been. If I deal with him eyeball to eyeball, Vandenberg told himself, I can maybe get him back to where he was in Sullivan . . . in Saigon.

As the governor dressed in his silk tuxedo, he began to go over the funeral idea in detail. Aunt Helga will be buried the day after tomorrow. I should attend, after everything she's done for me, it will be expected. I shall need a sophisticated alibi to cover the time I shall be missing. If I meet Daker in somewhere like . . . Fussen, I could have the whole thing covered in a couple of hours. The risks this time will be enormous. But I've taken great risks before. And I have no other choice.

For a moment, Ches Chesterfield looked like he'd been kicked in the head. Vandenberg's campaign team were brought to immediate silence. Chesterfield cleared his throat. "There's no way I want to come between you and your family commitments, Governor, but the timing is a bitch."

"I'm well aware of that, Ches," Vandenberg said. "But this is something I have to do. All we're talking about is thirty-six hours. Stella will stay on here and cover for me where she can. People will understand in the circumstances, I'm sure. The convention begins Tuesday. I'll be back from Switzerland Sunday night. I have all the drafts of the keynote speech. I have everyone's notes, including my own. I'll use the time on the plane to assimilate all the material . . . If you want the honest truth, I need this time to myself." He looked around at the fifty-seven people gathered in the conference room of Hague House and could sense momentum, built up over months, slipping away. Instinctively, he moved to take charge of the proceedings. "I needn't tell you what a drain this campaign has been on me, on all of us. And I haven't come this far to throw it all away now, I promise you. By Sunday night, I'll be ready for anything they want to throw at me, you have my word. I think it is vital we keep the issues in perspective at this time. So I want Larry to give you the update position with regard to delegate support."

Vandenberg sat down and Larry Kerkorian, the team's chief pollster, rose to his feet.

"You all know the mathematics involved here. We need the votes of 2,145 delegates to win the nomination outright at the first ballot." He put on bifocals and studied the sheet of paper in front of him. "We currently have 1,847, which means we'll need the support of 300 of the 772 super delegates to wrap up the nomination. My team have been on the phones all week, the last few nights, till three in the morning. I can tell you that we have the support of 203 of those delegates right now." There was an intake of breath around the room and some whoops of delight. He held up his hand. "Barring some kind of blocking coalition by the other party bigwigs, delegates already won by other candidates and the 'uncommitted' faction, which is extremely unlikely, it's mathematically impossible for the governor to be denied the nomination." This generated loud applause and more shouts of approval.

Kerkorian sat down and Vandenberg worked to lift his team's spirits still higher. "Ches has talked to the Bravington camp twice in the last twenty-four hours. If everything goes to plan, as a healing gesture, to give us political and regional balance, I shall invite Gene to join me on the ticket as the vice-presidential nominee. I've read a lot about him and I really feel we could work together . . . "

Marianne felt a creeping sense of unreality sweep over her as she tried to concentrate on what was being said. It was hard to equate the wholesome rhetoric of the man with the obscenities of the night before. Was it just the drink I heard talking? she wondered. Or is there a hidden, dark side to his nature? If there is, how come I never saw it before? God knows, the man has been under pressure. Few in the governor's inner circle had believed the "spin" that Chesterfield had put out, about the accident with the mirror in the hotel bathroom. It was clear to them that Vandenberg had had some kind of breakdown that night, as a result of the attempt on his life. Now Marianne was beginning to wonder whether the effects of that were escalating into something far more serious, something capable of distorting his judgment. She studied the composed figure holding forth opposite her. Or maybe the truth is that that side has always been there, but hidden from view. And now he's beginning to crack up, he's letting it show through.

Vandenberg looked around the room, taking care to make visual contact with everyone present. "You don't need me to tell you the difficulties the Republicans now face. I'm sure you've all seen the *Washington Post* piece with the transcript of the phone call between Governor Travanion and the mayor of Miami, the night of the riots there. The committee, investigating that matter, will publish its findings in September, which is perfect for us. The jury will still be out, so to speak, during the Republican Convention. This way, Travanion still takes the nomination in August—damaged or not, he's the best candidate they've got—and gets wiped off the political map a month later. I'm not saying for a minute our fight will be over then, but I truly believe this campaign trail," his face creased into a broad smile, "this grueling odyssey we've embarked on together, will end on the White House steps."

Vandenberg sat down to an eruption of applause. Chesterfield moved quickly to bring the meeting to order. He and Vernon Lacy began to hastily revamp the governor's schedule. Marianne shook away her thoughts and turned her mind to the subject at hand. She felt for the tiny dictaphone she always carried with her to take notes. It wasn't in her pocket or her purse, and she suddenly realized she must have left it in Vandenberg's private office, after their early-morning meeting. She slipped from the table and crossed the administration block into his study. For a moment, she couldn't see the little cassette machine, then she found it under some files on his desk. She retrieved it and hurried back to the conference room.

Two hours later, she sat in her own office, the governor's amended schedule in front her. All she

needed to do now was to add in his landing time at
Kennedy on Sunday night. Tim Matheson handled
all the governor's traveling arrangements. She had
called him at home from the office at 7:30 that
morning, to check on flights, and had recorded all
the details he'd given her straight on to the
dictaphone. Now she took it from her purse and
pressed "rewind" to spool the tiny cassette back to
the top. She copied the itinerary into her notes.

Suddenly the sound of her voice was replaced
by another; the governor's. He was talking on the
phone. For a minute, she was puzzled as to how it
came to be there. Then she remembered that the
machine was voice-activated. Any sound in a room
could cause it to switch on and record by itself. The
machine must have picked up a conversation the
governor had had after she'd left. She spooled
forward to where she judged her own notes from
the morning conference might be on the tape, and
pressed play. Again, Vandenberg's voice. He was
arranging to meet someone in Germany. Marianne
reached to move the tape on again, then she heard,
"And you're sure the Customs agent is staying on
where he is?"

Customs agent? They're a fairly rare breed,
Marianne told herself. As far as she knew, the only
Customs agent Vandenberg had ever had any
dealings with was her husband, at that one meeting
at Hague House. And he was in Germany right now.
Could Vandenberg be referring to Jack? What could
he want with him? Could it involve her? She turned
up the volume on the machine. A million dollars.
For what? she asked herself. " . . . to simplify the
end game." What the hell was that supposed to
mean? Were they planning . . . to bribe him? She ran

the tape again, this time from the beginning. It was impossible to know exactly what was being said, as she only had Vandenberg's end of the conversation, and much of it was clearly in reference to issues that had been discussed in an earlier call. But the tone of his voice . . . it had a hard edge to it, a callousness almost. She'd heard it before. She listened on. And then she remembered when. In the plane with the good ole boys: *"Round 'em up and fillet the fuckers!"*

She switched off the tape and sat trembling, stared unseeing out of the window. An animal feeling gnawed at her insides. There was no doubt what the money was to be used for.

TWENTY★EIGHT

The handful of mourners, gathered at the southern edge of the little Swiss cemetery, braced themselves against the wind and strained to catch what the priest was saying. Lowell Vandenberg stared at the small bronze coffin and asked himself, what would this woman feel for me now?

In his childhood years, Aunt Helga had been the only close relative prepared to show him love. To her, he was the last reminder of the family that had been snatched away from her forever, in the years when her Dutch homeland was overrun by the Germans. In truth, she had been more than a little over protective of the boy during the long summer vacations when he'd stayed with her at her island home on Lake Constance. But to the young Lowell, starved of affection and close family life, it was a small price to pay for a time which he regarded as an escape to paradise. The old baroque mansion, built on a chunk of granite barely fifty yards in diameter set in the center of the lake, was a place of everlasting enchantment.

In the evenings, she would sit on the balcony, overlooking the Alpine forests and peaks, and tell him of his mother. In those moments, Lowell had felt close to Anna Vandenberg, almost as though he could touch her. Some nights when the mist blew in, and the house was shrouded in an impenetrable wall of gray, it felt to him as though it existed in a place and time of its own. He slept in the room she'd slept in before the war. And here in the open window he talked with her. Here, he fancied she called back to him, across the water, with the answers to a thousand questions.

Now, it seemed, all that was lost. If she had ever been out there, he told himself, his was the last voice she would have heeded. Helga had loved him as much because of what he represented as for himself. Would she have understood the terrible accident of history that he was a part of, or, faced with the revelation, have turned away from him, horrified and disgusted? He watched as the coffin was lowered into the earth. Now he would never know.

Press photographers, stationed at the perimeter of the cemetery, began to move forward. Roddick, the bodyguard assigned to travel with Vandenberg, crossed to head them off.

Vandenberg's eyes never left the grave. My troubles are with the living, he told himself. By the time I fly out of here, they too will have passed.

The old couple who had run the island house for as long as he could remember crossed the gravel path toward him. "Will you be joining the others for some refreshment?" the man asked. "Or do you wish to go to the house now, Herr Vandenberg?"

I am him. I must be him.

"Is the gathering not to be held at the house, Josef?"

"No, it was felt that a boat trip would be too much for the older ones."

Vandenberg stared out across the village to the lake. "Oh yes, of course."

"The mayor of the Rorschach has offered his home. It is only a minute from here," the woman said.

"How thoughtful of him." Lowell put his arm around the housekeeper. "Well, we shouldn't let him down then, should we?"

The prospect of a few glasses of eau de vie and game pie seemed to cheer the pair, and they and Vandenberg joined the bent, shuffling figures negotiating the steep pathway to the town.

It was late afternoon when Vandenberg, Roddick, Josef and his wife reached his aunt's boathouse on the mainland. Several photographers had stayed on to get shots of the U.S. presidential candidate leaving the mayor's house, but had followed the car only as far as the end of the street. The caretaker parked the aging Citroën in the garage end of the building and began to carry the luggage to the wooden dinghy that was used as a shuttle. Vandenberg noticed that his bodyguard was fighting to stay awake. Good, the six-hour time change is slaughtering you. You'll sleep long and deep tonight.

Josef helped his wife down to the narrow wooden jetty, then looked around for the American.

Vandenberg heard Josef calling from below and

spun around. Satisfied that he was still alone, he unzipped a small sports bag and slipped the carving knife he'd stolen from the mayor's house in amongst the clothes. Plan B . . . Please God, it won't come to that. He slid it behind a pile of logs stacked by the window. When he got to his feet, a wave of tiredness hit him too. Had it not been for the two liters of water he'd drunk on the plane, he was certain that he would have fallen into a deep sleep at the wake. As it was, he knew that a good hot shower would revitalize him long enough to do all that needed to be done that night.

The couple knew Vandenberg's habits well enough, so there was no surprise when he announced, as they tied up at the island, that he would go straight to bed. Secure in the knowledge that he would not be disturbed until morning, he set about making his plans. He opened the French doors in the master bedroom, walked out onto the balcony and peered over the railings. Clear water lapped against the rock face, twenty feet below. In the fading light, he could just make out a rusty metal spike protruding from the granite beneath one end of the balcony. They're still there after all these years, he thought.

Even when Vandenberg had reached his teens, his aunt had expected him to turn in for the night when she did—often as early as 10:30. She would say that she could only sleep if she knew he was safe. The young Lowell, desperate to mingle with the girls around his age who frequented the bars of the smart hotels on the mainland, determined to develop an escape route. Once out of the house, he could swim the fifteen hundred yards to the shore with little difficulty, but his aunt, he knew, was a light sleeper: leaving by either of the main doors was to risk waking her. And there seemed to be no feasible way down the sheer wall of rock from his balcony. He had thought about a rope ladder, but that meant leaving it in place for his return and then there was the possibility it might be discovered in his absence.

One summer day, he'd swum around the island till he was directly beneath his balcony. He found there were good footholds for about the first twelve feet up to it, but the stretch above seemed unclimbable. He went down to where the trash was kept and found a broken section of old railing that had been left there. From it, he cut four short lengths of steel bar with a hacksaw. He climbed back up the rock face, as high as he could go, and hammered one into the granite above him. Then, using it as a foothold, hammered in another and repeated the operation until he could lever himself onto his balcony.

For the rest of that summer, and several to come, he would wait until he was certain his aunt was settled for the night, strip down to his shorts and climb down to the water's edge, then he would swim to the boathouse on the mainland. Here he would dry himself and change into clothes he kept hidden behind the logs. When the evening was over, he would return the same way with no one in the house any the wiser.

Tonight, Vandenberg would use his escape route again. Provided he followed the rest of the plan to the letter, his alibi—should he ever need one—would be in place. The boathouse, cut into the west side of the island, was always kept locked. The only keys to the thirty-foot fiber-glass cruiser

inside, and the wooden Riva power boat, were on
Josef's key ring. Even if it were possible to make
duplicates without his knowing, to take out either
boat at night, undetected, would have been virtually
impossible. Josef, who slept directly above the
boathouse, could be counted on to hear.
Vandenberg had decided that once his mission was
completed, he would return to his room the same
way he left it. He was satisfied that it would take a
giant leap of imagination to figure out how he could
ever have left his bedroom.

Neither would the transport he would use be
easy to trace. The previous summer, his boys and
four of their schoolfriends had come over to stay
with Helga. Anxious not to exhaust the old woman,
Vandenberg had arranged for three of the kids to
stay at the vacation home of a friend on the
mainland. He had meant to return the keys to the
place, months ago, but the friends had said nothing
and the keys had remained on his ring ever since.
Now the Morgensons were in Atlanta, so Stella had
said, so the place was certain to be empty. There
was a nondescript Volkswagen Golf in the garage
there, which the family used for shopping trips. The
keys were in a hiding place in the den. Provided
there was still enough gas in it to get him to the
filling station in the next village, it would suit his
purpose perfectly.

Soon, in the stillness of the bathroom, he was
turning his mind to his final problem: how to
change the face that millions knew to be his. In front
of him, on the glass shelf above the basin, lay the
remains of three lines of cocaine. Bringing it into the
country had been the biggest single risk he had
taken. While he waited for the inside of his nose to

become totally numb, he rifled through the contents of the envelope he'd found amongst Rathenau's things again and took out the Bosnian's passport with its German resident's permit. He stared at the battered face in the photograph and compared it with his own in the mirror. As a stratagem, it's by no means perfect, he thought. But it's the only one I have.

He glanced at his watch. Fifteen minutes; time enough. He took a safety pin from his toilet bag, took a deep breath and stuck the point of it hard into the flesh inside his nose. No pain. The cocaine had anaesthetized it perfectly. Then he took out a pair of tweezers and stood before the bathroom mirror.

It had taken the surgeon only ten minutes to put the silicone implant back in place when he'd knocked it out playing racketball with his sons, he told himself. He put the tweezers gingerly into his left nostril. How long could it take to get out?

The lakeshore boathouse was just a dark shadow in the early evening light. Vandenberg moved silently through the water in an even crawl, throwing his head to one side with each second stroke, to take in air. He scanned the jetty for movement. It seemed deserted. He struck out hard for the last few yards and clambered up the wooden steps. The sports bag lay where he'd left it behind the logs. After toweling himself dry and changing quickly into jeans, a denim shirt and a lightweight anorak, he emerged cautiously onto the narrow track that ran alongside the building and made his way up a series

of steep paths that lead to the Morgensons'
vacation home.

The only light visible in the house came from
the living room. Vandenberg knew that a table lamp
in there was wired to a timeswitch to ward off
thieves. He rang the back doorbell. When no
answer came, he let himself into the kitchen and
quickly checked the bedrooms. He was alone. He
unlocked the internal door to the garage; the
Volkswagen was where his elder son had left it
months before. So far, so good. He put the sports
bag on the floor and headed for the family den.
Behind the small built-in bar was a fridge. He
opened the door, pulled the empty ice trays out of
the freezer, and reached inside. His fingers closed
around a key ring.

Two minutes later, he slid the largest of the
keys into the Volkswagen's ignition, at the same
time revving the engine with the accelerator.
Nothing. He tried again. An overwhelming sense of
helplessness engulfed him. The battery was flat.
"Damn it, damn it to hell!" he shouted aloud. His
mind raced. The car was automatic so there was no
chance of bump-starting it. What the hell do I do
now?

He headed for the kitchen, but stopped in the
doorway to look back. There was something dark in
the corner of the garage, by the lawnmower. He
moved closer to inspect it. Something large covered
with a black tarpaulin. He eased his way through
some wrought-iron garden furniture and pulled the
cover away. Beneath it was a four-cylinder BMW
motorbike. It was far from new, but judging by its
condition it had been well looked after. According
to a label on one of the panniers, it had been bought

from a stockist in Munich, the manufacturer's base. Vandenberg felt for the smaller of the two keys on the ring, then he looked up. Above him, on a shelf, was a black crash helmet.

Until the Fall of 1993, the bierkeller that stood on the main road, east of the town of Fussen on the Austrian-German border, had been packed to the doors by 5:30 every night. But the motorworks that provided most of its custom had shut its gates for the last time in September of that year, and now the only customers were a few laborers from the surrounding farms.

Leland Daker downed another liter of pils, looked around the shabby little bar and wondered why Vandenberg should choose here of all places to meet. He had no doubt in his mind that the man was desperate—he'd heard it in his voice the last time they'd spoken. This place was off the beaten track, so maybe that was it. He wiped his mouth, the froth of the beer staining the new suede jacket he was wearing. He was glad that the governor was coming, that he was going to hear the key tape for himself. It's gonna focus his mind better than any words of mine, Daker told himself.

He crossed the bar and went out to the men's room. When he turned in the narrow passageway, he sensed movement at the far end. He strained to see. Someone was standing in the shadows by the door to the parking lot. Now, as his eyes grew accustomed to the light, he could make out boots. He stopped. "Who's there?" he called.

A tall man in black motorcycle leathers and a

helmet moved into the light. He lifted the black plastic visor. The nose was almost flat, the nostrils spread across the face. The eyes were dark and piercing. There was something familiar about the look. "Vandenberg?"

Silence. Daker peered at him. "I don't know what the fuck you've done to yourself, but it's you all right." Still the man didn't react. "You forget, I was one of the few who saw you after that VC busted your face the first time."

"Yeah, that's right." Vandenberg said at last. "I have very little time, Daker. Do you have the transcripts?"

"Sure." He took an envelope from his jacket pocket and handed it to him. Vandenberg flicked through it. Lassiter's current location in Munich was shown clearly at the top, along with the time and date of the surveillance. That was good.

"I didn't have time to transcribe it all," Daker said. "If you want the full thing you'd best listen to the tape."

"Yes, that would probably be the best thing." Vandenberg seemed to be having difficulty breathing through his nose. "Listen Daker, I don't see a lot of point in paying the kind of money you're asking to take care of a problem, if all I'm doing is creating another. I need to be very clear in my mind that the job will be handled properly and they'll be no comeback on me."

Daker feigned indignation. "Hey, if I wanted to be a problem to you, Lieutenant, you'd have felt my breath on your neck long ago. No; a million takes care of all loose ends."

"How can I be sure of that?" Vandenberg asked.

"Well, I can see it from your point of view, but

now I come to think about it, I guess you can't. I mean there'd be no point in my signing anything, would there? Look, I'm not a complicated guy. I just want to spend the rest of my life enjoying my money. Like you, I don't want to be looking over my shoulder."

"What happens when you've blown it all? How do I know you won't be calling me . . . maybe at the White House, asking for handouts?"

Daker shrugged. "Well, you're just gonna have to hope I hang on to a little, I guess."

Wrong answer. Very wrong. Vandenberg had no way of gauging the full implications of that remark, but warning signals started going off across his nervous systems. As his conscious mind worked overtime to rationalize them away, his subconscious began to make irrevocable decisions of its own. In an even deeper part of him, he was dimly aware that he was beginning to lose a grip on his sanity.

Vandenberg's voice was steady enough when he spoke. "You have the tape with you?"

"Sure. We can play it in the car if you want. Then we can talk business."

They walked out into the parking lot. Daker studied the man beside him and laughed. "Christ, you're not gonna pick up too many votes looking like that."

"Let me worry about it."

"And your eyes, you've done something with them."

"Colored contact lenses."

"You're not taking any chances, are you?"

"No, none."

They got into Daker's hired Renault. He put a

cassette into the stereo system and lit a cigarette.

The man's voice was muffled but the words were clear enough. So were the conclusions Lassiter had come to. The two men sat there listening for several minutes. Then Vandenberg began to cough. He put his hand to his crushed nose. "I can hardly breathe as it is," he snapped. "Smoke that fucking thing outside, will you."

Daker got out. "Okay, okay. Keep your hair on. Say when you've heard enough." He paced the parking lot as Vandenberg listened. Quite soon, the governor wound down the window. "What's happening here, Daker? I'm not hearing anything."

Daker turned around. "What are you talking about? I checked that cassette myself."

"I'm telling you, the sound just cut out. I'm just getting tape noise." Daker cursed, flung down his cigarette and crossed back to the car. Vandenberg got out and shrugged.

"It's nothing I did. Anyway, you can't erase a tape on a car system."

Daker slid into the passenger seat in his place. He spooled the tape back a little and checked it. Vandenberg moved up behind him. "That's crazy . . ."

Daker's head was around waist height now. Vandenberg's right hand closed around the ten-inch spanner in his jacket pocket. Daker ejected the cassette. "What the fuck . . ." The spanner smashed down into his right temple with such force it almost severed his ear. He slumped forward without a sound. Vandenberg checked that there was no one watching them and then hurried to the motorbike. From one of the panniers he took a coil of rope and a heavy-duty plastic bag and stuffed them into the back of the car. Then he got into the driver's seat, took out the blank cassette he'd put into the car stereo in place of Daker's, and slid it into his jacket. He started the engine and moved the car to the back of the parking lot. A short access road took him into the yard of a derelict foundry which had been turned over briefly to smelting pig iron after the motorworks had closed. A mountain of rusting engine parts blotted out the moonlight as Vandenberg guided the car over the uneven road surface and parked.

Vandenberg had been here before, two summers back. The family were on vacation at Aunt Helga's and he had brought the kids to ski off-piste, in the mountains above Fussen. Toward the end of the afternoon they got lost, and were forced to find their way down the mountain on foot. Finally, they'd come out at this derelict yard and sat in the bierkeller on the road till Stella brought the car round. The massive, funnel-shaped hopper, used to feed the smelter, deep in the body of the works, had stuck in Vandenberg's mind. As he dragged the body around to it, a low moan broke from Daker's lips.

Vandenberg took from the back of the car the plastic bag he'd found in the boathouse on the lake shore. It had been used for fertilizer or some such, but it was thick enough for what was needed. He pulled it over Daker's head and secured it tightly around the neck with a length of cord. The bag was immediately sucked in as Daker tried desperately to breathe. Vandenberg pulled his head in line with the rear wheel of the car and walked around to the driver's seat. Obliterating Daker's face and dental work was essential, he told himself as he started the engine, but at least the bag would localize the mess.

He put the gearbox into reverse and stepped on the gas. The car lurched back but there was no feeling of impact. He got out and walked around. Daker had somehow rolled to one side and was now halfway under the car. Vandenberg sighed irritably, grabbed the man's ankles and towed the body back into position. Daker's hands came up and he tried to pull at the bag. Vandenberg reached for the spanner and gave his head a couple of spirited whacks. Then he lined it up again. This time, the wheel connected. It actually rode up over the head for a second and then crunched downward, splitting it like a watermelon.

After Vandenberg had eased the car forward again, he took the rope, used originally for tying up Helga's boats, and secured one end of it around Daker's ankles. Then he climbed up onto the hopper and looked down. The chute that extended from it led into the works itself. Eight feet above his head was a heavy steel beam supporting a pulley wheel. The pulley itself was rusted through but the joist looked sound enough. At the third attempt, Vandenberg was able to throw the rope over it. Then he climbed down and tied the other end to the tow hitch under the rear bumper of the car. Satisfied that everything was in place, he put the gearbox into first and moved the car slowly forward. The beam began to creak as the rope took the strain.

Christ, this line held in a force-ten gale, a year back, Vandenberg told himself. It shouldn't give out now for a hundred and seventy pounds of Texas lard. One of the wheels broke free of the asphalt and spun wildly. Vandenberg slammed the dashboard with the heel of his hand. *"Goddamn it!"* He looked at his watch. This was taking far too long. He got out and made for the mountain of pig iron. Lying amongst it, in the baked earth, was the remains of a cylinder block. He stooped down and with considerable effort, carried it back to the car and laid it in the trunk.

This time the wheels held. As the car moved forward, Daker's bloody remains were slowly hoisted into the air. *If someone sees me now, I'm finished.* When the body lifted clear of the hopper, Vandenberg wrenched on the brake and hurried to the back of the car. He cut through the rope and Daker disappeared from view with a metallic thump. You were a damn fool, he thought as he coiled the rope. You could have had it all. Now you just get to rot.

He parked the car in the trees and resolved to drive it off one of the mountain roads later that night, when everything else was dealt with. Quickly he checked the yard. The bag that had covered Daker's head had leaked slightly and a small quantity of blood had pooled into the muddy tracks of one of the tires. Vandenberg stretched himself, worked his head around in his collar. Then he unzipped his fly.

For fifteen minutes he'd been Vandenberg the killer. *Silence this man and erase all trace of him*—no other thought had entered his mind. But now, as he watched the thin stream of urine wash away the last trace of the man he'd just slaughtered, some rational thought returned. Nothing stands between Lassiter and me now, he can come for me any time he wants. And the one man that might have changed that is at the bottom of a foundry with his head smashed in.

The part of Vandenberg's mind dominated by his real mother's genes had always believed that things with Daker would work out. The part dominated by his father's had planned meticulously to obliterate him at the first sign of trouble. Neither had worked in any practical way on the pressing problem of what was to be done next if events took the turn that they had. As the truth of the situation sunk in, Vandenberg's grip on reality loosened a little more. Quickly, an awareness began to form in his mind. Somehow, some way, I'm going to have to kill Lassiter myself. The risks this time will be enormous. But I've taken great risks before. And I have no other choice.

His breathing leveled. He zipped up his pants and began to walk back to the motorbike. His mind was in free fall now.

It's as though I have waited my whole life for this great trial. All the other risks I have taken, were merely in preparation for this.

The decision was taken and, even as momentous as it was, he began to feel better. Almost instinctively, he started to weigh up the probabilities. On the cassette, the Customs agent said he was going to be at the apartment in Munich tonight. I could be in there in an hour. If his plans haven't changed, if I act quickly and the kill itself goes smoothly, I could be back here in another two. The risk of my becoming implicated later is minimal. There is nothing that anyone but Lassiter yet knows to connect me with him. Apart from one routine meeting on another matter entirely, we are strangers. So what possible motive could I have for wanting him dead?

What *is* my name? Vandenberg thought idly, as

he kicked the engine of the BMW into life. My real name? Rathenau had said he and his wife had called their baby Rudy.

Well, Rudy . . . this is the one big one, wouldn't you say?

TWENTY-NINE

"The house in Würzburg is all locked up," Fraenkel said. "But there seems little doubt that Rathenau lives there at least part of the time. The police are watching the place in case he turns up."

A chance of getting a DNA sample at last! Lassiter thought.

Fraenkel sounded positively jubilant. "We need a court order to break in, of course. Hoffman's down at the Rathaus right now with an application. The court will sit tomorrow, so we're going to try and push it in at the end of the proceedings."

"What are the chances?"

"Not great. And if we don't get one tomorrow, we'll have to wait another week."

Way too late. Lassiter paced the little apartment that *Finanzamt* had provided for him in Munich. "Can't we get a hearing in chambers or something?"

"No. Our lawyers say that the issues are far too complicated. We're dealing with magistrates in a little country town here. Money laundering is not something they encounter every day."

"No, I guess not."

"We'll know if we're gonna get on by noon. I'll call you then."

Fourteen hours to wait. Lassiter hung up and began to pack. His options were clear enough. If the application was approved, there was every chance he would be able to get the vital sample he needed for a DNA profile on Rathenau without a soul being any the wiser. Erika had said that clothing, bed linen and furnishing fabrics could all contain fragments of the owner's hair. But clothing was the best source, as no one other than the owner would be likely to have worn it. Just a few millimeters of a single hair was all he would need to establish that Lowell Vandenberg was really Rathenau's son. If Hoffman failed to get the court order, then Lassiter knew he would go straight back to Washington. He had no clear idea as to how he would get hold of the two sets of samples he would need there, he just knew that all feasible sources in Germany would by then be out of reach within the timescale. If something did break over here, there was always the chance he could deploy Erika . . .

He closed his suitcase and took a tiny heart-shaped locket from his inside pocket. That last night he'd spent with her in Berlin, she had slipped the gift into his case without him knowing, along with a letter. He flipped open the lid and read the simple inscription inside: "My heart goes with you." An unbearable melancholia gripped him. The letter had ended with the closing lines of a poem by Theodor Storm.

Dass wenn des Tages Lichter schwanden,
Wie sonst der Abend uns vereint;
Und dass, wo sonst dein Stuhl gestanden,
Schon andre ihre Plätze fanden,
Und nichts dich zu vermissen scheint.

Erika knew all too well that his time in Germany was over and was clearly searching for a way to let go.

As the light of day is fading
When once evening would reunite us;
And the chair that you would set in place
Others come too soon to take
And nothing seems to miss you.

She seemed so certain he would go back to Marianne. And yet after that last conversation he'd had with his wife . . . His grandmother had always said, "You know someone's true nature by the choices they make." Marianne was working relentlessly for a lifestyle that seemed to exclude him and everything he held valuable. Whether Vandenberg rose to higher things and she with him was not really the issue. Faced with those kind of choices again he felt certain she'd make the same decisions. Whenever Marianne talked about their relationship it was always in terms of "you and me." He studied the locket. With Erika, it had been about "us."

The telephone rang. He was surprised when Marianne's voice broke though his thoughts. "I've been trying to reach you since yesterday." Her voice shook with anxiety. "I only got your number in Munich a few minutes ago . . . I had to speak with you . . . I don't know where to begin . . . "

"What on earth's the matter, Marianne?"

"I overheard a phone call . . . " They'd spoken simultaneously.

"What kind of phone call?"

"One of Vandenberg's. It got taped by accident . . . Look, this may not sound very rational, but . . . can you think of any reason why he might want to . . . harm you?"

Every reason! He's on to me . . . but how? He must be having me watched. "Why, what did you hear said?"

"This might be just my paranoia . . . I haven't slept for nights . . . In the call he talked about a Customs agent in Germany. The only Customs agent he's ever had any dealings with, so far as I know, and I run his whole life, is you. There was talk about a payment of a million dollars to 'simplify the situation.' At first I thought it might be they were talking about a bribe, but I've played it over and over . . . " She started to cry. " . . . Oh, I know this is crazy but . . . "

"You think he's paid someone to have me killed, is that it?" Lassiter said calmly.

She sounded very frightened. "Yes."

"Look, I can't talk over the phone. I'm leaving here right now. I'll be back in Washington in forty-eight hours at most." As he spoke, he let down the window blind, then peered between the slats, checking the street outside. "Nothing's gonna happen to me, I promise you."

"I've made such a mess of everything. There are a lot of things I should have said long ago, I know that . . . I wanted to, but the truth was I had so much I needed to straighten out in my own head . . . Jack, I do love you. For God's sake be careful . . . "

When she hung up, Lassiter lay back against the wall. *The whole time frame has changed.* He found an envelope and stuffed it with his handwritten notes and Max's printouts, scribbled a letter to his attorney in New York, asking him to take care of the documents, and sealed the package. He started to gather the rest of his stuff, and the locket fell out onto the floor. As he bent to pick it up, the solution to the DNA problem came to him.

He didn't need a tissue sample from Horst Rathenau. Mrs. Hofle, the sister-in-law in Brooklyn, had shown him that little picture frame of Rathenau's wife. Erika's locket had recalled it. The wife had been dead for more than fifty years, but hadn't Mrs. Hofle said that she herself had wound a strand of her sister's hair around the hand-tinted picture? *One hair was all he needed.* And if its DNA profile matched the impostor's . . . *One hair could stop Vandenberg becoming president.*

The matter would have to be handled with the utmost care. Only Lassiter himself would be able to convince the old lady to open the picture frame and give what he needed to an impartial forensic technician, in front of impeccable witnesses. Whatever the truth about the phone call Marianne had overheard, one thing was now clear: her blind loyalty to Vandenberg was gone. Once I'm face to face with her, Lassiter promised himself, I may be able to tell her enough to convince her to help me. How hard could it be for her to get one of Vandenberg's hairs, or a used table napkin with a saliva sample on it?

There was time enough. Just. Everything will have to go my way if I'm to make it, Lassiter told himself. He zipped up his suitcase. There was nothing to keep him in Germany a minute longer.

☆   ☆   ☆

Vandenberg reached the outskirts of Munich by late evening and began to edge the motorbike through the traffic toward the city center. A hundred yards ahead, drawn up in groups on each side of the carriageway, knots of policemen, armed with automatic weapons, scanned the traffic pouring north.

Someone saw you, Rudy. Saw you in the parking lot with Daker, Vandenberg's mind screamed. *Saw you hoist the body into the hopper.*

He pulled off right and moved down a side street that led to a flea market in a small square. Here he dismounted and pushed the bike carefully between the stalls. Poorly dressed peasants were hurrying to pack up their stocks, calling to one another in a babble of languages. There was fear amongst these people, Vandenberg could sense it. It mingled with his own as he edged forward. The way to his right led back onto the main street. He turned left and squeezed between two parked buses. Then stopped dead. All around him were police, maybe as many as three hundred of them. Some stood in huddles smoking, others waited in line as batons and riot shields were handed out. Through the tinted glass visor of his helmet, he could see buses in the distance disgorging still more uniformed men onto the sidewalks. It was clear, in an instant, that none were remotely interested in him. Vandenberg took a long breath. They'd obviously been shipped in to monitor some kind of demonstration. He turned the motorbike around and headed back to the main carriageway.

The center of the city had been closed. Steel railings had been used to cordon off most streets, and traffic had been diverted. Soon Vandenberg

parked and took out his map. When he had his
bearings he set off on foot across the square that
lay to his right. On every corner there were groups
of drunken youths. Many had their hair dyed
bizarre combinations of colors, others were shorn
completely, their noses and ears hung with metal
rings and other ornaments, their faces almost
obscured by patterns of tattoos. Standing out
against the rays of the dying sun was a forest of
banners and flags, reaching far into the distance
along Reichenbachstrasse. Everywhere, a sea of
red, white and black: the colors of the extreme
Right. Vandenberg spoke no German. To him it had
always been an ugly, guttural language. Now, as he
walked by, as one group spat oaths at another,
yelled execrations across the square, it became, as
it had for so many others, a language of hate. Here
was danger. Vandenberg knew the smell of it of old.
It had assailed him in the sweltering jungles of
Vietnam. He'd tasted it only weeks ago, standing in
a windy paddock, staring down the barrel of Daker's
rifle, then again, on that podium in Sullivan.

Until this moment, Vandenberg had had no firm
idea of how he intended to kill Lassiter, just knew it
had to look like an accident or some kind of routine
homicide—the work of a stoned mugger or bored
degenerate. Now, as he watched the skinheads
gather themselves into a disheveled army, a plan
began to form in his mind.

The street sign ahead told him he was in
Klenzestrasse. The apartment Lassiter was billeted
in had to be a short distance up on the right. He
lifted the visor of the helmet and looked at his
watch. There was really only one way to ensure
that the Customs agent was still in place and that

was to telephone him. As soon as Lassiter
answered he would hang up. It really didn't matter
if the call alerted him to danger, because by then it
would be too late. And if it flushed him out, so
much the better. Vandenberg ducked into the
doorway of a little supermarket, slipped a one
D-mark piece into a pay phone on the wall, dialled
and waited. No reply . . . Was he too late? Daker's
report and the tape he'd heard had said that he
was staying on here for another night.

Vandenberg was starting to sweat in the heavy
motorbike leathers. He took off the helmet,
unzipped the jacket and tried to calm down. Maybe
Lassiter had slipped out for something. If his car
was still here . . .

He flicked through Daker's report—where the
hell had he seen it?—found the registration number
of the Customs agent's car and, as he ran toward
the apartment block, began to check the license
plates of the vehicles parked at the roadside. Ahead
of him, to the right, was a mud-stained blue BMW.
The letters on the plate were hard to make out. He
squatted down and drew a long breath. *Gotcha!*

The street was deserted. In the distance he could
hear the voices of the skinheads, some chanting,
others howling like wolves. He looked around for
Lassiter once more and searched for his own key
ring. He eased off a key to one of his own cars, knelt
down and forced it into the driver's door-lock. He
used a stone he found in the gutter to hammer it in
as far as it would go. Then he broke the key off in the
lock. He hurried around to the other side of the car
and repeated the procedure. As he walked back up
the street, he jammed an American quarter into the
payphone on the wall, then hurried to the apartment.

☆   ☆   ☆

Lassiter turned into Blumenstrasse. He was certain he'd seen a post office on the left at the end. Across the road was a police cordon. A mob of chanting skinheads moved down between two lines of police. Lassiter walked up to the steel barrier and asked an officer where he could cross. "Nowhere, for the next couple of hours," he was told. He picked up his suitcase and started back to the car. I'll have to post the package at the airport, he told himself. He turned on the next street, walked up to the BMW, and tried to put his key into the door. And then the other door.

Marianne was right.

The only way out of here now was by taxi. And half the city center was closed off to traffic. The payphone on the corner was jammed up too. Goddamn it, I'll have to phone from the flat, Lassiter decided. He was ten feet from the door when it occurred to him that that was exactly what the killer wanted him to do.

The figure in black swung out of the shadows. Lassiter didn't see the knife, just a reflection of the streetlights on something metallic. Instinctively, he lifted the suitcase to cover himself. The blade cut through the canvas, and gashed the fingers of his right hand. Lassiter brought his foot up hard underneath the case, and caught his assailant in his right knee. For a second, Vandenberg lost his balance. He toppled back against the wall, twisting his body into a second thrust as he fell. The knife sliced straight through the case and deep into Lassiter's chest. He could actually feel the steel inside him. He pulled back and ran, felt warm blood pumping into the folds of his jacket, felt his mind detach from reality as his whole system, numbed by shock, began to succumb. He stumbled on toward a line of police vans. He called out—or perhaps the sound was only in his head. Something hit his right leg and he went down, skinning the hands and knees that scraped the pavement. Gasping for air, he scrambled to his feet and pulled himself upright against a shop front. A chunk of paving stone fell out of the sky above him, and smashed through the plate glass, a foot from his face. He felt his body begin to sink back through the few shards that remained, but steadied himself and peered ahead. The night air was filled with dust and smoke. Spikes of light shone through the feet of the marching mob as they pushed on toward the city center. Suddenly, silhouetted against them, was the man in the motorcycle leathers, oblivious to all around him, scouring the street for his quarry.

Lassiter snatched a breath and reeled giddily onward. The way ahead was cordoned off. With all the energy he could muster, he swung himself over the railings and plunged into the only cover there was—the shrieking mob, forcing its way down Wilhelmstrasse. The rhythmic pulse of its chanting merged with the crunch of broken glass beneath his feet as he struggled to keep up with them. He knew that if he stumbled, if he fell, he would be wreckage in their midst, trampled and crushed underfoot in an instant. But here he was hidden. Here at least perhaps . . .

The man in the helmet dived through the throng, slashing out with his knife. Lassiter twisted away and ran to the end of the rank. Others closed around him, pushing him now toward the gutter.

Ahead, on the ground, lay a policeman, his head tipped back toward Lassiter, his eyes rolling wildly like a trapped animal as he fought to regain his footing. Then his face distorted in pain as the mob began the long business of kicking him to death. There was no way out here. The youths had smelled blood. They closed in, trapping Lassiter at the center of the fray. Amongst them, he could see the motorcycle man. He was pushing too, but not to get to the policeman; to get to him. A skinhead was hacking at one of the policeman's limbs with a machete. Some piece of him detached and was brandished as a trophy to be admired by the mob. Here, it seemed, the fun was over. As Lassiter felt them pull back, he squeezed into a gap to his right and lurched on.

Ahead, was the heart of the battle zone. The air, between the blazing overturned cars, was rank with the smell of burning fuel and tear gas. Howling youths, their faces swathed in scarves, dodged the flames, and twisted through the fog in an attempt to regroup. Lassiter looked back again. The hunting man was no more than ten yards behind him. For five minutes, the two threaded unnoticed through a chanting army of skinheads. Through the red filtered light, Lassiter could see a massive detachment of police blocking the road ahead. Stones and missiles rained down on their riot shields as Lowell Vandenberg began to close with him, for a private reckoning of his own.

From the raucous shout that went up all around him, Lassiter gauged that the police cordon had broken. Now the mob moved faster and he too was forced into a run. The whole of his right side, he could feel, was soaked with blood. The red lights began to blur. Suddenly he slewed violently to the left, in a wild involuntary sideslip. His balance was going. He pushed between two skinheads in a desperate attempt to reach the curb. One screamed at him and punched him hard in the side of the head as he passed. He staggered blindly off to the left and found himself alone in a narrow side street. He was halfway down it before he realized that the end was blocked by a high wall. Echoing behind him, he could hear the smack of boots on the cobbles. Half-doubled in pain, Lassiter struggled on, looking to left and right for a bolthole. The wall loomed up ahead of him. Maybe, when he got closer, he would find there was an escape route, a little alley concealed to one side. Maybe . . . His eyes scoured every inch of the cul-de-sac. *There was no way through.* He stopped at the stone wall and turned around.

Vandenberg moved slowly out into the light and put his hands on his hips. His body heaved with the exertion. This time there would be no mistake. Lassiter could feel panic welling up inside him. He spun around and searched vainly for a foothold in the wall. Vandenberg moved in for the kill.

"Ausländischen Dreck, raus! Ausländischen Dreck, raus!"

Back in the main street, mounted police and water cannon were deployed in a furious counter-strike. The chanting mob fell back. A few, still shouting defiance, were split off into the cul-de-sac. Lassiter had managed to force his foot into a crack in the wall and had succeeded in levering himself up a few feet. With his last particle of strength, he swung his body out and with his injured arm, tried to make a grab for the coping that ran along the top.

He fell short and crumpled helpless at the foot of the rough-hewn stone. The man in the motorbike leathers closed the distance between them. Lassiter's senses were assaulted anew by the acrid stench of tear gas, and the old nightmare—the visions that had haunted his dreams for as long as he could remember—began to play out for real. Only this time the hostage marked to die was himself . . .

The skinheads moved farther down the street, their chants resonating against the buildings: "*Ausländischen Dreck, raus!*" Vandenberg circled the man slumped on the ground, hefting the knife, choosing his moment. Lassiter saw him lift his hand high to strike. He raised one arm in a last, pathetic gesture of defense. In that instant he started yelling, his voice loud and clear, rising above the din of the riot.

"*He, Spezi, kanns't ma mol bittschö helfa?*"

The broad, familiar, Southern German slang made a couple of skinheads turn. For a second, Vandenberg was thrown. Lassiter dragged himself forward a few feet, out of the shadows. One of the youths, his scalp and one side of his face tattooed with grotesque, swirling patterns, moved toward the man with knife. "*He Du da, bist vielleicht a Tschech a no?*"

Vandenberg froze. "I don't speak German."

Several of the other thugs, one armed with a chainsaw, moved in around the American. "*Papiere!*" one demanded.

Vandenberg shrugged. "I'm an American citizen."

"Speak German!" The youth behind him stepped forward and deftly tipped off the helmet that obscured Vandenberg's face. "You're in Germany, you know. Speak our language," he demanded in clear English.

Lassiter strove to focus his eyes on the face of the man sent to kill him. The features meant little to him . . . and yet something about the shape of the head . . . the set of the eyes . . .

They were filled with fear now. "I'm a tourist . . . " Vandenberg tried. Now the whole group, about a dozen youths in their teens, turned to face Vandenberg. One, carrying a pole topped with a crudely made head labeled, *"Helmut Kohl— Verrater!"*—Traitor!—spat, "Show me now!"

Before Vandenberg could reach inside his jacket, another youth grabbed the collar and pulled it down over his shoulders, pinioning his arms. The tattooed leader wrenched the papers from the inside pocket. Others gathered round as he flicked through the pages of the green passport.

"Bosnian!" he screamed to the others. His eyes bored into Vandenberg's. *"You Bosnian cunts! You take our jobs! Fuck our women! Defile our blood!"*

The tattooed skinhead held the passport aloft and let out a howl of triumph. Vandenberg moved back against the wall.

"Wait a minute. For God's sake . . . you don't understand."

One of the youths made a grab for Vandenberg's knife. The American sliced the air with it, catching the man's hand. For a second, there was a stunned silence in the little cul-de-sac. Then, without a word, the skinhead with the chainsaw jerked it into life.

The look on Vandenberg's face was one of raw terror. Lassiter pulled himself back into the shadows. The ragged hack of the chainsaw echoed against the high stone wall. The mob closed slowly around Vandenberg, all except the skinhead with the pole. Suddenly dissatisfied with the papier mâché head perched on it, he tossed it into the gutter. The tone of the chainsaw changed abruptly as it engaged flesh and bone. The skinhead seated himself on the curb, took out a knife and began to whittle the end of the pole to a sharper point . . .

THIRTY

The nurse cut through the last piece of surgical tape with a small pair of scissors. "There. Is that any easier across the chest?"

Lassiter eased himself off the bed and moved his arm around in a wide arc. "Much."

"Good. I'll give you a spare dressing to take home with you. What are you going to do with all this?" she asked.

Lassiter surveyed the line of white plastic laundry bags, filled with correspondence, manuscript paper, books and tapes. "God, it looks like I've been here for a year. Someone will come for it later."

"All right. Are you flying back to America today?"

"Tomorrow."

"Well, remember the physiotherapy and the medication." Lassiter nodded. "I understand you're going to leave by the staff exit?"

"Well, there are still a lot of press hanging around at the front."

"Do you know the way?"

"Uhuh."

She offered her hand. "Well, good-bye and good luck." He shook it firmly with his left and thanked her. She went to help him with his jacket but he pulled away—"I'm fine"—and she watched him struggle into it. "Do you have someone to look after you?"

"Yes."

He watched her walk off down the hospital corridor and began to gather up the papers on the bed. Amongst them lay a copy of *Time* magazine. Lassiter glanced at the cover once more. It showed a victorious Gene Bravington, waving to delegates at the Democratic Party Convention. The same edition carried yet another lengthy feature on the ongoing attempts by various U.S. agencies to unravel the mysteries of the late Lowell Vandenberg's secret life. The battered head recovered from a Munich gutter, identified as that of the governor of Virginia had, not surprisingly, created a media sensation with Jack Lassiter at its center, when the story had hit the newsstands three weeks before. Quite how the head had come to be there had been the subject of a succession of interviews that were soon judged by the Customs agent's doctors to be detrimental to his physical recovery. A bewildered Frau Hofle had surrendered some of her deceased sister's hair to FBI agents. Forensics had successfully matched DNA taken from it to a profile produced from Lowell Vandenberg's blood. But Lassiter was saying no more. Left to himself at last, he began to write. A sample chapter of his own version of events had been sufficiently well received by the publishing industry to leave him in little doubt as to what his next eighteen months would hold.

When CNN reported the collapse of the German government two days ago, Lassiter had found himself wondering whether Fraenkel had been right. Could the recovery of the Mielke billions have really made a difference? Certainly, the exposure of the Rathenau/Vandenberg connection in the press in recent weeks had spotlighted the issue of the missing money in a way that left Lassiter in no doubt that whoever did have it, had it where it would never now be found.

Lassiter put the magazine and the other papers into his attaché case and walked out into the corridor. There'd been plenty of time to think, cooped up in this sanitized little sanctuary. For that, at least, he was not sorry. Now, for the first time in a long while, he was sure where he was going. His pale face lifted into a smile as he watched her walking toward him. The words of the troubadour song rose to his lips.

Unter den linden	(Under the Lime trees
an der Heide	on the heath
da unser zweier Bette was,	there, we made our bed,
da mugt ir vinden	there you'll find,
schone beide	beautiful together,
gebrochen Blumen unde Gras.	broken flowers and grasses,
vor dem Walde einem Tal,	and before the wood a vale,
Tandaradei	Tandaradei,
Schone sang die Nachtigal.	How sweetly sang the nightingale.)

◼ HarperPaperbacks *By Mail*

Stories of treachery, heroism, espionage, and high-voltage suspense

Secret Missions
by Michael Gannon

A gripping espionage novel that takes place at the dawn of World War II about a German spy and an American priest . . . and two cunning operations destined to collide.

Alistair MacLean's Dead Halt
by Alastair MacNeill

A private schooner smashes upon the rocks of Nantucket and a cache of brand-new Armalite Assault Rifles tumbles out. It is the first clue in a deadly puzzle that will take two daring agents to crack open.

The Fighting Man
by Gerald Seymour

British Special Forces officer Gord Brown takes charge in a seemingly futile struggle against the Guatemalan military dictatorship.

City of Gold
by Len Deighton

A riveting story of espionage and high-voltage suspense, set amid the turmoil of World War II in Egypt, as Rommel's forces sweep across the Sahara and the fate of the free world hangs in the balance.

Name of the Beast
by Daniel Easterman

Ex-British agent Michael Hunt, and noted archaeologist A'isha Manafaluti, are driven to the truth about the mysterious Al-Qurtubi, who some call the saviour—others the Antichrist.

Buy 4 or more and receive **FREE** postage & handling

"So you're running away from it," Kizmin said. "You're turning your back on the forensics lab and going off to hide somewhere."

They stopped on the circular drive beside the detective's car. Iris watched the mourning family arrange the few small sprays of flowers to the side of the grave, out of the way of the backhoe that was lumbering into place as the area cleared.

"No," Iris said. "No more hiding. No more running away."

ACKNOWLEDGMENTS

I am most grateful to the following people:

Heather York, Anthropologist, for her many contributions (and Ben Fenwick for his patience).

Dan Brodt, Anthropologist, for sharing his enthusiasms with me and being such a good teacher.

Kent Buehler, Archaeology Lab Manager—Oklahoma Archaeological Survey Lab at the University of Oklahoma, for the fascinating session, and Dr. Lesley Rankin-Hill, University of Oklahoma Department of Anthropology, for her generosity.

Gerri Snow, for her time, and Dr. Clyde Snow for his kindness and inspiration—however indirect.

Deborah Olson of C.J. Olson Cherries in Sunnyvale, California, the fourth generation of the dedicated fruit-growing family that I have admired since childhood.

Elaine Koster for her continuing encouragement and support.

Audrey LaFehr and Aaron Priest, who try to keep me on the right track.

And Michael Bradley for so many reasons that I could fill another book.